Claudia Gray

The Perils of Lady Catherine de Bourgh

Claudia Gray is the pseudonym of Amy Vincent. She is the *New York Times*–bestselling author of *The Murder of Mr. Wickham*, and the writer of multiple young adult novels, including the Evernight series, the Firebird trilogy, and the Constellation trilogy. In addition, she's written several Star Wars novels, such as *Lost Stars* and *Bloodline*. She makes her home in New Orleans with her husband, Paul, and assorted small dogs.

claudiagray.com

THE PERILS OF
LADY CATHERINE DE BOURGH

The Perils of
Lady Catherine
de Bourgh

A Mr. Darcy & Miss Tilney Mystery

Claudia Gray

VINTAGE BOOKS
A DIVISION OF PENGUIN RANDOM HOUSE LLC
NEW YORK

A VINTAGE BOOKS ORIGINAL 2024

Library of Congress Cataloging-in-Publication Data
Names: Gray, Claudia, author.
Title: The perils of Lady Catherine de Bourgh / by Claudia Gray.
Description: First edition. | New York : Vintage Books, a Division of
Penguin Random House LLC, 2024.
Identifiers: LCCN 2023036875 (print) | LCCN 2023036876 (ebook)
Subjects: GSAFD: Detective and mystery fiction. | Novels.
Classification: LCC PS3607.R38886 P47 2024 (print) |
LCC PS3607.R38886 (ebook) | DDC 813/.6—dc23
LC record available at https://lccn.loc.gov/2023036875
LC ebook record available at https://lccn.loc.gov/2023036876

**Vintage Books Trade Paperback ISBN: 978-0-593-68658-4
eBook ISBN: 978-0-593-68659-1**

Book design by Steve Walker

vintagebooks.com

Printed in the United States of America
1st Printing

To all Janeites everywhere

THE PERILS OF
LADY CATHERINE DE BOURGH

Chapter One

September 1821

Forever will there be much discussion regarding the age at which it is most correct for a woman to marry. The simplest and truest answer—that this depends on each individual woman's temperament and circumstances—is unfortunately ignored in favor of sweeping prescriptions for the entire sex. There are those who advocate for an engagement to follow as swiftly as possible a girl's coming-out; and indeed, many are made brides at only fifteen or sixteen years of age. Yet even the most matrimonially minded mothers would generally prefer their daughters to be a little older before making the decision to marry, for it is a choice of unrivaled consequence in female life, one to be made in soberer thinking and stronger judgment than is common at fifteen.

Women of the genteel classes are widely believed to have no desire for any greater learning nor any profession, which if true would be most fortunate, as both education and gainful employ are denied them. They will remain in their parents' home until they wed or until those parents die, at which point—if she is still unmarried—it is the unhappy lot of a woman to be cast off upon a brother or a cousin, obliged to dwell in a house where her presence may be unwelcome, and the expense of her keeping will certainly be so. Those ladies with no male relation to support them may at least have inherited some small property but such as is unlikely to support them in comfort. They have little place in society. It is a most lamentable fate. The astute reader will have deduced that such outcomes might be prevented by means beyond matrimony—but matrimony remains the one curative acknowledged by society, and it is in this direction that young women shall ever be urged.

The nineteenth century is of course a more enlightened time than the eras that have preceded it; it is not considered strange for a girl to reach even the age of five and twenty before wedding, and the years of danger have not begun until near her third decade of life. Yet a girl of eighteen—as Miss Juliet Tilney of Woodston, Gloucestershire, had become— may certainly expect to soon find herself a wife. Like many such young women, Juliet had indeed begun dedicating some of her attention to the business of how a household is run; and on a bright day in early autumn of 1821, she had intruded into the kitchens of her grandfather's estate, Northanger Abbey.

Yet Juliet's curiosity tended in a rather different direction from that society would have expected.

"It is a fine haunch of meat," said Northanger's cook, the normally congenial Mrs. Ford, who currently stood near the kitchen worktable with her hands knotted together in worry. "Could roast it and serve it just as it is."

"Yet no one will mind if you serve a veal ragout rather than a roast." Juliet studied the many knives laid out for Mrs. Ford's use; the butcher had already worked his craft, but much remained to be done. "Far from it. My father quite likes a ragout, as you well know—and yours is very much the best I have ever tasted!"

This compliment soothed Mrs. Ford's concern. "Even your grandfather says 'tis his favorite, and he is not an easy man to please."

"Precisely. So the meat can be chopped fine, and no one will notice this." With that, Juliet took up a knife, held it over-head, and stabbed the meat with all her strength. Then she took up another—one with a shorter blade—and did so again.

Then a third, this knife almost as slender as a finger. This was in its own way a most savage attack—and it was precisely such that Juliet's efforts were meant to resemble. How did a cut in flesh look different when made with a curved blade instead of a straight one? How much force was required to penetrate an inch, or two, or five? Did the angle of the blow affect the appearance of the cut?

Such are not questions often considered by proper young ladies in society. But Juliet Tilney's curiosity had traveled in many unusual directions since she first took an interest in the investigation of murder.

She could not be faulted for such a morbid turn of thought, for the subject had been forced upon her. First, at a house party in Surrey, an uninvited guest by the name of Mr. Wickham had been bashed on the head and left lifeless on the floor in the dead of night. Then, during a trip to visit friends in Devonshire, the young Mrs. Willoughby had drunk a toast to her future well-being, which had proved to be laced with a fatal dose of arsenic. Both these crimes had been solved, not by the local authorities but by Juliet herself—in tandem with a young gentleman of her acquaintance, a Mr. Jonathan Darcy of Derbyshire.

Juliet's interest in criminal investigation was much honored by those who had benefited from her efforts but distrusted by her family and neighbor friends, even decried by those whose acquaintance, and compassion, did not reach such levels. Such a pursuit could not be considered ladylike; in theory, it might have even have proved dangerous—which those closest to her could not forget despite her many protests that she had never been at the slightest risk. How could her parents, her aunts and uncles, or particularly her stern grandfather, be expected to respond to such behavior without dismay?

The mention of Jonathan Darcy might, in other circumstances, have done much to alleviate any familial distress. Mr. Darcy was a handsome young man of good breeding and considerable property—no less than the heir to Pemberley, one of the greatest estates in the realm. In short, Mr. Darcy was a catch, and as Juliet Tilney was a young woman just at the age of marriageability, society deemed it her duty to catch him if she could. Even a bit of unladylike behavior could be excused, were this the inducement.

Alas, Mr. Darcy had shown no romantic interest in Juliet, much to her sorrow. She liked him—would have liked him even if he had possessed no estate at all—and had come to trust and confide in him more than many a wife ever did her husband. But for reasons she could not guess, it appeared he did not feel the same, and thus she remained unspoken for. It had been almost a year since they had last met, and neither he nor any other young man had made any overtures toward courtship in that time.

Her trip to Devonshire *had* attracted another potential suitor, who if not quite as wealthy, was also highly eligible. Unfortunately, this man had proved to be the very murderer she then sought. (Juliet had, at times, wondered disconsolately as to whether she attracted only criminal elements. If so, woeful years lay ahead of her.)

But she was not of a temperament to mope and sulk. The trait she had most admired in her false suitor was an interest in natural philosophy as it pertained to the commission of murder. Her finishing-school education would not allow her to test chemical substances, as he had done, but she had come to believe that other types of learning were within her reach. She had questioned the servants about the storage of guns, though she had not yet dared ask to fire one herself. She had read Lavater's translated essays on physiognomy, which proclaimed that a certain crook of the nose or emphasis of the brow might mark a face as criminal (though Juliet's experiences led her to doubt this). And she had managed to learn a great deal about knives and stab wounds without her family ever voicing any wonder as to why they were being served ragouts and fricassees more often.

Yet what does this avail me? Juliet thought as she rubbed her arm, somewhat achy from a deep strong stab that had hit the bone. *What is the likelihood I should ever use such knowledge again?*

With determination, she reminded herself that knowledge had merit, whether used or unused. "Very well, Mrs. Ford," she said to the cook, who stood there, clutching her apron as though it might save them both from Juliet's improper curiosities. "Let me try the cleaver, and then I shall be done."

But Mrs. Ford was delivered from witnessing this by one of the underservants, who had come seeking Juliet. "Miss, I thought you should know—a courier is come with a letter!"

A courier meant an urgent letter indeed. Juliet hastily rinsed her hands and hurried from the kitchen to find her parents, to whom the missive would be delivered.

Probably, she thought, the letter would be from her grandfather General Tilney, who spent much of his time in either London or Bath. He wished to feel himself of importance in the world. His military honors and his house should have sufficed for this, but the peace gave him few chances to exercise his rank, and Northanger Abbey was too remote from most fine society to be admired as often as her grandfather would have liked. If he was coming home, he would no doubt send many orders for the house to be put in order in his absence. (Juliet and her parents stayed at the abbey when he was gone for longer periods of time, due to General Tilney's unfounded distrust of his beleaguered servants. Otherwise they resided at the much more modest Woodston manor, some twenty miles distant.)

The note might also have come from her uncle, Captain Frederick Tilney—who would someday inherit Northanger Abbey and who often reminded his relations of that fact when he deigned to visit them, which was seldom. Juliet's greatest concern was that the note might be from her beloved aunt Eleanor, currently far from home in Scotland. What if she had come to some harm? (Juliet's assessment of the risks inherent in visiting Scotland had been much influenced by her reading of Sir Walter Scott.)

When Juliet entered the abbey's great hall, she found both her parents staring at the unopened letter her mother held in her hands. "Oh, is it from my aunt? Has she written to us?" Juliet asked. How strange that they had not yet opened it!

Her father wore a most peculiar expression upon his face. "The letter is not for us all," he said. "It is addressed only to you, and perhaps you can tell us who the sender is, for we know not."

In bewilderment, Juliet took the letter from her mother; it was written on fine paper, with a separate sheet used only for the envelope. These suggested a wealthy sender, as did the unfamiliar coat of arms pressed into the blue sealing wax.

"Open it," urged Mrs. Tilney, who relished all that was unusual and exciting. "Who can have sent it?"

Juliet broke the seal and unfolded the paper, looking first to the signature at the end. Her eyes widened as she took it in. "Why, it is from Lady Catherine de Bourgh!"

The title attracted her parents' respect but gave them no comprehension in return. "And who is that?" Mr. Tilney asked.

"Papa, I think . . . I think that is the aunt of Mr. Jonathan Darcy."

The aforementioned Mr. Darcy was, at that moment, at home in Derbyshire. To be precise, he sat upon one of the couches in the morning room at Pemberley—a room so awash in light, so beautifully decorated in shades of yellow and blue, that most of his family members could be found there long after morning had fled.

That day, all three Darcys currently at home were engaged in a favorite pastime at Pemberley: reading. Jonathan's mother, Elizabeth, sat with a novel, while his father examined the latest issue of the *Provincial Gazette*. At any point in the prior ten years, Jonathan would no doubt have been reading or rereading one of his beloved volumes of Gibbon. However—to his family's astonishment, and rather to their relief—he had in the past year acquired a new interest, one as fervent as his curiosity about ancient Rome: a devotion to the novels of Sir Walter Scott.

It was Miss Juliet Tilney who had first brought these to his particular attention. After they had last seen each other—in Devonshire, eleven months before—Jonathan had decided to read the books himself, in hopes of better comprehending Miss Tilney's mind.

How richly he had been rewarded! Scott's novels thrilled Jonathan in a way no fiction had ever done before, not even the plays of Shakespeare. Before he was even halfway through *Waverley*, he had asked his father to supply the Pemberley library with every volume of Scott's fiction that it lacked. The elder Mr. Darcy could be wary of his son's fascinations, and although he was a kind and loving parent, he was not an overly indulgent one. (He even argued that they could not be entirely certain Scott was truly the writer of these novels, open secret though their authorship was.) However, when Mother expressed her own interest in the new fashion for "historical" novels, Jonathan's request had been fulfilled.

He still did not know whether he had gained a deeper knowledge of Miss Tilney's thoughts and enthusiasms, but he harbored hopes that, in time, fortune would once again unite their paths—and that he should then have the chance of pressing his suit.

When this opportunity came, he intended to be ready in every sense. Jonathan knew that some of his habits were considered to be peculiar, laughable, even at times offensive. His interests tended to levels of enthusiasm that dominated his conversation, often to the dismay of others. His parents had come to comprehend that these habits were not willful petulance on Jonathan's part but an inherent element of his nature. However, society at large would never share that understanding.

Miss Tilney had come to see this about Jonathan as well, and he felt confident of her sympathy and loyalty. Yet it seemed possible that even her acceptance had limitations, that she would wish for more from a potential husband than from a friend. Thus, during the past many months, he had embarked upon an endeavor that he thought of as fashioning a "curtain."

This curtain involved forcing himself to meet the gazes of others, even when it caused him near-physical pain. It also called upon him to rock and thump his chair only when alone. He had taught himself a few more stock phrases and acts to help him endure louder, busier gatherings. His parents had not commented upon this, but he could tell that they were proud of what they considered greater maturity and self-control. In truth, it was a torment, and he felt sure it would ever be so. But if this were the price of winning Miss Tilney's affections, he was prepared to pay it.

For the time being, however, Jonathan could come no closer to Miss Tilney than enjoying the novels of Sir Walter Scott.

In this day's reading, the wounded Ivanhoe was being nursed back to health by the courageous Rebecca. As envisioned by Jonathan, Rebecca strongly resembled Juliet Tilney. He could imagine her in colorful medieval garb, proudly defying the contempt and cruelty of the prejudiced Normans. So absorbed was he in this scene that he scarcely noted the arrival of the butler with a letter for his father. As the elder Mr. Darcy received much correspondence relating to his tenants and lands, such deliveries were not unusual, nor were the other members of the household expected to hear their contents.

Today, however, Mr. Darcy said, "It is from my aunt Lady Catherine de Bourgh."

Mrs. Darcy could but scarcely repress a smile. "Does she write to express her astonishment at Pemberley's survival after two decades of my 'pollution'?"

"It seems she writes to command our son to her immediately." His father then began to read:

> *Dear Mr. Darcy,*
> *In the past year, nearly all the land has heard of your son's imprudent and impudent interferences with the law regarding not one but two killings. This is grievous, shocking, and ought not to have been allowed by any proper mother.*

"Your own role in Jonathan's upbringing is reckoned not worth the mentioning, it seems," Mrs. Darcy remarked. Her husband gave her a sharp look before continuing.

> *Yet as the young man has acquired such skills, let him cease to deploy them solely in the interest of strangers. What use is there in identifying a murderer only after the murder has taken place? Should not true vigilance*

extend to seeking out such villains before they have done
their worst? It shall be so in this case, for I demand that
your son set out for Rosings Park this very day. Several
shocking incidents have led me to believe my own life to
be in danger—

"Good G-d!" That was the first time Jonathan had ever heard his mother take the name of the Lord in vain. "Someone has attempted to take the life of Lady Catherine?"

"So it would seem." Mr. Darcy's countenance had gone pale, but he was not a man easily unnerved. "It is entirely possible that our aunt has mistaken the matter. She often finds fault where there is none; no great amazement would it be were she to also find danger when it does not exist."

No other topic would have possessed the power to draw Jonathan's interest away from *Ivanhoe*. Even now he felt an almost magnetic pull between himself and the volume he set down on the nearest table. "May I see the rest, Father?"

The elder Mr. Darcy hesitated. "Our aunt's view of you has never been charitable."

"As I am well aware," Jonathan said. "Nothing she writes will have the power to injure me." Lady Catherine's aspersions *had* hurt Jonathan during his childhood years; she drew attention to every difference that divided him from other young men. But as he had grown older, he had noticed that Lady Catherine's disapproval was generously dispensed to nearly all comers and thus was too common to be held of much value.

When Mr. Darcy then surrendered the letter, Jonathan read the remainder.

Your son's morbid curiosity may at least provide him
with a means of determining what wickedness conceals
itself about me, and should he succeed in bringing this

*wrongdoer to justice, I shall take a far more generous
view toward his future. But let him leave for Rosings
immediately. His clothes can be sent on later, and he
will lack for nothing else in my home. Make haste!*

Jonathan did not like his aunt's suggestion of departing
Pemberley, particularly in such a swift manner that he had no
chance to prepare himself, to bring clothing and other pos-
sessions with which he was familiar, and to disrupt the gentle
routine he so relied upon. In any other circumstances, he
would have pleaded with his parents to allow him to decline
the invitation or at least delay his journey until he could reconcile himself to the upheaval.

But this was his great chance to once more take up the
work of investigation that so fascinated him—and, even more
vitally, to see Miss Tilney again. Jonathan resolved that his
discomfort must be endured in the furtherance of these pas-
sions. And also for his aunt's safety . . . a consideration that,
he realized, ought to bear more weight with him than it did.

"You must go, of course," said Mr. Darcy. "If there is nothing to it in the end, well, then you have had an unnecessary
journey but no worse." Jonathan could not call any journey
that led to meeting with Miss Tilney *unnecessary*, but he knew
better than to say so to his father, who continued, "Yet if
there is any true risk to Lady Catherine, the cost of failing to
heed her letter could be grievous indeed."

"You cannot send him alone!" Mrs. Darcy protested.
"However unlikely the risk, if a murderer truly does lurk at
Rosings, our son will be in great danger."

"Indeed. I shall go with him." After a brief pause, Mr. Darcy
added, "My dearest, I believe it would be most conducive to
your own safety and peace of mind were you to remain at
Pemberley."

"You mean, it would be less provoking to Lady Catherine." Mrs. Darcy sighed. "Perhaps I shall write my sister Mary— I could travel with you into Kent, but leave you at Tunbridge Wells that I might visit Mary's family. Though I do not flinch from her ladyship's judgments, I would not further disturb her at a time when she must be much afraid."

Jonathan noted that Lady Catherine had said nothing of fear in her letter; and indeed, he could never recall his great-aunt's displaying that emotion even once. However, he trusted his mother's instincts in such matters far more than his own.

He would have gone to help his aunt at any time. Severe as Lady Catherine had ever been upon him, Jonathan paid her every civility that was her due. (She was well aware of what she was due, and not shy of reminding anyone of it.) At times, it seemed to Jonathan that his parents' patience and forbearance in Lady Catherine's company arose not only from familial duty but also from some other, more mysterious source, as though his father in particular felt himself indebted to her. Why this should be so, Jonathan had never been able to discern, nor had he dared to ask.

By this time, *Ivanhoe* was all but forgotten. The prospect of another investigation was far more fascinating—yet the principal attraction of this letter came at the very end, in a passage he had not read out loud:

> *The reports pertaining to your son's efforts in such*
> *matters have, one and all, linked him to a young girl*
> *from some family or other of Gloucestershire. I have*
> *no wish to encourage such an unsuitable match, nor*
> *to inflame the girl's avarice by raising false hopes*
> *pertaining to our family. Yet, it is said that she, too, had*
> *a hand in revealing the truth in these situations, and*

given his oddness, it may be that his success owes much
to her presence. Thus I have also summoned Miss Juliet
Tilney to Rosings immediately.

Miss Tilney's invitation to Rosings Park was, that very instant, the subject of conversation at Rosings itself.

"There is no saying to what heights the girl's ambitions may have risen," Lady Catherine declared in the sitting room, where she held court from an ornately carved chair that bore a rather studied resemblance to a throne. Certainly the mood in the room often held all the stiff formality of court with few of its attendant luxuries and none of its social whirl, for those drawn together there had varied but little during the previous two decades. "Too well have I seen to what lengths headstrong, impolitic young ladies will go in order to make themselves one day the mistress of Pemberley. Certainly my young nephew has not enough wits to escape being ensnared. But mark my words, his father will come with him. His vigilance and mine will make quick work of this Miss Tilney's scheming."

From the far side of the room spoke Lady Catherine's daughter, Anne, a woman in her forties, whose shawl was even then being adjusted about her shoulders by their ever-hovering servant. "Mama, if my cousin's vigilance could not keep him safe from his own imprudent match, how can it be relied upon to protect his son?"

"Do not speak of it!" Lady Catherine twisted her lace handkerchief in her hand. "Darcy's foolishness in that matter, his unkindness—never shall I cease to wonder at them. But many a man chooses more wisely for his son than he does for himself."

"I hope you do not still regret Darcy's choice, for that would suggest that you regret mine as well." Colonel Fitzwilliam had ever been connected to the de Bourgh family as Lady Catherine's nephew, yet upon marrying Anne de Bourgh sixteen years hence, he had become a resident of Rosings Park. Though husband and wife sat next to each other, they shared not a glance.

"Your kindness speaks well of you," said Lady Catherine, "and I have had no complaints about your conduct as my son-in-law. Yet I cannot but think how differently all might have been had Darcy only seen sense."

"How very penetrating your thoughts are, Lady Catherine," said the local clergyman, one William Collins. "To imagine an entire history unlived, all that might have taken place—it is a feat of the greatest insight and understanding." Lady Catherine's only response was a sniff.

Next to Mr. Collins sat his wife, Charlotte, who had attended her husband on most of his trips to Rosings throughout the entirety of their marriage. Long ago she had learned not to blush at his most fawning comments, even at times not to hear them at all. Today, however, she felt her cheeks flush at this particularly inept attempt, and she hoped her disquiet was attributed only to the heat of the fire, which had been stoked very high for this time of year.

"I shall be glad of seeing Darcy again," said Colonel Fitzwilliam. "And Jonathan, too. Say what you will of his habits, but I find him a good-hearted, honest young man."

"His good heart I have no need of," Lady Catherine replied. "It is good sense I require, and *that* I have seen little of from my young grandnephew. But I insist that this shall be one of the occasions!"

~

Gloucestershire and the Tilney family held little of Lady Catherine's esteem; she would have been most shocked to discover the sentiment was entirely returned by the Tilneys. "What is this Lady Catherine to us?" Henry Tilney said. The offending missive remained in his hands. "That she should summon our daughter to such risk, with so little feeling, such immense pride—"

"She is a woman in danger for her life," replied Catherine Tilney. Juliet watched her parents, not daring to interrupt either. Her mother continued. "She is afraid. Fear can wear the mask of arrogance; some believe that if they pretend no weakness, they will feel none."

"Nonsense, and all the more reason to decline her request, if a letter so impudent can be called by that name." Father glanced at the fire, and Juliet feared he might throw the letter there and burn it up, along with all her chances of another investigation.

And she longed for another chance so badly! Even before her first efforts in Surrey, she had sensed vaguely that life could and should hold more than endless piano practice, embroidery, and German verbs. However, she had not been discontented, for what else was there for a young woman to do? Since taking up her investigatory pursuits, however, Juliet had felt the thrill of fully employing her wits, the fascination of discovering more elements of human nature, and—perhaps more than any other sensation—the satisfaction of knowing that her endeavors had *purpose*. Always she had been told that the meaning of a woman's life was to be found in caring for her family, and this duty was not one Juliet wished to forsake. But she had the capacity for more besides, and she longed to demonstrate such capacity again.

"Papa, an elderly woman is in danger of losing her life," said Juliet. "Regardless of her manners of demeanor, she is a fellow Christian soul in need. How will you feel, if you refuse my going, and the murderer then strikes her down?"

Mrs. Tilney nodded. "This is my thinking precisely."

"Neither of you deceive me." Mr. Tilney smiled at them both; his good humor could rarely be eclipsed for long. "Catherine, my dear, you will always choose that which is unusual over that which is ordinary."

"I believe you mean that I will always choose what is interesting over that which is dull." Mrs. Tilney paused. "Granted, the one is very like the other."

Mr. Tilney turned to Juliet. "And you only want another chance to see that young Mr. Darcy!" He meant to tease her; he could not have guessed how his words lashed his daughter's heart.

Yet she remained composed. "Jonathan Darcy has no interest in me, Papa. I have no expectations from him. But he is a good man. I know he will do his Christian duty by Lady Catherine. I hope only to do the same."

Henry Tilney looked from his daughter to his wife and back again. "How is it the two of you always defeat me?"

"No good general reveals his strategy," said Mrs. Tilney, and Juliet managed not to smile.

Chapter Two

The Darcy carriage was not an uncommon sight in this part of Kent. Darcy had ever done his duty by his aunt, visiting her often and showing her every courtesy. Once, he had been her ladyship's favorite—spoken of as the genteelest, handsomest gentleman in the land, and possessed by far of the finest house (the only occasions on which she was ever heard to consider her own home, Rosings Park, as inferior to any other structure lesser than Chatsworth).

Her favoritism had ended with his marriage. Despite the displeasure Lady Catherine had never ceased to voice since, Darcy continued his visits. Elizabeth sometimes accompanied him, forbearing Lady Catherine's slights with considerable grace, though privately Darcy suspected Elizabeth endured this mostly for the sport she made of it afterward. His wife generally spent part, if not the entirety, of her time in Kent, at her sister Mary's home, and it was there he and Jonathan had left her the day prior. Darcy had brought all three of his sons on several occasions, but Jonathan less often than the others—for his son's peculiarities of temper were little respected at Rosings, and Darcy would not have him subjected to undue pain.

Jonathan has made no complaint on this present occasion, Darcy thought as the carriage rolled along the road leading to Rosings Park. *Perhaps it is his eagerness to conduct another investigation. Or perhaps he is desirous only of seeing Miss Tilney again.* Neither prospect was entirely welcome to Darcy.

"There is another carriage on the road some distance behind us," said Jonathan, peering from the window. "Do you think it may be Miss Tilney?"

"I do not believe the post coach travels this road." Darcy decided it would be as well to temper his son's expectations. "Nor are we certain that she will respond to Lady Catherine's summons. Our aunt is unknown to her, and her parents may not wish to further damage Miss Tilney's reputation for the sake of a perfect stranger to their family."

Jonathan looked at his father in evident dismay. "I do not think Miss Tilney would allow any person to be in danger when she might be able to help, whether known to her or not." Darcy nodded, granting this much; though he had doubts of Miss Tilney's delicacy, he did not question her decency. His son continued, "Why should her reputation be injured by taking part in these investigations? Is it wrong for a person to aid in the protection of the innocent, the capture of a murderer?"

"Indeed not," said Mr. Darcy. Jonathan's perceptions of the world differed from his own; here, he must ensure that his son viewed matters clearly. "However, Miss Tilney has seen much that no proper young woman should ever see. She has asked questions no gentlewoman should propose, and learned answers that should be entirely absent from polite discourse. She is no longer as innocent in thought as most men would wish in their brides. There is, perhaps, injustice in this, for Miss Tilney's proximity to such violent events was but a matter of circumstance. Unjust or not, however, society will judge, and its judgments are not easily ignored."

Jonathan sank back onto the carriage cushions. Darcy felt a twinge of conscience—Elizabeth argued that where society was wrong, it could be ignored quite easily indeed, and though she had never won him entirely to this view, he comprehended it far more than he had in his youth. But the guarding of Miss

Tilney's reputation was her parents' responsibility; Jonathan's reputation was Darcy's to protect. Such investigations could taint Jonathan only through association. Society's calumnies would always adhere more stubbornly to a woman's virtues than to a man's.

"It *was* the Darcys ahead of us," said Juliet as the Tilney carriage traveled through the imposing gates of Rosings Park. "Do you not see?"

"We have arrived together almost to the minute, though I would have expected familial duty to compel them to greater speed." Mr. Tilney smiled conspiratorially at his daughter. "Do you think Mr. Darcy is, perhaps, not terribly fond of his aunt?"

Juliet wondered whether her father's sense of humor would cause trouble for them upon this trip. Then she recollected the frosty, imperious tone of Lady Catherine's letter and corrected her wonderings; the question was only how much trouble, and when. She was determined to both minimize and postpone where she could.

How proud she was to be arriving in her grandfather's coach! At least by its use Juliet could demonstrate to this haughty Lady Catherine de Bourgh that she had family ties of worth and respectability.

The Darcys waited for them on the steps, civilly choosing for all to enter the house at the same time. Jonathan Darcy smiled at Juliet so openly that she could hardly help smiling back. (But why should she wish to refrain from smiling? The reluctance was strange, an impulse Juliet would have to consider at another time.) It seemed to her impossible that they had not seen each other in a year; his face had remained so vivid in her mind. The leaping delight she felt was, she told herself, the glee of undertaking a new investigation—that, and a natural pleasure in friendship. No more.

Although it was not generally the office of a young unmarried girl to make introductions, in this case there was nothing for it. She said, "It is such a pleasure to see you both again. I should say that I wish it were in pleasanter circumstances—but these circumstances are more pleasant than those when we last met, as here at least the murderer has been unsuccessful. May I introduce my father, Mr. Henry Tilney? Papa, this is Mr. Fitzwilliam Darcy and his son Mr. Jonathan Darcy."

"Greetings, Mr. Tilney, Miss Tilney," said the elder Mr. Darcy. "I see that you, like I, have seen the wisdom of leaving our wives well away from this unfortunate business."

"In truth, I believe Mrs. Tilney is somewhat disappointed to miss the excitement," said Mr. Tilney. "But she is very near writing the conclusion of her latest novel; and at such times, all other considerations of life are lost upon the author, entirely lost." This casual reference to her mother's authorship startled Juliet—women rarely publicly admitted doing anything so bold as writing novels, and never before had anyone in the family spoken openly of Catherine Tilney's work to any but their closest intimates.

If I did not know better, Juliet thought darkly, *I would think my father meant to* shock *Mr. Darcy.*

"A pleasure to meet you, Mr. Tilney," said the younger Mr. Darcy. Juliet noted with some surprise that he met her father's eyes and held that gaze for far longer than he generally did—even more so than most would do at such an introduction.

"Likewise," said Mr. Tilney, in such a measured tone that only his daughter could sense his wariness.

Juliet meant to ask the younger Mr. Darcy about his

journey—how they found the roads, which towns they had passed through; all the normal discourse between travelers, which though dull in itself could pave the way toward more open and congenial conversation. However, the butler had appeared to show them into Rosings Park.

The home of Lady Catherine de Bourgh was indeed a fine one, and most imposing. Although it was not as large as Northanger Abbey, much more expense had been lavished upon its fittings and furnishings, to rich effect. Juliet walked past long damask drapes held back with gilded cords and vast candelabra filled with fine wax candles, fully lit despite the brightness of the day outside on their way to the drawing room where they would be presented.

As they walked into the oddly shadowy room, the butler announced, "Mr. Darcy of Pemberley, Mr. Jonathan Darcy, Mr. Tilney of Woodston, Miss Juliet Tilney."

"Well!" came the response. "And you have come none too quickly, have you, nephew?"

"We first took Mrs. Darcy to Tunbridge Wells to visit her sister," said Mr. Darcy. "Though this delayed us but shortly. We are eager to assist you in this time of travail."

Despite the illumination from the candles, Juliet had required a few moments for her eyesight to adjust to the dimness of this grand room in which all the curtains were drawn on a fine day. Blinking, she could finally make out the figures seated there. First was a woman in her early middle years, small and delicate. The fair curls that peeped from beneath her fine lace cap were liberally streaked with silver, rendering her even more colorless than she would have been otherwise—which was very pale indeed. Her expression seemed pinched, and her hands were clasped tightly in her lap. A servant stood at her side, as if waiting for a command at any moment: a lady's companion, no doubt. This woman's obvious fragility made it clear such a servant was, for her, less affectation than necessity.

Next to this pale woman sat a man roughly her father's age, tall and correct in his person, with salt-and-pepper hair and a wide smile. Even as Juliet observed him, this man stood and held out his hand to Jonathan's father with great cordiality. "Darcy, my friend. It has been too long—six months, perhaps!"

Juliet had not known the elder Mr. Darcy could smile so broadly. "Mr. Tilney, Miss Tilney, allow me to introduce my cousins, Colonel Fitzwilliam and his wife, Anne, and my aunt, Lady Catherine de Bourgh."

Lady Catherine herself sat on an intricately carved and gilded chair, an embroidered velvet cap upon her head. Though elderly, she comported herself with great vigor and dignity. She gestured briskly toward Juliet. "Come, girl, let me have a look at you."

Mr. Tilney shifted on his feet; Juliet knew the thoughts running through his mind, likely indignation at his daughter being examined like a prize sow at market. But, contrary to expectation, the manners of the upper classes are often rather rougher than those of less exalted birth, and Juliet was neither surprised nor insulted. She stepped forward, saying, "It is only natural that you should wish to take my measure, given the gravity of the business for which you have summoned me. Thank you for the great trust you have already shown."

Lady Catherine raised an eyebrow as pointed as a gable. "You seem a pleasant, quick sort of girl. You may sit. And you, young Jonathan? Are you able to attend to important matters today?"

"I have come here with every such intention," said the younger Mr. Darcy. He took the chair between Lady Catherine's and Juliet's own. Happily, he seemed determined to use his familiarity with his aunt to shepherd the conversation to the point. "Now, dear aunt, please tell us—how is it that someone has been trying to kill you?"

"The first vexing incident," said Lady Catherine, "might have been nothing. *I* thought it of grave importance from the very start, but Anne and Fitzwilliam, the Collinses—all assured me that the carriage axle might simply have broken, rather than been sawed through, and I allowed myself to be persuaded. Lawson the stable master said it *looked* deliberately done, however. It was his words I ought to have heeded from the first." Her eyes narrowed as she took in the Fitzwilliams; Jonathan could not but sympathize with them, as he knew all too well the wretchedness of enduring Lady Catherine's disapproval. "My driver that day was thrown into the ditch and was thereby so bruised he could not work for a week. Had I been thrown with him, who can say what mischief might have been worked?"

Miss Tilney said, "You were entirely unharmed?"

"Harm was done to my dignity, and that is harm enough," her ladyship insisted. From her tone, Jonathan could tell that she considered herself far more injured than the hapless driver in the ditch. "Then came the second incident, not two weeks prior—a rifle fired through the window!"

Father sat up straight. "Someone shot at you from the grounds?"

"Missed her by a mile, but damage was done," said Colonel Fitzwilliam, gesturing toward the tall case clock that had ever held pride of place on the far wall. Jonathan realized its pendulum no longer swung back and forth; its face had been shattered, leaving the hands pointing at hours long past against a backdrop of immobile brass gears.

"And that clock has been in my family for three generations!" Lady Catherine seemed nearly as outraged about the clock as she was about the danger to her person. The heavy drapes concealed the window, but Jonathan wondered whether the broken pane had already been repaired. Yet there seemed little chance much could have been learned from it in any case. His aunt continued, "Finally, last week, I was prompted to write to Pemberley when the last attempt took place. In the afternoon, as I made my way from my chamber toward the stairs, some person unknown shoved me most violently—I very nearly toppled over the banister. It would assuredly have been the death of me."

Miss Tilney did not lack the courage necessary to speak to Lady Catherine. "You saw nothing, I take it, Lady Catherine? Not even a glimpse of the person who pushed you—a sense of whether this person might be male or female, even?"

"If I had seen who had done it, I should scarce require the two of you," Lady Catherine said. Her temper, rarely pleasant, was darkening rapidly. "No, not a hint had I. By such time as I could right myself to look behind me, the miscreant had vanished."

Jonathan knew he must be very cautious with his phrasing next: "Did you hear footsteps? A heavy tread, or lighter perhaps? Could you tell the direction in which your assailant went?"

His tact did not deceive her ladyship. "You suspect I conjured it all up in my mind after a mere fall, do you not? No, indeed. Whoever attempted such dark work made an escape quiet as a cat, but I assure you, the push was very strong. Undoubtedly deliberate. It was then I knew a killer to be far too close to my person, and thus I resolved to summon you both."

Three separate attempts! Jonathan thought. *Whoever has desired my aunt's death has desired it very much indeed.*

Anne de Bourgh Fitzwilliam had a stronger acquaintance than most with her mother's dark moods and tempers, as well as those few actions that might have the power of dispelling them. Quietly she turned to Mrs. Jenkinson, the servant who had served as a kind of companion for many years and thus had some expertise in this area herself. "If afternoon tea were to arrive early," Anne murmured, "I very much doubt Mama would take it amiss."

"Indeed, ma'am. Right away, ma'am." With that Jenkinson quietly scurried out to begin hurrying the kitchen maids in their duty.

"That was wise, my dear," said her husband as he sat by her side once more. "Besides, both our friends and our new acquaintances have had a long journey. No doubt they will appreciate some refreshment."

"No doubt," echoed Anne. She smiled at Mr. Darcy, who—as usual—turned away.

Jonathan she had known his entire life; he was in some respects an unusual young man, but Anne—who had always been of fragile health and also required particular attention and care—had more patience with this than most persons did, certainly more than her mother. She thought well of Jonathan's character and intelligence and could guess how he would undertake the strange but important work ahead.

It was Miss Tilney she did not know, Miss Tilney whose actions, and questions, could not be guessed.

Anne glanced at her husband, who seemed to pay her no mind. They had each learned to keep their own counsel.

"Forgive my raising another subject while we discuss one of such importance," said Mr. Darcy, "but where is young Peter?"

The name of Anne's son pierced her through like an arrow. How she missed him—how desperately she wanted him home! Her husband took her hand, either in sympathy or the appearance of it, as he replied, "Peter has gone to school. He is eight years of age now, you know."

"Few boys are sent to school so young," Mr. Darcy said. "Ten years is more common."

How often had Anne said just the same! And how often had her mother replied, as she did now, "There is nothing *common* about my grandson!"

Darcy frowned. "I had thought—the boy's health—"

"The boy's health," said Lady Catherine, "is unlikely to improve if he continues to be coddled and spoiled by his mother. No, a good proper education—play with schoolfellows—it is by far the best thing for him. I insisted upon at the first possibility."

Colonel Fitzwilliam nodded. "We heeded Lady Catherine in this—as we do in most things."

As we must, thought Anne. *As long as my mother lives.*

The cart with tea was wheeled in rather early, Juliet thought, but she was grateful for a pause in the conversation to collect her thoughts. As the others began complimenting Lady Catherine's excellent arrangements—usually as soon as Lady Catherine herself pointed them out—Juliet spoke in a low voice to the younger Mr. Darcy. "This is quite different, is it not? Multiple attempts for us to investigate, and Lady Catherine yet lives to give us insight as to who might have wished her harm. That only renders the situation more fascinating, do not you think, Mr. Darcy?"

"I do, indeed." He hesitated, as if he did not know what to say. Juliet had no idea what might lie behind this pause, and thus she was entirely unprepared when he added, "I say—

Miss Tilney, if on the balance you think it unwise that you should take part in the investigation, you need but say the word."

Consternation very nearly stole Juliet's voice. At last she was able to reply, "Unwise? I have come all this way, have I not?"

"It could as easily be said that this was a social invitation, no more," said the younger Mr. Darcy. "Given your acquaintance with my family, few would wonder at it."

"You do not want me to investigate these attempts with you?" Now it was a struggle for Juliet not to raise her voice, but she forced the words out at a mere whisper, so that none might be distracted from tea and politer conversation to witness this humiliation. "You do not think my assistance likely to be of use? After what we have accomplished together in the past?"

"Oh, it is not that at all, Miss Tilney!" He smiled at her, as though he did her some great favor. "But I would not wish to compromise your reputation."

Now she understood. Even Jonathan Darcy thought that her investigations had somehow coarsened her—worse, that they had detracted from her value as a woman, as a potential bride. Though Juliet had worked to disabuse herself of any hopes regarding the younger Mr. Darcy, she had scarcely expected such a blow as this. Her cheeks burned, and she wished for a fan that she might have sheltered her face. "My reputation, Mr. Darcy, is not yours to heed. My parents think it respectable, as you see from my father's presence. Or do you presume your judgment more correct than his as a clergyman?"

His face fell. "I did not—I would not— Forgive me, Miss Tilney. Yes, of course, we shall continue on together."

This concession seemed scarcely adequate to the insult

that had preceded it. Juliet spared herself the need to converse further by helping herself to a scone.

I have got it wrong again, Jonathan thought.

He had meant only to protect Miss Tilney from the kind of cruel gossip his father had hinted would be her lot were she to continue undertaking such investigations. Yet she seemed to look upon his interference as officious. His curtain concealed much, but it could not save him from every misstep. Bewildered and unhappy—how could their reunion have taken such a bad turn so soon?—he cast about in vain for some other, tamer topic of conversation.

Lady Catherine, however, had no need for tameness at present. "Well, young Jonathan? You and Miss Tilney were very much in discussion, though I dare not hope you have yet perceived much of value."

"No, dear aunt," Jonathan said, "but we must determine a course of action before we begin."

"How long will this take?" She sniffed again, then waved off Jenkinson, who had attempted to approach her with a linen handkerchief. "Will you be many hours at the task? Or days?"

Miss Tilney seemed to have recovered herself. "We cannot know how long the work will take until we start, Lady Catherine, and so we should begin as soon as ever we are able."

Jonathan had already determined the most likely obstacle to their plans would be Lady Catherine herself, unless this next were made to seem as if it were her idea, rather than theirs. "If we were able to ask questions, ma'am—of anyone and everyone who might have been present—"

With a wave, Lady Catherine said, "Yes, yes, of course. You may question all the servants. They can have no objection."

"We must question *everyone*," replied Miss Tilney. "Any person present might have seen something of importance, even if they themselves do not yet realize as much."

Any person resident in Rosings Park could also be guilty. Jonathan had recognized that even before setting out from Pemberley. He also recognized how wise Miss Tilney had been not to raise that point directly with Lady Catherine. How could he ever have considered doing this without her?

The next point, however, had to be raised, and Jonathan felt himself the best person to do so. "The questions we pose may seem . . . impertinent, even indelicate, at times. One must go beyond the boundaries of polite conversation if one is to uncover a truth so terrible."

"You will not be impertinent *with me*," said Lady Catherine, "as I shall not stand for it in my own home. But it is not my counsel you require, for if I had been given any clues in the matter, I should already have settled it entirely. No, no, it is the others who may have the answers you seek, and my commandment is given: All shall answer you entirely and honestly, the better to resolve this for once and for all!"

Chapter Three

Etiquette is so powerful that it can supersede near any other consideration, even the need to discover a would-be murderer. After tea, the guests could do nothing but settle into their rooms—though unpacking is of course done by servants, it is a rare traveler who does not wish to inspect the results in short order. After this, on their first night as guests at Rosings Park, they had of course to dine with their hostess, and she had ordered such rich fare it was as if they had gathered for a celebration.

"I had wished for the Collinses to attend," said Lady Catherine, "for the Tilneys will not know them, and must be introduced."

"Lady Catherine is the patron of Mr. Collins, who holds the living in this parish," explained Jonathan to Miss Tilney, smiling in the hopes that her ruffled feelings would be soothed.

Her expression remained too placid for him to read as she said to Lady Catherine, "Then I am most sorry they could not be present."

"It is most displeasing! They are always so attentive, but on this occasion, it appears a woman is very ill at her childbed, and both Mr. and Mrs. Collins felt their presence necessary."

"Indeed, that is an occasion of much trial, much suffering," Mr. Tilney said, with real feeling. "As a clergyman myself, Lady Catherine, I know well that the needs of the flock must ever be placed before the wishes of the shepherd."

"Do you remember that Christmas morning with the Davises?" Miss Tilney smiled at her father, who grinned back in the silent, mutual enjoyment of some story from their past. Jonathan longed to learn more—allowing people to tell their favorite memories was, in his experience, a useful conversational gambit, particularly when unsure about someone's mood. However, his curiosity was not shared by Lady Catherine.

"I do not see why the woman could not be attended after dinner just as well," she said as the servants began taking away the soup bowls in preparation for the next course. "Certainly Mr. Collins has not often missed any opportunity of dining at Rosings."

"In my memory," Mr. Darcy added, "he has never missed one."

"There, you see?" Lady Catherine said, reclaiming the conversation. "Suddenly in these past few months, he seems to value the invitation less than he should."

Jonathan found that difficult to believe, as Mr. Collins was ever ready with fulsome praise for his patroness. It would not be unlike his aunt to exaggerate, to turn one missed dinner into a supposed unfortunate trend. Yet before his arrival in Rosings, he had wondered whether Lady Catherine might have been exaggerating her stories of dangers to her person, and it now appeared that she had not. Her perceptions, while sometimes skewed, were not wholly false, and Jonathan had in the past heard her make observations of genuine insight.

If Mr. Collins had—after decades of constant attendance upon Lady Catherine—suddenly begun to absent himself from her presence, it would be prudent to ask why.

Juliet awoke in the vast four-poster in excellent temper. She was young and healthy—she had slept well, in highly comfortable surroundings; the sun shone; and she had work of purpose to do; such a morning cannot be resisted.

Yet one blot darkened her mood as the Rosings lady's maid swiftly prepared her for the day, namely, the unkind suggestion last night from Jonathan Darcy. *He thinks my reputation endangered by the same actions he proposes to take up without a second thought,* Juliet mused. It was very unfair—and maddening precisely because its injustice did not make it less than true. Men were allowed much that women could not assay. Her parents had hinted more than once that not all prospective suitors would look well upon Juliet's investigative experiences, had they not? She had long ago decided that such suitors were exactly the ones she would least like to marry; the right husband would not simply "overlook" her determination and curiosity but honor her for them. So why had Mr. Darcy's comment rankled so?

Perhaps because, deep within, Juliet had wished that Jonathan Darcy would be that suitor. Now more than ever, it appeared he would not.

"Ow!" The brush caught in her hair, and Juliet had exclaimed without thinking. Immediately she wished the cry unvoiced, for the lady's maid, a woman named Daisy, appeared aghast.

"Begging your pardon, miss," Daisy said. "I did not mean to tug at you."

"Of course. No, it is you who must forgive me, for making such a fuss. I was more surprised than hurt."

Daisy appeared much relieved. Juliet reflected that if even so august a personage as the elder Mr. Darcy could expect rudeness from Lady Catherine, the servants at Rosings Park probably heard far worse on a nigh-daily basis. She imagined asking Mr. Jonathan Darcy about this, then caught herself anew. Still, her thoughts tended toward him.

He does not care for you in that way, she reminded herself, *as was clear from his behavior in both Surrey and Devonshire. Besides, nearly a year has gone by—a year in which his parents would have invited me to Pemberley had they any intent of encouraging a courtship. This year may well have changed him—made him more stern, more austere. More like his father.*

Descending for the morning meal, Juliet met her father upon the stair; upon entering the breakfast room, she found a large part of those staying in the house—nearly everyone save for Lady Catherine. The Fitzwilliams sipped coffee without speaking much, though Juliet could not discern whether this silence sprang from comfortable familiarity or a lack of any such feeling. Meanwhile, the Darcys sat together at the far side of the table. It seemed to Juliet that one or the other of them, perhaps both, had specifically chosen a spot where it would be graceless for her to directly join them.

Am I so disreputable? Juliet thought, in no good temper. *Well, let them both see how little I care for their attentions.* She sat as far away from them as possible; spoke with great animation to her father; and inwardly prided herself on being so evidently, obviously dedicated to investigation alone. If Mr. Jonathan Darcy would be so easily distracted by other concerns, all the more reason for her to act from purer motives.

(It will be noted by the attentive reader that Juliet was, in fact, extremely distracted by the Darcys, but we all must at times take considerable effort to not care about that which is disagreeable before that effort bears fruit.)

In the end, after the Fitzwilliams had gone about their daily business, the younger Mr. Darcy took the first step to begin their investigation in earnest by addressing her across the table. "Well, Miss Tilney, we should, I propose, begin with the first attempt," he said, seemingly oblivious to the earlier slight. "Only after we have learned all we could from it should we move on to the second, and then to the third."

"We are in accord, Mr. Darcy," Juliet replied. If he could pretend nothing was amiss between them, so, too, could she. "The first attempt was the sabotage of the carriage, was it not?"

"To the stables we go, then." Mr. Tilney smiled at his daughter, who could scarcely contain her dismay. From the corner of her eye, she could see that the younger Mr. Darcy shared her consternation. In this, at least, their feelings were the same.

But Juliet knew she must be the one to raise the objection. "Papa, the work we embark upon is delicate in nature. To have other persons present would prove a distraction from our purpose."

Mr. Tilney raised an eyebrow. "I should have thought two young people together on their own far more distractible."

Juliet knew her father's larkish humor, but the elder Mr. Darcy did not, nor did he seem pleased by it. "Do you doubt my son's purpose?"

"Indeed, no." Mr. Tilney gave Juliet a look, an invitation to join him in silent disapproval of such humorlessness. She only wished her mother were there; Mama always knew how to smooth over such moments.

Yet the elder Mr. Darcy seemed to consider the matter soothed already. "There is no impropriety in going together to the stables, provided the groom and other servants are present."

Mr. Tilney looked as though he had thought of another witticism to utter, but it remained unspoken. Juliet silently thanked the Lord for this mercy.

❧

Jonathan had thought that his first moment alone together with Miss Tilney would be a happy one, but it appeared that she still harbored some displeasure regarding his comment the evening before. She was entirely matter-of-fact as they strode from Rosings Park onto its verdant grounds. "I believe that yesterday I heard Lady Catherine refer to the stable master as a Mr. Lawson?"

"Yes, Lawson is the man. I have ridden here since my childhood." Briefly, Jonathan felt a pang for his beloved horse Ebony, left by necessity at Pemberley. "The stables are this way."

Rosings's stables offered accommodations to its equines nearly as grand as the house did for humans. The straw was kept fresh, and the horses drank from troughs of water clean enough to suggest constant refreshment. Lawson, a gray-haired fellow with large ears, greeted Jonathan with cordiality befitting their stations and acquaintance, and was most civil when introduced to Miss Tilney. All such congeniality was threatened, however, upon mention of the broken axle.

"It was deliberately done, of that I assure you," Lawson said with some heat. "Never should a carriage in my keeping fall into such disrepair as to break apart, though it amused someone to make it appear so."

"Do you believe yourself to have been a target, Mr. Lawson?" Miss Tilney asked. "Do you think that the fiend behind this meant not only to endanger Lady Catherine, but to impugn you?"

Lawson's shoulders slumped. "No, miss. It was my hurt pride answering you, not my good sense. Nay, the other attacks on her ladyship had nothing to do with my stables, and so I reckon it more likely that the wrongdoer thought not at all what such an incident might mean for me. Had Lady Catherine died, the local constabulary might have placed the blame squarely upon my shoulders, though I nearly broke my head open in the ditch."

That, Jonathan thought, was another facet of a murderer's wickedness, one often overshadowed by the heinousness of the killing itself: always married with it was the willingness for another human being, some innocent person wholly unconnected with the business, to hang for the murderer's crime. He said only, "It was you who drove Lady Catherine that day?"

"Myself and no other," Lawson replied. "Her ladyship prefers a full complement of servants with livery for most purposes, but she was going no farther than Hunsford Parsonage, a journey she takes regularly. Nothing seemed at all amiss at any point before the axle's break."

"Had you examined the axle that day?" Miss Tilney asked.

Lawson's shoulders sagged. "No, miss, and oft have I repented of it. But until that day, it was my practice to inspect carriages after each use, not before. Perhaps I would have taken a look earlier had the carriage been out of use for some extended period of time, but such was not the case here."

Jonathan knew enough of stable keeping to be aware that Lawson's methods were neither negligent nor uncommon. In fact, those habits were probably considered—and relied upon—by the wrongdoer they sought. He asked, "Who has access to your stables, besides the servants? Do all three residents of Rosings Park come often to take carriages or ride? Are any guests allowed that right?"

"Lady Catherine herself, of course," said Lawson, "and both the colonel and Mrs. Fitzwilliam, though I must say Mrs. Fitzwilliam rides but rarely, and never without Mrs. Jenkinson at her side. She lacks the strength for it."

"Which would suggest that she lacks the strength to saw through a carriage axle," interjected Miss Tilney.

"Colonel Fitzwilliam rides nearly every day, when the weather is fine, and conducts most of his business on horseback," Lawson said.

Jonathan felt he understood the implication. "Therefore the colonel has little to do with the carriages?"

Lawson hesitated. "As a general rule, Colonel Fitzwilliam takes a carriage only in inclement weather or when he is traveling a considerable distance, and he rarely travels far without his wife and Lady Catherine present. The lone exceptions that come to my mind were when he would go to visit your father at Pemberley. Of late, however . . ."

Jonathan and Miss Tilney shared a glance—one with the true conspiratorial fascination he remembered from the past. His heart thrilled to it for that first instant, but she swiftly averted her eyes. Oh, how he must have blundered! Despite his dismay, he kept to their purpose. "Yes?" he said. "Go on?"

"On some few occasions of late, yes, the colonel has taken the carriage for trips that require less than a full day. The last of such was the day before the incident that so distressed Lady Catherine. There has not been one since." Lawson shook his head. "Do not confuse my meaning, for I do not accuse the good colonel. He was properly accompanied by a driver on all such occasions, and how a man could damage a carriage axle while riding upon it, I cannot begin to think."

"It would require a most extraordinary effort," said Miss Tilney, but her expression remained thoughtful. "Yet it may be worth noting that Colonel Fitzwilliam would have had opportunity, on these trips, to make a more thorough study of the carriage than he had before."

This insight pained Jonathan, who was fond of his cousin Fitzwilliam, but he could not but admit the justice of it.

Miss Tilney continued, "So only the members of the household or their houseguests would come to the stables."

"Only one exception to that," said Lawson, nodding toward the open stable door, "and it appears they are coming this moment, so you may ask them yourself."

Miss Tilney turned to see a party of four persons coming up the walk. "And who are they?"

Jonathan said, "It is time now for you to meet my cousins, the Collinses."

Mr. William Collins was cousin to Jonathan's mother. In fact, the house of Longbourn—in which the former Elizabeth Bennet had grown up, and in which her parents still dwelled—would upon the death of Mr. Bennet be inherited by Mr. Collins, thanks to an entail upon the property in favor of the male line. Yet Mr. Bennet remained hale and vital despite his advancing years, and thus, Mr. Collins required another house and source of income, which he had received in the form of the living at Hunsford from Lady Catherine de Bourgh.

Rarely has such a gift found a more grateful recipient. In the eyes of Mr. Collins, Lady Catherine could do no wrong—as he proclaimed frequently to all who would listen and many who attempted not to do so. Her manners, her taste, her wisdom, her condescension: all were considered equally fine in his sight and equally worthy of constant praise. Even her household fittings attracted his fulsome admiration. Such fawning regard would have been unendurable if feigned; but to most who knew him, Mr. Collins's adoration of Lady Catherine de Bourgh appeared both genuine and absolute. This did not make his paeans to her virtues much easier in the listening, but at least they were not compounded with the sin of falseness.

Juliet's unprejudiced first impression of the Collinses was that they looked like any other genteel family strolling to see a neighbor: a middle-aged couple, simply dressed, neither handsome nor plain; a daughter close to Juliet's own age; and a son perhaps three or four years younger. The daughter more closely resembled her father, and the son his mother, these inheritances more flattering for the children than their parents.

As they approached, Mr. Collins's smile widened, far past the point of reasonable happiness in meeting; to Juliet's astonishment, when they came within paces of herself and Mr. Darcy, he actually bowed deeply, as though being presented at court. "My dear Mr. Darcy! It is ever a pleasure to see my cousin. How tall you have grown! The very figure of his father, is he not, Mrs. Collins?"

"They are very like," replied Mrs. Collins. She also smiled, but more sensibly than her husband.

"I have been the same height for these past two years at least." Mr. Darcy looked down at his shoes, as if wondering whether he would suddenly resume growing and render them too small for purpose. Juliet could not help smiling; she was not wholly satisfied with Jonathan Darcy at present, but she remained fond of his small foibles.

Mrs. Collins interjected with swiftness and courtesy: "Will you not introduce us to your friend?"

"Of course," said Mr. Darcy, recollecting himself. "Mr. Collins, Mrs. Collins, this is our friend Miss Juliet Tilney of Woodston, Gloucestershire. Miss Tilney, these are Mr. and Mrs. Collins and their children."

"Yes, yes," said Mr. Collins, holding out his hand to present his children as though they were to be on display. "Allow me to introduce you to our daughter, Catherine, and our son, De Bourgh."

"We go by Katy and Deb," said the daughter, with a smile that seemed both more sensible than her father's and warmer than her mother's. "It will be good to have more young people near."

Deb added, with an honesty lost to those over the age of fourteen: "It's been dull as a churchyard since little Pete left."

"To speak of Peter Fitzwilliam, the grandson of Lady Catherine de Bourgh, with such familiarity—" Mr. Collins stopped himself, evidently unwilling to upbraid his son before a new acquaintance. "But I digress. We have come to invite you to luncheon at our cottage now. Of course our humble abode cannot compare in grandeur to Rosings Park, but rest assured, Lady Catherine herself has advised us on all our arrangements!"

"If our host will excuse us, we will be only too delighted to come." Juliet was hungry . . . but more important, if the Collinses had access to the grounds and the stables at Rosings, she needed to learn more of them. Luncheon provided the perfect opportunity.

And whatever else Mr. Darcy might think of her—however more stern or conventional the past year had made him—in this, she felt confident they agreed.

From the window of his study, Colonel Fitzwilliam saw the Collinses departing with Miss Tilney and the younger Mr. Darcy. He had known the luncheon invitation would be forthcoming—Mr. Collins had written the day before for Lady Catherine's permission—but he had believed the Collinses likely to be refused. Were not these young people here to investigate? Perhaps they did not believe the danger to Lady Catherine was real; perhaps, like some of their age, they were too easily distracted by ready pleasures to turn their thoughts to more serious matters. Unlikely—they had solved two murders before—but Colonel Fitzwilliam could not watch them walking away through the fields without wondering.

He looked down at the letter he was writing, blew away the sand, and carefully set it aside in a drawer, where it would not be seen by any who might intrude into his study. Then he walked to the stables. After many years of visiting Rosings Park, followed by many more years inhabiting it, he knew the habits of every resident, including his wife's tabby cat. None would cross his path, and indeed the first person to see him after leaving his study was Mr. Lawson, currently brushing the brown mare. "Colonel Fitzwilliam! Do you plan to ride today? The weather is fair for it."

"I should make the most of the days before autumn's chill, no doubt," said the colonel, "but that is not my business here. You spoke, I think, to our two younger visitors?"

"Yes, sir. I did, sir." Lawson's posture stiffened. "They asked who had occasion to take out the carriages, and of course I had to say you were among them."

"I would not expect you to lie, Mr. Lawson. Nor would I expect you to betray a confidence. You did not tell them where I went?"

Lawson shook his head, and Fitzwilliam felt some of his inner tension ease. "No, sir, and the young Mr. Darcy did point out that no man could damage a carriage axle while sitting upon it."

"Not unless he was far heavier than I!" Fitzwilliam clapped his hand on Lawson's shoulder. Truly, a faithful servant was a treasure richer than gold.

Fitzwilliam's knowledge of the goings and comings of his family and servants was indeed thorough but not beyond error. His own wife, though generally predictable in her habits, was ever pleased when she had both strength and sunshine in the same morning, and had elected to spend this one in the small gated garden on the east side of the house—the one close enough to the stables to hear conversations there.

Anne Fitzwilliam stood holding her basket, very still, puzzling over the words her husband had spoken. Where would the colonel have gone, and why had he done so in secret? Yes, he had been absent a little more than usual lately—but she had attributed this to preparations for the coming harvest. Apparently there was more to the matter.

"Do not fret, madam," said Mrs. Jenkinson, who held the garden shears and the knife to pare away thorns, keeping them ready for Anne's use. "Husbands often have business of which their wives need not know."

Anne would have liked to snap at Jenkinson, to remind her that the *Mrs.* in her title was but customary, one adopted by female servants past a certain age even if they had never married. What did she know of husbands? But Anne's irritation was held in check by the fear that she herself knew nothing of husbands, either.

Blithely unaware of her mistress's pique, Jenkinson continued her reassurance. "Be sure, madam, there is nothing at all to it."

"Of course not, Jenkinson." Anne turned her face back to the roses. With luck, her servant would assume her mistress's attention had turned, too. She took the shears and snipped the stem of a white rose, which tumbled into her basket.

The reader will at this juncture perhaps entertain some curiosity as to the activities undertaken by the two visiting fathers—Mr. Darcy and Mr. Tilney—while their children were so engaged in their investigation. Under normal circumstances, any visitors without pressing tasks would have been expected to put themselves at Lady Catherine's disposal, to listen to her every thought and share relatively few of their own in return. Neither man was of a disposition to enjoy this; thus they must be forgiven for finding some relief in the fact that Rosings Park's circumstances were far from normal, even given the distressing cause. Lady Catherine kept more to her room than was her custom, and this freed both Mr. Darcy and Mr. Tilney to do as they wished.

Any two other guests would have, perhaps, taken pleasure in making each other's acquaintance. However, both men had come to Rosings as fathers first, and each father felt himself to have good reason for doubting the other. Protectiveness of one's child, however laudable in general terms, can lead to shortsightedness, unfairness of opinion, and even undue dislike. It was sadly thus for Darcy and Tilney.

They had each taken themselves to the library that morning to read the latest papers. To do Tilney justice, it must be noted that he attempted to make conversation with Darcy, beginning with "Your aunt takes several London papers, it seems, and yet she does not strike me as taking an avid interest in current events."

"I believe it was my late uncle who first subscribed to them," said Darcy, "and Lady Catherine has simply never taken the trouble of cancellation."

"It is, I think, considered rather stylish to take the best papers. Perhaps it is there that Lady Catherine's true interest lies?"

Tilney's humor had rarely been worse timed. For all Darcy's comprehension of his aunt's foibles and shortcomings, his sense of familial pride made such a remark offensive—even though it was also just. "If you consider it so, I wonder that you take such pleasure in the results," Darcy said, a pointed reference to Tilney's having taken up a paper.

For his part, Tilney could find the humor in almost anything save for humorlessness. He felt unduly judged for a mild remark, attributing this to Darcy's possession of an overweening sense of pride. "Forgive my comment. It was not unkindly meant."

"Respect is due one's elders," said Mr. Darcy, who had greatly honored his own excellent father, which inculcated this particular virtue.

"Respect, like all else, must be measured by truth, not by aphorism," said Mr. Tilney, who had always done his duty by his father despite his father's vanity, coldness, and even cruelty, which had in turn made him dubious of unthinking obedience to older relatives.

Thus it was that Tilney came to consider Darcy a prig, and Darcy to consider Tilney disrespectful. The discussion might have continued—and, perhaps, shown each man the error of his first judgment—had there not been a faint commotion in the entry hall, which led them both to rise and investigate.

A woman from the village of Hunsford—likely a farmer's wife, to judge by her attire—was pleading with McQuarrie the butler: "But Mr. Collins must be here. If not at the parsonage or the church, he is ever here!"

"I tell you that he is not, madam," said McQuarrie, not best pleased to be doubted.

Darcy said, "What is the meaning of this?"

The woman wiped tears from her cheeks. "Forgive me, sir, but my father—he is surely soon to breathe his last, and we have no clergyman to attend him."

"You do indeed," said Mr. Tilney. "I am a man of the cloth also, and if your local rector is not to be found, I am most willing to undertake this office myself."

"Oh, thank you, good sir! Thank you so very much."

The woman's relief was plain to see, as was Mr. Tilney's generosity. This act might have greatly improved Darcy's opinion of the man, had Tilney not then handed his paper to Darcy—as if putting him in his place. Darcy instead thought Tilney rather officious. He was not sorry to see the man fetch his coat and leave in that woman's company; any time Tilney spent time away from Rosings was entirely as Darcy wished.

Indeed, the unfortunate lady had missed her intended clergyman by only minutes, for he was at that moment occupied in escorting his two young guests to his home, Hunsford Parsonage. This house, like Mr. Collins's position as rector of the parish, had been given to him by Lady Catherine de Bourgh, an act of such singular generosity—in Mr. Collins's opinion—as still to excite his wonder nearly thirty years after the fact. On their walk to the parsonage, he informed Juliet of her ladyship's goodness three separate times. He also informed her of the worth of Lady Catherine's horses, her carriages, her best china, her second-best china ("though still, to be sure, far superior to that which is seen in most homes of nobility, so we are reliably informed"), and even the lace that trimmed her favorite bonnet. The younger Mr. Darcy seemed wholly unsurprised—rather, to have heard it all before—which affirmed Juliet's opinion that Mr. Collins was ever thus. To her, his endless effusions regarding Lady Catherine seemed as though they must be insincere, for who could sustain any genuine admiration at such a pitch, least of all for the many years Collins proudly reported in this position?

Nor was his topic of conversation merely carried on to entertain Juliet along the journey, for her arrival at Hunsford Parsonage was marked by yet more information from

Mr. Collins: Lady Catherine had approved of this very mirror, what did she say to that?

"Indeed, it is lovely," said Juliet in all honesty. All the fittings and furnishings of Hunsford Parsonage struck her as exceedingly fine. Perhaps Mr. Collins's paeans to Lady Catherine arose because of her great generosity as a patroness; Hunsford was indeed an enviable living for any clergyman.

Mr. Collins seemed ready to show Juliet every other item in the house, but his wife's politeness prevented them. "We must have another subject, my dear," said Mrs. Collins as she led them to the luncheon awaiting them.

Mr. Collins frowned in consternation, clearly unable to comprehend anyone wishing to think upon a topic beyond Lady Catherine. "Should we not honor her ladyship's exquisite taste? The liberality of her advice upon every topic?"

Sagely, Mrs. Collins continued, "You would not wish to take the pleasure of the telling away from Lady Catherine herself."

"Indeed not." Mr. Collins had caught himself already. "How wise you are, my dear!"

Deb Collins made a face; his sister, Katy, stifled a laugh. Juliet pretended not to see, but was glad to know the other young persons present were more sensible than their father.

Mrs. Collins next turned her attention to Mr. Darcy. "Pray, how is your mother? I have not had a letter from her since midsummer."

"My mother is very well, thank you. During the past few months, she was much occupied with preparing Matthew and James for school."

To Juliet, the easiest topic of conversation to follow seemed clear. "You are educated locally, Deb? Or will you go away to school in a year or two?"

Mr. Collins went very still; Mrs. Collins, more circumspect, was almost able to conceal her haste as she said, "We employ a tutor. You may not know, Miss Tilney, that Mrs. Darcy and I were great friends in our youth. Our houses were not two miles apart. I have known Elizabeth Darcy longer than any-one else in my life, save for my parents and siblings."

"Mrs. Darcy is singularly charming," said Juliet. This was the least Mrs. Darcy was due—her intelligence, and her insight, had much impressed Juliet in Surrey—but the precise circumstances that illustrated as much could not be discussed at table, pertaining as they did to the murder of Mr. Wick-ham. "Would that she could have joined us at Rosings Park!"

Juliet expected Mr. Darcy to explain his mother's absence, but he kept to the most important matter at hand: "Miss Til-ney and I were speaking to Mr. Lawson about her ladyship's carriage. The incident with the broken axle unnerved her exceedingly."

"Which one was it that broke?" asked Katy. "The chaise or the landau?"

"I thought it was the landau," said Deb.

Mr. Collins said, "It was the chaise, and a very fine equi-page it was. The damage can be repaired, one hopes, for the coach cost three hundred pounds!"

"Three hundred pounds!" Deb whistled, which drew his mother's displeasure.

"*De Bourgh*. Manners. If you know not how to comport yourself at luncheon, I cannot fathom how you will ever con-duct yourself with grace in other situations."

The boy hung his head, dejected at the rather mild rebuke. Juliet, who had a little brother roughly Deb's age, knew well how changeable moods of the young could be. (Her own mer-curial spirits at the same age were best forgotten.)

"We just purchased a new carriage, very fine indeed," said Katy. "Though it is not so elegant as her ladyship's, to own even one seems to me the height of luxury, so I cannot imagine owning so many from which to choose!"

Mrs. Collins folded her hands in her lap, restoring proper calm and propriety. "Miss Tilney, will you pass the bread?"

Juliet did so, but not without the suspicion that Mrs. Collins had sought to change the subject for a reason, though what that reason was could not yet be guessed.

Chapter Four

After luncheon, Mr. Collins accompanied Jonathan and Miss Tilney back to the gates of Rosings Park, with the intent both of preserving propriety and availing himself of the opportunity to praise those of Lady Catherine's shrubberies, trees, and paths he had not described before. These were few in number—Mr. Collins was ever thorough in his admiration of all that pertained to her ladyship—but he could not bear to neglect a single one. Only through understanding Lady Catherine's magnificence, munificence, and condescension could others come to realize the importance her patronage granted to Mr. Collins himself. To Miss Tilney, all was new; Jonathan Darcy, of course, had seen Rosings's wonders on previous visits, but it often seemed to Mr. Collins that the young man failed to attend. Many had been severe upon Jonathan for the peculiar divide in his attentiveness, which often led to fascination with irrelevancies at the expense of more appropriate points of interest. Mr. Collins, however, looked benevolently upon the young man, for it was in Jonathan and his brothers that the bloodlines of Collins and de Bourgh entwined. He left the two young persons some steps within the gate, disguising his haste to depart until after he was well concealed behind a particularly fine hedge.

"They seem a pleasant family," said Miss Tilney, "and proclaim themselves happy to have Lady Catherine as patroness."

Jonathan replied, "I do not know whether that happiness is shared equally among all the members of the family, but to be certain, Mr. Collins's gratitude would suffice for all."

"They have access to Lady Catherine's stables and live so near that they might easily intrude within," Miss Tilney said, "but what reason would they have to attack the woman from whom they have their position, their living?"

"It is unthinkable to me that Mr. Collins would harbor any animosity toward Lady Catherine," Jonathan said, but Miss Tilney's statement made him consider. "I suspect, at times, that Lady Catherine's"—how to put this?—"liberality with her opinions is less welcome to Mrs. Collins and her children than it is to Mr. Collins himself. But that seems an unlikely motive for murder."

"In the matter of Mrs. Collins and the children, I agree entirely, Mr. Darcy." Miss Tilney did not seem wholly satisfied with this, though Jonathan did not see why. "However, Mr. Collins—no man wishes to be servant rather than master. The fulsomeness of his praise beggars belief. Surely he cannot be in earnest."

Jonathan replied, "If his praise be false, then he has maintained it with the same fervor throughout my memory, and through my parents' as well. No, I believe Mr. Collins's admiration of Lady Catherine to be entirely genuine."

Although Miss Tilney appeared unconvinced, she spoke on that point no longer. "I gathered from the conversation at luncheon that Mrs. Collins is a great friend of your mother's. You must all have met very often at Rosings Park through the years."

"We have indeed. I believe that in their earlier lives they were very nearly inseparable."

Miss Tilney seemed to hesitate, but overcame her reluctance to speak before Jonathan could urge her past it. "They strike me as unlikely friends, for your mother has such wit and vivacity, and Mrs. Collins—I do not speak ill of her, she seems a most respectable matron—but her conversation does not flow so brightly."

"I had not considered that before," Jonathan said. The friendship of his mother and Mrs. Collins had forever been a fact in his life, one it had never occurred to him to question. "Perhaps Mrs. Collins was of a merrier temperament before she married."

"It is true that not all women are settled with equal happiness."

Miss Tilney became quiet then, and Jonathan was overcome by chagrin. How could he have been so thoughtless, reminding her of her dashed hopes regarding Ralph Bamber? He knew himself to be tactless at times—not by temperament but only by misunderstanding unspoken social cues—but this was exceptionally hurtful; and on this occasion, he should have known better. The distance between them (for he had noted it with concern) could only be increased by such blunders!

Yet Miss Tilney had spirit enough to turn her thoughts back to that which was most important. "We have determined that many persons have access to the stables at Rosings, so no one might mark their presence there. But we are in agreement that Mrs. Fitzwilliam lacks the strength to saw through an axle, and that the Collinses appear to have no possible motive to do Lady Catherine a harm. The colonel, however—he has been taking unusual journeys lately, enough so that Lawson felt the need to speak of it."

"But what motive has he?"

"As we just touched upon—men expect to be masters of their own households, do they not? Even if Mr. Collins is an exception to this rule, Colonel Fitzwilliam may not be. There can be no doubt that Lady Catherine reigns at Rosings."

Jonathan had never looked upon his potential future as a husband and estate owner in that light. However, when he tried to envision Lady Catherine as resident in Pemberley, giving commands with her usual zeal, he could well imagine the detrimental effect upon his father's temper (though his mother's would surely be equally darkened). "This I must grant. Yet I have known Colonel Fitzwilliam all my life, and he has never seemed to bristle under Lady Catherine's authority, even when he would have been well justified in doing so. Ever has he appeared to be a fair, just, congenial man."

"All of our potential suspects appear entirely respectable," Miss Tilney observed. "Yet we have learned that reputation is but a facade, behind which one's true character may or may not be known."

This seemed another reference to Mr. Bamber. Jonathan reckoned it best to remain silent.

Miss Tilney did not let any painful memory preoccupy her for very long. "Let us turn our attention to the second attempt on Lady Catherine."

"Yes. It is time that we investigate the rifle shot."

They began with Lady Catherine.

"'Twas a Sunday evening," she said to her two young guests. Juliet noted that, yet again, Lady Catherine had ordered her sitting room windows' curtains closed, considerably dimming the abundant afternoon light. "The Collinses ought to have been in attendance on me, but they were not present. What kept them I have yet to learn, for I was exceedingly put out after the event itself."

"Please, Lady Catherine," Juliet said, "tell us more. Were you seated in this room?"

"The very same. I was speaking to Colonel Fitzwilliam about young Peter. Both he and Anne obstinately wished for him to attend a day school nearby. A day school! A son of Rosings Park, to be educated with local boys of no particular family or connections! It shows a willful blindness to the first purpose of boys' education, which is the cultivation of appropriate friends." Lady Catherine's eyes narrowed, as though she were preparing to deliver a full lecture on the topic, but not even this could distract her from the far more important story she had to tell. "Our talk was of some duration, and I rang the bell that Mrs. Jenkinson might bring me some refreshment. No sooner had I done so than I heard the most fearful report. The window shattered, as did my clock."

Lady Catherine pointed at the window in question. Belatedly, Juliet realized that the curtains were now kept drawn to conceal her ladyship's person from anyone who might be standing in the garden outside . . . in particular, one holding a weapon. She was not certain that this preventative was as foolproof as would be hoped, given Lady Catherine's penchant for sitting always in the same chair, but both a good aim and good memory would be required to make the same attack again.

More significantly, the curtains were the first evidence that Lady Catherine—for all her imperious pride—was indeed worried that someone wished to take her life.

Mr. Darcy said, "Was anyone seen on the grounds?"

"I saw no one, nor did Fitzwilliam. He dashed outside in the hopes of capturing or at least identifying the person responsible, but either the colonel was not swift enough, or my attacker is very swift indeed, for not a person was to be spotted there. As I said before, the Collinses were one and all late; they arrived soon thereafter, first the parents each alone, then the boy and girl together. What scattered them to places far and near, I cannot guess. Anne was upstairs resting—as you know, her health is delicate. Nor did any of the servants witness the event, not even Daniels."

"Who is Daniels?" Juliet asked.

It was Mr. Darcy who answered her: "The groundskeeper. Since the marriage of the Fitzwilliams, he has also had charge of the gun room."

This struck Juliet as vitally significant. "You believe the gun to have been one of the family's own?"

"We are certain," Lady Catherine said, "for the weapon was found afterward lying on the floor of the gun room. The colonel also recognized the shot found in the clock workings afterward. The lock on the gun room door had been forced open; you may see for yourself the evidence of it."

"We should do so immediately," agreed Mr. Darcy, "and speak to Daniels as well."

As they rose, Juliet asked her final question: "Colonel Fitzwilliam is the only gentleman of the house? And no servants beyond Daniels have use of the weapons?" She knew that sometimes servants were allowed use of guns for the purposes of gathering game for the table or ridding the gardens and fields of vermin.

Lady Catherine drew herself upright. "You shall not find me one of those who allow servants every liberty. Nor have we need to hunt for aught but amusement in this household, whatever you may be accustomed to in Gloucestershire."

Juliet wondered if Lady Catherine thought of her as some sort of wild creature eking out a perilous existence in the forest primeval. "Thank you, ma'am."

She allowed Mr. Darcy to precede her into the hall, as he knew the way to the gun room. Once they had moved out of earshot of the sitting room, she ventured, "It seems as though Colonel Fitzwilliam was the only person likely to have both access and ability to damage the carriage axle—and yet he is the only one who absolutely cannot have fired the shot at Lady Catherine."

"It is confounding," Mr. Darcy agreed. "My hope is that

Daniels's information will reveal more to us, perhaps, than it did to Lady Catherine. I do not mean that my aunt is not clever—her attention can be most perceptive, where directed—"

"And yet she may fail to ask the correct questions? Do not fear, Mr. Darcy. I realize that no slight on your aunt was intended."

Mr. Darcy led her through a side hall, one that would be used more regularly by servants than by residents or guests. Juliet turned a corner just in time to almost collide with Mrs. Jenkinson, who carried before her a coffeepot, a cup, a sugar bowl, and all other coffee accoutrements upon a tray. "Oh! Miss Tilney! Do forgive me. Lady Catherine has taken to coffee in the afternoons—"

"It is we who should beg your pardon," said Juliet, "as you could not have anticipated us here." Jenkinson did not acknowledge this beyond a brief nod before scurrying along her way. Thoughtfully, Juliet watched her go.

"My aunt is not the most congenial employer, I suspect," Mr. Darcy said. "I do not believe her to be grossly unfair, and her standards, however exacting, are at least fixed and clear. Yet she can be quick to find fault."

Of this, Juliet had no doubt. "We have not yet discussed even the identities of our suspects. In the past, we have seen servants wrongly brought under suspicion solely because of a reluctance to assume the higher classes capable of such acts. However, we cannot assume that no servant could ever do harm. You know Rosings Park far better than I will ever be able to claim; do you think we should consider Lady Catherine's servants among our suspects?"

Mr. Darcy must have reflected upon this question previously, for his answer was immediate. "I do not think they should be first or most important among that number. Although my aunt may be a difficult mistress, as I said before, she is neither capricious nor cruel. Lady Catherine often complains of the wages she pays, and in truth the amounts are generous enough for most servants to overlook her particularities. Furthermore, there is great constancy in the household—Jenkinson, I know, has been in service at Rosings since before my birth, as have many of the other senior members of the staff."

A household unfairly and unkindly run was a household with frequent quittings and hirings. Juliet nodded. "That constancy does suggest that the servants here are mostly content with their lot. Surely it is unlikely that one should attempt to avenge some perceived wrong upon their employer in such a manner rather than simply finding another station. Why risk the noose when an easier method of escape is ever possible?"

"I agree entirely. The motive of the individual we seek must be a more personal one." Mr. Darcy's expression faltered, became uncertain. "But that means the would-be murderer must be among the family or their closest companions—all of them people I have known my entire life."

Juliet silently noted that Mr. Darcy, like herself, implicitly classed the Collinses among those to be suspected. She had wondered whether she was being overly wary—a country rector? his respectable wife?—but the luncheon conversation at Hunsford Parsonage had taken so many odd diversions, swerved away from so many paths, that she could not but believe that at least one person in the family wished to conceal something.

But what?

In Jonathan's experience, groundskeepers tended to be bluff, hearty fellows as earthy as the land for which they cared. Daniels, however, was cut in the same fine mold as Rosings's delicate topiaries: slim and short. He spoke more genteelly than many a member of the merchant classes: "Indeed, sir, miss, you must examine the door. The marks are most curious."

The door to the gun room was not secured any more or less stringently than any other in the house; a simple brass knob and keyhole, such as would be found anywhere in the house, formed its close.

Miss Tilney ran one fingertip along the scratches in the door, which surrounded the brass lock. "These are the damages done by the person who broke in to take Colonel Fitzwilliam's gun?"

"Yes," said Daniels, "but the pattern . . . it is peculiar, is it not, miss?"

The scratches formed a kind of spiderweb in all directions from the lock. Jonathan saw the difficulty right away. "If one were attempting to force the door open, one's efforts would cause damage nearest the lock—not elsewhere. But this has been scratched all over."

"Could it have been done in an attempt to remove the doorknob and lock entirely?" Miss Tilney asked.

"Perhaps an attempt, but any success would have required the shooter to replace the knob after the fact, with all the house in alarm and uproar. Why take such an unnecessary risk?" Jonathan gestured to the intact doorknob before turning back to Daniels. "Did you find anything within the gun room that might be of use to us?"

Daniels shook his head. "No, sir. The gun lay on the floor, and the cabinet with the shot was left open. A fair bit of powder had got scattered around, but I expect the villain acted in haste."

"No doubt," said Miss Tilney. "Do you alone have the key to access this room, or do others?"

"Me and no other, miss. I leave it in my quarters most days, as the gun room need only be accessed when Colonel Fitzwilliam elects to hunt, which he does but seldom."

Jonathan asked, "Can anyone else access your room to find the key?"

"No person but my wife could unlock our door—she works here as well, you see—and certainly *she* is not the author of this mischief."

"Of that I am certain, for surely no person would choose a weapon so readily connected to their family, particularly not when we know this villain to have made trial of many possible methods of doing harm," Miss Tilney said, a conclusion with which Jonathan silently agreed. "On that day, do you recall any unusual behavior or happenstance? Did you see anyone near whom you would not normally see?"

Daniels considered this thoughtfully before answering. "No particular event drew my attention, miss, and the only persons I saw unusually out of place cannot possibly be the villain you seek."

Jonathan knew they must press. "Those people may have seen something more pertinent, possibly without even realizing as much, and therefore we should know their identities, in order that we might question them."

"Of course, sir. Well, immediately after the shot, I spotted the Collins children hurrying from the far end of the hall." Daniels pointed past the gun room door, toward an ill-lit area that led into a corridor that would surely be used only by servants. "Both Miss and Master Collins, and they were in some haste. No one in the Collins family was announced at Rosings until some minutes after the shot was fired, when the whole house was in an uproar, so I cannot say precisely when—but the young people should not have been anywhere but the entry hall before being announced. They would have to have been present a few minutes to have made their way down here, sir; but again, it is impossible that mere children should ever do such a thing as shoot at Lady Catherine!"

"Thank you, Daniels," said Miss Tilney. "You have given us much to consider."

She gave Jonathan a look, one which he knew meant *We should discuss this together, out of the hearing of others.* He had not realized until this instant that he would recognize such a look from her, nor that she would anticipate his understanding. Perhaps this heralded a thaw in their relations. This realization was so thrilling that it took him a moment to comprehend that action was required. "Thank you for your assistance, Daniels. Miss Tilney and I will come back if we have further questions—and we hope you will come to us if something else comes to mind that might shed light upon the matter."

That allowed Jonathan to escort Miss Tilney away from the gun room and upstairs into Rosings proper once more. Lady Catherine was so fond of her sitting room that she quite neglected others in the house, including the library, to which he directed their steps. It was not improper for him to be alone with Miss Tilney here, provided this occurred only during daylight hours and the door was never fully shut; Jonathan had a conviction that their discussions must be held privately, for the interference of others would be more likely to confuse matters than to enlighten them.

But he did not at all mind the chance of being alone with Miss Tilney.

No sooner had he taken a seat than she said, "The marks were feigned, were they not?"

"On the gun room door?" Jonathan turned to see her upon the settee, the late-afternoon light tracing gold into her dark hair. "Perhaps. Otherwise I cannot account for them, except for an extraordinary and unlikely clumsiness. But why should someone feign the need to break in?"

"To conceal that they had access to the room, though if the key is truly only to be had by Daniels or his wife, then I do not see how such access is possible."

Jonathan thought upon this. "Perhaps—perhaps if the guilty person planned ahead and deliberately distracted Daniels after the colonel's last hunt, they might have kept him from properly locking the door. If so, it could have remained unlocked for some time before being detected, if at all."

"I must acknowledge that is feasible, but I cannot think it likely. As Daniels said, gunpowder was scattered about. Would this be the act of one who had arranged for hours or days of unimpeded access to the gun room?" Miss Tilney frowned in consternation. "Perhaps that very haste is our true answer. The guilty party may have been very near a state of panic, and thus flailed about the lock uselessly before gathering the presence of mind to act with efficacy."

"It may be so. But that explanation does not entirely satisfy, does it?"

"No, Mr. Darcy, I confess that it does not." Miss Tilney sighed. "Let us instead number our suspects. First, Colonel Fitzwilliam—"

"But he cannot have fired the shot."

"No, he cannot. That does not absolve him from having damaged the carriage axle."

This, Jonathan felt, went a step too far. Was she disagreeing with him for the sake of disagreement? Perhaps his hope of a thaw had been premature. "Do you honestly think it likely that Lady Catherine should, in the span of a few weeks, attract the ire of *two* would-be killers?"

"It is unlikely but not impossible." Yet Miss Tilney's countenance showed less conviction than her words. "Let us do this instead. Let us number the suspects based solely on their motives, as we understand them at this time. Having done that, we can then determine who had opportunity. Your greater acquaintance with Rosings Park and those who dwell within makes you by far the expert in this area, but based on my first impressions, I feel confident that Colonel Fitzwilliam has such a motive: he is a man who is not master in his own home, and he could be driven to taking drastic steps to acquire Rosings Park for himself."

"He and Lady Catherine have oft been at odds, though he smooths over troubles soon after they arise." Yet Jonathan could imagine how Fitzwilliam might tire of such, given enough years. He still strongly believed the colonel's character would not admit of such wrongdoing, but at this point, they spoke of the theoretical. "So I will grant you the potential motive."

Miss Tilney nodded, clearly satisfied to have won the point. "Next we must add Mrs. Fitzwilliam."

"Anne? But Lady Catherine is her mother, and a most attentive, solicitous one. Anne is a frail creature, one I can scarcely imagine even holding a rifle, much less managing to fire it without injuring herself."

"An attentive mother can be either blessing or curse, or both at once," said Miss Tilney. "We are both, I think, fortunate to have mothers who are women of sense and feeling. Lady Catherine, however—her attentions may not always be welcome."

Jonathan had always been acutely thankful that Lady Catherine was not his mother. This was due both to her frequent disapproval of him and her constant pronouncements as to what his cousin Anne wanted at any given moment, often issued with very little consideration of any desires beyond her ladyship's own. "Therefore both the Fitzwilliams are among our suspects. Next it appears we must count the Collins family, though Mr. Collins, at least, would never wish harm upon Lady Catherine."

"I am not as certain of the sincerity of Mr. Collins's devotion as you are, Mr. Darcy. The presence also of Miss and Master Collins in the house, before being announced—surely that is strange indeed," said Miss Tilney. Her expression betrayed doubt, which Jonathan understood. "But they are younger even than we, and is not Lady Catherine their benefactress?"

"Indeed she is. Yet—if you will allow me to continue your thought from earlier—Lady Catherine is as benefactress quite as she is as mother, which is to say, generous in all senses of the word. Her attentions can be overweening, and her opinions must be heard and heeded."

"And they are entirely reliant upon her?"

"They have been for many years and will remain so until such time as Mr. Collins inherits Longbourn." Jonathan caught himself. "That is my grandparents' house. My mother was one of five sisters born into a home entailed on the male line, and Mr. Collins will therefore be its next master."

Miss Tilney hesitated before she asked, "Is your grandfather in good health?"

"Exceedingly so, for a man of his years."

"So the Collinses cannot expect to inherit soon. I am quite at a loss, Mr. Darcy: You believe that Lady Catherine may interfere too frequently into the Collinses' lives and thus earn their resentment, at least that of Mrs. Collins and her children. Yet none among them strikes me as a likely killer, particularly not when the family must expect all its welfare to depend on Lady Catherine's generosity for a long time to come."

"Do you wish to exclude them, then?" Jonathan felt they

should not, but it was always interesting to hear Miss Tilney's thoughts. "To look only upon the Fitzwilliamses at this time? None other but the Collinses visit Rosings Park often enough to know it as well as our would-be killer must."

Miss Tilney shook her head. "No, impossible though it seems, we must include them among those to be investigated. At luncheon, I was quite certain that they changed the subject frequently—even innocent questions were denied an answer. You noted it, too, did you not?"

"Indeed." Quite the puzzle lay before them. "We shall be at this for some time, I think."

"I fear you are correct, Mr. Darcy."

They were experienced investigators, and yet they were still very young, whose experience of the world's evils—though broader than would be hoped—was still rather small.

For only innocence could have led them to believe that a would-be killer who had already made three attempts would refrain from assaying a fourth . . .

Chapter Five

The young persons so earnestly discussing potential reasons for murder in the library believed themselves to be doing so entirely free from the scrutiny of others. This was not entirely the case. Someone else was listening—in point of fact, was eavesdropping, in defiance of all proper manners. In a household where some among the residents were suspected of attempting to kill one of the others, it might have been surmised that such eavesdropping was nefarious in nature. To Mr. Henry Tilney, however—recently returned from his errand of mercy—it seemed the only prudent course of action.

He had little concern for the welfare of Lady Catherine de Bourgh, not out of any lack of Christian feeling but rather because of her ladyship's demeanor, which showed far more irritation and arrogance than fear. Indeed, Mr. Tilney half thought the answer would prove to lie in a series of strange, unfortunate happenstances—a servant cleaning his rifle at the wrong moment and angle and fearing to admit it, perhaps, or the sort of accident that might befall any carriage, even ones so finely made as those kept at Rosings Park. No, his worry was reserved for his daughter and her tender heart.

Juliet had told her father that she had no expectations of Mr. Jonathan Darcy, and he knew her to be a truthful girl. But many often speak what they believe to be true, yet communicate to others the lie they themselves do not recognize. Mr. Tilney comprehended that his daughter's feelings had been touched by a young man of wealth and distinction; from long observation of many such young men, including his elder brother, Mr. Tilney had learned that among their number are those who take a positive pleasure in the breaking of young girls' hearts. Thus he had been wary.

Many of his fears had faded as soon as he met Jonathan Darcy, who seemed open and artless in his manner. Somewhat stiff, yes—but this appeared to be more a matter of ungainliness than snobbery. As Juliet had said, nothing in his manner suggested he intended to court her, even though his liking for her was evident. All this was to the good. Yet when he heard the two of them speaking to each other late in the afternoon, while alone together in a room, even one with a door properly left ajar . . . suffice it to say, the opportunity to listen could not have been resisted by any father so loving.

In addition, like many clergymen, Mr. Tilney felt that his profession gave him a stronger sense of right and wrong than the layperson could readily claim. This was truer for Mr. Tilney than for many clergymen, though perhaps not so much as he preferred to think.

What he heard was a rather animated discussion about the gun room, which was enough to put his mind at ease. Nothing of flirtation, nothing presumptuous on the part of the younger Mr. Darcy—nothing, in short, in which Mr. Tilney could find reason for concern. He strolled away with a smile on his face, and when he passed the elder Mr. Darcy in the hall, he gave him a cordial nod before taking the stairs up to his room; it would soon be time to make ready for the evening meal.

Mr. Darcy returned the nod—in politeness he could do nothing else—but he was not so congenially inclined. His earlier ill opinion of Mr. Tilney now seemed fully justified. From his vantage point down the hallway, he had clearly observed Mr. Tilney listening to the private conversation between Jonathan and Miss Tilney. Certainly Darcy understood a father's need for caution, in the general sense; in the particular case, however, he could not accept that such caution should be necessary regarding his son. Jonathan was surely in greater danger of being preyed upon than Miss Tilney! Thus one father's relief had become another father's displeasure.

Lady Catherine set a fine table for her guests, as she herself pointed out as the assembly took their seats. Had she not pointed it out, Mr. Collins would have done it for her; he had been on the very verge of doing so when Miss Tilney belatedly realized it was time to praise the white soup. And such soup it was! As excellent a soup as could have been asked for even in a royal palace. Mr. Collins thought of saying this, too, but his patroness responded to Miss Tilney first.

"It is the fashion, I believe, to reserve such fine dishes for balls and other grand occasions," Lady Catherine declared, spoon in hand. "In *some* households, the mistress is convinced by her housekeeper that it is too taxing upon the staff, to regularly serve that which requires so much preparation. At Rosings, however, it is understood that we shall never present less than our best."

"Indeed, ma'am," said Mr. Collins, seizing this opportunity for praise. "Who among those fortunate enough to have dined at Rosings Park can deny the magnificence, the exquisite nature of—"

"You cannot still be growing, Jonathan," said Lady Catherine. Mr. Collins instantly fell silent. At Rosings, his sentences often went unfinished. "You are exceedingly tall. *That*, I suppose, comes from your mother's side of the family. The men in our family, though not deficient, cease growing when they have reached the appropriate height for a gentleman and no more."

Jonathan Darcy required a moment to reply. "No, ma'am, I believe I am the same height as when last we met."

"You *look* taller," Lady Catherine insisted.

Mr. Collins could not allow her assertion to go unsupported. "Indeed, Mr. Darcy, you have quite outdone yourself. But one who carries the blood of this family in his veins can never fail to appear less than a gentleman."

He saw his children exchanging glances, as though he had done something foolish. They did this very often when he praised Lady Catherine, which showed only that they still had no understanding of how much they owed to their patroness. It was her word to the bishop that had given their father the living at Hunsford, and it would require no more than this for the living to be taken away. At least his children had learned from their earliest youth to treat her ladyship with deference and respect; Mr. Collins trusted time to do the rest.

Lady Catherine herself had never ceased staring at Jonathan Darcy. "No, I have discerned it, and even if I had not, I would have known after sitting to table with you. For how can you eat so quickly, if you no longer have need of it?"

The younger Mr. Darcy had not been eating with undue haste, in Mr. Collins's opinion, but he must have been incorrect. He slowed his own spoon as the elder Darcy said, "Aunt, we would not have been tempted were the soup not so excellent. You must share our compliments with your cook."

"The cook merely boiled and stirred and threw this and that into a pot," said Lady Catherine. "It was *I* who decided this soup should be served!"

Her guests absorbed this in silence.

Mr. Tilney, when he next spoke, appeared somewhat amused, not appropriately awestruck given the grand occasion of dinner at Rosings. "You entertain us most beautifully, Lady Catherine. If this is the meal you present to us of an everyday evening, I can scarce imagine what would be served at a ball! One envisions delicacies and marvels out of a Tudor banquet—fruits spun of sugar, perhaps, or eight types of fowl baked into the same pie."

Lady Catherine did not care for such flights of fancy. "We have no need of spectacles here. Nor will a ball be thrown in your honor unless and until the villain in the matter is caught. We shall have no special guests for your amusement—no guests at all, save Guinness, who makes his journey here in slightly more than two weeks' time."

"That is precisely as we should wish," Miss Tilney said. She deferred to Lady Catherine most promptly; Mr. Collins decided he liked the girl. "We intend to concentrate our efforts on the important matter at hand; and for the purposes of our inquiry, it is best for all at Rosings Park to continue precisely as it did before."

Jonathan Darcy nodded. "Deviation from normal patterns of behavior—those may point the way to the guilty party."

That would not do, Mr. Collins realized. That would not do at all.

As Lady Catherine held forth on how far the standards of elegance at balls had fallen since her youth, Mr. Collins sought to catch his wife's gaze. This proved difficult. Charlotte—ever temperate, ever attentive, continued nodding at Lady Catherine; never before had her husband disliked this habit in her! He was ultimately driven to letting his fork clatter too loudly against his plate. The nuance granted by two decades at the Rosings table allowed him to do this in such a way as would draw Charlotte's eye without alerting Lady Catherine at the far end of the table.

Charlotte Collins had, in point of fact, been aware of her husband's vague gesticulations and starings. Little occurred around her that she did not observe, and she knew Mr. Collins's concerns as well as he did himself, if not better. It was most unwise of him to attempt to draw her attention only to emphasize a point she already knew: that their own deviations from routine must become more subtle, lest they alert Jonathan Darcy and Miss Tilney. To do so in public, at table!

But Charlotte was not a woman given to despair; she could scarce have endured twenty-four years of her marriage if she were. So she put an end to it by meeting his eyes and nodding, firmly and just once, before turning back to Lady Catherine.

After dinner, instead of performances at the pianoforte or a couple of tables of whist, the party was to hear Lady Catherine's retelling of the most recent attempt upon her life. Juliet appreciated the expediency, but thought it rather poor entertainment for all others in attendance. As at least one of these persons must be to blame, however, that individual did not deserve a congenial evening, and with this small justice, the others must be content.

"It was after morning hours, though before tea was served in the afternoon," said Lady Catherine. "As Miss Collins was to attend one of her first country dances that evening, Anne made free to lend her a dress—one far finer than any Miss Collins would ever own, of course."

Katy Collins bore this degradation better than Juliet could have in her place, merely lifting her chin. Deb Collins seemed to feel the ire his sister did not, mouth twisting into a scowl, before a glance from his mother wiped the expression away.

Mr. Collins interjected. "We have recently purchased fine new things for Katy, very fine indeed, precisely as you suggested, Lady—"

"I did not take part in this, as Anne told me naught of it,

even though I should have thought they would wish my counsel on what dress would be most becoming," Lady Catherine continued. "However, I heard some stirring downstairs and believed Miss Collins had descended the stair, perhaps to show herself to the servants or others in the house. Propriety demanded my presence. I therefore emerged from my room and walked toward the stairs—it was a cloudy day, one that had darkened most precipitously, so candles were not yet lit, and I made my way in the dark. Just as I would have begun my descent, I felt the shove! A most brutal, deliberate shove it was, across both my shoulders, and one that sent me down several steps. Had I not caught myself upon the banister, I could well have tumbled to my death."

"It sounds most shocking, ma'am." Juliet had realized that the only way to work with Lady Catherine was to flatter her, though the young lady was determined to do so only when her compliments were genuine, as this one now was. "How fortunate that you were not overcome."

Lady Catherine lifted her chin in apparent pride. "Ever have I kept my head in time of travail."

"And you neither heard nor saw your assailant?" the younger Mr. Darcy asked. When Lady Catherine shook her head, he continued. "Who besides the servants has access to the upper floors of the house?"

Although Colonel Fitzwilliam began to answer, Lady Catherine would have no detail shared that she herself did not offer. "Myself, of course, as well as Anne and the colonel, and on rare occasions, the Collins family." Her eyes narrowed as she looked toward the Collinses . . .

In particular, toward Deb Collins.

Lady Catherine believes Deb to be the guilty party! Juliet could hardly credit such a theory as this, nor imagine a murderer so young, yet she did not know the persons present nearly so well as did her ladyship. Where she suspected, Juliet in turn must suspect.

But it was no more than a suspicion, far less than true conviction. This Juliet surmised from the simple truth that, if Lady Catherine de Bourgh had been fully persuaded of Deb Collins's guilt, she would not have failed to declare so, at length and volume, to any who would listen. The younger Mr. Darcy and Juliet herself would never have been summoned.

Whence could such doubts spring?

Jonathan Darcy did not appear to have recognized his aunt's wariness, nor who had caused it. "We will speak to everyone in turn about the events of that morning, if that is congenial to those present."

Those present did not look particularly delighted with this request, but Colonel Fitzwilliam was the first to say, "We will be only too happy to help. Will we not, my dear?"

Anne Fitzwilliam's gaze remained downcast. "Of course," she said, so weakly—so unwillingly—that Juliet knew who they must question first.

The next morning dawned gray and cool, the windows revealing a foggy view speckled with mist. Anne prepared for her conversation with Miss Tilney and Jonathan by choosing a seat near the fire in the library and instructing Mrs. Jenkinson to make sure the blaze was stoked high. Probably the instruction had been unnecessary, for Jenkinson knew Anne nearly as well as Anne knew herself; she even brought a thick lap blanket for her mistress just in case. Anne was grateful for it, less for the warmth (for the library fire crackled with heat) and more for something to clutch or rearrange with her hands should this talk prove difficult.

"Your mother will be expecting me," said Mrs. Jenkinson. Although the woman had for some time served primarily as Anne's companion, Lady Catherine had considered such companionship less necessary after her daughter's marriage to Colonel Fitzwilliam; Jenkinson's duties had accordingly increased in breadth since that time to encompass both ladies of the house. "Yet if you feel I should stay with you—"

"Go to Mother. I will not find it difficult to speak with them alone." But this was spoken with no confidence in its truth.

When Miss Tilney and Jonathan were shown in, Anne could not resist a moment of envy—deep, sinful envy—upon regarding the young woman's evident health and strength. What would it have been like to spend her youth rosy cheeked and carefree, confidently moving through the world without fear? To attract others to her without having to rely solely on those from one's own family for support, friendship, even love?

No doubt Miss Tilney had problems of her own, at which Anne could only guess from within her filigree cage.

"Good morning, cousin," said Jonathan as he ushered Miss Tilney to her seat, then took his own directly opposite Anne. He smiled without artifice, one of the reasons Anne had always liked the young man far more than her mother did. "It is a difficult conversation we are to have, but in the end, all will be the better for it."

If only everything could be fixed so easily! "Forgive my uncertainty—you see, it is very rare that people choose to speak to me rather than to my mother or my husband, even rarer that I do so without their presence. I speak to the Collinses, of course, but they are always here, and by now I consider them very nearly a part of the family."

"And that," Miss Tilney asked, "is why you wished to lend the gown to Miss Collins?"

"Exactly. Mama considered it overly familiar, but I think it wise for a family to do their best by their daughters. On their marital prospects, so much depends, and to improve those, a girl must look her best. Love seems to follow beauty rather more closely than it should." Anne felt her cheeks flush warm and hoped the young investigators would attribute this to the high stoke of the fire. "The Collinses are very attentive to such things. Since Katy, I mean, Miss Collins, came out, they have spared little expense for her garments. But handsome as the Hunsford living is, it is not equal to every fancy or desire. I had a fine dress made up last year but have not been in health to wear it. Why should not Miss Collins have use of it?"

Jonathan said, "I see no reason to deny such a generous impulse, but I take it from your eloquent defense that others disagreed."

Anne could not but sigh. "One cannot oppose all of Mama's wishes. It is in fact very hard to oppose any of them. Where I can get my way, I sometimes do. Does that make me a disobedient daughter?"

Miss Tilney's expression had gentled. "If so, then we are all disobedient, for everyone wishes to have their own way *sometimes*. Did your mother know that the others were upstairs, or had you chosen not to disturb her?"

"How tactfully you put it, Miss Tilney!" Anne exclaimed. "Mama knew, but chose to reserve her disapproval for another time, when it might be shared with a larger number of listeners." She had meant this purely as a statement of fact, but could not be much astonished to see both Jonathan and Miss Tilney stifling smiles. "So Mrs. Collins and Miss Collins came to Rosings in the afternoon. I took them up to my rooms, so that Miss Collins might try the dress for herself. It was a terribly dark day, as Mama said, threatening rain but never shedding it, and we all wished to see the dress in as much light as possible. As Jenkinson was helping Miss Collins with her laces, both Mrs. Collins and I went to seek more candles. Mrs. Collins walked toward the east wing, I toward the west."

Jonathan's attention was instantly drawn. "In which direction were the main stairs?"

"That stair is to the east of my room," Anne said. "But I do not accuse Mrs. Collins—we were separated from each other only briefly, and to me it seems outrageous that she should attack Mama, to whom she owes so much."

Miss Tilney said, "In all confidence, and in all honesty, whom do you think most likely to be behind the attacks on Lady Catherine?"

"I have pondered and pondered the matter, and I am no closer to an answer than I ever was."

Anne hoped that would be the end of the interview, and felt the greatest relief when she realized it was.

Charlotte Collins might have been expected to be fond of Jonathan for his mother's sake, and indeed she had always behaved kindly toward him, even during the early years of his childhood, when his more curious patterns of behavior had been so much more pronounced, so very disruptive. However, she was a woman of cool, considered opinion, and so her feelings toward the boy would never outweigh the more important facts: that Jonathan Darcy was Lady Catherine's grand-nephew, and heir to one of the greatest estates in the realm in Pemberley. In the unlikely, but not impossible, event that De Bourgh should fail to inherit Longbourn, her entire welfare in her dotage might depend upon Jonathan Darcy's charity, a truth Charlotte never forgot for an instant.

She did not curry favor in the manner of her husband. Charlotte understood that praise is more highly valued where it is judiciously given. As she came into the library, only recently quitted by a wan-looking Anne Fitzwilliam, she smiled but slightly at Jonathan. "It is good of you to concern yourself with your aunt's safety, Jonathan," she said. "And of you, Miss Tilney. Many would turn from such an ugly business, but it must be faced."

"What can you tell us of that afternoon, Mrs. Collins?" Jonathan asked.

"Mrs. Fitzwilliam had most generously agreed to lend Katy a dress for a ball that was soon to be held. Jenkinson took us upstairs and helped Katy to dress. The day was very drear, as it is today, and so we wished for more light. Mrs. Fitzwilliam and I went in search of candles or lamps, or another servant to fetch the same."

"In which direction did you search?" Miss Tilney said.

"I went to the right—the east, I believe it is—but only into the next room, the bath, as I knew that Lady Catherine has a lamp kept in that room at all times." Charlotte did not feel certain of this next, but it must be said. "I heard a strange sound from the farther end of the hall, the west. So I walked some paces in that direction, all the way around the corner, seeking out the source of the noise. Behind me, I heard Lady Catherine's door open, and moments later, her shout of alarm. I ran back toward her, as did all of us on the first floor—Katy, Jenkinson, Mrs. Fitzwilliam."

Jonathan had begun to frown. Charlotte refused to worry, simply preparing herself for his next question, which proved to be: "Who reached Lady Catherine first?"

"Not I," Charlotte replied. "It would have been Katy, I suppose, and Jenkinson with her, of course."

Miss Tilney asked, "And you saw nothing farther down the corridor? No movement, no other person?"

"No one at all. I confess, I quite forgot the peculiar sound I had heard once we had all rushed to Lady Catherine's aid. The significance of it did not occur to me until much later." Charlotte smiled civilly. "Have you any other questions for me?"

Fortunately, they did not.

As they waited for their final conversation of the morning, Jonathan said to Miss Tilney, "The accounts we have been told do not entirely agree. If Mrs. Collins heard something upon the first floor, would not Cousin Anne have heard this as well?"

"It may have been Mrs. Fitzwilliam herself that Mrs. Collins heard," Miss Tilney said, "and regardless, whatever it was that happened to the *west* cannot have immediately led to Lady Catherine's fall, as that occurred to the *east* of Mrs. Fitzwilliam's room. Yet we must note all we have heard carefully; even if we have but one small piece of the puzzle, it may prove the piece that ultimately will reveal all."

How pleasant it was to be investigating with Miss Tilney again. Jonathan wondered whether it would be politic to say so—after all, in this situation, no one had perished, and so enjoyment was not so unseemly. Best of all, their shared work seemed to be restoring him in her estimation after his early blunder. Before he could decide how to begin, however, the servant showed in Katy Collins.

Katy had grown up with Jonathan as an occasional playmate, and she was a peer to Miss Tilney, so her demeanor was unsurprisingly different from those of the two matrons with whom they had already spoken. She smiled more easily as she took her seat before them. "Were the situation any less dire," Katy said, "it would be—why, it would almost be *fun*, would it not?"

Miss Tilney said, "It will become much more so when we have identified the guilty person, and Lady Catherine is safe once more."

"I do not think I shall be able to help you very much," said Katy. "On that day, Mrs. Fitzwilliam took us upstairs, I tried on the dress, the ladies went in search of candles, and then Lady Catherine cried out in alarm, which brought all to her side." A faint smile played upon Katy's lips. "Forgive me, but— when I saw her on the stair, her skirts rumpled almost to her waist, and I believe I was too shocked at the sight of Lady Catherine's petticoats to heed much else!"

"I quite understand," said Jonathan. Indeed, he normally thought of his aunt less as a human being with all the limbs and underclothes of such, and more as a kind of extraordinarily animated sculpture. "You recall no other details of that day?"

"Only Papa's great fear when he arrived, though that was some time after the danger had passed," Katy said. "His horse was deep with mud, so I suppose he must have galloped all the way from our parsonage."

"But how did your father learn of it?" Miss Tilney asked.

Jonathan answered for his cousin. "No doubt one of the servants carried the word. The two households are much connected on a daily basis; little happens in one house that is not swiftly learned in the other."

Katy added, "My father has always made it clear that he wishes to be informed immediately of important happenings at Rosings. So word would be brought quickly, and he would respond with equal alacrity. I would expect no less, given the regard in which he holds Lady Catherine!"

Miss Tilney said, "No doubt his benefactress holds him in esteem as well." Jonathan was not nearly so certain of this.

Katy laughed. "I suppose we shall know once Mr. Guinness comes to visit!"

"What do you mean by this?" Jonathan asked. "Who is this Mr. Guinness? Lady Catherine mentioned him last night."

"Her solicitor," said Katy. "She means to amend her will— she has told us all of it often enough these past two months— but cannot do so until his arrival. I believe he is to be here in about a fortnight. She has not told us what changes she wishes to make, but no doubt she will tell once it is done, and no one can question it. Not that she is much discouraged by questions!"

At this, Jonathan turned to Miss Tilney; in her face he saw the mirror of his own comprehension.

They had already known that someone wished to kill Lady Catherine. They did not yet know why. But now, at least, they understood why the attempts had begun at this point in time: a person who believed themselves likely to benefit from Lady Catherine's current will, and thus likely to be deprived by any material alteration to it, wished to put an end to her ladyship's life before the will could be changed.

He grasped one further truth as well—that this person knew they had roughly two weeks before the will's alteration. If the guilty person was sufficiently determined . . . there would be another attempt on Lady Catherine's life, and soon.

Chapter Six

Upon the realization that the impending change to Lady Catherine's will likely lay at the root of the attempts on her life, it became crucial to discover what her will currently said, and what material alteration was anticipated. The young investigators thus requested a private audience with her at the soonest opportunity. This was granted, though not in especially good humor.

"Your ladyship," said Miss Tilney, "your solicitor, a Mr. Guinness, is to visit you soon. You wish to amend your will. Can you explain to us what manner of amendment you have planned to make?"

"I wish merely to add a codicil, making a small gift to Miss Pope. She was Anne's governess, a very genteel sort of girl. There was some talk of her marrying, but I heard nothing in the end had come of it, so I wish to settle a small sum upon her that will allow her to live independently in her dotage."

Jonathan and Miss Tilney seemed far too surprised at this evidence of Lady Catherine's thoughtfulness. This she considered exceedingly ill-bred of them, but before she could say so, Jonathan said, "Then I must ask to whom you intend to leave the remainder of your estate."

"To whom would I leave it but my daughter? Our family estate is such as can be inherited by heirs female, and from her naturally it will pass down to Peter in the fullness of time."

"That is the rational assumption," said Miss Tilney, though

she looked confused. "You left it to Mrs. Fitzwilliam in its entirety? No other bequests?"

"Indeed not. That is how family fortunes decline—one generation not fulfilling its duty to the next. Miss Pope is an exception only because of her extraordinary efforts on my daughter's behalf. As you see, there is nothing remarkable in my will, nor shall there be after Guinness's visit."

"Indeed there is not," Jonathan said, his dismay evident. The Tilney girl comported herself better, but her shoulders betrayed that she, too, had expected to learn much from the contents of the will. To Lady Catherine it had been obvious all along that *this* could not be the trouble. Silently she resolved that, if they made such a poor show of themselves for too much longer, she would let it be known that she was *most* put out.

Had her ladyship but known of it, the dismay of Juliet and the younger Mr. Darcy was equal to her own. As they sat before the fire, readying themselves for the next investigative conversation they would have, they looked as crestfallen as any wallflower at a dance.

"Her will is entirely as I would have thought it to be," he said as they sat together in the library. "Surely the bequest to Miss Pope cannot be substantial enough a sum for them to resent its loss."

"Were it so, Lady Catherine would have told us of it, I am certain." Juliet had already discerned that her ladyship preferred for her generosity to be known and acknowledged, as widely and often as possible. "What about the Collinses? Might they have expected to inherit from her?"

To her this seemed an excellent notion, but Mr. Darcy

shook his head. "Mr. Collins will inherit his own estate in time, so he would have no need for such. Besides—the change in the will does not affect the Collinses' standing. If any among them felt a murderous resentment at being excluded, why should they act only now? Mr. Guinness's visit does not, will not, change their fortunes in the slightest."

Juliet had to admit the justice of this. "Might she have failed to mention any smaller bequest to us? A piece of jewelry, one or other of the furnishings—this might seem as nothing to her, while having great value or meaning to someone else in the house. An heirloom going to one of the servants, rather than to Mrs. Fitzwilliam, for instance."

Mr. Darcy mulled the question over ere making any reply. She liked this about him, the careful consideration he gave to replies others might make without thought. It was most inconvenient, Juliet felt, to be reminded of what she most liked about a young man who did not show the same sort of liking for her, but *that* disappointment was to be dwelled upon at another time.

"I think not," Mr. Darcy at last replied. "Lady Catherine does not seem to take these attacks as seriously as she should, but she would not fail to answer us fully. Can it be that the alteration to her will is not at the root of all?"

Doubtfully Juliet said, "That may be so—but we must proceed under the assumption that it is, for if so, as the solicitor's visit draws nearer, the danger to Lady Catherine will become the greater."

It was then that Colonel Fitzwilliam entered. Juliet had not been certain that the colonel would respond to their summons; the midday meal was soon to begin, and he had, by every report, been absent from Rosings Park at the time of Lady Catherine's near fall upon the stairs. Yet reports could be mistaken, or deliberately incomplete; thus she considered it important to speak with him on the matter. She set her surprise aside to greet him. "Colonel, it is most good of you to come."

"We must get to the bottom of it, must we not? I am ready to answer questions, hear theories—whatever is required in this investigative effort, up to and including the use of my very own quizzing glass." He sighed as he took his seat opposite them. His hand rested for a moment on the lap blanket that Mrs. Fitzwilliam had left behind. "Lady Catherine must be kept safe from any danger, though I hope the miscreant has seen the error of their ways and ceased any attempts."

Mr. Darcy said, "We hope that as well, but we must not make rash assumptions, not with her ladyship's life at stake. And such clues as we have are not those to be examined under magnification."

Colonel Fitzwilliam could not entirely stifle a smile. "The offer of the quizzing glass was but metaphorical, Jonathan. I mean only that I intend to help in any way I can."

Juliet remained struck by the colonel's earlier suggestion. "Do you truly think a person already so corrupted as to think of murder can reform their own character, without any intervention of either law or clergy?"

"It sounds unlikely, I know," said the colonel, "but I have come to consider the first attempt—the sabotaged carriage—as rather unlikely to succeed. The shove might have been intended to be delivered with less force. The rifle shot might have gone wide by design rather than chance."

Juliet comprehended his meaning. "You mean, you think the would-be killer is not a would-be killer at all. That this person has meant only to harass and frighten Lady Catherine."

The colonel nodded. "It is possible, is it not?"

"Possible," said Mr. Darcy, "but we cannot afford to assume it to be so."

"How may I help you, then?" Colonel Fitzwilliam asked. "I understood you to be learning more about the shove upon the stairs, as of today I mean; and as you know, I was not at Rosings Park when that occurred."

Juliet hoped she was wording this correctly. "We do know you were not present, but what we do not know is where you actually were at the time."

"What can it matter where I was," said Colonel Fitzwilliam, "so long as I was not at the top of the stair?"

If it does not matter, why will you not say? Juliet knew she could not ask that bluntly, so she pressed again: "We simply wish to understand the events of the day. Depending on where you were, you might have seen an event or person of interest to the inquiry."

Colonel Fitzwilliam did not reply at first. Juliet perceived Mr. Darcy regarding his cousin with some dismay, no doubt disappointed by the lack of a ready answer, and all that this lack implied.

But the answer, when it came, surprised Juliet with its firmness. "I was in the town of Faxton, some ten miles from Hunsford," Colonel Fitzwilliam said, his tone most decided. "One of my property agents handles some of my business there, and I wished to discuss matters with him. His name is Baker, and if you wish to speak with him to confirm the veracity of my account, you may do so. What matters these were, I must reserve the right to keep to myself."

Mr. Darcy did not find his cousin's demeanor so surprising as Juliet did. "I can well imagine," he said, "that it is difficult to keep anything to one's self while living under Lady Catherine's roof, and what privacy can be had is therefore all the more precious."

"You understand me well," said the colonel with a smile. It was a smile Juliet trusted. Could she do the same for the man?

Once, Colonel Fitzwilliam would have thought himself more likely to accept transportation to Australia than to willingly live under the roof of his aunt Lady Catherine de Bourgh.

Yet he did not actually consider the question, back in those days. He visited occasionally, usually with his cousin and dear friend Darcy, and it was Darcy he thought more likely to someday dwell at Rosings Park. The match between Anne de Bourgh and Darcy had been the wish of both their mothers, as the entire family knew . . . though what was to Mrs. Darcy more of a passing fancy had been taken up by Lady Catherine as very near a holy crusade. Colonel Fitzwilliam knew Darcy to be very particular about ladies, so much so that he seemed unlikely to make a match in the conventional way. (Many young women would have had it otherwise, as would their mothers, but Darcy was not a man to be taken in by a fortune hunter.) He had always thought that Darcy felt a sense of duty to Anne, and so in those long-ago days—despite no evidence of ardor between the two—it did not seem unlikely that they would indeed wed.

Then, after some weeks visiting his friend Bingley, Darcy had returned home with much to say about a Miss Elizabeth Bennet. At first Fitzwilliam could scarce believe that Darcy would choose a girl of little family and no fortune, but the more Darcy spoke about her wit, her dancing, and her fine eyes, the more his strong sentiments toward her became evident. Once Fitzwilliam met Miss Bennet for himself, he became a firm supporter of the match; her intelligence was the equal of Darcy's, her temper most amiable, and her strength of character evident. Her vivacity would temper his cousin's too-frequent somberness.

Yet the colonel had been ever aware that Darcy's happiness came at the price of Anne's enduring solitude.

Anne de Bourgh's delicate health was, to Fitzwilliam's mind, worsened by Lady Catherine's strictures that prevented exercise, fresh air, and a more varied diet. She would never be presented at court; Rosings Park would never host a ball at which she could expect to lead the first dance. The announcement that Anne was "out" had been only her hair one day being worn up when before it had ever been down. Lady Catherine's vocal disapproval of every other family in town—including those that contained young, marriageable males—meant that they had few guests save for family and the omnipresent Collinses. What chance had Anne of finding a husband?

This question crystallized in Colonel Fitzwilliam's mind when he considered his own matrimonial prospects. As a younger son, he would inherit next to nothing; he could not expect to come into a house. This called for taking a wife with more money than he, but as rich young ladies wished to marry even richer young men, Fitzwilliam was ever at a disadvantage. His good sense, appealing person, and gentle humor won many female admirers, but such charms were not sufficient to persuade their parents that they should encourage his suit. It came to him that he and Anne de Bourgh might solve each other's difficulties quite satisfactorily, as long as he could endure living at Rosings Park with Lady Catherine for however long she might survive. (He was younger then, young enough to believe that, at more than sixty years of age, Lady Catherine's life could not long endure.) Thus he proposed to Anne, believing himself to be doing that which was best for all concerned. She accepted, no doubt in much the same spirit.

Lady Catherine would have preferred a more illustrious match for Anne, one that would have put Darcy and his upstart bride in their places. Yet Anne was then well into the years of danger, and the obstacle of her poor health was not lost upon her mother. (Indeed, few realized the tenderer aspect of Lady Catherine's desire for Anne to wed Darcy—for was that not her ill child's best chance at happiness?) Colonel Fitzwilliam was amiable and respectable, and after all, Anne could scarcely marry into a more illustrious family than her own. Her ladyship therefore blessed the union and urged them to wed soon, from Rosings.

Only one person had ever spoken against the match. Shortly after the banns were first read, the Darcys visited Rosings Park to make their congratulations. Mrs. Darcy had wished them joy, but Darcy, while saying all that was appropriate to the occasion, seemed to Fitzwilliam rather subdued. One night, after the two gentlemen had withdrawn to the study to smoke cigars and drink port, Darcy had finally come out with it: "Fitzwilliam . . . though it may be too late for my caution, I must speak. I urge you, do not wed for the sake of pity. That is no favor to any person involved. The marital union can be the making of one's life, or its ruination. It was the making of mine, to be certain. I would wish no less for you, nor for my cousin Anne."

"What chance has she of another attachment, Darcy, with Lady Catherine guarding the door to her cage?" Fitzwilliam had sighed and clapped his friend on the back. "Anne will make me a good wife, and I intend to make her a good husband. It is an advantageous match for us both. You must consider it in that light."

"And so I shall," Darcy had said, his brief smile indicating that he would take no further liberties, say no more upon the subject. How often Fitzwilliam had considered Darcy's words, in the years that followed!

The Collinses came to dinner. Jonathan saw Miss Tilney take note of this; he resolved to inform her, at their first opportunity, that the Collins family took as many as five or six meals a week at Rosings Park. Their appearance this evening was hardly unusual. Miss Tilney seemed to pay especial attention to Deb Collins, which Jonathan found puzzling. Then again, many found Deb puzzling. He kept to himself more than most boys, often absenting himself at the strangest and most inconvenient times. Jonathan had upon occasion been grateful for this behavior, as it distracted others from Jonathan's own peculiar habits.

On this night, for instance, Deb ate very little. When Lady Catherine remarked upon it ("most obstinate to refuse good food, far better than he could have at home"), Deb blurted out, "I feel not at all well, not at all."

"That will do," said Mrs. Collins, rising abruptly from the table. "Forgive me, your ladyship, but if our son is unwell, he should no longer trouble you at table."

Lady Catherine waved them away, but she watched Deb go most pointedly. Miss Tilney watched Lady Catherine and Deb both. Jonathan watched Miss Tilney.

Maybe Miss Tilney's interest sprang from the information that both Deb and Katy Collins had been sighted near the gun room on the day someone shot at Lady Catherine. Indeed, they needed to speak together alone again, soon. Why had they not devised a time and place to do so each day, as had been their habit in both of their previous investigations? Miss Tilney seemed to wish more distance from him, it seemed. Jonathan could scarce blame her, given how she had received his suggestion that she leave the investigation; beyond this, he thought it very likely that her heart was still much wounded by the loss of Ralph Bamber. After such an extreme circumstance, no doubt any young woman would be more circumspect, less trusting.

Jonathan knew the only way to truly win trust was time; this, at least, they had, thanks to Lady Catherine's misfortunes. He would suggest a more regular meeting and see what she said to it. Beyond that, he could not yet hazard any guess.

"Well?" Lady Catherine said, glaring at Jonathan, then Miss Tilney. "What have you learned thus far?"

Jonathan and Miss Tilney shared a look of equal dismay. In their past cases, the victims had not been alive to express any curiosity about their efforts. No doubt they, too, would have been impatient for the answers to be made known. Miss Tilney had the courage to reply, "We should say nothing until more is known, Lady Catherine. Until we are certain. For discussion invites speculation, and speculation invites confusion."

Though this was excellent reasoning, her ladyship did not seem much swayed by it. "Well. If you insist. But it is most vexing, to remain in ignorance after you have both been summoned for answers."

"We hope to have answers for you shortly," said Jonathan. Although he was not certain, he wondered whether his great-aunt's desire for prompt resolution was not rooted in fear. Granted, she showed few signs of terror, but his mother had said Lady Catherine would be afraid, and Mother was generally correct about such matters.

No, he and Miss Tilney could not make a practice of sharing their information and theories with her ladyship, but Jonathan inwardly resolved that—if his great-aunt's fear ever became apparent, if there ever came a point when she truly appeared to be suffering from her uncertainty—he would share any information they had found that might have the power of reassuring her.

Assuming, of course, that such information was to be had.

Lady Catherine's attention had already been diverted. "You, Miss Collins, are dressed very fine this evening."

Katy, who indeed looked very pretty in her pink dress, smiled to show her dimples. "Thank you, your ladyship."

"It is not praise to point out when one has overdressed for an occasion," Lady Catherine said with a sniff.

"Last month you did say that my muslin was not fine enough, ma'am." Katy cast down her gaze. "I only thought—"

"Be silent, child!" Mr. Collins cut in before his daughter could any more oppose Lady Catherine. "We are of course ever grateful for your insight on the finer nuances of society, which are most completely understood only by one so perfectly situated as yourself, your ladyship."

Lady Catherine did not seem to be fully placated, Jonathan thought. His father quickly took the opportunity to begin a conversation about the harvest, to which Mr. Tilney could knowledgeably contribute, and in which Lady Catherine would fully participate with knowledge or not. Jonathan, like most others at the table, could fall silent for a time. He knew not how the others might feel about this turn in the evening's talk, but he himself was grateful.

The conversation about the crops and yields endured through the afternoon dinner. Afterward, the men were to retire for cigars and port, but Mr. Collins begged her ladyship's leave to depart with Katy. "It is to be a very early day tomorrow, very early indeed."

"I do not see why, as it is not a Sunday," said Lady Catherine, "but go as you will."

Jonathan did not see why, either; his attentiveness to routines and rituals had taught him that Mr. Collins usually lingered at Rosings as long as possible, well into the evenings. This might mean nothing, but it was worth noting.

As farewells were said, Jonathan found an opportunity to whisper to his father, "Do you think we could convince Lady Catherine to leave Rosings for her own safety?"

"If she thought that advisable, I assure you, she would already be gone," Father said.

"Yet we cannot be sure the attempts have ended."

Immediately Father shook his head. "None here is such a fool as to make another attempt while so many more people are present, nor, for that matter, while others are actively searching for the wrongdoer. Lady Catherine's safety is assured so long as we remain. Your efforts, I hope, will ensure that we need not remain too long."

Jonathan wished, rather than believed, his father's statements to be true.

The Collins family spent that night with very different feelings about the evening that had passed.

Mr. Collins could not but count any time spent at Rosings Park—regardless of what might have transpired there—as assuredly, unquestionably, superior to time spent anywhere else. To pay Lady Catherine such small attentions as ladies enjoyed was a small price for all the blessings he had thereby received. Were Lady Catherine to guess, even for an instant—but she had not. She *must* not. Else all would be ruined.

Much the same thoughts occupied the mind of Charlotte Collins, albeit with greater nuance and complexity. She had kept secrets from Lady Catherine before, primarily on such topics upon which Charlotte did not wish to hear any advice. (To hear Lady Catherine's advice was to be expected to take it. No disagreement would be brooked. The best way to avoid disagreements, Charlotte had found, was to avoid troublesome conversations altogether.) The secrets she kept now, however . . . these were of a different nature than any she had possessed before. At times, to Charlotte, it felt as though she were forced to transport hot coals without a scuttle, her very being burning with the need to be done with them.

But Charlotte was not a woman to entertain such dramatic

notions for long. That which must be concealed would be concealed. She would do what was required. She wished only that she knew how much longer the pretense must be maintained.

Katy Collins was in high dudgeon. *Overdressed! I wear no trim beyond a small ruffle at the hem—no lace, nor a sash—only to be called overdressed by an old woman wearing silk and pearls!* This was even more outrageous to Katy's mind than Lady Catherine's disdainful comments the month before, for Katy had worn that muslin dress with no particular object of looking well. After her ladyship's disapproval, however, her father had insisted that new dresses must be had. Mama had taken her to the shops at Faxton, fabrics had been selected, a seamstress employed and then hurried, and for what? Merely to err again, in the opposite direction!

(Some readers may derive from the previous paragraph certain beliefs about the importance of fashion in the minds of young ladies, believing Katy's ire to spring from outraged vanity, no more. Such would be in error. Young ladies are entirely capable of both reflecting with thought and depth about the persons nearest them and the issues of the day *and* choosing the perfect gown for an upcoming ball; the breadth of these topics strains their minds no more than it does those of gentlemen who argue both politics and who shot the most grouse at the last hunt. In the particular case of Katy Collins, her anger with Lady Catherine was not newly minted. The disapproving comments upon her dress were but salt poured into a wound carved over a long period of time, cut very deep.)

Deb Collins remained lost within his own thoughts, almost sick to his stomach, dreading what was surely to come. Lady Catherine's eyes had darted over to him many times during dinner. She had said nothing, but she had not had to; Deb felt certain he understood her purpose.

She knows, he thought. *She knows.*

The ladies of the house were expected to retire to the parlor, but Anne Fitzwilliam admitted to feeling somewhat ill. Juliet was most heartily sorry for this, not only because she pitied the frail woman, but also because this left Juliet alone with Lady Catherine, to bear the full heat of her all-seeing gaze. She did not feel equal to asking her ladyship about Deb Collins, not least because she suspected no response would be forthcoming unless and until Juliet and Mr. Darcy had already proved Lady Catherine to be correct. Thus the topic would be entirely of Lady Catherine's choosing.

"You are a prettyish sort of girl, Miss Tilney," her ladyship said as she settled into her throne-like chair. "You have not let yourself become too brown while traveling. Many young ladies do not take sufficient care and will end with freckles." This last word was pronounced as though it were a terminal disease.

Juliet knew she was expected to respond to this, though she was not entirely certain how. "We enjoyed fortunate weather on our journey, Lady Catherine," she said. "The skies held enough clouds to provide shade and a respite from heat, but not so many as to slow our progress with rain and the muddy roads that follow."

"You sound a very experienced traveler." Lady Catherine squinted as Juliet, as if attempting to better take her measure. "But you cannot have been often from home at your age."

"Not often, ma'am. Once to London, when I was much younger, once to Bath not long after—and then last year, to both Surrey and Devonshire."

"Of *those* trips, I have heard quite enough. You are not, then, one of the young ladies who cannot bear not to make a spectacle of themselves in faraway places? Gadding about to Bath or Brighton, husband hunting?"

Juliet felt her situation had become even more precarious. "No, ma'am. I am in no great hurry to marry." She would not wed until she found a man who treated her with respect, who spoke to her with true honesty—such as she had once had with Jonathan Darcy. In the lack of any declaration from him, her thoughts could tend only toward an abstract ideal, one Juliet felt certain would be difficult to find.

She braced herself for far more to come, for this seemed a subject on which Lady Catherine might potentially hold forth at length. Instead, however, her ladyship merely shook her head. "So many are in a rush to go around and about. To spend more and more time away from their home and their properest concerns. My son-in-law spends one or two days a week away on horseback or in a carriage. To what end? What can be meant of it? Every time I ask him, and every time, his answers are wanting. It is restlessness, be sure of it, restlessness and no more."

But Juliet was not at all sure of that. Why was Colonel Fitzwilliam so often away from Rosings Park these days? What business was he at such pains to conceal?

Chapter Seven

However novel or strange or grand a house may be to a visitor upon arrival, there is no place so foreign that people cannot adapt. The awe of the first day inevitably shifts into familiarity; even a farmer transported to a palace would be, within a few months, quite as easily at home as any prince to the manor born.

Juliet Tilney was no farmer, and Rosings Park no palace; Northanger Abbey, though more remote and rustic than Lady Catherine's house, was not rendered shabby by comparison. Yet its elegant decoration had still made her flutter in the first moments of her stay. By breakfast on the fourth day, however, she descended the stairs with a sense of ease. (One might expect the proximity of a potential murderer to banish any hope of calm—but even this can be got used to through repetition, and Juliet was at this point all but inured to it.)

As she reached the lower hall, she saw Jonathan Darcy standing there, presumably waiting for her. They would begin their investigations right away, which—she told herself—was the only reason her heart gave a tiny leap. Her tone of voice hinted not at this as she said, "Good morning, Mr. Darcy."

"Good morning, Miss Tilney. You are later to breakfast today; I believe we are the last persons remaining who have not eaten."

Already, he saw fit to upbraid her for not beginning earlier. "Perhaps I was awake later, for my mind was busy with thoughts about what we have learned thus far. To me it still seems as though the information we have points in every direction at once. I will endeavor to rise earlier tomorrow, however, that we may resume our efforts more promptly and make better progress."

"You misunderstand me, Miss Tilney. I intended no chastisement." Mr. Darcy fell into step beside her as they walked toward the breakfast room. "I instead saw an opportunity. In our past investigations, we chose a regular time to meet and discuss all that we had learned. Here, we are able to work and speak more openly, yet I feel that our progress would be swifter if we returned to our earlier habit."

Juliet had had the same thought but had not spoken to Mr. Darcy of it for fear of seeming too eager for his company. She resolved that instant to allow no further silliness of this sort to hamper their efforts. "I entirely agree, sir. When and where do you propose?"

"I have visited often enough at Rosings to know that breakfast is most often taken early, and my father does likewise when he is here." Mr. Darcy's eyes met hers with more than common directness, almost as though he were trying to hold her gaze. Briefly Juliet wondered why, when she knew him to dislike such. "Sometimes my cousin Anne will have something brought to her on a tray, but even when she comes downstairs for the morning meal, she does so in its first half hour. If your father does likewise, then we could simply resolve to come down slightly later each day, ensuring that we will have the breakfast room to ourselves."

From past investigations, Juliet had learned that few combinations were more delightful than investigations and scones. "Then let it be so."

As Mr. Darcy had predicted, the breakfast room was empty when they arrived, save for a silent footman in the corner who would neither speak nor move unless and until his assistance was required. The trays with cold meats, bread, cheese, and pastry remained at the ready, of course, as did silver pots of both coffee and tea. Juliet's satisfaction at the sight had little to do with her hunger (eager though she was to break her fast); somehow, this investigation had not felt as natural, as important, as their previous efforts, until this very moment. This had less to do with the inherent value of Lady Catherine's life, however so valued, and more to do with Juliet finally feeling that she and Mr. Darcy need not tiptoe around each other—their old ease might not have returned, but from this point all would be simpler.

Yes, much can be accomplished as we now have a pleasant place to talk without being overheard! Juliet thought as she filled her plate. *Well, the footman will hear, but we need not fear the servants gossiping. Lady Catherine will have put a stop to* that, *I feel certain.*

Yet no sooner had they sat down than Juliet heard a visitor arriving. Moments later, the butler McQuarrie ushered Mrs. Charlotte Collins into the breakfast room; she bore a basket with some cloth-wrapped bundle inside. "Good morning to you both," she said. "I come bearing plum cake, you see."

"That is most kind of you," said Juliet. She wondered whether this was the work of Hunsford Parsonage's cook, or whether perhaps the Collinses practiced more economy than they let on, obliging Charlotte to do some baking herself. "I fear the residents of Rosings Park have finished breakfast already."

Charlotte did not seem surprised; no doubt she knew the habits of those at Rosings even more thoroughly than did Mr. Darcy. "I shall take this up to Anne, then, that she might enjoy a slice on her tray. Plum cake is a favorite of hers."

Once Juliet and Mr. Darcy had both taken slices for politeness, McQuarrie led Charlotte upstairs. The plum cake was in truth very good. "Are little gifts such as these brought to Rosings often?" Juliet asked.

"No," said Mr. Darcy. "I cannot remember any other similar occasion. Nor do any of the Collinses regularly go upstairs at Rosings. They are intimates of the family, yet Lady Catherine wishes to preserve the distinction between their situations."

"Do you think—can it be a subterfuge, a mere ploy to allow Mrs. Collins to go into other parts of the house?"

Mr. Darcy did not seem to think much of this idea. "All those we suspect are not at all the sort we think of as being capable of murder, so we cannot discount Mrs. Collins solely due to her temperate nature and her respectability. However, it seems most unlikely that she would announce herself so openly before making another attempt . . . and before lunch, at that."

"There is no reason not to commit murder in the morning as opposed to later in the day, and yet it feels most unusual, does it not?" Juliet wondered at it. "Perhaps we imagine a murderer would require more time to ready for the task, to bolster courage. But be the killer cold-blooded enough, and any hour would be possible. That said, not even the earliest riser among villains would announce themselves as Mrs. Collins just did."

Mr. Darcy remained puzzled. "I cannot imagine her reasons for this, then."

"Could she—might this be some manner of diversion meant to conceal the wrongdoing of another?" Juliet asked.

"How might this do so?"

"I admit, I can think of no specific possibility," she admitted, "but there was much in Lady Catherine's looks last night to make me think she has some suspicion of the Collins family . . . in particular, of the younger Mr. Collins."

"Deb?" Mr. Darcy frowned. "Whatever could his reason

be for wishing to murder Lady Catherine? She is his family's patroness, and though her demeanor is not such as to appeal to a boy of his age, he must surely be sent to school soon and thus away from her."

"I cannot say why he should do it, nor why Lady Catherine should think so. But so she does think, of that I am sure, and we must determine why." Then Juliet discerned an inconsistency, one that might mean nothing or everything. "Mr. Darcy, it seems to me that Mr. Collins and his family are very eager to follow Lady Catherine's example in every possible way."

"Indeed they are," said Mr. Darcy.

"And yet, Peter Fitzwilliam has been sent away to school at only eight years of age, while De Bourgh Collins remains at home though he is turned twelve. Did Lady Catherine suggest differently for him than for her grandson? Or do they oppose her, alone in this among all other things?"

Mr. Darcy considered this. "I do not know whether the discrepancy in their actions is meaningful or not—but a discrepancy it is, and one we must account for."

Jonathan Darcy had known both Katy and Deb Collins their entire lives. Not as intimate friends—he came to Rosings Park perhaps three times a year, and the Collinses had only visited Pemberley twice in Jonathan's recollection. Among children, however, but a few hours' acquaintance can be sufficient for great familiarity.

Of course, Jonathan was the oldest of the children, but Katy fell between the ages of his two younger brothers, Matthew and James; Deb was only two years younger than James. Thus the pack of them had been able to make merry mischief together. Most of this, Jonathan remembered vaguely as a series of events altogether too loud and sudden for him to enjoy, save for the rare occasions when they would help him line up his toy soldiers into review ranks, then into battle lines for imaginary wars.

Yet one day in particular stood out in Jonathan's memory, one in which a shared afternoon at Pemberley had taken the shape of the game all children, everywhere, have ever played and ever will: hide-and-go-seek.

Jonathan's mother had impressed upon him that he had natural advantages as both the eldest and a resident of the house, and that he should not unfairly use these to the detriment of the other children's fun. So he had taken it upon himself to seek, allowing the others to hide. He found James first, in the ballroom, poorly hidden behind some draperies. (James, ever indecisive, always put off choosing his place until the last minute and thus always chose very ill.) Katy had turned up next, holding a blanket over her head in a closet. Matthew had shown early signs of shrewdness by secreting himself behind the pigsty, a place generally avoided due to its stink. Deb, however, had proved elusive.

"Deb?" Matthew had called after the group's repeated searches of the ground floor turned up nothing. "Deb, stop it! You win! Tell us where you are!"

"You win!" James had repeated, chortling at their bewilderment.

Katy, however, had not laughed. Jonathan remembered how quiet she became, how her footsteps quickened the longer they looked. When she called her brother's name, he detected what he believed to be a note of true alarm. But he must have been wrong—misunderstanding, as often he did—because what would there be to fear at Pemberley? Besides, Deb often chose unusual comings and goings, fre-

quently deviating from the calm, orderly habits that gently
ruled Pemberley; Jonathan, even fonder of order in his youth,
had noted Deb's deviancy with dislike. Still, it could hardly be
a cause for greater concern.

Finally, out upon the grounds, Katy cried out and ducked
beneath a thick topiary hedge. After a few moments, she
emerged with Deb by her side; Deb had been utterly filthy,
with dirt all over his clothes and face and his hair so disheveled he might as well have been in a windstorm. He had not
met any of their eyes. Matthew had laughed and laughed.
"Did you burrow beneath the ground to defy us? Like a mole?"

The joke was kindly meant—if anything, such a stunt would
have won the admiration of Jonathan's brothers. But Deb had
looked away, and Katy had made a reply that was no reply at
all: "Let us have another game. Buffy gruffy, perhaps?"

Jonathan could not abide buffy gruffy, which would require
him to be blindfolded. So he took himself off to read, while
the others squealed in play for hours more. It was but one of
countless such afternoons spent in childhood with neighbors
or friends, the specifics of which fade in the cloudy memories
of the young. Jonathan might have forgotten it altogether,
but the day stood out in his mind because the next morn was
when they had discovered all the chickens murdered in the
coop, no doubt the work of a fox. The grass of Pemberley's
gardens had been daubed here and there with feathers, and
with blood.

Juliet could tell that Mr. Darcy was much preoccupied with
a thought or memory he did not seem inclined to share. She
trusted that he would tell her were it significant to their investigation, so she did not inquire. Their next steps seemed clear

to her. "We must call upon the Collins family at Hunsford Parsonage," said she. "Perhaps by spending more time in their company, we will get a better sense of why Lady Catherine suspects De Bourgh Collins—and whether she is unjust in doing so."

Mrs. Collins came downstairs at that very time, which made it all the easier to suggest walking with her back to the parsonage. Upon stepping out onto the grounds, Juliet saw that the Collins children had accompanied their mother as far as the garden gate and waited for her there. None of the Collinses appeared to detect any ulterior motives behind this impromptu visit. "Is it not frightfully dull, when the weather is so bleak?" Katy said. "We have a new puzzle, if perhaps you would wish to try that. Or we might sketch or make silhouettes of one another."

The clouds made the day very dim, yet not quite dark enough for silhouettes. Juliet regretted this until she realized she had been hoping to take one of Mr. Darcy. Such a sensibility was not to be allowed. Sketching won the day, and they all set about doing their best to draw one another—with highly varied results. Drawing was not among Juliet's modest accomplishments, but she had through extensive practice learned how to create likenesses that outraged neither truth nor the person depicted. Katy Collins had never studied drawing at all—"Lady Catherine says it is the least useful of all female accomplishments, and that instruction would be time wasted"—and thus could scarcely produce more than a scrawl. Mr. Darcy possessed some degree of ability; from his pencil issued drawings that lacked vitality but possessed an accuracy of scale and fine attention to detail. Juliet suspected Mr. Darcy would make an excellent draughtsman, in the unlikely circumstance that he might need to earn a living.

(For a moment she remembered Lawrence Follett, whom

she had so briefly known in Devonshire. During all their sit-
tings, she had been half convinced that he was the murderer
they sought, and thus only at the end had she been able to
fully appreciate the excellence of the portrait of her that he
had produced. Where might that picture be now?)

However, it was Deb Collins they had come to study; and
much to Juliet's surprise, his talent far outstripped the rest.
He would not be serious, producing only caricatures—but
the cartoons possessed as much justice as wit. "I suppose I
should not laugh," she said, attempting not to giggle at Deb's
creation, a small sketch of Lady Catherine sitting upon an
actual throne, her crown bedecked with emu feathers. "Yet it
is indeed very like!"

"She is my great-aunt, and deserves my respect," said
Mr. Darcy, "but I cannot deny the similarity."

"I have to look at Lady Catherine enough, so I hope by now
I should know her face, whether I wish it or not, and I *do not*,"
Deb said. "I know you like her no better than we do, Jona-
than, so I speak plainly."

Mr. Darcy did not seem to know what to say. Finally he ventured, "Certainly there have been occasions when I believed
Lady Catherine not to be fond of me."

It was Katy who laughed, though she covered her mouth
quickly. "Forgive me, cousin, but . . . has there ever been an
occasion when you believed that she *was* fond of you? Do
not be offended, for I believe she is not truly fond of anyone in God's creation save her daughter, and even then only
when Mrs. Fitzwilliam does exactly as Lady Catherine wishes
in every respect."

The lack of an answer from Mr. Darcy was as telling as any
affirmation could have been. Juliet studied Deb closely. He
kept tracing over and over the wrinkles in his sketch of Lady
Catherine's face, carving them deep until she looked so aged

as to be even beyond death. "She is our patroness but also our burden," he said. "A burden we are all obliged to endure, so long as she lives."

Katy's smile faded. Juliet and Mr. Darcy exchanged a look. At that moment, however, all attention was distracted by another carriage driving up to Hunsford Parsonage. Juliet peered from the drawing room window with surprise as she saw Mr. Collins emerge. His carriage was a fine one, nearly as much so as Lady Catherine's or the Darcys'; Juliet idly wondered whether her grandfather ought not to be more generous with her family, if this were the manner of equipage most rectors could expect.

Mr. Darcy asked, "Has your father traveled far today?"

Before either Katy or Deb could speak, Mrs. Collins passed through the room toward the front door. "He was but visiting a parishioner. As a clergyman, Mr. Collins must attend to the needs of his flock, a duty that can arise any time of night or day."

As the Collins family gathered together for greetings—and rather pointed comments to Mr. Collins to inform him of the visitors' presence—Juliet dared lean closer to Mr. Darcy and murmur, "Surely Hunsford is not so large a town that he would require a carriage to visit anyone who dwells within it."

"He may wish to display the carriage, so that Lady Catherine will hear that he conducts himself in the style she has suggested," Mr. Darcy replied. "That, or Mr. Collins is meeting with someone beyond this village . . . for reasons he wishes to remain concealed."

Another homecoming occurred later at Rosings Park, whither Colonel Fitzwilliam was returning.

He went upstairs, wearied from a trip along a road made treacherous by rain. Too many of these rides had he taken of late; at least, soon he would have no more need. As he passed his wife's bedchamber, he saw that she had left her door ajar. Was that to keep note of his comings and goings?

Or did he dare consider it an invitation?

Fitzwilliam rapped upon the doorframe. Anne looked up from her embroidery and smiled at him, but her smile was uncertain as she asked, "Is all well?"

"It soon will be," he said.

They might have spoken much more to each other, had Jenkinson not that moment appeared behind the colonel. "Forgive me, sir, madam—but Lady Catherine wished to be promptly informed of Colonel Fitzwilliam's return."

How kind of her to come to them first! "Mrs. Jenkinson, might you delay your message to your mistress a bit longer?"

He believed Mrs. Jenkinson would have agreed to all, but Anne had risen to her feet. "We ought not lie to Mama," she said. "Go and let Lady Catherine know at once, Jenkinson."

The servant left to obey, and Fitzwilliam followed her. There would be no peace, no conversation with Anne, not so long as Lady Catherine's dictates governed his every action, his every hour!

Chapter Eight

Nothing increases our desire for anything, be it activity or object, more acutely than the knowledge that we cannot have it. Thus it was that, after a chilly, blustery morning in the vicinity of Hunsford, a brighter afternoon drew many out of doors who might otherwise happily have spent this time inside. The wind was held to be no hindrance; extra shawls and scarves were looked upon more as ornaments than as mere shields against autumnal chill. Miss Tilney was among those so tempted, for as she and Jonathan left the parsonage, she said, "Oh, what a pity that we must go back directly. Would not it be refreshing to take the air?"

"Then let us do so," said Jonathan. Hunsford surrounded the estates so closely that he and Miss Tilney would not go unobserved, and thus they might walk without a chaperone. "We could walk through the village. I do not think you have yet seen much of Hunsford beyond these two houses."

Were her cheeks already reddened by the cool breeze, or was the walk more improper than he had reckoned with? But Miss Tilney said, "Your suggestion strikes me as an excellent one, Mr. Darcy. Let us do precisely that."

At last, he thought, *we seem to be making friends again.*

Thus Jonathan guided Miss Tilney into Hunsford. Luckily there was no mud to speak of, and the way was a pleasant one. "Hunsford is not very sizable," he explained as they entered the outskirts of the village, "but it is busy enough to satisfy both needs and caprices. They have an excellent lending library, I am told, and I have considered joining."

"Rosings has rather a large collection of books in its library," said Miss Tilney. "Can you not find enough to suit? Or—no, I have guessed it—Lady Catherine lacks sufficient classics for your taste. Perhaps not even a single volume of Gibbon?"

This was, in its way, teasing, and Jonathan was too accustomed to being teased. Yet this humor struck him as far gentler, not aimed as a weapon, but intended to be shared. He found it easy to smile back. "The de Bourgh library contains a very handsome complete set of Gibbon's works. However, I have recently expanded my interests in reading. When we were in Devonshire, you showed a very marked interest in the historical novels written by Sir Walter Scott—or, at least, that we believe to be written by Sir Walter Scott."

Her evident delight warmed him through. "I am very flattered indeed, Mr. Darcy, that you should take an interest based on my opinion alone. Best of all is that my example does not appear to have led you astray."

"Not at all, Miss Tilney! His stories are so exciting, so thrilling—" Jonathan struggled for words. He could praise the books with the same phrases others did, but he wished to say what he truly felt. "I feel as though I am there. In the wilds of Scotland, or back in the days following the Conquest, when the Normans oppressed the Saxons. I had just reached the part of *Ivanhoe* where Isaac and Rebecca rescue him, and then Lady Catherine's letter arrived. What with the uproar this caused, and the hurry to depart, I entirely forgot to pack the book. Of course we must reserve most of our time to the resolution of this mystery, but I had thought, if I could borrow *Ivanhoe* to read in my spare time—"

"That you could return to the story. I should not mind the chance to reread it myself. Yes, let us seek the library."

By now they were walking through Hunsford proper. They saw milkmaids carrying pails, a cobbler shaping leather through the window of his shop, even Jenkinson hurrying from store to store, no doubt to fetch some bow or trim for one of the Rosings's ladies' bonnets. The added sounds of boots and hooves upon cobblestones, the creaking of hinges, the murmuring of conversation, provided the necessary auditory concealment for Jonathan to feel safe to say, "Certainly Deb does not care for Lady Catherine."

"I should say he greatly dislikes her," Miss Tilney replied, in the same low tone. "And Katy is nearly as irked by her ladyship, or perhaps as much or more—but is older and more able to conceal it."

"Yet as he said, she is their benefactress," said Jonathan. "All they have, they owe to her. Lady Catherine can be imperious, and harsh in her judgments, but does this truly negate all the good she has done them?"

Miss Tilney considered this for a few moments. "Sometimes, I believe, in such situations, we are even quicker to anger than we would be otherwise. There is the old saying, that we should not bite the hand that feeds us—but the saying's very existence hints that many people do indeed feel that desire. We do not wish to be dependent. We wish, insofar as it is possible, to choose our own fates, to earn our good fortune."

Jonathan could understand this. "And yet, for so many people, this is not possible. We are all of us confined by the society in which we belong, by our families, by the laws of God."

"All the more reason to long for freedom, do not you think?" Miss Tilney sighed. "I am beginning to sound as ungrateful as any American."

Before Jonathan could reassure her otherwise, he spied Miss Tilney's father in the town square, a newspaper folded beneath one arm. He waved to the two younger persons and began making his way toward them. Miss Tilney began, "If he asks about the investigation—"

"I shall reveal as little as possible," Jonathan finished. They could not make progress with opinions and theories from all and sundry; short of Lady Catherine falling prey to panic or irrationality, he would not speak.

Mr. Tilney had struck Jonathan from the first as a most amiable, easygoing fellow, but on this day his countenance was grave. "Juliet," he said. "Mr. Darcy. Thank goodness I caught you myself."

"Papa?" Miss Tilney seemed to find her father's demeanor as unusual as Jonathan did. "Whatever is the matter? Oh—it is not Mama?"

"Your mother is safe and well," Mr. Tilney said, quickly taking his daughter's hand. "But I came into town today for the paper, because I knew that a certain date had come and gone, occasioning news you must both hear, though it may be difficult."

By now Jonathan's concern was mounting. "What do you mean, sir?"

"The murderer you caught—Mr. Ralph Bamber—" Mr. Tilney removed his hat. "Yesterday Bamber was hanged."

It is quite one thing to pursue justice. It is another to enact it. One may feel with all one's being that the price of murder should be death and yet balk when that price must be paid: this was Jonathan's frame of mind, more or less. He could not bear to see even an animal be needlessly shot, avoiding the hunts that so many other gentlemen delighted in; the thought of the execution of a person—any person, but particularly one he had known from boyhood, one whom he had briefly considered a friend—made him go pale and cold.

It is also possible to look at the matter from entirely a different perspective, as did Juliet. Having twice now seen murder with her own eyes, she had come to feel most strongly that deliberately taking life was wrong, regardless of the reason. How did society prove murderers wrong by murdering them in turn? Should not a regard for life extend as far as could be imagined and in every possible direction? (After all, Marianne Brandon had been spared punishment and execution despite her killing of Mr. Wickham—there, the law had shown understanding and mercy—though Juliet knew the comparison was poor. Marianne had struck at Wickham solely to defend herself, an act entirely unlike Bamber's cold calculation of poison.)

As a clergyman's daughter, Juliet also thought leaving such persons in prison at least gave them a chance for repentance and salvation. She had hoped as much for Ralph Bamber but would never know whether this had come to pass. The knowledge that he had been hanged made her cheeks flush hot and dizzied her almost to the point of swaying.

This was an inevitable circumstance for Jonathan Darcy and Juliet Tilney, as any outside observer could have anticipated. If one is to make a habit of catching murderers, one will eventually see those murderers meet their fates. Yet how often our reactions change when "eventually" becomes "now"!

So Mr. Tilney shepherded both younger persons back to Rosings Park, *Ivanhoe* entirely forgotten.

Juliet spent the late afternoon largely in her room. This room contained a broad window seat, from which Juliet could look out upon the grounds at everything and nothing at once. Dully she watched squirrels romping in the trees; two servants walking hand in hand during a brief moment of leisure amid their work; Mr. Collins appearing at the exact hour when he might most likely be invited to stay for dinner. She hoped very much he would not be. She was of no mind to pay attention to detail, as the investigation demanded, and beyond this purpose, she had no interest whatsoever in spending more time with Mr. Collins.

A soft rap near her open door made Juliet turn, half expecting a servant with tea on a tray; instead she saw Anne Fitzwilliam. "Forgive my intrusion," Anne said. "But I heard of—of the event mentioned in the newspaper, and I wished to be certain that you were well."

"You are very kind to do so," answered Juliet. "I fear I cannot say. At moments, it seems to me that all has transpired as it must, and that I ought not to feel any shock regarding an event that all anticipated from the first revelation of Mr. Bamber's guilt. At others—oh, at others, it feels as though I had plunged a dagger into his breast for no purpose but meanness, that I am the murderer and he the victim—I am sorry. I should not say such things."

"Even Mama would find it difficult to quote etiquette in such a matter as this," said Anne. "So I believe you are free to say whatever you will, or nothing at all, should you prefer."

One aspect of Mr. Bamber's fate had particularly disturbed Juliet's mind, one she felt she could discuss only with another woman. Until this moment, she had intended to withhold these thoughts until she wrote to her mother the next morning—but with a willing listener at the ready, Juliet found she could resist no longer. "It is especially distressing for me to recall that, while we were in Devonshire, before the truth was known, Mr. Bamber . . . I believe he was courting me."

"*Oh.*" Anne looked much astonished, as well she might. "Had he declared himself?"

"No, though once he came very near it."

"Were you very much in love with him?"

"Not at all," Juliet said. "At least there is that mercy. But he was a young man of fortune and family, amiable in his address and correct in his person, and so I had wondered whether I ought not to *try* to love him. Instead, through my actions, he has gone to the gallows."

"That is not so," Anne replied, with more firmness than Juliet had ever heard from her before. "Mr. Bamber's own actions led him thither. You are not to blame merely for telling the truth, for that which can be destroyed by truth deserves its destruction."

These sentiments struck Juliet most forcefully. *Can that be the belief of a murderer?* she asked herself, before realizing, *It can be the statement of a murderer who wishes very much to be believed.* She said only, "We are asked, as young women, to consider every eligible young man as a potential husband, little guessing what may lie behind his fortune and reputation. To promise ourselves, often before we even know the true character of the men who ask for our hands. I have always thought this unwise, but now I see that, if the wrong gentleman asks, it can be dangerous as well."

"You speak the truth," said Anne, "and I doubt even Mama would argue against it. As you know, she will argue against a great many things . . . but not this. She never wished for me to marry a stranger."

"That is fortunate. Colonel Fitzwilliam is also your cousin, is he not?"

"Yes, he is." Anne ducked her head. "But he was not my mother's choice. You see, it was her intention that I should marry Mr. Darcy."

Juliet experienced a moment's confusion before realizing that they spoke of the elder Mr. Darcy. "Do you mean to say that he courted you?"

"Not at all. I assure you, such a thought was never in his mind. Both of our mothers desired it, but with his mother, I think, this was more a jest than a matter of seriousness. Mama, however, considered us as good as engaged from the time I had turned five years old. She kept me apart from other children and young persons, fearing for my health; this obliged me to play dolls or archery with Mrs. Jenkinson, or checkers with McQuarrie, when he could be spared—and kept me from meeting any boys who might have grown later into suitors. Mama saw no harm in that. Her thoughts, her attentions toward my future, were entirely for Mr. Darcy as my husband."

"Lady Catherine is most formidable," said Juliet. "Where she wishes her way, I believe she usually gets it. In this case, however, it seems she did not."

Anne smiled crookedly. "Mr. Darcy is not a man to be forced. I believe he would never have married anyone merely to oblige the wishes of his family. Once he met Miss Elizabeth Bennet—the future Mrs. Darcy—his intentions swiftly became plain, much to Mama's displeasure."

"But to your relief, I think." Juliet studied Anne, trying to take her measure. She was so little, so silent compared to her mother, and her features were so slight as to almost appear pinched. Yet she possessed a quiet, delicate sort of prettiness, like the small white flowers that go forgotten amid large bouquets of showier blooms. "You were then free to marry a man you loved, one who loved you." When Anne remained silent for many moments afterward, Juliet added, "If I have spoken out of turn, I most humbly beg your pardon."

"It is a day for confidences, I think," Anne replied. "In truth, I believe the good colonel did precisely what Darcy did not: he married to oblige our family, to do me a kindness. He knew my health would never permit me to be presented as

other girls were, and I was nearing the age past which courtship becomes all but impossible. His own position in the family obliged him to marry wealth, so why should he not do so in
a way that would satisfy the needs of so many others as well?"

These were not uncommon sentiments toward matrimony,
yet they were so unlike Juliet's own feelings upon the matter!
"We are so often told that love will come later, if we choose
well at the start."

Anne stared out the window, but without seeing, more
occupied with memory than with the view. "Truth be told,
I had always been rather taken with Colonel Fitzwilliam.
Mr. Darcy—forgive me, I do not wish to cast aspersions—but
he is so firm, so decided in his ways. It is a trait he and my
mother have in common, though neither would ever admit it,
and Mr. Darcy is generally guided by good principle. Mama's
dictums arise from more opaque sources. Regardless, I was
always drawn to the colonel's gentler, more amiable temper.
This was what my life lacked; this was what I wished for from
a husband."

Juliet believed she finally understood. "So you loved him
from the beginning. His love came later."

For a few long moments, Anne struggled with her response.
Juliet thought her more likely to end their conversation, and
so was surprised when the reply came: "I thought that perhaps it had. My husband has ever been kind to me. So solicitous, so thoughtful—and after we had Peter, we became such
a happy little family! Our rooms, and the nursery, belonged
to us alone, and we spent so many days with just the three of
us together. But then Mama insisted that Peter must go to
school at the soonest possible opportunity, and—ever since,
Miss Tilney, a terrible silence has fallen between us. It is as
though neither of us knows what to say any longer. I miss my
boy so very much, and surely the colonel does as well. But we

do not condole together. Instead, Colonel Fitzwilliam now seems to grasp at any chance to be far from . . . from Rosings."

"My father says that all human wisdom can be expressed in one proverb: 'This, too, shall pass,'" Juliet said. "Perhaps the colonel's wanderings are the way he grieves your son's absence. Every room of Rosings Park must hold memories that are, for now, too painful for him to consider. This cannot last forever. At the very least, Peter will come home for Christmas, will he not?"

"Yes, and already I am counting the days." Anne put one hand to her chest; her fingers were trembling. What a fragile creature she was! "Forgive my unburdening myself to you."

"There is nothing to forgive, for you have paid me the compliment of honesty," Juliet said. "I shall endeavor to deserve it."

She meant this in all sincerity, even though she would have to betray Anne's confidence—for this conversation must inform the investigation. Yet she knew Jonathan Darcy would never speak of this to another unless it proved to be pertinent . . . unless Anne or Colonel Fitzwilliam was revealed as the villain they sought.

Jonathan was granted no such distraction from his remembrances of the late Ralph Bamber. Not even a volume of Cassius Dio from the Rosings library had the power to draw his attention from memories laced with old pain and new guilt. He had not followed Bamber's trial closely, primarily out of a sense that it would be highly unseemly to do so. (Would Bamber believe him to be gloating? Would those around Jonathan who knew the role he had played in Bamber's capture think it, too?) Yet from snatches of newsprint Jonathan had gleaned that Bamber's family had managed to delay the trial for some months. At times Jonathan had been greatly afraid that he would be called to testify, a prospect he did not relish. In the end, however, Bamber had confessed, saying he could not endure the waiting.

What was it like, spending months in a cell comprehending that the only way you would ever again see the world beyond it was by walking to the gallows? Jonathan both wished to know and was profoundly glad he never would.

Father found him in the library not long before dinner. "You should dress for the evening meal," he said.

"I need but change coats," Jonathan replied, not moving.

His father came to the couch and took a seat next to Jonathan. "You are much distressed by the news about Bamber, are you not? I saw it in the newspaper myself. It greatly shocked me, though I never met the young man—and thus I can imagine the information's effect upon you."

"I know not how it affects me. At times I am horrified to have played any role in the end of a man's life, even if that is more truly the result of his own wrongdoing. At other moments, it seems not to concern me in the slightest, as though I had never met Ralph Bamber at all. Is that not cold? Unchristian?"

"Before your trip to Devonshire, you had not seen him in many years," said Mr. Darcy, "and Bamber's own crimes were his undoing. Your actions were in the interest of justice, no more and no less. Thus it is entirely correct for you not to feel undue responsibility for this event. Yet I sense that this is not all currently troubling you."

It was not. Deep within, Jonathan wondered if his relative lack of distress regarding Bamber's death had anything to do with Bamber's interest in Miss Tilney. For a brief time, they had been romantic rivals—though neither Bamber nor Miss

Tilney ever knew it. Jonathan disliked Bamber nearly as much for wounding Miss Tilney as he did for committing murder, an equivalence that could not be justified in any proper reckoning of morality.

Yet Jonathan did not wish to discuss these points with his father, whose opinions regarding Miss Tilney seemed unduly strict. (Perhaps this sprang from the unfortunate incident in Surrey, when Father had caught the two of them in the Churchills' library; although they had been doing nothing more improper than searching for potential clues in *Debrett's Peerage*, had they been seen by anyone else, Miss Tilney's reputation would have been ruined and Jonathan's would have been scarred.) So he said only, "I distrust both what I feel and what I do not feel. It is a conundrum, Father, one from which I doubt I shall ever see my way clear."

Mr. Darcy's hand rested on Jonathan's shoulder. "Trust in justice, my son, both that of the land and that of our Savior."

And yet, Jonathan thought, *Miss Tilney and I are called upon to ensure yet again that justice shall be done. How strange that the creator of all in heaven and earth should need help from us!*

It was a small joke, but easier to think upon than the image of Ralph Bamber swinging from a noose as his life faded.

Chapter Nine

By the time Juliet descended for breakfast the next morning, she felt steadier. Though the burden of Mr. Bamber's fate would ever remain with her, she held fast to the knowledge that this had fundamentally been the work of the Crown and of Bamber himself. She was much relieved, upon entering the Rosings breakfast room, to see that the younger Mr. Darcy sat there waiting for her as they had previously arranged, and that his prediction had held true: no one else was in the room at that hour aside from the footman.

"Good morning, Miss Tilney," Mr. Darcy said, rising to greet her. "I trust you are well? The shock of yesterday's news was . . . I find I have no words for it. But I have spoken with my father and prayed upon the matter, which surely you have done also."

"Yes." Juliet had ultimately taken dinner in her room; apparently even the formidable Lady Catherine de Bourgh considered this an acceptable excuse for declining the society of the house for an evening. "Difficult as it is to reckon with, I have taken from the event this resolution: the gallows shall not be employed in this case, for we shall catch the person attempting to do harm to Lady Catherine before she suffers any injury worse than a broken clock." She hesitated. "Does it sound as though I did not consider her ladyship's life reason enough before? For that is not at all what I intended."

Mr. Darcy smiled. "Have no fear, Miss Tilney. I understand you perfectly."

It seemed to her that he was studying her very closely this morning, as though searching for some further response from her regarding Mr. Bamber. If Mr. Darcy had, during the past year, become more concerned with notions of women's delicacy, he might see her current behavior as lacking in that regard. Perhaps he expected her to swoon, to weep, to be unable to carry on?

But no. Her ire over his comment had run its course. Mr. Darcy's words had greatly displeased Juliet, but proof is not in words but in actions—and he had treated her as a true partner and equal from the first day of their inquiries. His heart had not changed so much as she had initially feared.

Furthermore, Bamber's death and their shared reactions to it had shown her that the bond between them—even if not of the nature she would have wished—remained strong. Juliet would not squander it.

"Let us not think about the past," said she, "but the present matter to hand."

"And the future we wish for Lady Catherine." Mr. Darcy smiled at her, and she felt that he, too, was glad that the chill between them had ended. He took from his pocket a piece of paper on which he had written a sort of chart. "Last night, I found it did not do to let my attention wander. So I took the liberty of creating this."

The chart was entitled, *Those with Opportunity to Harm Her Ladyship*. Within it was written:

The Carriage

<u>Access to the stables:</u> Colonel Fitzwilliam, Mrs. Fitzwilliam (though the latter lacks strength to perform the mischief), Mr. Collins

<u>No access to the stables:</u> Any other member of the Collins family

The Shot

<u>Access to the gun room at the pertinent time:</u> *Deb Collins,*
    Katy Collins, potentially Mrs. Fitzwilliam
<u>No access to the gun room:</u> *Colonel Fitzwilliam (present with*
    Lady Catherine at the time of the shot), Mrs. Collins,
    Mr. Collins

The Push Atop the Stair

<u>Access to the upstairs of the house on that day:</u>
    Mrs. Fitzwilliam, Mrs. Collins, Katy Collins
<u>No access at that place and time:</u> *Colonel Fitzwilliam,*
    Mr. Collins, Deb Collins

"This sets out our problem with admirable but daunting clarity," Juliet said. "Not one of our suspects was even capable of all three attempts upon Lady Catherine's life. We have fundamentally misunderstood something important, but what?"

The dismay on Mr. Darcy's countenance was no doubt the mirror of Juliet's own. "My proposal is that, for the time being, we examine motives. When we have found the most compelling motive and can concentrate our efforts on only one of our suspects, that person's method may make itself more readily known."

Juliet had thought long upon what Anne Fitzwilliam had told her the day before. This needed to be shared with Mr. Darcy—but not here. The footman who stood at the ready in the breakfast room did not speak, but even if he did not actively listen, he could scarce help overhearing them. Confidences so intimate about one of his mistresses were not for his hearing. Surely Anne would not wish it so. "Yes, Mr. Darcy, we have much to discuss. Shall we take a turn in the Rosings gardens?"

Given the very few opportunities society presents for young men and women to be respectably alone together, the popularity of gardens cannot be wondered at. Here, strolls may be taken; here, conversations may be had. Although a garden path lacks privacy in the fullest sense, would-be listeners are generally very far away. Jonathan felt glad for this as Miss Tilney told him what his cousin Anne had revealed about her marriage to Colonel Fitzwilliam.

He found he was not greatly surprised. "Not, that is, by the information itself," he said as he explained this to Miss Tilney, "rather I am surprised that I should never have wondered what circumstances brought them to marry."

Miss Tilney merely shrugged. "You have known them since your earliest childhood, have you not? We rarely question that which has always been a part of our lives, for to us it can never be curious."

"True," said Jonathan, "and yet, my mother has occasionally joked about Rosings Park, and under what circumstances my father might have come to live there. Always I believed this to be merely a fanciful notion of hers, no more. Now I realize that she was referring to the supposed engagement between Anne and my father."

"When next she does so, you will be able to inform her that it was the colonel Anne preferred all along," said Miss Tilney.

"I predict this will refresh her wit on the subject anew. However, it is my father's reaction that most occupies my thoughts." Jonathan knew that Miss Tilney could not in politeness inquire further, but he understood her curiosity, for it was not so very different from his own. "Father has always seemed to feel himself . . . indebted to this family, and in particular to Anne. I used to think that it was as though he had done them a great wrong, even though I knew this to be impossible, given his character and his respect for our aunt. It must be this of which he thought—his decision to marry my mother."

"He did no wrong by Mrs. Fitzwilliam!" Miss Tilney protested. "The 'engagement' was nothing of the sort; and if she herself did not desire the match, he in fact did her a service. She married a man of sense and breeding, one who was willing to live under the same roof as Lady Catherine. There could be few such gentlemen."

Jonathan nodded. "My father is certainly not among that number. Yet I believe the guilt plagues him to this day. When all is resolved in this matter, I might speak to him of this, so that he might understand how well Anne has always been reconciled to his choice of wife."

"Say nothing as of yet, Mr. Darcy. We must consider what this information means for the situation at hand." Miss Tilney paused, her countenance uncertain. "Mrs. Fitzwilliam confided in me out of kindness, I believe—to distract me from the news about Mr. Bamber—so it pains me to say this. But her history convinces me that both she and her husband have ample reason to resent Lady Catherine and to wish themselves the master and mistress of Rosings Park."

Jonathan could well imagine it. He found his great-aunt difficult company at the best of times, and he had never been obliged to endure her presence more than three weeks in a row. To be under the reign of such judgment, such officiousness, day in and day out—it would tax the gentlest soul. "Lady Catherine is not intent upon disinheriting them. She told us so herself, in my belief, honestly so."

"So they have no cause to fear the solicitor's visit." Miss Tilney considered this. "We may be wrong about that visit being the spur behind these attempts on Lady Catherine's life.

Instead of preventing something in the future, either husband or wife may be revenging a wrong done in the past—by which I mean their son's being sent away."

"I could scarcely wonder at their displeasure," Jonathan said, memories of the miseries of his school days very much with him. "Peter is a quiet, shy child. He cannot be happy among boisterous crowds of older boys, and I am sure his parents know it."

They walked on for a few paces in silence before Miss Tilney nodded. "Very well. We have established strong motives for both of the Fitzwilliams. So we must look more deeply into the potential motives of our other suspects."

Jonathan took her meaning immediately. "Shall we for Hunsford Parsonage?"

He crooked his elbow for her, and Miss Tilney took his arm. Respectable as their pursuits were, and uncertain as he was regarding the state of Miss Tilney's heart, Jonathan could not help feeling a small thrill at the touch of her gloved hand upon his sleeve.

Charlotte Collins glanced out her window and saw Jonathan Darcy and Miss Juliet Tilney walking up the path. She very much did not desire callers, least of all these two, but there was nothing to be done for it. She straightened her mobcap, called to her husband, "We have visitors!" and swiftly descended the stairs so that she might receive them in her drawing room.

"Mr. Darcy!" Mr. Collins said, hurrying in moments after their arrival. He breathed too quickly, and he still held his hat in his hands. "Miss Tilney. How good of you to return to our humble abode. De Bourgh, I fear, is unwell today, but Katy will join us shortly."

Jonathan pointed immediately to the hat. "You have just been out, sir?"

Charlotte possessed sufficient discipline not to wince. However, her reaction might have been gleaned by Miss Tilney, who swiftly added, "I hope our visit has not kept you from your gardens, sir."

This opportunity must be seized. Charlotte said, "My husband was preparing to visit our beehives. They are of interest to you, are they not, Mr. Darcy?"

"Indeed they are," said Jonathan. He had been enamored of them as a boy, staring at them sometimes for hours on end. A peculiar young man, indeed: sometimes Charlotte could see nothing of Elizabeth in him at all. "May I join you, Mr. Collins?"

Mr. Collins looked at his wife almost plaintively, as though she could provide further help than she had already. "Ah, yes. Yes, of course. Certainly. Right this way, Mr. Darcy!"

As the two men quitted the room, Charlotte turned her attention to Miss Tilney. One guest, and one guest's questions, could be more steadily handled. "Please do sit down, Miss Tilney. To what do we owe the honor of your visit? I presume it relates to your quest to learn who has been attempting to harm Lady Catherine."

"You speak plainly, madam. I will do you the honor of speaking likewise. Yes, I need to determine your whereabouts, and those of your family, on the day before her ladyship's carriage accident."

My whereabouts are known on the day of the incident upon the stairs, Charlotte thought. *She does not ask about the day of the shooting. Why not?* None of these thoughts disturbed her visage. Charlotte Collins had long ago mastered, if not true serenity, then the appearance of it.

"We may consult the house diary to check," said Charlotte, "but I believe I remained at Hunsford Parsonage all day. Our figs had ripened—and you know how quickly you must then act, lest the birds steal them all away. So I was supervising my kitchen staff as they made fig butter. The previous week they had made our apricot preserves, and I spent much of my time labeling the jars properly. One does not wish to serve the wrong accompaniment to tea, particularly when Lady Catherine comes to call. She is decided in her preferences."

"Indeed." Miss Tilney appeared somewhat taken aback by the swiftness and thoroughness of Charlotte's reply, which was entirely as Charlotte had intended. "Did Katy help at the task? I often assist my mother in similar endeavors; when I left for Rosings, she teased me that I was only going to avoid our fall's raisin-making."

"She did indeed, as did Deb—though as a growing boy, he did more stealing of fruits than preserving them!" Charlotte allowed herself a small smile.

Miss Tilney would not be distracted for long, it seemed. "And your husband? Surely Mr. Collins had nothing to do with the kitchen."

"Of course not." Charlotte knew what her husband would say when he was asked, and thus she must say the same: "My husband took a day's trip to Faxton—that is a village to the east, more than an hour by carriage—to purchase some lace for me."

"Lace?"

"Yes. I wanted to trim my caps anew, and add a ruffle to Katy's green dress. Ruffles are becoming quite the fashion, they say."

Miss Tilney's hand brushed against her neckline, as though suddenly aware of her own attire's lack of both ruffles and lace. "That is an uncommon errand for a husband to undertake, as opposed to a wife."

"Yet I had no opportunity to go, and he did. He chose well, I think." Charlotte touched the lace at the edge of her mob-cap. "Do not you agree?"

"The lace is very lovely indeed."

Of course Miss Tilney was not convinced; Charlotte could easily discern as much. But the girl was, for now, silenced. That would do.

Mr. Collins was, at that moment, standing at the beehives with Jonathan Darcy, who had just frowned in confusion and asked, "Lace?"

"Lace indeed, Mr. Darcy. When the time comes for you to take a wife, you will learn how many concerns of the feminine sphere a husband is obliged to attend." The bees hummed through the air, a constant low buzz that set Mr. Collins quite on edge. By custom, beekeeping was more commonly a male pursuit, but in their household, Charlotte had much more the nerve for the task. "Such information can be useful, however, as Lady Catherine's interest in all such details is very great. I pride myself on being able to engage her ladyship in conversation on any topic she may desire! You will find that genteel ladies are much engaged with these matters."

The young Mr. Darcy seemed to be reckoning whether this was true of all ladies. Unfortunately, he realized it was not. "Aunt Mary does not concern herself with clothes at all. She says Mr. Wheelwright believes the finest ornaments of woman to be learning and piety."

"Ah. Yes." Mr. Collins's mood soured in an instant. The former Miss Mary Bennet—sister and current host of Elizabeth—had married a clergyman named Mr. Wheelwright, who now held the position of Dean of Tunbridge Wells. This put him in some authority over Mr. Collins, a circumstance that affected his daily life very little. Yet whenever Mr. Collins found himself in the company of Mary and Elizabeth's parents—the same Mr. and Mrs. Bennet who occupied Longbourn, the home Mr. Collins had been waiting to inherit for more than twenty years—Mrs. Bennet lorded Mr. Wheelwright's position over Mr. Collins as though this fact could undo the entail in an instant.

Yet if discussing Mr. Wheelwright would distract Jonathan Darcy from his other inquiries, let it be done.

So skillfully did the elder Collinses distract their guests, they were able to go the entire visit without once producing either Katy or Deb to be questioned. Jonathan enjoyed again visiting Mr. Collins's bees, but he could scarcely credit that as a worthwhile use of the afternoon. As he and Miss Tilney walked back to Rosings Park, he found she shared his dismay.

"Katy and Deb are undeniably hiding *something*," she said. "They were near the gun room on the day someone shot at Lady Catherine, when they never ought to have been. And neither of them can abide Lady Catherine, who in turn distrusts Deb. It seems so unlikely that a girl of my age and a boy some years younger could turn to such violent acts, but I believe they would be our main suspects were it not for the strangeness of their parents."

"You did not believe the story about the lace, either," said Jonathan. It was a relief to see that her judgment in this matter matched his own. "Many men do sometimes purchase such things for their wives—more, I believe, than is commonly admitted—but I cannot see Mr. Collins being among them."

"I can see Mrs. Collins as being the sort of woman who

gives not one whit about the lace she wears," Miss Tilney said, "and thus I could envision her entrusting the errand to her husband. I might not have thought anything of the story had she not insisted on it so strongly. It seemed to me that she wished for us to believe that Mr. Collins was in Faxton on the day when someone must have tampered with Lady Catherine's carriage."

Jonathan considered. "We must remember that she would impress that information upon us strongly regardless of its truth or falsehood. Yet we can in fairness say that our investigation disquiets them—which means that we must in fact investigate even more thoroughly."

The dining room at Rosings Park had been built to accommodate a far greater number of guests than ever actually enjoyed the hospitality of Lady Catherine's table. Even Pemberley—which sometimes hosted balls for more than one hundred persons—could not boast such an enormous table. Lady Catherine had once mentioned how much the table had cost, and this information was repeated at least once a fortnight by Mr. Collins. All Jonathan could think was that it was exceedingly awkward for all the dinner guests to be grouped together at one end of a table that stretched out blankly empty so far past them.

He sat to the end of table, with Mrs. Fitzwilliam on his left, Mr. Tilney between her and Lady Catherine, who of course sat at the head. Jonathan's father sat in the position of pride at Lady Catherine's right, with Miss Tilney next to him, and finally Colonel Fitzwilliam. Mr. Tilney appeared to be a man who sought lively conversation, though at Rosings he was obliged to seek it very hard indeed.

"A fine cut of meat, indeed," he said. "Roasted over apple-wood, was it not?"

Lady Catherine stared at Mr. Tilney as though he had said something highly offensive. "Never should I deign to inquire as to the sort of wood used in our ovens. Do you always converse so much with your servants that you should know such a thing?"

"The type of wood used affects the flavor, madam." Mr. Tilney appeared amused by Lady Catherine's ignorance of this fact; Jonathan could scarcely blame him for this, but would have wished for the man to display his amusement less openly, as this could but stoke her ladyship's temper. "Apple-wood imparts a lighter, sweeter taste, and is especially good with pork such as this. For more savoriness, however, and a darker color, one might instruct one's kitchen staff to burn hickory wood instead."

"How very interesting," said Anne, though perhaps more from politeness than true engagement with the subject.

Lady Catherine would not be so easily entertained. "How the cook achieves the desired results is beneath the notice of any person of gentility. That is a matter for kitchen staff."

The elder Mr. Darcy interjected, "Mrs. Darcy often says that the mistress of a home must understand her house-keeper's needs and habits in order to supervise her correctly."

As ever, the mention of Jonathan's mother deepened Lady Catherine's frown. "*She* may count twigs as she pleases, but I shall not stoop to such!"

He noted that Anne and Colonel Fitzwilliam exchanged a glance then, one of shared amusement—but then Anne's expression swiftly clouded, and her gaze drifted down to her plate. Jonathan could not but interpret this in the light of what Miss Tilney had told him this morning: that, at least on Colonel Fitzwilliam's side, theirs was not a marriage of love.

It was, however, one of mutual endurance, even mutual suffering, under the petty tyranny of Lady Catherine de Bourgh. What might two decades of such treatment have driven the colonel to consider?

And what might a lifetime have done to Anne?

Chapter Ten

As the sixth day of the Darcys' and Tilneys' visit dawned, a greater sense of calm had settled upon Rosings. Although both young investigators strongly believed the danger to Lady Catherine had not passed, the hopes of others in the house were more sanguine . . . and even Jonathan Darcy and Juliet Tilney could not maintain the same sense of alarm after having watched her ladyship go for nearly a week entirely unmolested. Perhaps, had they been able to conduct their morning discussion as planned, their fears might have been stoked anew. Instead, however, at the first moment callers could in any decency show themselves at the house, the knock at the door sounded: Katy and Deb Collins had come not only to call but also to play.

"Let us have a day of archery," Katy pleaded to Lady Catherine. Many tendrils of her curly hair had escaped their bun, which had the effect of making her seem more like a little girl than the young lady she had become. (Charlotte had tugged these curls loose for entirely that purpose.) "It is always such fun. Do you shoot with bow and arrow, Miss Tilney?"

"I have done so at friends' houses," Juliet replied, "though never so often as I would wish. It seems an excellent sport for ladies and gentlemen alike."

Mrs. Fitzwilliam also expressed her desire to join them. Frail though she was, she did not lack the strength necessary to use a light bow. This was one of the few areas in which she had some physical prowess to display, and one of the few pastimes beyond gardening which gave her an excuse for more time out in fresh air—and archery allowed her to travel even farther from the house, sometimes entirely out of Lady Catherine's earshot. What could be more appealing?

Even the gentlemen were inclined to join in, and thus it was that, within twenty minutes of the young Collinses' arrival, their entire company was to be found camped on the far north lawn (save the elder Mr. Darcy, who first had letters to compose before he could join the party). As Daniels directed his underlings to and from the gun room for the setting of the targets and the dispensation of bows and arrows, Jenkinson and the lady's maid named Daisy set out a chair, a little table, and a footstool for Lady Catherine, from which setting she would be able to witness and remark on all from the comfort of shade. Yet even her ladyship smiled with the brightness of the day and the prettiness of the lively young people on her lawn. Had she not done well in bringing them all together?

(Except of course De Bourgh. She would never forgive Mr. Collins's impudence in so naming his son, which she found so mortifying that she was, uniquely in her experience, unable to speak a word upon the subject. And she was sure the boy's rascality lay behind all this, just as she felt confident that he had not in fact wished to kill her. His pranks had simply gone too far; Jonathan and Miss Tilney had been brought here to expose him, at which point Lady Catherine expected De Bourgh's terror and repentance, each of which she would find extremely satisfying.)

As for the young investigators: They did not know how little Lady Catherine felt herself to truly need their services, but they had begun to sense it. This did not make them relax their vigilance, however; each was keenly aware of the potential implications of bows, arrows, and targets both inanimate and otherwise. Yet neither Deb nor Katy made any rash turns toward her ladyship—they were both intent upon the game, and soon everyone else was also.

"I shall hit my target," said Anne Fitzwilliam, with uncommon spirit. "Watch me, dear!"

Colonel Fitzwilliam did at that moment seem to greatly admire his wife, particularly when she let her arrow fly and it landed very near the red. Katy and Deb shot even better, which made Juliet's turn all the more intimidating. Still, she braced herself, pulled back as hard as she could, and—

"There!" Juliet cried in delight as her arrow struck the bull's-eye, dead center. "There, do you see?"

The Fitzwilliams applauded her; the Collinses cheered. Juliet's face fell, however, as she realized that the young Mr. Darcy had become particularly fascinated by a knot in a nearby tree and had not attended her at all.

It signified little, really. What troubled her more was her father watching this as a frown appeared on his face.

Henry Tilney, like many fathers, felt no particular hurry to see young men courting his daughter. Also like many fathers, however, he was very much displeased to see a young man *not* courting his daughter, especially as the young man in question was one who seemed to have captured Juliet's imagination. When the day's sport allowed him a few moments to stand by Juliet, somewhat away from the others, Tilney murmured to her, "Your Mr. Darcy is not very gallant."

"He is not my Mr. Darcy," Juliet said, more placidly than he would have expected. "It does not matter how I . . . it does not matter. I told you before that he did not regard me in that way. Do you now believe me?"

"It is *he* who moves me to disbelief." Mr. Tilney's outrage was touching for his daughter to behold, for she would never have thought him so moved by her disappointments of the heart. "How can he ignore what is before his very eyes?"

"Do not believe him unkind or unfeeling—nor unobserving, though his attention sometimes alights on peculiar things. Mr. Darcy is a kind, thoughtful, upstanding young man who simply is not as other young men. His oddness of temperament should not be mistaken for a lack of character. His attention may wander from time to time, but I am most certain that it will always return to the place where it most properly belongs, which is to say, assuring Lady Catherine's safety."

Often we can forgive offenses against ourselves more easily than those committed against others, particularly when those others are persons very dear to us. So it was with Henry Tilney that day. Grateful though he was to see his daughter unaffected by Mr. Darcy's inexplicable neglect, Tilney's determination to think ill of the Darcys gained even greater force through Juliet's arguing against it.

As Katy and Deb jokingly coached Jonathan Darcy on the proper handling of a bow, the Fitzwilliams had a moment when they stood near each other and no one else could hear. The colonel said to his wife, "Your mother seems happy today."

"She does, does she not?" Anne's smile did not reach her eyes. "The fresh air and exercise must do us all good, and I cannot but enjoy the sunshine. Still—how can we help imagining Peter playing here? It has not been a month since he was tossing horseshoes and laughing."

Colonel Fitzwilliam's memory had brought to him a different time, a different game: Peter, still very small, toddling across the lawn with his hobbyhorse. "I hope he has no idea how little his grandmama misses him," the colonel said. Anne winced, but she could not dispute the fact. He continued, "I shall be away this afternoon, but rest assured, I will return by dinnertime."

"Are you leaving Hunsford *again*?" Anne could only look at her bow; the sun felt too bright for her eyes. "What business can possibly draw you away so often?" She spoke carefully, as though she did not truly wish an answer to the question; in truth she longed for any revelation from her husband that would give her some insight into his mysterious comings and goings.

"When it is complete," he said, "you will know." Rather than explain further, he strode away in the direction of the stables. Anne knew he would be gone within minutes, and wondered what he would do while he was absent—and whom he might see.

Was it Jonathan's imagination, or was Mr. Tilney casting dark looks in his direction? He very much hoped for the former, for he could think of no cause for the latter. Although his long practice had taught him more how to behave as others did—to draw the curtain—this practice had not yet been perfected, as he was all too aware. He had redoubled his efforts to be pleasing to Miss Tilney during this visit to Rosings, and yet somehow he seemed to have made matters worse. Had he also blundered somehow with Mr. Tilney? If so, that would harm any later chance of—

This thought was interrupted when Mr. Tilney uttered a small sound of pain. The taut string of his bow had scraped his finger deeply—nearly a cut. Miss Tilney seemed concerned, but already her father had recovered himself enough to jest. "Surely this is the least dignified injury one can receive from bow and arrow. How King Harold's men would have mocked me! I am lucky indeed not to have lived in the days of the Normans and Saxons, when I might have been obliged to take up the bow more often."

Lady Catherine expressed her concern by gesturing for Mrs. Jenkinson to approach the Tilneys, which she hurriedly did. "Will you need a bandage, sir?"

"I fear it does." Mr. Tilney offered his hand to Jenkinson, who swiftly yet carefully wrapped his hand in a handkerchief—an older, faded one, no doubt inherited after it had become too shabby for either of the ladies of the house. "Well done, madam. I see that in addition to being a companion, you are also a skilled nurse."

"Through practice, sir, through ever so much practice." Jenkinson had brightened at Tilney's praise. She received little enough of it from Lady Catherine.

Miss Tilney had taken a step closer to him. How bright was her complexion in the fresh air and sunshine; how rosy were her cheeks! "Is there any way in which can justify our playing at archery today, Mr. Darcy? Or are we merely playing truant?"

Jonathan would have answered her, but at that moment his eye was drawn to the bottle of reddish liquid next to Lady Catherine's chair, and the glass of it, which had just been placed in her hand. A small vial sat but inches away. At this angle, the afternoon light streamed through the liquid in both vial and glass, beams of scarlet.

And beneath that—

He hurried forward, bending toward Lady Catherine just in time to snatch the glass from her hand. A small quantity of wine splashed upon her ladyship's gown; Daisy the lady's maid began hastily mopping Lady Catherine with a handkerchief, quick attentions that did nothing to soothe that lady's renewed temper. "What is the meaning of this? What can you intend, Jonathan, behaving in such a manner?"

"The vial," he said, holding it up to the sunlight. Visible now to all was a powdery residue left at the bottom, thick as the silt of a riverbed. "The amount of opium in your laudanum—it should not be nearly so much as this, Aunt. Someone has greatly increased the dose."

Miss Tilney had hurried to his side. "Do you think the dose would have been fatal?"

"Only a doctor could tell us," Jonathan replied, "but I suspect that whoever added the opium to this bottle of laudanum very much hoped that fatality would ensue."

Lady Catherine's eyes widened. "Do you mean to say that this is yet another attempt upon my life?"

Jonathan nodded. "It appears your attacker is unwilling to rest while you remain alive."

Chapter Eleven

We often say we are frightened when we feel no actual fear. It is easy to imagine a threat in the abstract, quite another to confront it as true danger; all the rational calm we applied to the former heats, bubbles, and boils away when confronted with the latter. Lady Catherine's terror had this effect on herself and all the household on that fateful day when the laudanum often added to her wine was seen to have been poisoned with far too large a dose of opium.

Even the attentive Juliet Tilney found it difficult, later on, to recount the next hour's events with any degree of certainty. More voices were raised in shouts and cries than had been permitted at Rosings Park in many a year. Residents, guests, and servants all found themselves hurrying from place to place with more urgency than direction. Later, when Juliet attempted to recall this time, she had many vivid memories but could not quite put them in order—as though all the illustrations in a book had been ripped out and tossed in the air to fall into whatever order they would.

Definitely she recalled holding the near-fatal vial in her own hands, observing the thick muck that had collected at the bottom. Limited though Juliet's experience with laudanum was, she had leafed through her mother's medicine book enough to know that a pint of laudanum would contain no more than two ounces of opium dissolved in canary wine. Yes, cinnamon, cloves, and saffron were generally mixed in as well, but those, Juliet would have recognized. This could only be opium, many ounces of it, too much for it all to dissolve, certainly enough to stupefy, and perhaps enough to kill.

(She could not help but remember Ralph Bamber talking with her so confidently about his "experiments" and "discoveries" regarding arsenic, when really he had been making up false scientific innovations in the hopes of convincing everyone that his crime had been committed by another. That made her think of Mr. Bamber hanging dead from a noose. Then she could scarcely think at all.)

Juliet also recalled the bustle to get inside—inexplicable, even ridiculous in retrospect, for how was Lady Catherine any safer indoors than out? Yet all had felt the need to absent themselves from the place where the poisoning had so nearly occurred. Lady Catherine, her dress stained with the wine, had leaned heavily on the arms of Mr. Tilney and Mrs. Jenkinson, while Daisy assisted a ghostly pale Anne Fitzwilliam. The archery targets and bows rested upon the green lawn, the pleasant hour they had inspired now forgotten. Lady Catherine's chair lay on its side, its mistress agitated beyond the ability to sit still.

"Murder!" her ladyship had cried out, much like a minor character in a Shakespearean drama. "Murder most foul!" This had the effect of drawing forth the elder Mr. Darcy (who had been in the study composing his letters) and—more surprising to consider later than it had seemed in the moment—Charlotte Collins, who declared that she had come to Rosings Park to see whether her children would be home for luncheon. The midday meal at Hunsford Parsonage seemed likely to be forgotten entirely, as Mrs. Jenkinson was swiftly dispatched to collect Lady Catherine's smelling salts.

Katy and Deb had very little to do of any assistance to her ladyship, but that did not prevent them from remaining close by her side throughout. Juliet wondered whether their father's coaching had taught them to attend to her ladyship's needs whenever and however they could.

The first event Juliet could fix in her memory with certainty was the moment when—after Lady Catherine had been settled upon her favorite chair in the sitting room and tea was being fetched (and watched most carefully)—the younger Mr. Darcy drew Juliet aside. "We must consider the servants again," he said in a low voice. "It was Jenkinson who fetched the vial, who put the drops of laudanum in her ladyship's wine."

"But what does that signify, if the vial was itself poisoned? The mischief may have been done ere she touched it." The offending vessel had been brought in and set upon a table; although the light within this room was not so bright as outdoors, it provided illumination enough to silhouette the ominously thick sediment at the bottom.

"Quite true," admitted Mr. Darcy. "You have kept your head better than I, it seems."

This statement pleased Juliet greatly, though she attempted, for politeness's sake, to mediate it. "Lady Catherine is your great-aunt, whom you have known all your life, and it is only natural that danger to her should disquiet you far more." How good it was, to have this truce between them, to return to their comfortable ways of conversation and discovery? "Your great-aunt does not strike me as a frequent user of laudanum, which induces a stupor quite unlike her liveliness of mind."

"My father once inquired about this in concern for her well-being," he replied. "Apparently her laudanum solution is mixed to be very weak indeed. As different as is possible, it seems, from today's mixture, which might well have killed her."

In Juliet's home, either she or her mother might mix up the medicines. She doubted very much that either Lady Catherine or Anne Fitzwilliam took on this task themselves. "We must consider the servants again, for they have much freedom within a house."

Yet Mr. Darcy did not seem wholly convinced. "That freedom is not absolute. Neither Jenkinson nor Daisy, for instance, would have any access to the gun room; Daniels alone has the key. So we should not assume them all to have had opportunity."

"I suppose they may in fact have had less," Juliet said as the realization sank in. "Servants' time is not their own. How could they plan any events so precise as the shot or the shove, when they cannot know at what instant they will be called for and given some task to be completed immediately? No, we cannot exclude them entirely, but without any known motive . . . let us say that I believe we must continue investigating our principal suspects."

Mr. Darcy nodded. "Another part of our reckoning has almost certainly been proved true," he said. "The would-be killer still means to put an end to Lady Catherine's life before she is able to revise her last will and testament. It is less than two weeks until Mr. Guinness is to arrive."

"Which means our killer is becoming desperate." Juliet felt a queasy shudder of fear. "We can expect more attempts, Mr. Darcy."

"Not only that," he said, "but those attempts will likely not be as carefully considered. The killer must act in haste—and some of the methods already used could have done harm to more than Lady Catherine."

Juliet realized he was right. Anne Fitzwilliam was so frail, so slight; what if she, too, had requested a few drops of laudanum to help her rest this afternoon, after her exertions at archery? The gunshot had been fired either without due caution or by someone without very good aim, which meant the bullet could well have gone astray and struck a target more animate than the tall case clock. Colonel Fitzwilliam had been equally as endangered as her ladyship.

Who knew where the next attempt might fall?

To one person at Rosings Park, this event was more disagreeable than to any other: Lady Catherine herself. She had believed these attempts on her life to be clumsy pranks. This, however! To put too much opium into her laudanum—*that* was meant to cause her death, and she had come within a hair's breadth of drinking it.

Many would have become fearful after only one such attempt upon their persons. Almost anyone would have done so at this point, when the danger appeared imminent. Lady Catherine, however, could not easily picture a world that continued to turn without her presence. To her it still seemed self-evident that the blackguard responsible would be stopped, shamed, and severely dealt with. Yet on this day she experienced the wider range of sentiments that might be anticipated upon such a turn of events. Astonishment: that anyone should wish to deprive themselves and the greater world of the company and wisdom of Lady Catherine de Bourgh. Anger: that impudence could rise to such extraordinary heights. Determination: that this miscreant should not only fail but be humiliated in their failure.

Deepest down, where no one else could see and even Lady Catherine did not permit herself to look: hurt, that one of the few intimate companions of her life should secretly wish her ill.

"This, then, is the answer to all my generosity!" Lady Catherine proclaimed as she sat in her chair, being fanned by the tremulous Mrs. Jenkinson. "A viper has made its nest amid my home, strikes at me again and again. Was Egypt ever thus plagued? No, it shall not be borne, I tell you, it shall not!"

Anne sobbed once. Lady Catherine would have patted her daughter's hand, were she any closer; the killer showed no consideration for Anne's frailties, to put her to such a shock as well. Charlotte Collins performed this office instead, her face as serene as that of a medieval Madonna. The Collins children and Miss Tilney had all withdrawn to the far side of the room, obviously uncertain what best to do; the elder Mr. Darcy observed all with dismay.

"Consider it in this light, great-aunt," said Jonathan, kneeling by the side of her chair. "This further attempt upon your life gives Miss Tilney and myself more information to consider, more hints as to the identity of your would-be killer. This person comes nearer exposure with every act."

"Then let this be the last such action necessary!" Lady Catherine gathered herself and waved away Jenkinson. She would not be seen to swoon and sputter the rest of the day—certainly not in front of the person who did her harm, who might well be one of those observing her that very instant. "We will have no more of this, I say. I am most put out!"

It took some time for the hubbub to quiet, and thus nearly half the afternoon had fled before Jonathan was able to speak privately again with Miss Tilney. They took another turn upon the grounds. As it happened, they emerged just as the servants finally began putting away the accoutrements of archery. Miss Tilney pointed to the targets being taken away. "I spent the first part of the morning's amusement afraid for Lady Catherine, but I believed that if any risk were to arise, it would come from the bows and arrows. They were not involved in the slightest! We are all very lucky that you spotted the strangeness of Lady Catherine's laudanum in time."

"Indeed, miss." This was Mrs. Jenkinson, who had emerged from the house; she appeared as weary and as wary as might be expected under the circumstances. "In the past, when I have mixed her ladyship's draught myself—well, the weak dosage used here at Rosings is not a tenth of what had been put within. Surely this would have killed Lady Catherine. I did not see the difference—oh, how could I have been so foolish?"

"You must not blame yourself, for the difference was only visible in bright light," Jonathan said, as soothingly as possible. "Be certain to give my aunt no more laudanum for the duration of this trouble. We cannot be certain the killer will not try the same ruse again. It is unfortunate to deprive Lady Catherine of her sleeping draught at the very moment that uneasiness must make rest more elusive for her, but I believe it must be done."

"To be certain, sir," Jenkinson said, "even if I were to offer laudanum to Lady Catherine, I do not think she would drink it, and if she did so, her terror would overcome any of her draught's sedative qualities."

This was an excellent point, in Jonathan's opinion. Her ladyship might not yet be safe from her would-be killer, but she was at least safe from death by laudanum.

A window opened, and Daisy appeared, calling out, "Oi, if you want a rest in our room, you had best hur—oh! Excuse me, Mr. Darcy, sir! I did not see you there."

Jonathan shook his head, hopefully indicating that he was unoffended by witnessing an informal moment between two servants. Daisy must have called from an empty room, believing no one save Mrs. Jenkinson would see or hear her.

Or . . . had Daisy *meant* to interrupt his conversation with

Jenkinson? Nobody would know one servant's methods and habits better than another servant, particularly one who seemed to be a friend. Equally, someone in the house—one of their prime suspects—could have ordered Daisy to call Jenkinson, in order to disrupt Jonathan's questioning.

Mrs. Jenkinson, however, seemed to have no thought beyond the opportunity to seize a rare moment of rest. "If you'll pardon me, sir—"

He nodded, releasing Mrs. Jenkinson to retrieve Lady Catherine's kerchief from the lawn where it had fallen amid the tumult of the poison's discovery.

When he turned back to Miss Tilney, she seemed lost in thought, to have scarcely observed the conversation between the servants. After only an instant, she attended to him again, but she said, with great feeling, "It is possible, surely, to rely on sleeping draughts too much. Our household has opium for medicines, like any other house, but in some others I have seen—oh, it is very unfortunate indeed to become too accustomed to opium."

Jonathan was not sure, but he sensed that possibly Miss Tilney was considering a very particular incident, one involving a person close to her. The subject was not one that could be inquired about without greater certainty than he possessed, so he turned his attention to surer terrain. "We agree that Jenkinson's handling of the laudanum should not be considered evidence of her guilt. Who else should we look at instead?"

"Colonel Fitzwilliam had departed beforehand," Miss Tilney replied, "but I do not know that this works in his favor, as he could easily have poisoned the laudanum ahead of time. Mrs. Fitzwilliam must also be considered to have had the opportunity—again, not during the archery match itself, but immediately beforehand."

Jonathan nodded, thinking upon this. "I cannot see how Katy and Deb could have done this. Occasionally they have access to the higher floors and inner rooms of Rosings, but they did not today, and they were much occupied with archery throughout."

"Yes, that seems unlikely, does it not? But did you note Mrs. Collins's sudden arrival just at the time of crisis?"

"I did," Jonathan said. "Although it is possible she had some other errand that brought her here, an errand entirely respectable, she would have been allowed into the house and would have been quite alone for some minutes, save for a few servants who would have had tasks to perform and would not have spent all their time observing her."

"Mrs. Collins is a frequent guest at Rosings, I believe," said Miss Tilney. "Surely she knows Lady Catherine's habits and routines as well as any other person living."

"Lady Catherine would not have it any other way."

Miss Tilney nodded. "Do you take my meaning, Mr. Darcy? Mrs. Collins would have known that Lady Catherine was soon to take her afternoon dose of wine laced with laudanum. Presumably she knew her children had set out for Rosings Park with a plan that would keep all others much occupied out of doors. If she wished to add more opium to the laudanum vial, that would have been a perfect opportunity."

"I cannot deny it," said Jonathan, "though I wish I could for my mother's sake. Charlotte Collins is her friend of many years. This news would upset her greatly."

Jonathan was not the only person considering his mother's feelings at the moment. His father had in fact finished a letter of business that morning, and just at the time of the contretemps arising from the attempt on Lady Catherine, he had been beginning his second letter of the day—one to his wife.

By the time he was able to return to the task, his first paragraph of general information about the weather and the health of all present had fully dried. Thus he had no need of sand before he could pick up his pen once more and resume:

> *Since writing this last, Rosings Park has been in an uproar occasioned by what appears to be yet another attempt to murder Lady Catherine. The laudanum she takes as a sleeping draught every afternoon and night seems to have been contaminated with a far larger dose of opium than necessary—whether it be enough to cause death, I know not, but the act was deliberate, to be sure. What other purpose could the opium have been meant to serve?*
>
> *Earlier in our stay, I had come to suspect that the first attempts on Lady Catherine were hardly worthy of the name. This I believed principally due to her ladyship's own conduct and demeanor. Her tone in her letter to Pemberley on the subject was a fair representation of her temper upon our arrival through to this very day—disquieted, yes; angry, certainly; but <u>frightened</u>, not in the slightest. Jonathan's presence, like Miss Tilney's, seemed to me to be calculated primarily for the focusing of attention on her ladyship, which we both know to be her strong preference at all times.*
>
> *Today, however, I am chastened for such nonchalance. Someone of this household—or, strange though it may seem, of Hunsford Parsonage—truly wishes to see Lady Catherine dead. Although I will of course do all within my power to watch and protect my aunt, her principal defenders are our son and*

Miss Juliet Tilney. Though I still find their interest in such matters morbid in the extreme, in the current circumstance I must admit their usefulness. I find I wish to say that I hope Jonathan will turn his efforts to other endeavors in future, but what I truly wish is that his path should more seldom cross those of people wicked enough to seek to end the life of another.

Do not be concerned on our behalf. There is not the slightest suggestion that harm is intended upon any other person, myself and Jonathan included.

Jonathan has taken to the task with his customary zeal. Presumably Miss Tilney has done so as well. Her conduct toward our son remains correct, and not that of a flirt, so we need have no concerns on that score. This is more a relief to me than it would have been before, as Miss Tilney is currently being chaperoned by her father. Mr. Henry Tilney, though a clergyman of good family, displays more of his wit than his sense or feeling. Theirs is not a family to which we should wish to be attached.

As soon as more is known, I shall write to you posthaste.

Mr. Darcy signed his name at the bottom, pleased with what he had written, little suspecting the effect this missive would have upon its reader.

When Colonel Fitzwilliam, who had departed that morning to conduct business of his own, returned to Rosings in the final half hour before sunset, he observed that the servants were scurrying about with more than their usual haste. As he entered the foyer, the uncanny silence confirmed his belief that the calm of the house had been greatly upset. To the butler, Mr. McQuarrie, he said, "Is something amiss? Is Lady Catherine well?"

"There was another attempt upon the life of Lady Catherine," McQuarrie said with his usual calm, crisp voice. "Far too much opium had been mixed into her laudanum. Rest assured that she did not drink it, and the caution of the house has been duly heightened."

"Indeed," said Fitzwilliam. He knew he should display concern, or anger perhaps. Probably Lady Catherine would expect him immediately at her side to provide reassurance and comfort. But thence, he found, he could not bring himself to go. Instead, he went to find his wife.

As was usual in the early evening, Anne sat in her comfortable place by her bedchamber window, embroidery in her hands. How like her not to have deviated from routine even on such a day as this. When Colonel Fitzwilliam entered the room, she looked up; there was nothing of routine in her stricken look. "McQuarrie has told me all. Are you well? How has Lady Catherine endured the shock?"

"Mama is very much unsettled, more than ever before," Anne replied. "Until now I do not think she believed the attempts were in earnest. I myself doubted it more than I had realized until this, when all is shown to be terrible and true."

"No," Fitzwilliam said evenly. "After this, there can be no denial."

Anne gazed searchingly up at him. "Do you know, it was Jonathan who saved Mama? As we were all out upon the lawn with our archery, the sunlight shone down upon the laudanum vial through it—and thus he was able to see that the liquid was opaque where it ought to have been translucent."

Fitzwilliam shook his head. "How often does Lady Catherine take her draught out of doors? I cannot recall even a single such instance."

"Had she taken her draught inside as so usually does, the opium would not have been visible, and I doubt Mama would still be with us." Anne set her embroidery aside with a crooked attempt at a smile. "Jonathan is greatly in her favor at the moment, a place I doubt he has ever been before."

"That can be cause for congratulations or for pity," Fitzwilliam said. Anne seemed calm enough, given the circumstances; he could retire to his own room for an hour before the evening meal, to consider many of the matters currently pressing upon his thoughts. "I will knock to bring you down for dinner."

Anne held up a hand, as if to stop him. She wanted to ask where he had been—Fitzwilliam could sense it—and still, he did not know whether he was ready to tell her. (Would he *ever* be? At moments, he doubted it. They were not so different from many other married couples in their lack of intimacy; Fitzwilliam sometimes felt as though he were taking a great liberty using his wife's first name, for many husbands did not.)

But Anne had grown up with Lady Catherine de Bourgh for a mother, in a house where intimacy was all but unheard of, where questions were no more welcome than the opinions of those besides its mistress. She turned back to her embroidery, making the most of the last few minutes of daylight.

Chapter Twelve

The next day, the seventh of the visitors' stay, was the Sabbath. Juliet, like the rest of the company, rose a bit earlier and dressed for church. This alteration in their routine meant that she and the younger Mr. Darcy would have no opportunity to talk about the investigation together in the breakfast room; she found this most vexing, as they now had so very much to discuss, but there was nothing for it. No clergyman's daughter would deny her Savior his due, which was most reasonable at the rate of one morning per week.

Mr. Tilney's status as a clergyman did not go unmentioned, for as the party set out toward the church in Hunsford, the weather cool and gray, Lady Catherine said, "You, Mr. Tilney, attend our church today while neglecting your own?"

His good humor was not to be undone by such a minor slight. "Shameful of me, is it not? Rest assured, Lady Catherine, that I have engaged a vicar from a nearby parish, who will hold services in my absence. His living is not an ample one, and he has a large family, so I believe him to be very grateful for the position."

Lady Catherine sniffed. "True, the practice of taking on another vicar to cover ecclesiastical duties is not an uncommon one in some places, but in this parish, we do not hold with it. Mr. Collins would never dream of neglecting his duty to *me*."

Juliet's temper, quicker than her father's, burned at a very unladylike heat. Before she could say anything untoward, however, the younger Mr. Darcy said, "The Collins family has visited us at Pemberley for longer than a week. Were there no services in Hunsford at that time?"

He spoke utterly without guile, Juliet thought, which made the rebuke more perfect. Lady Catherine colored as she said, "That is never done without my permission, and I personally approve the young men who will read sermons in his absence!"

"Mr. Collins is fortunate to have such a conscientious patron," said Mr. Tilney. Juliet hoped she was the only one who could detect how much wit lay within the word *conscientious*. "I have my living from my father, also a thorough man in his way, but his thoroughness does not extend to his piety. Thus he is content for me to choose where I will. The young man in question has both an excellent character and many mouths to feed, so all is well for everyone involved."

"Indeed," said the elder Mr. Darcy, who agreed with Mr. Tilney's take on the matter but did not wish to be seen agreeing with undue strength. Such might be taken as encouragement—an invitation of sorts toward the family. Had he realized that he thought rather more of Miss Tilney's marrying his son than Miss Tilney did herself, Darcy would have been much better at making conversation.

For his part, Jonathan thought far more upon the matter than either of the other parties. He could not tell whether his efforts toward Miss Tilney had had their desired effect, nor whether they were noticed at all. He had kept the curtain drawn—had not rocked in the presence of any other, had conversed about Sir Walter Scott only so much as was appropriate, had met gazes and shaken hands as required. Did she not see this change in him? Would that not lead her to consider Jonathan as a potential suitor?

Perhaps this investigation—rare opportunity though it was—had proved a poor time to press his suit. Jonathan knew that patience was necessary, given the heartbreak Miss Tilney had endured. Given what had become of Mr. Bamber, no doubt her mourning would be extended. But by how great a measure? If he were importunate and raised the matter ere she was ready, she would reject him as unkind, unfeeling. Yet if Jonathan waited too long, another young man might win her heart as Bamber had, and it was unlikely that her second suitor would also disqualify himself, particularly in such extraordinary fashion. It seemed to him an unsolvable conundrum.

He was, however, no longer mystified by his sentiments toward her. The thought of being so physically close to another person—particularly to the point of marital congress—had always felt ungainly to Jonathan at best, deeply unpleasant at worst. The desires other young men joked about regarding women had been totally alien to him. Although he had always known it was his duty to marry and further the family line, he had desired only to put that day off as long as possible, and that Matthew and James might marry early and well, so that his parents did not see so great a need for Jonathan to do likewise. This resolution had endured until the journey into Devonshire the previous October, when suddenly he realized that the idea of taking pleasure in physical touch was no longer strange to him—not when he imagined the touch to be Miss Tilney's. His imaginings were very nearly chaste, no more than a waltz and a stolen kiss, but those thoughts alone were enough to dizzy him. How splendid marriage must be!

As we have seen, even a group composed of faithful Christians, with a clergyman as one of the party, may enter church with thoughts running rampant on every subject except the goodness of the Lord. Into this devotional spirit they would have to be coached by Mr. Collins.

This he did not do with very great skill. Mr. Collins,

though sincere in his faith, did not expend unnecessary thought regarding the Almighty. To him the Lord was a hazy figure of great power, whose opinions entirely agreed with those of Lady Catherine on all matters, and who would at the Last Judgment welcome the faithful into an even more paradisical version of Rosings Park. Although Mr. Collins did not simply read sermons from a book, as the laziest rectors and vicars did, he used such a book as a guide, inventing only as much phraseology as necessary to claim the result as his own. Some patrons would not have been satisfied with this, but Lady Catherine principally judged Mr. Collins's efforts by how much they flattered her, and at this, his excellence was incomparable.

"Today's sermon," he announced gravely, "is drawn from the book of John, chapter fifteen, verse twenty. 'Remember the word that I said to you, the servant is not greater than his lord. If they have persecuted me, they will also persecute you.'" The allusion to Lady Catherine's predicament was clear, to those who knew of it. The rest of the congregation could listen and take from the lesson what spiritual comfort they could.

After services, as Mr. Collins paid court to Lady Catherine and the other parishioners filed out unheeded, Jonathan found himself in step next to Katy Collins. She said to him in a low voice, "Do not think me unfeeling toward her ladyship, but I am a selfish enough girl to also feel disappointment that we shall be able to have no other games out of doors at Rosings Park—certainly not while this remains unresolved, perhaps ever."

Jonathan *did* find this somewhat unfeeling but knew better

than to say so. "If we wish such sport, surely it can be had at Hunsford Parsonage."

"We will invite you for some fun very soon, I am sure." Katy retied the ribbons of her bonnet more snugly beneath her chin, a concession to the blustery breeze. "You and Miss Tilney are engaged in the search for the wrongdoer, and I know you are concerned for your aunt, but it seems very hard that poor Miss Tilney should not have any amusement while here."

"I am certain she is grateful for what amusement is to be had," said Jonathan, "particularly given the burden she must bear. Yes, by all means, let us distract her from such concerns where we can without neglecting Lady Catherine's predicament."

Katy frowned. "Burden? What do you mean?"

Jonathan wished he had not spoken so, but having done it, he judged it better to explain than to leave the question open. In that case, Katy might take her question directly to Miss Tilney, and how much worse that would be! So, while Miss Tilney stood with her father talking to Mr. Collins, Jonathan quietly explained that the last murderer they had caught, Mr. Ralph Bamber, had in fact been courting Miss Tilney while plotting yet more evil, and how cruelly her sentiments had been abused. Katy listened in mounting dismay, finally exclaiming, "I should not have expected anything so terrible as this! She carries on as though her heart were not broken at all."

"Miss Tilney is courageous in the face of it," said Jonathan. "Given that Mr. Bamber was hanged only this week, the pain will be all the more acute."

"Then we shall certainly amuse her, distract her, do whatever is within our power to make her forget the villain entirely," Katy said. "In fact, let me speak quickly to Mama. Perhaps we can have her to visit this afternoon."

Jonathan recognized that he was not included in this particular invitation—disappointing, but upon consideration, possibly for the best. Certain condolences could be uttered only by and among women, which his presence would inevitably forestall. Besides, this would give him the opportunity to speak directly with Colonel Fitzwilliam. There would be, he thought, no need for a pretext in the matter; Fitzwilliam was an intelligent person who understood why Jonathan had been brought to Rosings Park—and that even he must answer questions in the matter of the attempts upon Lady Catherine. Granted, Fitzwilliam's answers had not been complete at their first conversation on the topic, but it was possible that the colonel might be more forthright when no young lady was present to hear that which might potentially be indelicate.

These plans held true so long as to allow Miss Tilney to walk toward Hunsford Parsonage with the Collinses, and for Jonathan to fall into step by Colonel Fitzwilliam as their party returned to Rosings Park. Their progress was not swift—Anne had said she would not need the carriage that day, and indeed she did not, but the half mile took her longer than most, and they were obliged to slow their steps to match hers.

As soon as they returned to the house, McQuarrie announced, "A rider has brought a letter from Master Peter."

"Peter!" Anne cried. "Oh, let us have it!"

"Yes, let it be read," said Lady Catherine. "We shall gather in the sitting room."

Most appeared happy to listen, though Peter remained unknown to them. Anne and the colonel, however, looked at each other with open reluctance. Jonathan was unsure how to interpret it, but if forced to guess, he would have speculated that father and mother would have preferred to read their son's letter alone, without the household guests present or even his grandmother. But letters among friends and family were held to be of common interest and were read aloud to all unless circumstances dictated otherwise. Thus Jonathan would have to be among those intruding upon this communication—and any discussion with Colonel Fitzwilliam would have to wait.

As it happened, every word of Peter's letter was exactly what a parent would expect and hope to receive from a child at school. Peter liked his schoolfellows. His marks were good, and he had received no scoldings nor canings. He hoped the weather would allow them to continue playing at sport after lessons. He said his prayers every night. He missed them all very much and looked forward to Christmas.

Anne listened to her husband's reading with tears in her eyes, for she understood every word to be false.

She knew her son, how he spoke, how he wrote. These phrases and sentiments were so unlike him that she could very nearly see the schoolmaster standing at Peter's shoulder, dictating precisely what he should say. It was possible of course that this was done with all the boys, but Anne could not help imagining what torments and sorrows were thereby concealed. The colonel had told her some wretched stories of his own schooling—and he had gone when he was an older boy, and he had been tall and healthy, had been good at sport, had in short possessed all the advantages that help a boy to be liked by his fellows. Dear as Peter was, Anne knew him not to be equally blessed in such respects. Her own experiences as the invalid daughter of an imperious mother had taught her all too well how it felt to be ever excluded from the fun and comradeship of others. Like many a parent, the pain she had borne for herself was one she could scarcely stand to imagine being suffered by her own child.

Her mother lacked such insight, pronouncing with satisfaction: "It is entirely as I anticipated. Peter is excelling, distinguishing himself already among his peers."

"Perhaps," said the colonel, "but he does not say how well the other lads are faring."

"I assure you there have been canings and scoldings aplenty," Lady Catherine insisted. "The school chosen is known for discipline! That Peter has as yet required none— that alone tells us that he is understood to be an exceptional child."

In Lady Catherine's voice, Anne could hear her pride in her grandchild—even her love for him, just as she had always understood the strong maternal love Lady Catherine held for herself. But her mother did not understand that such sentiments could be expressed through means other than constant command.

"If that is so," said Jonathan, "then I am pleased for Peter, for his schooling was more pleasant than mine."

Mr. Darcy rested his hand on Jonathan's shoulder—a brief touch, but nonetheless remarkable for her taciturn cousin. "We considered bringing Jonathan home to study with tutors often, but he expressed his willingness to endure. Yet we had wished for better than mere endurance for him."

"All is well, Father." Jonathan smiled at Mr. Darcy, and in that instant, Anne could see the little boy he had been not so very long ago. If only she might someday witness a similar moment between Peter and his father! "I did endure."

"*Peter* shall have no need of mere endurance," Lady Catherine said. "Mark my words, he shall continue to excel!"

Anne held her handkerchief to her face, the better to disguise her anger and to suppress her desire to scream.

Juliet had been surprised by the invitation to Hunsford Parsonage, or at least by its having been extended to her alone and not to the younger Mr. Darcy as well—particularly given that he and the Collins children had all been friends of a sort since their early childhoods. However, she soon reasoned that this connection inevitably led to less urgency for visits, as both the Darcy and Collins households would meet many times more. She herself was the novelty, likely never to come this way again.

Unfortunately, all hopes of a pleasant afternoon outside were dashed by the elements, for the cool gray morning became cooler and grayer as the day went on. Summer sun could no longer be relied upon to burn away early clouds; although no rain fell, it seemed constantly as though it might begin at any moment. Thus they busied themselves in the parsonage parlor, where Charlotte Collins embroidered and Deb read while Katy and Juliet attempted to make a filigree basket, with little success. Mr. Collins had left shortly after the family's return home, on some clerical errand or other.

"I have never made much of a study of filigree," Juliet admitted, trying to curl silver paper in a pleasing whorl instead of the shabby little crumples she had produced thus far. "As must be evident to you by now!"

Katy winced at her failure of her own paper-curling efforts. "Nor is it my principal accomplishment, but Papa insists that all proper young ladies should make a study of filigree. I should much rather play my harp."

"Oh, the harp!" Juliet exclaimed. "No one in my family plays, and it is such a beautiful instrument. Mrs. Collins, may I not plead my privilege as a visitor, so that I might hear Katy play?"

"Of course," said Charlotte. "I am sure she will be only too happy to oblige you."

Katy gave Juliet a look that betokened her deepest gratitude before hurrying to the beautiful instrument where it sat in the corner. The harp proved to need a new string, a delay for which the household's guest was herself grateful. With both Katy and Deb occupied with their separate concerns, Juliet had a few moments to speak with Charlotte Collins.

"I confess," she began, "that I have scarce recovered from the shock of yesterday's terrible incident at Rosings Park."

Charlotte's stitches did not slow. "It was most perceptive of Jonathan to have noticed the difference in the laudanum. He is an intelligent young man, when he attends properly."

Her use of Mr. Darcy's Christian name reminded Juliet that this woman had known him from birth. "Your families have always been friends, I understand, as you and Mrs. Darcy have been since childhood. I became acquainted with Mrs. Darcy in Surrey last summer."

"During the events surrounding the death of Mr. Wickham," Charlotte said, openly acknowledging that which Juliet would have left unspoken. "I knew Wickham in his youth, when he was very wild. It was no great astonishment that he should end as poorly as he had lived."

Juliet was uncertain how best to reply. "At the time, I assure you, it was very shocking indeed that such an act should take place at Donwell Abbey. Mrs. Darcy knew him best, and perhaps mourned him least, but even she was much taken aback by what had occurred."

"The immediacy of the event was no doubt unpleasant," said Charlotte. Her demeanor was so calm, so measured, that Juliet could have imagined that—had it been Charlotte Collins who had found Mr. Wickham's body, instead of Juliet herself—she would have simply stepped over it and gone to fetch a servant to see to the attendant mess.

Not knowing how best to steer the conversation in the direction of the questions she most wanted to ask—namely, how it was that Charlotte had appeared uninvited at Rosings Park just before the poisoned bottle had made its way to Lady Catherine—Juliet decided simply to stay on safer ground and trust ingenuity for the rest. "Mrs. Darcy is a most lively and engaging person. I greatly enjoyed making her acquaintance."

"Elizabeth possesses more wit than any other person I have encountered," said Charlotte. "She always has, even as a girl."

"How wonderful it is when women are able to remain friends after they marry, even when their husbands take them into new towns or counties," Juliet said. "Which of you married first?"

Charlotte finally looked up from her sewing. "You have not heard the story, then."

Although Juliet had no idea to what Charlotte was referring, she was curious to know. She phrased her next words with caution: "There have been allusions, but ones I poorly understood. Will you not tell me?"

"Well may you wonder how our matrimonial fates might be spoken of in the same breath. Mr. Collins is of course Elizabeth Darcy's cousin, and the heir to Longbourn, where her parents still reside. And her husband is the nephew of our patroness, Lady Catherine de Bourgh. Yet the source of Mrs. Darcy's witticisms on the subject no doubt arises from the fact that Mr. Collins first proposed marriage to her, and she refused him."

"Oh!" Juliet would never have imagined the clever, sophisticated Mrs. Darcy as the wife of a figure such as Mr. Collins: so openly supplicant to Lady Catherine, so punctilious, so pointedly pious. Yet she could hardly say so aloud, least of all to the woman who had married him. "But he could not have been very brokenhearted by it, as he then fell in love with you."

"He proposed to me but days later," said Charlotte, "and I accepted him."

Surely she had not heard this correctly. "You do not mean to say that Mr. Collins proposed twice within a matter of days."

"Indeed I do. I have never been of a romantic nature, and I am convinced that those who marry in fevered spirits do not fare any better than those who choose rationally. I knew Mr. Collins to be a respectable young man who would in the fullness of time inherit a fine house. Why should I refuse him?"

These feelings regarding matrimony were so very different from Juliet's own that she scarcely knew how to respond. Timidly she ventured, "How fortunate that your marriage and Mrs. Darcy's have both been so happy!"

Charlotte said, "Whatever happiness is."

Before Juliet could even wonder what this meant, Katy, having readied her music, began to play the harp, and in politeness there was nothing to do but listen.

For his part, Jonathan fully intended to ask questions of Colonel Fitzwilliam that afternoon—but in order to do so, he would have to gain an audience alone with the colonel, which proved maddeningly elusive.

The other gentlemen at Rosings Park determined that the only amusement for such a gray, chilly afternoon must be billiards. Jonathan's proficiency at billiards was such that he felt obliged to decline the invitation; if he played, he would win every match, and many who were good sports at their first or

second defeat had soured greatly by their fifth or sixth. Both
Father and Colonel Fitzwilliam, who had lost to Jonathan
many times before, had to persuade Mr. Tilney to allow the
younger man's departure. "Very well, I concede for today,"
Tilney finally said, "though these protests have made me
more curious to see your prowess for myself, rather than less.
I promise now, I shall not leave Kent without having at least
one game with you."

"I am available to beat you at your leisure," said Jonathan.
He did not understand how this sounded until Mr. Tilney
laughed out loud; he was fortunate that Juliet's father was a
good-natured sort of person, unlikely to take offense at either
the comment or his ultimate inevitable defeat at billiards.

Lady Catherine and Anne had both gone for afternoon
naps—presumably taken without the assistance of drops of
laudanum. This left Jonathan quite on his own. With the sky
threatening rain, he dared not excuse himself to join Miss Tilney at Hunsford Parsonage; besides, the invitation had been
issued to give her some opportunity to take comfort among
other women for what he assumed was a very feminine sort of
heartbreak. What, then, ought he to do?

Father had written Mother yesterday, so there was no need
for Jonathan to compose a missive of his own just yet. He
had thought of investigating the poisoning of the laudanum,
but that was futile; all the ingredients, including the opium,
would be kept in the house stores, accessible to any servant
or resident of Rosings at virtually any hour of the day, and he
knew from past visits that the vials were mixed to contain
several doses at any one time. So it would be impossible to
determine any one person as having a greater chance to add
the lethal amount of opium. Perhaps, in the end, there was
nothing better for him to do but to read. Was it possible that
Lady Catherine had added any volumes of Sir Walter Scott to
the Rosings Park library?

As it turned out, she had. The book, *Rob Roy*, had been out for some years, and Jonathan had already read it several times. However, he was happy to do so again. No doubt Miss Tilney would enjoy discussing the story over dinner.

The grayness of the day worked against him, though, providing scarcely enough light to read by. The library hearth was not lit, so Jonathan took the volume into the Rosings study, where a blaze already burned and could be stoked higher. *Much better,* he thought, *though I could well do with a quizzing glass.* He was not one of the smart young persons who wore the magnifying glass on a chain as a fashionable accessory— but had not Colonel Fitzwilliam offered them the use of a quizzing glass? Therefore the colonel must have one, probably kept in the desk of his study.

So Jonathan went to the desk in good faith, and he opened the drawer to search for the quizzing glass with no intention of reading any documents he might see inside. But Jonathan was a quick reader, one who could no sooner have a piece of paper before his eyes than he had already interpreted the majority—and so it was with him that day, and the letter that rested within the colonel's desk, from one Mr. Baker.

> *It is my pleasure to inform you that you have been offered tenancy of the house at 3 The Paragon, in one of the finest neighborhoods in all of Bath, for the price of five hundred pounds per annum. The house is fully furnished, though at present employing only a cook, two maidservants, and a man-of-all-work. You may either bring the remainder of your own staff or, if you wish assistance in hiring—*

Jonathan pulled himself away before he could read any further, as he would then have crossed the boundary between that which is accidentally learned and that which is dishonestly sought. Quizzing glass and even *Rob Roy* forgotten, he sank into one of the chairs near the hearth. *Colonel Fitzwilliam intends to leave Rosings Park, to establish a home of his own,* he thought.

And I do not think my cousin Anne knows aught of it.

Chapter Thirteen

Ordinarily Juliet would never have lingered so long at Hunsford Parsonage as she did on that Sunday, but the ever-threatening sky made her reluctant to walk, and the younger Collinses unwilling to release her. "You must not worry about remaining here," said Katy. "A servant could be sent to fetch your clothes, should you even need to stay the night!" Juliet's thoughts about some poor servant getting drenched by a downpour did not so distract her that she failed to notice the sharp look Charlotte gave her daughter. Katy's hospitality was genuine, but the lady of the household wished their guest gone.

Juliet did not resent this; only the most intimate friends could be entertained in all the comfort and relaxation of home, and she had not even known the Collinses for two weeks. She did, however, wonder that Mr. Collins did not return home. To her it seemed most natural that he might drive her back to Rosings Park in his carriage, even that he would be proud to display its elegance yet again. As the hours went on and he did not reappear, she surmised that but two explanations existed for this: either a parishioner or parishioners were suffering very greatly from ailments, both physical and spiritual, for which a clergyman might be expected to condole with them—or that this excuse was merely a pretext, that Mr. Collins's business was something altogether different that he wished to conceal.

She concluded that she should hurry the short distance to Rosings and trust that the clouds would not burst in those few minutes' time. Before she could say so, however, she caught sight of Deb. He stared blankly forward at nothing, his body oddly rigid.

"Come, Deb." Charlotte rose swiftly, allowing her needlework to drop to the floor. "We should review your lessons before tomorrow."

Deb scarcely seemed to comprehend her. He rose, but his motions were jerky and strange.

"Oh, Miss Tilney, you must come with me." Katy had already stooped to collect her mother's embroidery, and she now smiled too brightly up at Juliet. "You are a lover of books, are you not? Our library can scarce compare to that of Rosings Park, but we may have something to tempt you."

"Of course," said Juliet, who in politeness could but follow. She glanced over her shoulder as they went to see Charlotte hurriedly ushering Deb from the parlor. He stared at his mother fixedly all the while, an uncanny fixation that made her shiver. *Is he soon to lose his temper?* Juliet wondered. *It seems as though Mrs. Collins and Katy are . . .* afraid *of him.*

As they entered the tiny parsonage library, Juliet heard a loud thump, then a louder thud. She whirled about. "What is that? It sounds as though someone has fallen?" *Or been pushed.*

Katy, however, shook her head and spoke in a tone of voice she no doubt hoped would sound careless. "Most likely that is Deb. He can be most clumsy sometimes!"

The next sound was fainter, but Juliet would have sworn it was a groan of distress or pain. "Are you certain all is well, Katy?"

"Yes." Katy's hand around her friend's arm tightened, all but pulling Juliet into the library. "Now, let us find something fine to read."

✒

Next morning, near the end of breakfasting, Jonathan heard Miss Tilney's account with great interest. "Did you see Deb again before you left?"

"I did not. He did not emerge to bid me farewell, when at last I was able to leave. This as you know was not until near sundown, as Mr. Collins still had not come home—Mrs. Collins walked me back to Rosings, which is after all not so very far." Miss Tilney sighed. "Lady Catherine demanded to know why I had not sent word that I should need a carriage, which was rather a kind impulse, really. She is an imperious lady, but one thing that can fairly be said of the imperious is that they are attentive."

"Indeed, they must attend, for how else would they know when to issue commands?" Jonathan did not mean this as a joke, but Miss Tilney laughed, and he was grateful for having accidentally proved himself a wit. "What you say about Deb and Mr. Collins is curious. Certainly both are hiding something—no, the entire family is doing so—and I doubt it is only one secret they conceal. The only question is whether any of their secrets pertain to murderous intent toward Lady Catherine."

"To me it seemed very much as though Deb were angry, though what inspired his wrath, I cannot say."

Jonathan said, "I feel I should tell you of an incident I witnessed in our youth. This I never shared before, because I understand it no more at the present than I did at the time, but the similarity to what you witnessed is very great indeed."

He explained Deb's odd absences, the ways in which the Collins family sometimes suddenly withdrew him from all others, and the damage to property sometimes found afterward. The story of the henhouse alarmed Miss Tilney exceedingly. "Do you mean—do you believe it was Deb who truly did the harm?"

"This I do not know," Jonathan replied. "The juxtaposition of the two events struck me very forcefully at the time, and still does. However, I must in justice admit that they may be wholly unrelated."

Miss Tilney shook her head. "Surely it cannot be Deb. He is still but a boy."

"As one who has attended a boys' school, I know too well that boys can be cruel, some of them as coldly as any grown man." Jonathan did not want to think about his schooldays any longer, nor to remind her of Ralph Bamber, and so he chose this moment to tell Miss Tilney of his inadvertent discovery in the study the day prior.

She was even more thunderstruck by this information than he had been. "The colonel intends"—Miss Tilney leaned closer, so as to speak so softly not even the footman could overhear—"to leave his wife?"

"I must believe it so, for he has kept this information a secret, even from my father, to whom he is both cousin and friend," Jonathan said. "Were they both departing, the news would surely be known to all, through Lady Catherine's vocal displeasure if via no other means."

"Mrs. Fitzwilliam would have told us of it. The servants might well be involved in the preparations, and they, too, would have spoken, would they not?" Miss Tilney sighed. "As neither she nor any other knows of the colonel's plans, he must intend to go alone. Did he make no reference to his wife in his letter?"

"I cannot say, for I did not read further nor pry into what else might be within Colonel Fitzwilliam's desk. Had what I saw pertained more directly to any of the attempts to harm Lady Catherine, such a search might have been morally justified—but it did not."

"Nonetheless, this information may prove important to

us," said Miss Tilney, echoing Jonathan's own thoughts—until her next sentence surprised him. "This makes it much less likely that the colonel could be the attacker."

"Less likely? When he is concealing such a secret—certainly from his general society, and likely from his own wife?"

"I do not say that he is right to withhold such a significant fact, but consider, Mr. Darcy. If Colonel Fitzwilliam finds the rule of Lady Catherine in this house so burdensome that he intends to leave it—why then attempt to kill her? He will make his escape without risking his life nor committing such a terrible sin."

Jonathan had to admit the justice of this. "Granted, we can absolve him of merely wishing himself rid of Lady Catherine." They had lowered their voices, so that the servants would not hear all, but he still glanced nervously to the side of the room. The lone footman present to attend on breakfast seemed more in danger of falling asleep than of eavesdropping. "However, there may be a financial motive to consider. Lady Catherine may have perceived the colonel's intent and be determined to take action. What if Mr. Guinness comes not to amend the will but to somehow restrict Fitzwilliam's rights to the family fortune?"

"Would not all that be set out in their marriage settlements? Unalterable?"

"Yes," Jonathan admitted. "My knowledge of such matters is limited, however, and perhaps there is some other manner of legal limitation she would make . . . if Lady Catherine knew of his departure, and on balance, I must admit, it seems that she does not."

Miss Tilney's face fell. "How sad for Mrs. Fitzwilliam."

Although Jonathan had not been unaware of what the colonel's plans meant for his cousin, Miss Tilney's remark made him consider it afresh. To have been married for pity was one thing; to be left in contempt another. "This seems so unlike the colonel."

"Matrimony has its own secrets, I believe," said Miss Tilney, "at which others cannot begin to guess."

Mr. Collins never required a reason to visit Rosings Park; Lady Catherine was pleased to see him at nearly all occasions, principally because *he* was always so delighted to see *her*. However, he liked to craft such reasons regardless, even if only as an appealing thought for himself to mull upon during the walk to and from her ladyship's house. We all of us like to feel ourselves needed, and the more we think of the person who needs us, the more we are able to think of ourselves.

On this particular day, his reasons were rather more important than was usual, and more immediate as well. So his usual eager step was more of a scurry as he made his way along the elegant walk that led to the Rosings Park door. (The shrubberies alone had cost more than seventy-five pounds!)

He was received by McQuarrie and taken immediately to the sitting room, where Lady Catherine sat in her customary chair, attended by the Fitzwilliams, Mr. Darcy, and Mr. Tilney. How inappropriate for the two young persons charged with safeguarding her ladyship to be the last to wait upon her in the morning! Yet their absence provided Mr. Collins with the opportunity to make up for their shortcomings in attentiveness, so he did not much regret it.

"You are prompt this day, Mr. Collins," her ladyship said by way of greeting. "We would have thought to see you yesterday after services, though it appears you had other concerns."

His absence had been noted! What a compliment to him, what a mark of her exquisite condescension! "Indeed, the demands upon a clergyman are unpredictable. Believe me, Lady Catherine, no greater desire had I than to be by your side yesterday as in—"

"You traveled much about the town yesterday, did you?" Lady Catherine sniffed. Jenkinson produced one of her seemingly countless lace handkerchiefs. The younger Mr. Darcy and Miss Tilney entered at this time, but Mr. Collins took what comfort he could from the fact that Lady Catherine did not look away from him to acknowledge them.

That might change at any instant, however, so he hastily replied, "Yes, your ladyship, and very muddy and wet was I from my wanderings. The roads throughout Hunsford, you know, are not so well kept as those of Rosi—"

"The town officials do not keep them so well as they should," said Lady Catherine, warming as ever to the topic of another person's negligence. "How are we to feel safe from being thrown from our carriages into the ditch?"

"It is appalling indeed," said Mr. Collins. "Shocking and shameful."

"The roads here do not strike me as being so very much worse than in most villages of similar size," ventured Mr. Tilney, who had lost his battle to remain solely attentive to his newspaper. "Nor have I seen much of mud since my arrival—rain has *threatened* more than it has *appeared*. Granted, I do not know Hunsford as the rest of you do."

"I will not brook contradiction!" Lady Catherine declared. "No, sir, you do not know Hunsford's roads, or you should know them to be in as shameful a condition as we have described, if not worse."

Mr. Collins at last felt at ease. Her ladyship's attention was on the roads, nothing more, and the questions he feared were unlikely to be asked.

❧

Juliet watched Mr. Collins flatter and indulge Lady Catherine that morning with an increasing sense of wonder . . . and of alarm.

No man can truly be so obsequious, so servile, to another who does not actually hold the power of life and death over him, she thought. *This cannot be sincere. It cannot be real! It is but a pretense, and a pretense that must outrage every principle of pride and dignity within the human heart.*

Like any child, Juliet had once played with the reeds by the river, bending them back, back, back until they would take no more and snapped forward (ideally to strike an unsuspecting playmate nearby). She could not but help of imagining Mr. Collins's spirit as that reed, unnaturally bent as low as it could possibly go. What might happen if—no, when—that, too, snapped?

The elder Mr. Darcy declined Mr. Tilney's invitation to walk about the grounds that afternoon. Although he appreciated the gesture—very clearly an attempt to be less satirical and more civil—it would not do to encourage too much familiarity between the Darcys and the Tilneys. Give the girl her due, her attention seemed all for the perils faced by Lady Catherine; not a moment of coquetry had he detected in her. Yet, however modest Miss Tilney's amibitions, there was no saying what the expectations of her father might be. Darcy did not intend to raise them.

He remained with Lady Catherine as much as possible throughout the day, observing closely, less with an eye toward actually apprehending the villain who wished harm upon his aunt, more with hope of discouraging any such homicidal efforts by his mere attentiveness. When she retired for her afternoon nap, however, he was free to take himself to the Rosings library, there to lose himself in a volume of history or essays.

As is often the way, however, no sooner do we achieve our perfect pleasure in solitude than another person arrives. In this case, it was Jonathan who approached his father. "Am I disturbing you?"

Mr. Darcy set aside his history without a sigh. "Certainly not. How progresses your efforts to find the attacker of Lady Catherine?"

"At times I think we have learned much; at others, nothing at all. Or, rather, we are uncertain whether what we have learned is pertinent to the matter of our aunt's safety."

"Your coming here, I surmise, is an effort to determine such. In what way can I help?"

"I am not certain that you can, Father, but I must ask," said Jonathan. "Have you not, in the past, noted a certain . . . peculiarity about Deb Collins?"

Mr. Darcy's first thought was that he had been too worried about others rejecting Jonathan for his own peculiarities to worry about those of any other child. But Jonathan's habits and rituals, however odd, were of no harm to anyone. With Deb Collins, he had never been as certain. "They have long been secretive about the boy. Your mother has remarked often on how long Mrs. Collins's letters are while actually saying very little, and on the subject of her son, Mrs. Collins is particularly quiet. That said, I have never seen any harm in the lad myself."

Jonathan considered this. "At times, when we were all younger and he was but little, we would sometimes try to include him in games only to have him vanish for long periods, after which his parents and sister often appeared to be in considerable distress. Others did not note this much, though

I was ever curious about this habit of Deb's. Then, yesterday, he withdrew from company at Hunsford Parsonage, and Miss Tilney heard shouts and thuds from a nearby room, almost as though a physical altercation was taking place between Deb and Mrs. Collins."

"This is shocking indeed, if true, though more terrible events occur within families than society at large will ever concede." Darcy was a wise enough man to comprehend how great was the difference between the inner and the outer life of both individuals and families. "Your mother has observed a kind of cautiousness in Mrs. Collins pertaining to her son. Whether that be fear for him or fear of him, I know not. I can provide no greater insight."

"You already have," said Jonathan. "You have told me that Miss Tilney and I are not merely imagining this, that our perceptions of some oddity at work within the Collins family are correct. Upon this foundation, we can proceed to determine greater truth."

However much Darcy despaired of his son's interest in the investigation of murder, in this moment he could see clearly that these experiences had matured Jonathan's reactions and reasoning. He had ever been aware of his son's intelligence, but increasingly Darcy had come to believe that Jonathan would in the fullness of time match cleverness with true wisdom. His dislike of the subject matter kept him from saying as much; instead he simply patted Jonathan's shoulder. Yet that was enough for his son to smile back at him in the full knowledge of paternal pride.

Although Anne Fitzwilliam often took an afternoon nap at the same time as her mother, on this date she did not. Her husband was home for the entire day, an increasingly rare thing, and she did not wish to waste the opportunity. To her it seemed as though, during the past several months, the distance between herself and her husband had slowly but inextricably lengthened until he was almost out of reach. Peter's letter had almost built a bridge between them—she had felt it—and if Fitzwilliam had but spoken of his own concerns about their son, his own understanding that the letter sent could not in the slightest be genuine, Anne believed they might have opened their hearts to each other as they had not in so long.

(Not fully. Never fully. This was denied them, now perhaps more than ever, but Anne wanted whatever of his heart she could have.)

Colonel Fitzwilliam's general habit on gray days at Rosings Park was to either take care of business in the study, read in the library, or spend time with Daniels in the gun room, helping to clean and oil the rifles and pistols found therein. Such labor could never be purely menial to a man who had been in the army, or so Fitzwilliam said. But she spotted Daniels walking on the lawn with his wife during a respite from their labors, and from the library she could hear the voices of Mr. Darcy and Jonathan discussing she knew not what. Ergo, she went to find her husband in his study.

He was not there, but to judge by the cigar he had left burning in a nearby tray, he would return at any moment. Anne reflected upon what a pleasantly masculine, useful spot this was. During her father's lifetime, the room had always smelled musty, and the curtains had been kept drawn as though sunlight were an enemy. The colonel, in taking the study for his own, had added touches that testified to his unique personality and history: a few fine paintings of horses, a portrait of herself that had been painted as a wedding present, and a new leather footstool so that he might lean back in his chair in comfort.

I do not think Papa cared aught for comfort, Anne reflected, recalling her straitlaced father. He and her mother had been so perfectly suited! Yet she did not recollect much happiness or trust between them, for all that.

Always, Anne had put so much faith in her husband—ever believing in his sense of rightness, in his goodness. But his many unexplained absences had worn her trust thin. The many attempts on Lady Catherine's life had further taxed Anne's restraint. So it would be wrong, perhaps, to judge her for the terrible temptation that came over her in that moment of opportunity. How could she not wonder what secret he had been keeping? How could she not seize her chance to know?

Anne went to the desk and began opening drawers; it did not take long for her to find an unsent letter in her husband's handwriting. She took it up and read the entirety very deliberately, then twice, then yet again, attempting to comprehend the truth: that her husband had already found a new home, so intent was he upon leaving her.

Chapter Fourteen

Let it never be said that the mind of Lady Catherine de Bourgh lacked perception, nor that her intuition was not as sharply honed as a fencer's sword. Though her attention might tend in certain directions to the neglect of others, in those directions her acuity was unparalleled.

One of those most favored as the subject of Lady Catherine's thoughts was her daughter, Anne. All who knew them were aware that her ladyship's attentions toward her daughter were and ever had been exacting. Very few understood that this sprang from the first days of Anne's life, for she had been an infant so frail, so small, that midwife and physician alike had despaired of her survival. In an era where many women of higher station and nobler birth sent their infants to wet nurses at the soonest opportunity, Lady Catherine had kept Anne in her arms or next to her unceasingly as she fed her; warmed her; and, with all the vigor of her considerable personality, willed the child to live. In this first of many such instances, Anne had done as her mother wished.

This motherly devotion, however, soon took on a highly proprietary quality. In the opinion of Lady Catherine, Anne had not merely been born of her; Anne *belonged* to her, and all her concerns and thoughts were as much her ladyship's property as the mantelpieces of Rosings Park. Although Anne had never fully obliged her mother in this, her mother had never perceived as much; her ladyship believed that outward daughterly obedience was both the path to, and the surest sign of, inward contentment.

Lady Catherine had felt some faint tremors of concern upon her daughter's marriage. The colonel was neither so highborn nor so wealthy as she had hoped for the man to whom she would grant her daughter's hand; after Darcy's cruel spurning, her ladyship had hoped to find a future son-in-law of even greater fortune and position, so that Darcy might be humbled thereby. Yet how was such a man to be met with, when their habits and Anne's health kept them so near Rosings? Nor was Lady Catherine unaware that Anne had been near thirty, which meant many chances had already fled and the rest would soon follow. Colonel Fitzwilliam would do. What had distressed Lady Catherine was the knowledge that someone else would have a share of Anne's affections and obedience. Yet in practice, most seemed to have gone on much as it did before. Peter's birth had changed matters— making the house rather louder, for one—but there, too, the will of her ladyship, in all its wisdom, had been allowed to govern. If asked, Lady Catherine would first have upbraided the questioner for impertinence, then replied that, yes, she still felt that Anne shared all her dearest concerns with her mother.

Early that evening, however, as she made her way through the upstairs hallway, her ladyship noticed Anne sitting at her familiar window seat, trembling as though with cold. Peering closely allowed Lady Catherine to see how very white Anne's face had become. "And what is this?" Lady Catherine said, striding into her daughter's room. "What troubles you so?"

In truth, Anne had always been much more skillful in hiding her emotions from her mother than Lady Catherine had ever dreamed. What privacy was to be had in Rosings Park had to be closely guarded, lest it vanish completely. But in that hour, when the news of her husband's plans felt as though it had torn her open, there could be no restraint. How could she not tell all?

Colonel Fitzwilliam sat in the drawing room with his cousins Darcy, whiling away the last minutes before dinner, when he heard Lady Catherine's voice call out: "Colonel Geoffrey Fitzwilliam, you will explain yourself *this instant!*"

Both Darcys looked at Colonel Fitzwilliam with true sympathy as he rose to his feet. The colonel, by now a veteran of both the Napoleonic Wars and more than a decade of Lady Catherine's rages, was not a man to frighten easily. Yet could he be blamed for blanching when Lady Catherine descended upon them, such a fire in her eyes as had never been seen before? "My dear aunt," Colonel Fitzwilliam began, "whatever is the matter?"

"You dare to ask this, when you know perfectly well the sin you have committed against me, against my daughter, against the house of de Bourgh!" Colonel Fitzwilliam had but time enough to note that her ladyship had not felt the need to mention Anne's name before she concluded, "You dare to abandon us! To flee from your marriage under cover of darkness like a thief! To flee to Bath, there perhaps to take up residence permanently."

Colonel Fitzwilliam felt all the shame Lady Catherine would have wished for him to feel—more, he would later conclude, then he rightly deserved. But as is so often the case, secrecy created its own shame and meted out the punishment for its own demise. Acutely aware was Colonel Fitzwilliam of the shocked, disapproving stare of the elder Mr. Darcy;

he can be forgiven for failing also to note that the younger Mr. Darcy did not seem so very surprised. "Lady Catherine," he began, "there is much we must—I had intended first to speak with Anne—"

"Your deception does not confound *me*," Lady Catherine retorted. "You had no intention of speaking to anyone until your trunks were packed, or did you instead intend to abscond in the night and leave us entirely unawares?"

In the doorway behind Lady Catherine, Colonel Fitzwilliam became aware of the shadowy form of his wife. How had she learned the truth? (He knew Lady Catherine herself had not informed her, for her ladyship's ire had undoubtedly brought her to Colonel Fitzwilliam in the very next instant.) Anne's face was a pale oval in the darkness—a cameo portrait—until the instant she turned away and vanished into the darkness.

"You decline even to answer?" Lady Catherine's dudgeon continued to swell. "This, then, is the contempt in which you hold me?"

"Lady Catherine," Fitzwilliam said, in some desperation, "at the moment I will say only this: that I intended, and intend, to discuss this with my wife before I speak of it to any other person."

"I am her mother!"

He shook his head. "It is to Anne I must speak. Excuse me."

"You are not excused—" Lady Catherine began, but, for once, the colonel did not allow her to finish. He hurried past her, up the stairs, toward the door to Anne's room, which he reached at the very moment the key turned, locking them on opposite sides. Knock and plead though he might, he won no reply. Anne remained silent, and alone.

Some amount of good cheer generally accompanies a gathering at the dinner table, if for no other reason than the expectation of food. That night, however, the spirit at Rosings Park was rather bleaker. Both Anne and Colonel Fitzwilliam remained upstairs; Jonathan was unaware whether they were speaking together or sequestered apart. He had not managed to converse with Miss Tilney before the meal; his intention had been to ask her whether she had informed Anne of the colonel's plans. This, at least, had proved unnecessary, for Miss Tilney's pale countenance and shocked demeanor strongly suggested she had said nothing. The likeliest explanation, Jonathan surmised, was that Anne—whether through suspicion or mischance—had found the same letter that he himself had found in Colonel Fitzwilliam's desk.

Father, who considered Colonel Fitzwilliam one of his dearest friends, appeared nearly as cast down as Miss Tilney. The Collinses had not been invited to dinner that night, if only because the early-evening hubbub had prevented it. This left only Mr. Tilney to make conversation with the outraged Lady Catherine; in this matter, almost uniquely, the two of them were in perfect accord.

"'That which God hath joined together, let no man put asunder,'" Mr. Tilney quoted. Jonathan could imagine Mr. Collins saying the same words in a rather priggish manner, but Tilney sounded merely solemn, perhaps sad. "Husband and wife have taken a vow before the Almighty to do all within their power to provide love, aid, comfort, and trust for each other. Some cannot find happiness together despite great efforts, and for them I have sympathy—I have seen the tragedy an ill-suited marriage can bring. But abandonment? Without any attempt to heal the breach? This, I cannot sanction."

"None has asked you to," Father said somewhat sharply.

Lady Catherine did not heed this; Mr. Tilney was quite the only soul at Rosings who currently pleased her. "One only knows what sort of person this 'agent' may be, and to whom he may have shared our family's concerns. To be spoken of with scorn in Hunsford and Faxton—no, it shall not be borne!"

"If the colonel continues on his intended path," said Mr. Tilney, "the temper of the community will condemn him, and support your daughter."

This was not the sort of forbearance Lady Catherine had in mind. "We shall . . . we shall have a large supper. Two nights' hence—that is enough time for the cook to make ready. We shall invite all the local families of any prominence, and they will witness Fitzwilliam and Anne in harmony. That will silence wagging tongues for some time."

"Your solution seems incomplete," Jonathan said. "What is seen to be so at one dinner can be contradicted by later events."

Lady Catherine remained obdurate. "What is seen holds more sway than what is heard. *That* you may rely upon."

"But"—Miss Tilney appeared as confounded as Jonathan felt—"the attempts upon your life—can this be the time to—"

"You are very free with your opinions, young lady," said her ladyship, "and you cannot have considered the question at any length, for if you had, you would have concluded, as I have done, that I shall be safest where I am observed by as many people as possible."

Jonathan could see why Lady Catherine thought so. Yet he had in the past seen a woman die of poison at a party thrown in her honor, falling down to breathe her last amid all those who had gathered to celebrate her. Where a murderer was determined, witnesses could be ignored.

Equally true, however, was that where Lady Catherine was determined, no refusals would be brooked.

Darcy slept little that night.

He was not a man to unduly involve himself in the affairs of others unless honor so demanded. Yet he could not determine whether honor had a hold on him in the present situation. Colonel Fitzwilliam was both his cousin and one of his closest friends, the confidant he had known longest in his life. All that would be as nothing if Fitzwilliam behaved abominably to his wife. Anne was Darcy's cousin, too—one whom he felt he had perhaps wronged and certainly wounded—and if she were abandoned, Darcy would stand behind her with all the rest of the family.

These truths were not in question. However, Darcy could not believe that the colonel would behave so. Such an action ran contrary to every action, every principle, every deed of goodness Fitzwilliam had evinced before, and these were many in number. As Colonel Fitzwilliam had not disputed Lady Catherine's account of his plans to leave Rosings Park, there must be *something* in it . . . but as dawn neared, Darcy resolved that they did not yet know all the particulars of the matter and that to pass judgment before learning all would be premature. Fitzwilliam's account might not absolve him, but it would, Darcy felt, at least make the action comprehensible in light of the colonel's character.

He saw naught of Colonel Fitzwilliam at breakfast, though Darcy lingered long in that room (to the apparent discomfiture of Jonathan and Miss Tilney). Doubt suggested that perhaps Fitzwilliam had proved himself false already by fleeing the house, but a trip to the stables and a conversation with Lawson confirmed that the colonel had withdrawn neither horse nor carriage. Finally Darcy set out to walk in the woods, recalling that the pleasant patch nearby so well-liked by Elizabeth was a favorite of Fitzwilliam's as well. This approach bore fruit, as it was not above a quarter of an hour before he came across his friend wandering amid the trees.

"Fitzwilliam," Darcy called. "Hold. I would have a word with you."

"Come to box my ears, cousin?" Fitzwilliam walked toward him, neither uncertain nor resolute. His face was haggard, so much so that Darcy first wondered if his valet had failed to shave him that morning. "I might welcome it, for at least then I should be preoccupied with matters beyond the ones which currently torment me."

Darcy fell into step beside him, the concord of their movements gentling the effect of his words. "You speak of your torment but not your wife's."

"I never intended to leave Anne," said Fitzwilliam. "She has misconstrued the letter she found. I could reassure her if she would but speak with me!"

"Could you? For merely denying her own perceptions will not have that effect. You have caused your wife to doubt you, and you will have to reassure her in more ways than one, if you can."

"If I can?"

Darcy sighed. "Let us be frank with each other. You explained to me before your wedding that you had married Anne out of pity."

"It was you who chose that word. I would not call it pity. I would call it . . . compassion, in the true sense of fellow feeling."

"But you were not in love with her."

"No more than she with me," said Fitzwilliam. "As I told you then, my hope was that Anne and I could be friends. Is not friendship a good place to begin a marriage? Many matches are made from mere infatuation, and surely a friendship has more meaning than that."

"This, I cannot say," replied Darcy. "My own courtship was of a most unusual nature."

"Well do I recall." The ghost of a smile departed Fitzwilliam's face almost as soon as it had appeared. "You speak of repairing a marriage, but you and Mrs. Darcy—I have long considered you the most perfect union of all those I have known."

Darcy would not admit that he took any pleasure in being so described, but he allowed himself to anticipate the happiness Elizabeth would feel when he told her of it later. "You mistake the matter if you believe that the mark of a good marriage is the absence of repair. Even the best of us, with the finest ideals and purest intentions, will cause harm where we would least wish to do so. Even those we love best will at times fail us as we have failed them. No, I would say that the mark of a good marriage is regular, sincere repair of the inevitable injured feelings that must arise on occasion between any two persons so intimately connected."

"This, however—" Fitzwilliam sighed. "My error may be beyond repair."

Privately Darcy agreed, but it would serve no purpose to say so. "You cannot know this until you have made the attempt."

Within Rosings Park, all was uproar, commotion, and activity. A dinner for twenty persons would normally be an event long planned for by host and guests alike, to say nothing of the servants whose actual labors would bring this dinner into being. Yet Lady Catherine had decreed that one should take place on very short notice indeed, and thus every room of the house hummed with activity. Juliet saw rugs being beaten upon the lawns and every hearth being swept; she could but imagine the pandemonium in the kitchens. For Juliet's part, she had little to do beyond wishing that she had bought a finer gown, appropriate to the occasion.

When she expressed this to her father, Mr. Tilney became grave. "You are, I think, possessed of too much sense to concern yourself with the opinions you will encounter in this company. Lady Catherine may be a respectable woman, and certainly her desire to shield and console her daughter is laudable. But her set and ours shall never be the same, and I daresay all parties involved are equally glad of it."

"It was but a small joke, Papa, nothing more," said Juliet. "I am of course present for a purpose far more important than any fine gown, but Lady Catherine's plans have rendered Mr. Jonathan Darcy and me unable to pursue those ends."

"Take heart—her ladyship's reasoning is sound, so the dinner will provide her with protection for that time at least. And if the colonel's deception had aught to do with the darker deeds here at Rosings, then its revelation must also work to the good."

Mr. Tilney might have continued at greater length had not the butler appeared at that instant. "Mr. Tilney, sir—Mr. Portman, a farmer in our parish, has come to Rosings Park in search of you."

"Of me?" Then Tilney frowned. "Mr. Collins is around and about again, is he not?"

McQuarrie nodded. "So it would seem, and the lady of his house is very ill, only able to be comforted by a clergyman."

Already Tilney had risen to his feet with a sigh. "I am doing more work here than I would in my own parish! But it is not work to be ignored, not when the need is so great."

This left Juliet alone for a time, so she had ample time to consider why, despite her father's wise counsel, the idea of the dinner still dissatisfied her greatly. Finally she came to the conclusion that her concern was primarily for Anne.

Mrs. Fitzwilliam must be heartbroken, she thought, and surely in that state, nothing could be less desirable than an obligation to spend hours in the company of persons who do not and cannot know the true concerns of one's heart. To have to dress in one's best, make polite chitchat, and—if all went as planned—remain in the company of the husband who might soon be departing: it was cruelty indeed.

Lady Catherine does not intend cruelty, Juliet decided, *but if cruelty caused harm only where it was deliberately intended, our world would be far happier than it is.*

As she and the younger Mr. Darcy had been prevented from their usual breakfast conversation by his father's lingering over coffee, they had been unable to further discuss what this revelation portended for their investigation. Juliet believed that her father had hit upon one truth: that this information being known could not put Lady Catherine in more danger and could potentially make her less at risk of harm. But if the attempts had ceased . . . did that mean they assumed Colonel Fitzwilliam to be responsible? For they had no proof, none that would allow any crime to be prosecuted . . .

She was jolted by the thought of Ralph Bamber with his hands tied behind his back, mounting the steps of the scaffold. Juliet caught herself upon the stair, grasping the rail—not in a swoon but in the need to feel something solid and unyielding.

No, there was no need for prosecution. Juliet was not a member of the constabulary, and unless the role of woman was to be even more radically redefined than Mary Wollstonecraft had dreamed, it was impossible for her to become one. Her place was not to marshal the law, merely to see that Lady Catherine remained alive and well.

Balance restored, Juliet continued her descent. Although much of the house's furor took place within the rooms frequented by the servants or their back stair, the clamor now was too great to be entirely so confined. McQuarrie the butler strode purposefully through the foyer, past Jenkinson bustling along with a key to some room or other; all the finery that could possibly be displayed within a house, it seemed, would be employed in service of the illusion that all was well at Rosings Park.

Then Juliet thought again on the matter of locked rooms, and a spark of inspiration came to her. She hurried after Mrs. Jenkinson, catching up with her in the hallway. Jenkinson startled at Juliet's approach, then put one hand to her chest. "Forgive me, miss, but you gave me a start."

"I suppose none of us at Rosings can rest entirely easy these days," said Juliet. (Privately she had doubts that "resting easy" had little to do with anyone living or working under Lady Catherine's purview, but this was not an opinion to be voiced aloud.) "It is I who should ask forgiveness, for I am interrupting you at your labors, but I realized that I should ask about the keys to the house, and who has the keeping of them. Usually the housekeeper performs that office, and yet I am much surprised to see that Rosings Park has no true housekeeper in that sense. Or have I simply failed to make her acquaintance?"

"You perceive rightly, miss. That is one way in which Rosings Park is unlike other great houses—or so I am told, for I have worked here thirty years and lack experience of any other place," Mrs. Jenkinson said. "The late housekeeper, Mrs. Prowse, was ailing for several years before her demise; she wished to continue working, but was quite unfit to do so. So Prowse's daughter Daisy and I took on more and more of her tasks as time went on. When Lady Catherine became aware of it, she allowed the arrangement—Prowse was a great favorite of hers, and she greatly dislikes change. We thought that when Mrs. Prowse finally passed away, another house-keeper would be hired, or that one of us would be given the position, but instead we have gone on as we were."

This was more of a history than Juliet had wished, though she inwardly noted that Lady Catherine had shown more leniency in the matter than many mistresses would have done in her place. "So you have the keeping of the keys?"

"No, miss, that's Daisy. Keeps them in her room when they're not on her person." She held up the key currently in her hand to add, "She lent me this so I could complete my work, but I shall return it to her promptly once I am done."

A proper housekeeper would *always* have had the keys on her person, save when she washed and slept; Daisy, it appeared, took more irregular care of them. For someone, this had proved an opportunity. "And this is known to every resident of the house, that the keys are often to be found in Daisy's room?"

Jenkinson had to consider this before replying. "Lady Catherine knows, of course, and Mrs. Fitzwilliam. The colonel does not concern himself with such things." Juliet was on the verge of thanking her for what seemed a complete answer when the next words came: "As for those outside the house, Mrs. Collins knows of it, too."

"Mrs. Collins? It seems very irregular that she would be aware of the household arrangements."

"Lady Catherine . . . has many thoughts about the proper running of a house, Miss Tilney, and these thoughts she is generally eager to share. She spoke of it to Mrs. Collins, and to be sure, that knowledge came in handy when we had the influenza in this house last winter. Mrs. Collins came then to assist in such nursing as she could properly do, and the keys aided her in that endeavor."

Daniels keeps the gun room key in one room, and Daisy the other house keys in another, Juliet surmised. *The only ones among our suspects who knew about the keys—who could perhaps have used that knowledge to devise a way to acquire them—were Charlotte Collins and Anne Fitzwilliam.*

Chapter Fifteen

The town of Hunsford, though not large, comprised persons enough to have a greater variety of society than is common in most of the countryside. Its location made travel to London quick enough that many could be heard to consider it, and yet of such a distance that few turned consideration into action. The preeminence of Rosings Park and the family of de Bourgh was unquestioned, though comparisons enough existed for this preeminence to have some meaning.

Thus, while dinner guests in a smaller town or village might be safely guessed, some suspense accompanied the rare invitations to Rosings. Families felt themselves obliged to win Lady Catherine's favor, lest they be overlooked on the next illustrious occasion. In this situation, however, invitation and announcement were as one, and the fortunate were not made to suffer the wait. (Those passed by took consolation in the fact that a dinner party so hastily given was unlikely to be among the finest.) Several houses in Hunsford were in nearly as much an uproar as Rosings Park itself, as gowns and suits not previously known to be needed were hastily made fine. Every shoe-rose in the shops had fled by the afternoon before the dinner was to occur.

Those closest to Lady Catherine anticipated the event in varying states of mind. Mr. Darcy, who had much passing acquaintance in the area, looked forward to hearing what news they might have. Mr. Tilney, who had previously possessed no acquaintance in the area beyond Rosings Park and

Hunsford Parsonage, had met a few others while conducting pastoral business in the absence of Mr. Collins, and he very much hoped to be introduced to yet more persons with easy tempers and liberal views, so that he might return home with at least one new joke to tell his wife.

The Collinses were in a state of high anxiety. They knew the ebb and flow of Lady Catherine's tempers better than most, and such an unexpected, abrupt gathering seemed to them an ill omen. Mr. Collins in particular privately fretted about the timing of it all, but was resolved to appear at the proper place and time. Deb, it was decided, should remain at the parsonage and plead ill health. Details would not be offered, and given the general hubbub, most likely they would not be sought.

Juliet Tilney warmed to the idea of the dinner more as time elapsed. She believed that Lady Catherine was likely to be safe for the duration of the gathering, and observing the suspects in a new milieu might prove a revelation. Once again she regretted not having brought a better gown but philo-sophically concluded that it is through such experiences we learn the value of preparation.

Jonathan Darcy's astonishment at the announcement of a dinner had soon deepened into dread. He easily became overwhelmed by a surfeit of noise, light, and commotion, by overfamiliarity (which he considered as virtually any atten-tion given him by those whom he did not consider intimates), and by unexpected and intrusive touches. None of these were necessary ingredients of a dinner party, many of which he had successfully navigated in the past. However, in the town of Hunsford there was a family called Fisher, and the Fishers were nothing if not noisy and overly familiar. They were given to handshakes, slapping backs, touching arms, and many other disagreeable behaviors, and they appeared to know of no other way to speak than loudly. The Fishers' adoration of Lady Catherine was eclipsed only by that of Mr. Collins, which meant they were often invited to the Rosings table—and this was to be among the occasions. Jonathan very much hoped their presences would not unsettle him so much that he could no longer wear the curtain he had fashioned so carefully for Miss Tilney. All depended on maintaining it to perfection.

Justified though Jonathan's foreboding was, it could not come close to that experienced by the two persons most responsible for the party: Colonel Fitzwilliam and Anne. Neither wished to be with any person besides the other; Anne did not feel strong enough for the inevitable confrontation; and Fitzwilliam, having first pleaded to explain himself, now felt that no explanation would be accepted. Yet how could they join a merry party for dinner with such a breach between them, so violent as to be almost visible? In the end, it was Anne who determined that something must be said before the gathering, or else something might be said *at* the gathering—an eventuality that would complete her humiliation. *No,* thought she, *let the subject be broached now, while I yet have time to collect myself before the meal.*

Anne summoned Daisy to prepare for the dinner with even more care than usual; as little a difference as it might make, she wished to face her husband looking her best. Almost all her gowns were white or the faint grayish-green Lady Catherine thought most suitable to her complexion, but Anne had been able to exercise independence enough for a few in blue and one in a soft pink—and it was this one she wished to wear that night. The blush gave her a healthier glow, she thought, and while this might be illusion with no basis in truth, she allowed herself this vanity. Once her pearl necklace had been fastened around her neck, Anne excused Daisy, gathered her courage, and knocked on the door that joined her chamber to her husband's.

At first no reply came. Had she been mistaken, when she believed sounds had issued from his room only minutes prior? Finally, though, Fitzwilliam called out, "Come in, if you now will."

She opened the door to find him sitting in the chair near the window. He had removed a few pieces of his own clothing rather than waiting for the valet—military men, he had explained, sometimes valued expediency over propriety—but shirt and breeches remained, which made this conversation possible. "Colonel Fitzwilliam," she said. "I see you have not yet begun to pack."

He closed his eyes, a habit of his when he sought to control his temper. "You have assumed the very worst without bothering to ask me whether it is true."

"You have inquired after taking a house in Bath without bothering to ask me whether I should wish to accompany you. Do you believe we are equally in error?"

Fitzwilliam sighed. "No. The greater fault is mine. I ought to have spoken long ago—"

"Now your actions have spoken for you."

"Anne, look at me." The colonel rose to his feet. "I intended to ask whether you would come with me to Bath."

"Leave home?" Living beyond the walls of Rosings Park was impossible. This Anne had been told over and over, since she was too young even to comprehend. Fitzwilliam might have asked her to fly through the skies with him and been more easily believed. "I see. You meant to ask me such a question so that the refusal, the fault, might be mine alone."

Fitzwilliam rarely grew angry, but Anne could see the signs in him now. He said only, "Anne, there are times where you are too much your mother's child— No. That is not true. At all points, you are too much your mother's child. But there are moments you cannot help, and moments when you could be different if you but chose. Rarely do you so choose. Are you not ready to be your own governor for once?"

How dare he be angry with her, when the error was wholly on his side? "You seek to govern me as much as Mama," Anne cried. "If not, you would have spoken to me of all this before taking the house, and not after!"

Fitzwilliam's anger dimmed, replaced by resignation. "This I should have done. Does my failure then doom us to failure forever?"

It was then that both heard the clip-clop of horses' hooves on gravel. Anne felt a moment of pure fury toward the Fishers, who were always ill-mannered enough to arrive early, then so fawning toward Lady Catherine that they earned future invitations regardless. "I must go down."

"Go, then," said Fitzwilliam. He seemed weary, then—perhaps sad. Anne could not think of that now, could not think of the rest he had told her. That was all for later. She turned and left to join Mama, greeting all comers to the dinner.

"Wherever can the Collinses be?" Lady Catherine asked. "It is unlike them to be late."

"I hear he attended to the baptism of a babe not expected to survive," said Mr. Tilney. The guests were milling about to converse before dinner. "Or so I was informed, when I was fetched to pray with an infirm elderly woman this morning. I imagine he has remained with the child's family in their time of trial."

Lady Catherine was not convinced. "He has never failed to

consider this house and its occupants as his first concern. I am astonished that he should fail to do so now."

Mr. Tilney thought little of this, as anyone observing him could see. To preserve the gentler tenor of the evening, Jonathan would have made an ordinary sort of excuse for the Collinses, blaming the unwillingness of horses or some small domestic mishap, except that he was already surrounded by dinner guests—most particularly, by Fishers.

"You see," said the matronly Mrs. Fisher, curls bobbing around the edges of her cap with every nod of her head (and she nodded her head with every word), "one cannot but sympathize with the late queen, no matter how terrible her behavior might have been. To have her turned away from the coronation? Before all the crowd? No doubt it was the death of her."

"To be sure, the king's edict was discourteous," Jonathan said. He had learned that the safest conversation tactic, when in doubt, was agreeing with people in words only slightly different from their own. After such a restatement, he sometimes had the chance to escape from company he found oppressive, and he hoped for such a chance here.

This hope was in vain, for the eldest Miss Fisher immediately replied, "Of course, she was not invited. She knew she was not invited. But I believe her point—that the queen should not *require* an invitation to her husband's coronation—to have been a sound one."

"I supported her as long as I could, because she was a woman," said her younger sister, Miss Lettice. "But I can hardly forgive her for having called herself 'attached and affectionate' to the king when it was so surely not the case."

The youngest sister, just this year out, was Miss Maria; she was perhaps the most formidable of the lot. "As she is gone to Judgment, I am resolved at least always to think she would have been respectable, had the king behaved only tolerably to her at first."

Mr. Fisher, meanwhile, had already drained his second cup of wine to the dregs. "Dead of shame. Dead of shame. And the king cares not one jot."

Under other circumstances, Jonathan might have been interested, even delighted, in the company of women who were both informed about and interested in politics. His mother was so, and she swore many other ladies to be as well; she claimed that they were discouraged from expressing such interests, their conversation unnaturally limited to the domestic and the trivial. However, this circumstance involved being surrounded by the Fishers, each of whom was very tall, very slender, and possessed with riotously curly blond hair that might have passed for a particularly garish wig. The effect was not unlike being surrounded by a wall of firecrackers, all at the moment of explosion. To Jonathan it seemed very nearly that loud.

Young Miss Maria Fisher had by this time wandered away from Jonathan, which he would have perceived as a blessing were it not for the fact that she had gone in the direction of the pianoforte. Although this was not a time for the proper exhibition of one's accomplishments, musical or otherwise, in such a setting some light music would generally be considered a delightful ornament to the occasion. She began to play a lilting Irish air, to the pleasure of all . . . save Jonathan. It was noise atop noise, combining with the gathering of people to make him feel crowded, hot, confined.

Miss Tilney managed to push her way through persons Fisher to come to his side. "Mr. Darcy?" she asked. "Do not you think it overly warm? Perhaps you might step out and speak to a servant about the fire."

"Why should he do it?" Miss Lettice asked. She did not

appear to appreciate the interruption in Jonathan's attention. "Surely that is Lady Catherine's office—and I do not think it so warm at all."

Jonathan did find it warm, but that was not the point. The point was that he was on the verge of becoming overwhelmed and losing all ability to function normally, politely, or perhaps at all. Miss Tilney had glimpsed his distress, understood it, and managed to tactfully bring him back to himself in time for him to take the appropriate steps. "I shall see to it right away, Miss Tilney," he said. He could not focus on her face, on the Fishers, on anything else except the need to leave immediately.

Swiftly he walked toward the door, eager to step outside not just the room but Rosings Park itself. As he did so, he very nearly collided with the Collinses, both parents and Katy, who had belatedly appeared. Mr. Collins's voluminous explanations filled his ears further, but Jonathan ignored him and stumbled out of doors, around the house, into the blessed quiet dark. Here he remained for several minutes, collecting himself, allowing the silent tides within his mind to ebb at last.

Once he was himself, however, Jonathan still could not bring himself to return. The failure of his efforts stung too sharply. Miss Tilney had seen him having trouble; she had been obliged to help him. He would not go back until he could show her the perfect drawn curtain once more.

At table, Juliet found herself seated between an elderly gentleman who smiled genteelly but said little because he heard even less, and a young gentleman who was most interested in making her acquaintance until he determined that her father was but a country parson, at which point the connection seemed less desirable to him. Nor was she seated close enough to either of the Fitzwilliams to make much study of them; both were pale and quiet, as might be anticipated, but nothing else could she deduce.

Would that the younger Mr. Darcy sat nearer, so at least they might converse—but he was as far from her as the table permitted, and his countenance was nearly as troubled as that of the Fitzwilliams. She hoped his earlier constitutional had done him some good.

"How lovely a table has been set," said Mr. Collins, beaming at Lady Catherine. Once again Juliet wondered at his performance: the pretense at admiration so exaggerated Lady Catherine's merits—surely such a tremendous artifice could only be meant to conceal an equally tremendous hatred. "How excellent your arrangements are yet again, your ladyship. To have provided such splendor on such brief notice! Truly, it is a rare hostess who could—"

"You have become rather tardy of late, Mr. Collins," said Lady Catherine, not beaming at him. "Punctuality was once among your virtues, but very remiss have you become."

"'Tis the roads and the vile condition they are in." This was Mr. Fisher, who had marked himself to Juliet as a person whose discussion circled mainly around that which he disliked. "We have been fortunate here, with little rain, but Faxton and its environs have been repeatedly drenched. That road is nigh impassable not two miles from Hunsford."

Lady Catherine would not be so easily placated. "Mr. Collins has no business in Faxton. Whyever should he be there? He has been busy with some other errand of his own, no doubt, which takes precedence over his appearance at the home of his patroness."

"Indeed not, Lady Catherine!" Mr. Collins could scarce

have looked more horrified. Juliet remembered that the Collinses had both said he went to Faxton to purchase lace; she had little believed that before, but at this moment could well imagine that this was not the sort of errand he would ever admit had been of more importance to him than his patroness's wishes. He continued, "I assure you, my lateness was but a matter of—of household—"

"What my husband is reluctant to reveal," said Charlotte Collins rather smoothly, "is only that which must be apparent to all—that our daughter, now that she is out, is much more particular about gowns and hair and all other such things. We are three times as long leaving the house these days!" Many around the table chuckled. Katy Collins did not; she frowned at her plate. Juliet wondered whether her displeasure was related to the embarrassment occasioned by that comment, be it true . . . or the injustice of the comment, be it false.

Once again she attempted to catch the younger Mr. Darcy's gaze, to see if he detected the peculiarity of the moment. However, he stared straight forward, as though determined to perceive nothing, and to be perceived by no one. Had he come to the same realization that was upon her now?

For Mr. Fisher's words had made one thing very clear: Mr. Collins had lied to Lady Catherine. He had claimed the roads in Hunsford to be muddy and wet, yet—though rain had threatened often the past few days—none had actually fallen. The roads remained dry.

It was Faxton, she had heard, where torrential rain had fallen. Therefore she considered it likely that it was to Faxton Mr. Collins had gone—and likely not in search of more lace for Mrs. Collins. What purpose might he have had in doing so that he would lie to conceal it?

To what extent Lady Catherine's dinner achieved her goal of establishing the family's harmonious reputation, no one within Rosings Park was in a position to say. Had those in attendance been observing closely, they would no doubt have noticed Colonel Fitzwilliam's uncharacteristic silence, but when people are presented with a fine table and new acquaintances, they are unlikely to take note of words unsaid. (Anne's quiet paleness was common enough at such gatherings that it would draw no comment.) On the whole, Mr. Darcy wished that the dinner had not taken place, as it seemed to have discomfited Jonathan and interrupted the investigation, all while failing at its perceived social purpose.

Thus he was in no good temper that following morning, until a courier arrived with a letter. As soon as Darcy saw the address written in Elizabeth's fine, sloping hand, his spirits improved. He tipped the courier handsomely, took the letter to the library, and proceeded to discover that he was in trouble.

> *Dearest—*
> *Your news from Rosings Park is shocking indeed, and equally as astonishing is your manner of revealing it. Perhaps it is I who am mistaken, for I am not present and cannot judge for myself, but the renewal of attempts upon the life of Lady Catherine is most distressing. Yet you speak of it almost as a trifle, and you assure me that no one else is endangered. How can this be, when anyone taken ill within the house might be dosed with laudanum, or happen to be walking through the room into which the rifle was fired? I believe, my husband, that your view upon the matter has been too much shaped by Lady Catherine's own belief in her invincibility. (Which cannot be absolute—and here*

*I chide you, my dear, for assuming that her motive is
only to focus attention upon herself. Someone is most
certainly attempting to murder her.)*

   *I note also that you have time to write waspishly of
Mr. Tilney. You must admit that, in the past, you have
at times judged others too sharply for wit, then warmed
to the individual in question considerably—one proof of
this, I particularly recall. Whether this shall be another
such occasion, none can know, but I must take exception
to your declaration that the Tilneys are "not a family
to which we should wish to be attached." This suggests
that you are, once again, judging young women one and
all to be nothing more than fortune hunters—a harsh
ruling in many cases, but particularly unjust as regards
Miss Tilney, who after all was commanded to Rosings
precisely as Jonathan was and whose interest in solving
the case is, I doubt not, entirely genuine. If she does
look to Jonathan as a potential match . . . can that be so
terrible? The Tilneys are respectable, unless you believe
an excess of wit in a clergyman diminishes his place in
society; furthermore, Miss Tilney's liking for Jonathan
has always struck me as natural and unaffected. She
may be the one girl in all England who would not first
see Pemberley before even thinking of the man!*

   *If I react with too much spirit, my love, I hope you
will forgive me. But your life may be at risk. My son's
life may be at risk. And you may be working against
the best match our son could possibly make. These three
potential disasters command me to pack my trunks and
set forth for Rosings. (Sister Mary, Dean Wheelwright,
and our nieces and nephews are all very well and
happy, and have made me most welcome in their home,
but I have already stayed longer than should any guest*

*who issued her own invitation.) I shall arrive in two
days' time, reckoned from your receipt of this letter.
Whatever risk may lie in it for me, I am determined to
brave, for there is too much risk to the rest of you for me
to rest easily anyplace else.*

   *Despite all the travail, my heart will fill with joy
when I see you again—*

Elizabeth

Colonel Fitzwilliam had left almost with the dawn. Jonathan overheard the butler McQuarrie quietly mentioning to Mrs. Jenkinson that the colonel had taken nothing with him; such reassurance was now necessary, Jonathan realized, to ascertain that Fitzwilliam had not left Rosings Park—and Anne—for good. Otherwise the morning began much as it would have before, beginning with his late breakfast and conversation with Miss Tilney . . . and her, he could barely face.

Yet she showed no evidence of dismay, and had even deduced valuable information from the conversation of the Fishers—an accomplishment, Jonathan suspected, no other had ever achieved. "We know, then, that Mr. Collins has been deceiving Lady Catherine, and likely his many delays and absences can be attributed to travels to Faxton or its environs. Yet I do not immediately see how this can be considered any proof of his complicity in the attempts upon my great-aunt's life."

"Indeed, it seems more likely to exonerate him, for if he was in Faxton, he could not have been here to commit these attempts," Miss Tilney said, between her delicate nibblings at a strawberry scone. "Yet the very fact that his travels are secret makes me wonder whether he might have some darker purpose there."

"Yes, we must consider this," he said. "I believe that to be the one valuable fact gleaned from last night's dinner. I am glad you were able to attend." Should he apologize for having become overwhelmed? No. If Miss Tilney was determined to ignore his faltering the night before, then he should do likewise.

Indeed, Miss Tilney's thoughts had taken an entirely different direction. "I also hoped to observe the Fitzwilliams, but they were so very quiet, so very distant from each other. I do not think the party achieved Lady Catherine's aim of projecting marital harmony."

"We are in agreement," said Jonathan. "Furthermore, no dinner, however successful, will have the power to prevent gossip if one spouse later leaves both domicile and marriage."

"It is so very sad. Mrs. Fitzwilliam cares very much for her husband. One would hope he had similar sentiments toward her—or, failing that, at least the loyalty a man is meant to show to wife and family."

Jonathan had intended to agree with her further, but at this juncture his father entered the room. Did Father intend to interrupt all morning discussions between him and Miss Tilney henceforth? If so, they would have to find another place and time to meet.

As it turned out, his father had come for quite another purpose. "Your mother arrives," he said. "Her concern for us and for Lady Catherine will not allow her to stay away. I thought to write and discourage her coming . . ."

"But that would not work," Jonathan said. "Where my mother is determined, she will not be gainsaid."

Father sighed. "I have succeeded in diverting her path once or twice—but no more."

Miss Tilney very civilly said, "I shall be delighted to see Mrs. Darcy again. It was such a pleasure making her acquaintance at Donwell Abbey last year."

Father looked as though he would like to respond to this but was uncertain how. The moment passed, though, for Jonathan realized what must happen next. "We need to inform Lady Catherine at once," he said, turning to Miss Tilney to add, "Her ladyship can be very ungenerous toward my mother, the reasons for which you have already learned."

"So you wish to tell Lady Catherine sooner rather than later," Miss Tilney ventured, "in order that her initial wrath will have subsided before Mrs. Darcy's arrival?"

Jonathan could not help smiling. "You see things very clearly, Miss Tilney."

The three of them took themselves to the sitting room, where Lady Catherine had settled herself. Yet she was not prepared to be attended upon, for she turned to see the trio and frowned. "What is this? It does not appear that you have all happened to find yourselves here. No, you have a purpose, do you not?"

"Indeed, madam." Father had readied himself for this next. "I must inform you that—"

Glass shattered. Lady Catherine seemed to toss her head—light shone through—china trinkets on shelves on the fall wall broke and clattered in shards to the floor. At first Jonathan could no more than blink in astonishment. Then he saw Lady Catherine lifting her hands to her head, which, for the first time in many years, was devoid of both mobcap and wig. Said accoutrements were pinned to the far wall by an arrow, its shaft still quivering.

"Someone has tried again to kill Lady Catherine!" Miss Tilney hurried forward with a blanket, which she draped over Lady Catherine as a kind of shawl, all the while draw-

ing her ladyship down and staring at the window—with its
newly ripped curtain, through which weak sunlight shone.
Jonathan ran to pull back the curtain, but nothing there was
to be seen upon the lawn except an abandoned bow, lying in
the grass where its assailant had left it, with no clues as to who
that person might be.

Chapter Sixteen

This latest attempt on Lady Catherine's life created an uproar that surpassed any that had come before. Both the Darcys rushed downstairs in hopes of locating the offender, but no sign could be found save the abandoned bow and the door of the gun room (where the archery equipment also was kept) that had been left ajar. Jonathan noted that the gun room had apparently been broken into when the rifle was taken, but this time, a key must have been obtained (or if the key had been used before—and the marks made on the door had been intended only to suggest its absence—no similar subterfuge had been used on this occasion).

They returned some minutes afterward, bringing with them Anne Fitzwilliam; she had apparently been out of doors, and had a gardening basket still on one arm. "Did you see anyone at all?" Miss Tilney asked as she remained by Lady Catherine's side. "Or hear anyone as you did your gardening?"

"No," said Anne. She showed very little shock in the matter, though Jonathan could not tell whether this was due to the sheer number of unsuccessful attempts on Lady Catherine's life by this time, or whether her lack of astonishment sprang from more sinister sources. "I was quite alone there, which it appears is precisely as my mother would wish me to be."

"Have you any idea what that bonnet cost?" Lady Catherine had drawn the shawl over her head like a medieval

Madonna. "It was among my finest! And now it is ruined, ruined entirely."

"Lady Catherine," said Miss Tilney, "you might have lost much worse than a bonnet."

"Do not think to scold me! You forget your place, young lady."

Jonathan knew that Miss Tilney had spoken, not to upbraid Lady Catherine but to make her fully comprehend the danger she was in, a realization that seemed far too slow in coming. Yet he believed the comment to be unnecessary, for despite all her ladyship's protests, her gaze had become fixed and her face exceedingly pale. Fear had finally found Lady Catherine; she simply refused to acknowledge it.

"It seems impossible," Jonathan said, "that anyone should attempt to shoot Lady Catherine with an arrow through closed curtains—and even more so, that the arrow should come so close to its target!"

Miss Tilney answered, "I have been thinking on precisely this point, Mr. Darcy. Then I realized—the attempt with the rifle shot broke a pane of glass newly replaced. All the assailant would need to do is aim at that exact same pane, which could be distinguished from the others by a sharp eye."

"I believe you have put your finger upon it, Miss Tilney." Jonathan had previously noted the new pane, which in itself looked very like the others—but the damaged mullion surrounding that pane had been repaired and repainted. That white paint, still lacking the mellowness of age, gleamed a shade brighter than those around it. Never had he considered that this could serve as a target to a determined murderer. "There can be no other explanation."

Anne sat on the other side of her mother, as she must have felt obliged to do, but she offered not even the comfort Miss Tilney did. Instead, she stared down at her basket, which held both shears and new-cut roses. Was it possible to have carefully chosen flowers for cutting, paused, tried to kill one's own mother, then gone back to gardening? Jonathan believed Anne would have had time enough, but he could scarce believe his cousin so cold-blooded.

And yet—if Anne believed it to be Lady Catherine's fault that Colonel Fitzwilliam was leaving—

"We should inform the local constables," Father said. "This is too much, Lady Catherine. The law must be involved."

"Nay, I will not have it!" Her ladyship's anger had returned along with her hauteur. "To have all Hunsford aware of our shame? No, it shall not be endured."

Jonathan realized that no one had yet informed Lady Catherine of his mother's imminent arrival—and, further, that it would be highly unwise to do so until his aunt had regained some semblance of calm.

Yet I am not sure calm will arrive, he thought, *before Mother does.*

And there will be little chance of calm after that!

Charlotte Collins waited near the gate to Rosings Park impatiently. What could be taking her husband so long?

She had had many frustrations with William Collins through the years of their marriage—more than many wives have with their husbands, but, it must be said, fewer than many wives would have had with *this* husband. They had no great concordance of opinion and belief, though Charlotte conversed with her husband so skillfully that he remained unaware of this. (Her contrivances would not have deceived a man sincerely interested in learning his wife's thoughts, but to Mr. Collins, no surer sign of harmony could exist than verbal agreement, which was given in precisely the quantity he desired.) However, Hunsford Parsonage was a comfortable home; their situation was a respectable one; and in the full-ness of time, they could expect to inherit Longbourn, which would allow Charlotte to live the rest of her life within an easy walk from her beloved family. All this had been deliv-ered unto Charlotte at a time in life when such things seemed to have eluded her forever, and so she felt all the good fortune of it.

Her determination to make the best of all things had served her well when Mr. Collins had begun to express cer-tain . . . discontent some months prior. This discontent, she shared and had in fact been enduring for many months, so she was only too happy to discuss with her husband the ways in which they might be able to remedy their situation. He had been difficult to persuade, but Charlotte spoke so tactfully, so carefully, that he was well on his way before he even knew he had begun. Only at moments such as this—when he was taking so very long!—did Charlotte wonder whether they had chosen the correct path.

However, he did hurry toward her at last, sweaty from the exertion. "Forgive me, my dear," he said. Among Mr. Collins's many illusions was that his wife adored him; she liked him well enough not to disabuse him of that notion. "Let us make haste." Together they proceeded to Rosings Park, when they were shown in and promptly told of another attempt on Lady Catherine's life.

"It is most grievous," Charlotte said to the company, "but I cannot call it shocking, for whoever wishes harm to Lady Catherine has shown great determination."

She would have felt this sufficient, but Mr. Collins could not resist adding greater sympathies. "The base inhumanity of it! One's mind struggles to comprehend the depravity that must lie behind such actions!" *Too much,* thought Charlotte, *it is too much!* She thought this often.

"What brought the two of you here this morning?" asked Juliet Tilney, all politeness . . . or so it seemed. Was the girl considering the short duration of time that had passed between the arrow's flight toward Lady Catherine's head and the arrival of the Collinses? As Charlotte made a polite, meaningless reply about neighbors, she realized she had been wrong to wish her husband faster. Better that he had walked more slowly.

The commotion and clamor meant that Juliet could find no moment to speak with the younger Mr. Darcy alone until the early afternoon, when Lady Catherine went to take her nap. (Given the circumstances, Juliet suspected it more likely that Lady Catherine would simply spend a few hours lulled to unnatural calm by laudanum-laced wine—which, for the time being, she was proudly mixing herself and thus avoiding any future risk of poison—but who could begrudge her ladyship even this respite from terror?) Where her father or Mr. Darcy was, she was not certain, but she found the Darcy she sought in the sitting room. After a moment's consideration, Juliet not only joined him there but sat in Lady Catherine's own throne-like chair. He raised his eyebrow in inquiry. She said, "I mean no disrespect to your great-aunt, Mr. Darcy. My only wish was to learn how it felt."

"I admit, I have had some curiosity on that point myself over the years," he replied. "How is it?"

"Not entirely comfortable. A pity, given how much time she spends in it." Juliet shook her head in dismay. "Yet another attempt! We are failing utterly in our object, Mr. Darcy."

"The guilty person is failing in their object as well; it is greatly to my great-aunt's benefit that this unknown person's ingenuity is apparently unmatched by skill. Yet that ingenuity is successfully hampering our investigation. We have learned much about the hidden currents of feeling within and around Rosings Park, but the attempts are coming so quickly—and so variously—that we scarce have time to examine the one before the next occurs."

Juliet felt a small quail of despair, but she refused to give way to it. "Very well," she said with firmness, "we must take what encouragement we can from the fact that, where our would-be killer strikes, more evidence must be left. It is up to us to find it."

Mr. Darcy very nearly smiled. Not since the dinner party the day before had Juliet seen him more like his usual self. How good it was to see! How grateful she was for their restored congeniality! He said, "We can at least absolve Colonel Fitzwilliam, as he left Rosings Park this morning not long after dawn."

"We cannot absolve him until we know where he went. The colonel could have declared himself to be going, ridden his horse some measure away, then taken care not to be seen as he returned and fetched the bow and arrow."

"The bow and arrow, I would argue, firmly establish that this was not the work of Colonel Fitzwilliam," insisted the younger Mr. Darcy. "Why would a military man, proficient with firearms, reduce himself to using a bow and arrow—weapons with which he is not especially adept?"

Juliet saw the good sense of this immediately. "The archery equipment is kept in the gun room, so he could as easily have taken a rifle as arrow and bow. And yet—perhaps this is a scheme to disguise his involvement? Though I suppose that is overly fanciful."

Mr. Darcy said, "The colonel appears to have no great skill at archery. You outshot him handily—for he had not one bull's-eye, did he?"

This remark caught Juliet by surprise, for she had believed Jonathan Darcy not to be attending to her on that day. Yet he had been watching her after all. A blush marked her cheeks as she thought, for the first time, that he might pay her more attention—an attention of a particular sort—than she had previously reckoned.

To disguise her momentary discomfiture, Juliet averted her gaze to instead look at the evidence of the morning's assault. Lady Catherine's cap and wig remained affixed to the wall by the arrow. It was to her ladyship's benefit that she had clung to the fashions of her youth, which piled the hair high atop the head. Juliet winced to look at the pinned things—but that was not the only reason her head was beginning to hurt.

Horse's hooves on the gravel path alerted them both to an arrival at Rosings. Juliet and Mr. Darcy moved as one to the hallway, where from a window they would be able to see who it was that approached. As she had hoped, it was Colonel Fitzwilliam; so far as could be observed from this distance, he seemed subdued—as certainly he had reason enough to be. "If we are to redouble our investigatory efforts, Mr. Darcy," said she, "we should do so immediately."

"We are in accord, Miss Tilney. Allow me to lead the way."

Quickly as they acted, they were not the first to encounter Colonel Fitzwilliam at the door; this honor fell to McQuarrie, who had evidently just delivered the news in the moment before Juliet and Mr. Darcy entered the front hall. "Again?" Fitzwilliam exclaimed. "Again, another attempt upon Lady Catherine—and this with a bow and arrow? They hunt her as though she were a creature of the wood!"

"It is indeed barbaric," Mr. Darcy said. "It appears this person will stop at nothing until Lady Catherine has been killed."

Juliet shook her head. "I would not call it 'barbaric,' but 'desperate.' There is no *logical* pattern that explains the methods used against Lady Catherine at every turn. Although some element of planning has to have been at work, I believe the person responsible is seizing whatever methods of inflicting harm can be obtained."

Vitally important though this discussion was, Fitzwilliam's thoughts must have been elsewhere, for he said, "What of Anne? Where was Anne, when this took place? Was she harmed?"

"In the flower garden . . . we think," said Mr. Darcy, giving Juliet a look of much significance. "She came to her mother shortly thereafter, but Lady Catherine is now taking her afternoon rest."

Colonel Fitzwilliam looked upstairs, as though debating going to his wife's room, her likeliest location. Yet he then turned and walked toward his study, saying absentmindedly as he went, "Thank you for informing me. Good afternoon."

Once the study door had closed, Mr. Darcy said, "His reaction suggests that he played no role in this attempt. Though I suppose it is possible he pretended at surprise for our benefit."

"Yes, pretense might have been at work," replied Juliet, "but we nonetheless learned much."

"Much? Of what do you refer?"

Juliet blushed somewhat to speak of it—it was such an intimate subject on which to speak—but much that was private had been aired within Rosings Park often enough during the past several days, and no doubt more was to come. "The very first question the colonel had after learning of an act of violence in this house was about his wife. His demeanor, the manner in which he spoke—he was *frightened* for her. Why should he pretend at that? I can think of no reason, so I presume that his fear was quite genuine. Colonel Fitzwilliam may have formed a plan to move away from Rosings Park, perhaps even away from his wife, but . . . despite all this, I believe that he loves her."

Henry Tilney might have been the person at Rosings least immediately affected by the various perils of Lady Catherine, for he bore neither familial sentiment nor any especial share of the danger. Yet none could be present for such events without deepening dismay. For this reason he wished an audience alone with his daughter—but this took some time in coming, as she was much engaged in examining the gun room and archery equipment, walking the lawn to determine the likeliest position of the person who had let fly the arrow, and hurrying back and forth between that location and others about the house and grounds. Accompanying her throughout these endeavors was the younger Mr. Darcy, whose animation appeared to have fully returned. What sort of young man was it who found conversing and dining in company to be disagreeable, yet enjoyed himself thoroughly when presented with such a diabolical act? Not the sort Mr. Tilney would wish to marry his daughter.

(In this reasoning, Tilney ignored his daughter's own enthusiastic participation in the activity. Juliet he could look upon as a father, replete with memories of her childhood playfulness that allowed him to consider her in a more generous light than he could one not already beloved. A broader view of any individual invites more generous interpretation, just as a narrow acquaintance, or none, may lead more quickly to condemnation. It must be the reader's to determine which prejudice induces the greater misunderstanding.)

While observing all this, Mr. Tilney once spied the elder Mr. Darcy standing in the rear of the house, watching the young persons together in much the same way. He comprehended that this gentleman's view of the potential match was as negative as his own. Common feeling might have been the foundation of some manner of alliance between the two, but instead Tilney disliked Darcy the more for it. The insult to his daughter's eligibility and character was all too plain, and each father laid the scandal of their investigations at the feet of the other's child. Yet another element played upon Tilney's feelings, one he was loath to admit even within himself: the knowledge that he could not be sure of providing Juliet with the dowry and society she deserved.

Tilney's family, though not so wealthy as the Darcys, nor as advantageously situated, was prosperous—even illustrious, thanks to General Tilney's rank. However, Henry Tilney was the second son. He had not inherited richly from his late mother, and could expect even less from his father. Both the law of primogeniture and General Tilney's own preference decreed that Mr. Tilney's elder brother, Frederick, should acquire all. To what extent the general had ever concerned himself with his younger son's welfare, he had felt that Henry could make his own fortune by marrying well. When instead Catherine Morland, of little dowry, had been chosen, General Tilney had resolved that Henry should reap as he had sown.

Never had Henry Tilney been inclined to regret his choice for his own sake; he was a clergyman whose tastes were as modest as his needs, the living in the parish of Woodston provided such means as were necessary, and his union with Catherine remained an exceptionally happy one. Yet as both his daughters and his son grew older—with Juliet now of marriageable age—he was considering anew the consequences of his decision upon his offspring. What if Juliet was unable to make a match that would support her in even the humbler means to which she was accustomed? When Tilney was in darker temper, he considered that her greatest hope lay in her grandfather's pride; General Tilney might yet be persuaded to enlarge her dowry in order to encourage a more advantageous marriage. However, the general's generosity was a scarce and changeable resource, uncertain in timing and depth. He could not be relied upon until the promise was made—possibly not even until the money had been paid, and vows spoken at the altar.

Catherine was more sanguine about Juliet's prospects, saying that grace and good sense were worth as much to a wise man as any number of pounds might be. Henry Tilney could not forget that grace and good sense did not purchase houses, furnish carriages, or support the next generation. No bachelor of means would forget that, either.

Jonathan Darcy as a suitor would have put an end to all cares. Juliet would have been united to one of the most prosperous families in the realm; she would in the fullness of time become mistress of no less an estate than Pemberley. General Tilney's satisfaction at such a match would have been boundless, hearty enough to ensure that some provision would be made for Theodosia and Albion in turn. Most important of all—despite all her protestations, Mr. Tilney knew his daughter to be very fond of Jonathan Darcy, and no father could wish better for his daughter than a match that offered both wealth and love. And the young Mr. Darcy clearly appreciated Juliet—but not as a potential wife. Why? Whatever could the young man be wishing for?

The answers seemed clear: money and family connections.

After nearly two weeks' acquaintance with Jonathan Darcy, Mr. Tilney suspected that any such inclinations were not the work of the young man himself (who seemed guileless), but of his father. To desire more fortune than Pemberley could be naught but avarice.

Rest assured that Henry Tilney was generally not so severe a judge, particularly on so little evidence! But where our children's fortunes and hearts are at stake, the worst is brought out in even the best of us.

Juliet, along with the young Mr. Darcy, had run from the garden to every other spot imaginable, then back again, only to surmise that anyone on the lower floors of Rosings Park, or upon its grounds, would have had time to retrieve the bow and arrow swiftly from the gun room, then time again to hide themselves in haste and create the illusion of having been elsewhere. She was much relieved when Mr. Darcy suggested assembling some chairs in the flower garden, that they might speak to several people in turn. First came poor Mr. Daniels, whose gun room had now been robbed twice over, rendering him in a grievous state.

"It appears very much as though, this time, the attacker possessed the key to the gun room," said Mr. Darcy. "No one had asked for that room to be opened?"

"No, sir, indeed they did not," insisted Daniels. "No one had spoken to me of the gun room all day, nor the day before, either, and I went in especial last night to judge whether I ought to purchase more powder. Mr. Guinness is to visit us soon, you see, and he likes to go shooting with the colonel when he comes. I had to unlock the gun room to enter, and certain am I that it was locked again as I left!"

"Did you speak to any of the residents of the house in that

span of time?" Juliet asked. Any inquiry, however, general, might have been an effort to determine Daniels's comings or goings.

"Briefly I spoke to Mrs. Fitzwilliam, but only in passing, for she visited this garden in the morning, even before she took breakfast, I believe. What passed between us was no more than a pleasantry, you might say, miss. Oftentimes when she does her gardening, Mrs. Jenkinson is with her, but this morning, Mrs. Fitzwilliam was on her own."

Juliet exchanged glances with Mr. Darcy, who appeared to hold her gaze for an unusually long time—for any person, but most particularly for him. Whatever did he mean by it? Regardless, she could tell that he, too, found it significant that Anne Fitzwilliam had been in that place at that time. That he further had seen the question this begged: Why had she gone alone that day, without her trusted servant? Then to consider Anne's lack of sympathy for her mother afterward . . .

"Daniels, you mentioned having seen the Collins children near the gun room around the time of the shooting incident," said Mr. Darcy. "Were they anywhere near the house today? Mr. and Mrs. Collins arrived very soon after this morning's event."

"No, sir, I saw neither hide nor hair of the Collinses," Daniels said. "Mr. Collins has gone shooting a few times with the colonel, so he would know where the gun room is to be found, but I doubt Mrs. Collins could find that place were her very life depending on it."

What little evidence they had regarding this incident thus far pointed strongly toward Anne—more so than any other attempt had indicated any one suspect. Yet could such a fragile creature truly be responsible for such a heinous act? And Anne had been suffering under such a strain since the revelation of Colonel Fitzwilliam's plans.

Then it occurred to Juliet with a start that the colonel's

wish to leave could be seen in quite another light. What if he were not an unloving husband abandoning a helpless woman— instead, a husband who had realized his wife was not at all the person he had believed her to be?

One capable of murder?

Chapter Seventeen

Some would question how much longer Lady Catherine could continue to defy the danger in her path. Long after most would have given way to petrification with terror, she had sallied forth—not oblivious to the trouble but treating it less as a threat to her very life and more as an impertinence that continued to plague her. However, this fifth attempt to kill her had come closer than any other, the arrow within mere inches of penetrating not her wig but her head. Would her courage be shaken at last?

"Perish the thought!" Lady Catherine declared that afternoon, when her elder nephew Darcy suggested that she might wish to return to her room and have her meal brought in on a tray. She defied the evidence of her own quavering voice and, by implication, demanded that he ignore any sign of fear. "It is not for *me* to quail and shiver and tremble—no, it is for the blackguard responsible, who shall be given reason enough to tremble when all is known, I assure you!"

"This I do not doubt," said Darcy. "I mean only that you should preserve your strength until such time as we have come to more resolution of the matter."

Lady Catherine's eyebrows, already raised, climbed near to her wig (which, thanks to the ministrations of the clever Daisy, showed no sign of its wound). "And how much time will that be? Young Jonathan and that Miss Tilney ask many questions but have as yet obtained no answers. The delay is most inappropriate."

Darcy, not a man easily baited, could not resist asking, "What, madam, would you consider an appropriate delay to be?"

"None at all, of course! Though I suppose the recent upsets are responsible for some measure of that. Fitzwilliam does not dare show his face this afternoon, I understand."

Mr. Darcy believed that his cousin had sequestered himself in his study, but he did not wish to speak upon that subject, as it would further excite Lady Catherine's irritation—and at this juncture, he had need to give her ladyship news she would not like. At least this blow would, for a brief time, supersede all others; the distraction would serve her ladyship well, loath though she would be ever to admit it. "I received a letter from my wife yesterday. Her concern for you has persuaded her that she must be with the family at this time. She will leave her sister in Tunbridge Wells to join us at Rosings the day after tomorrow."

"Concern for me, is it? Elizabeth was not so animated by this concern to accompany her husband and son in the first place."

There was the extra element of Elizabeth's concern on Miss Tilney's behalf, but this was not a point Darcy intended to raise with his aunt. "Since your letter summoning Jonathan, there have been two further attempts upon your life, madam. The concern of all is greatly heightened."

"Is there no end to my burdens?" Lady Catherine asked the skies. "Very well, let her come if she will, but I will have much to say to her about her son and the slowness of his investigation!"

Darcy suspected Elizabeth would not lack for any response . . . but that, he would leave to his wife.

∽

Colonel Fitzwilliam had indeed sequestered himself in his study, but only while he considered carefully what he had to say, and how it best should be said. He had reached his resolve too close to the hour of dining, but the colonel decided he could not wait until the meal had ended. Delay had already taken its toll; he would give it no more. Thus he went upstairs and rapped upon his wife's bedroom door. "Anne?" Fitzwilliam said, pitching his voice that so she would certainly hear, while Lady Catherine downstairs certainly would not. "Anne, it is I. We must speak. Please let me in." The adjoining door between their bedrooms was never locked; he could have entered there had he wished, and was determined to do so if Anne would not respond. But how much it would mean to him if she would but consent to open the door!

This she did. Anne stood before him, so silent and pale that Fitzwilliam could scarce believe she remained standing. She said only, "You are going? You have come to tell me farewell?"

"Why should you think so?"

"How could I not?"

Fitzwilliam had to admit the justice of this. "Please, let me come in. If, after we speak, you wish me to depart—whether that be your chamber, Rosings, Hunsford, or even England— that I will do."

"England?" The corner of her mouth curved, a weak imitation of a smile. "You are willing to be transported to Australia, then. Penitent indeed." But she stepped aside to allow him entrance.

He took the chair nearest her favored window seat, to which she obligingly returned. A memory came to him then with sudden clarity. "I recall speaking with you here shortly before Peter came to us. You sensed your time was near. Do you remember, how we could not agree on a name for a daughter?"

"I said Mama would countenance nothing other than Catherine. You said I should choose a name that I wished for myself, nothing less. Then Peter settled the question with his appearance."

"Tell me, Anne—did you ever choose a girl's name? Even if you never meant to breathe a word of it to me or to any other soul?"

She studied him for a long moment, then whispered, "Leah."

Fitzwilliam felt an ache for this daughter who would never be. "That is a beautiful name indeed."

"Why do you ask me this now? What meaning can it possibly have? Were we ever to have been blessed with another child, it would have been long ago, and as things are—" Anne's voice quivered, and she fell silent once more.

How much courage it took, to reach out and clasp the hand of she who had been his wife these many years! Fitzwilliam squeezed her fingers between his as he said, "I spoke the truth earlier. Yes, I wished—I still wish—to leave Rosings Park, to take another house. But I always hoped that you would come with me, and that the two of us would make a home together there, with Peter."

"You know Mama would never allow it."

"She cannot stop us! We are free adult persons. Let her disapprove as she may—let her disinherit us, even Peter if she be so cold—but she cannot prevent us going, Anne." Fitzwilliam had researched their accounts many times, which allowed him to make the next statement: "Although your mother controls most of the family wealth, some sums were settled upon me outright upon our marriage. You have your private inheritance from your grandmother in trust, which would sustain you in the absence of Lady Catherine's support. We might not live so ornately as we do here, but we could have a very comfortable situation. And we would be *free*, Anne. We could make our own decisions. Live as we see best. Do you not wish to escape her rule?"

"But—Mama means well—"

"I know that she does," Fitzwilliam said. "Her love for you is plain. Never have I doubted that all her strictures and lectures are, at the heart, intended to help. Yet they do not help. They confine you, and me with you. I believed I could endure it forever, that these were the terms on which we wed; all these years I have borne it, and were it my welfare alone at stake, I could bear it longer still. But then—when she insisted that we send Peter away—"

Anne made a small sound in her throat; Fitzwilliam knew the mere mention of Peter had nearly brought her to tears.

"I realized I could not endure my son's absence, not when I know he would be happier and better educated *with us*. It is the same for you, is it not, Anne? Do not you share my convictions, my concern for our son?"

"Yes, yes, of course I do." Anne wiped her cheek with her kerchief. It scarcely fluttered; Lady Catherine decreed a great deal of starch in the linens. "Why have you not spoken to me of this before?"

"I wished to be sure that I could find a house we would like, within such means as we would have alone. Bath struck me as the properest place—you could take the waters often, for your health, and it is not so far that we could not be able to visit your mother, and she us." He took a deep breath. "If, of course, we part on terms that would allow for visits, but I believe that will come in time." His belief was not rooted in the malleability of Lady Catherine's principles, for of this quality there was none. Rather, Fitzwilliam relied upon the fact that her ladyship would soon feel the emptiness of life with neither child nor grandchild. Love would do what rational persuasion could not, and change the conviction of Lady Catherine de Bourgh.

Anne considered his words many moments before she said, "Yes, those are among your reasons, and they are all good ones. But they are not the whole truth, are they?"

The bell rang. Fitzwilliam groaned even as Jenkinson, exactly on her daily cue, rapped on Anne's door. "Time for dinner, Mrs. Fitzwilliam!"

Husband and wife looked at each other in mutual chagrin. To delay responding to the summons to dine would be to bring Lady Catherine to them within moments, demanding to know their purpose in deviating from the set pattern of the day. This instant encapsulated all that was entailed within living under Lady Catherine's authority.

Dinner at Rosings Park that night was a most awkward affair. Juliet, inwardly taking measure of all at table, knew the first and foremost reason for this: all the suspects in the attacks on Lady Catherine were seated in the same room, every single person aware than one among them must be responsible for a great evil. Yet other hidden sentiments demanded recognition. She particularly noted that Anne and Colonel Fitzwilliam—who had, for the past several days, been exceedingly cold with each other—now showed small signs of mutual warmth. (It is possible, of course, to ascribe too much meaning to such dinnertime incidents as passing the salt cellar, but as Juliet had noted the lack of such interactions before, she noted their presence as well.)

The Collins family had returned to Lady Catherine's table; and as usual, Mr. Collins gave every indication that nothing on earth could have pleased him more. "Partridges!" he exclaimed, well after the birds' presence on the table had been made known to all. "What a delicacy you have presented to us—rest assured, Lady Catherine, that we feel all the honor of it."

Mr. Tilney murmured to his daughter, "I doubt any of us felt it as acutely as the partridges did." Juliet bit her lip so as not to smile, returning her attention to the Collinses.

"Yes, yes, it is most delicious, most refined," Mr. Collins kept on, reinforcing Juliet's belief that some measure of his enthusiasm must be feigned; surely no human possessing any sense of dignity could so prostrate himself over such commonplace courtesies as Lady Catherine offered. "I do not know when we have had a finer repast! . . . save of course, the elegant dinner your ladyship so recently hosted for us all, which shall forever linger—"

"De Bourgh," said Lady Catherine, "why do you stare so?"

Deb's attention was, in fact, very fixed on the table. Slowly he said, "We have had this meal before, have we not? All of us seated together, with partridges?"

The younger Mr. Darcy, who had a fine memory for such details, shook his head. "Not since the Tilneys' arrival, I am sure. Partridges appear but rarely at table here."

"Or anywhere, when the gentleman of the house goes shooting so rarely as ours does," said Lady Catherine. This jab, blatant though it was, did not affect Colonel Fitzwilliam one jot. He was watching his wife as though studying her every action.

Similarly attentive was Katy Collins to her brother. Her nervousness was disguised well enough for most of those at table, but Juliet's careful watch over all had shown her Katy's sudden trembling. "You are thinking of some other occasion, Deb. I am sure of it." Deb nodded, but absently, not truly attending his sister's words.

Mr. Collins could not repress his delight in the evening any longer. "And what delight, to be here on such a pleasant evening, after so much infernal weather. Do not you think so, my dear Charlotte?"

"Fair is always more welcome than foul," said Charlotte, but she stared at Deb as fixedly as her daughter did. Juliet could not be similarly attentive to him without drawing notice, but she could no longer doubt that it was Deb around whom the family's fears circled, Deb whom they . . .

"Distrusted," Juliet whispered to the younger Mr. Darcy once the meal was over; the gentlemen and ladies would soon separate, so their conference had to be held swiftly and immediately. Not everyone was staying for the after-dinner pleasantries; Katy and Deb were being sent home with a servant. Given Deb's youth, this was no remarkable action, but in the light of what Juliet had observed earlier, she could not help but infer deliberate meaning. "They distrust Deb in some way. But why should they do so?"

Mr. Darcy considered this. "I have noticed their behavior regarding Deb in the past, but their *wariness* of him has never been so pointed as it is at present."

"Tomorrow, perhaps, we can find opportunity at breakfast to review our list of suspects, their opportunities to strike, and see whether we can make more progress."

"I agree that we should do so at the next opportunity," Mr. Darcy said, "but that will not be tomorrow morning. You see, I have told my aunt that I wish to have one of our horses reshod, as I know from experience that she thinks very highly of a blacksmith in Faxton. As I anticipated, Lady Catherine suggested that I should go there with the horse, and I am doing as she recommends."

"That was most ingenious," said Juliet. His answering smile—oh, he seemed like himself again, like himself *with her*, and she was so glad of it! "You can speak to the agent and find out whether there is more to Fitzwilliam's story than he is telling."

Mr. Darcy said, "I believe there is more to learn, besides."

"Yes, the village of Faxton has been noted by too many persons, at too many moments, for this to be merely coincidence. Our minds are much in concord, Mr. Darcy."

How he looked at her then! Juliet felt a treacherous but irresistible hope as Mr. Darcy replied, "I believe that they are, Miss Tilney."

Anne bore the dinner as best she could, which was not very well. *Only Mama would insist upon fulfilling every proper element of an evening on the same day upon which she was nearly murdered*, she thought, waving away Jenkinson's third offer of a glass of Madeira. In the next room, as the men smoked cigars and took port, Colonel Fitzwilliam must be as anxious as she to continue their conversation.

She had reflected upon his words throughout dinner, over and over. What had seemed impossible to her at first—that all his actions had been intended to bring about a change not for *him*, but for *them*—became more credible upon further consideration. This was more in keeping with his character, was it not? He had invited her to join his plan to leave Rosings Park forever, as he had apparently wished all along.

Fearsome thought! Anne had been told since her infancy that she could not survive in the harsh world beyond Hunsford, that her mother's constant vigilance was necessary to ensure that her delicate health did not collapse. She had so little experience of life outside Rosings. From this, was she to establish an entirely new household, furnish and equip it, hire and supervise an entirely new staff of servants—well, perhaps she could bring Daisy and—?

It would kill Mama, Anne thought. *It would strike her dead, a surer weapon than rifle or arrow.*

When her fevered imagination would allow her to pretend interest in the women's chat no longer, Anne feigned a headache so that Jenkinson would be allowed to escort her to her bedroom. There she submitted to being undressed, but as soon as her maid had left her tucked in, the covers were thrown off and her oil lamp turned back to full brightness. She knew not how long Fitzwilliam would remain occupied with the men, but she trusted that he, too, meant to excuse himself as soon as possible. Her trust was rewarded, for it was not half an hour more when the soft rap came at the door that joined their bedrooms.

"They said you were unwell," he said, taking her hand as they sank down together on the window seat. "I suspected it might be only a pretext, but if I am wrong—"

"No, I am well." Anne feared the conversation to come, for upon it the whole of her future, her entire happiness, would rely. Yet the moment had arrived for her to open her heart fully to her husband, and to endure what she learned thereby. "I must ask *why* you wish me to come to Bath."

"You are my wife. You are Peter's mother. We are a family, are we not?"

"That can mean everything or nothing. I have always been aware of why you asked to marry me. Then, we each thought it enough that you should feel pity and I gratitude. After Peter came, though—we were so much more in each other's company, and we shared such delight in him—"

"Yes," said Fitzwilliam softly. "Peter's coming changed much. I learned more of your tenderness, your insight, your devotion."

Anne wanted to cry out, *Why did you never speak of it before?* But she knew the answer; it was the same reason she had never opened her heart to him. Neither had dared to dream that their marriage of convenience could become more, and so neither had been willing to risk the comfortable lie that had been the foundation of their marriage, not for a perilous truth.

Fitzwilliam continued, "The hours we have spent together as a family—these are the happiest of my life. I have come to believe that our marriage could possess some measure of this happiness as well, if your feelings are like mine."

"They are so very like yours," Anne said, near tears. "So very like, we might share one mind. I would wish this above all things."

He clasped her hand. "This shall be so, if you but say the word."

"The word, then, is yes, for if you still desire it, I will come with you to Bath."

Fitzwilliam's smile brightened the night almost to day. He kissed her hand quickly. "We can be happy there. This I strongly believe."

"We can write Peter tomorrow and let him know that he shall be at that dreadful school but a short time longer. In Bath we will certainly be able to find a good tutor for him or a good day school."

"Yes, I imagine Peter will be overjoyed indeed." Fitzwilliam's expression became somewhat graver. "As Lady Catherine is already displeased with me, I will tell her of our plans and bear the brunt of her unhappiness. Rest assured that I will make it clear that all aspects of this plan were mine alone, that you merely consented to join me to preserve our marriage."

"This is my choice, too. I will face her with you, and

together we will endure what comes." Greatly daring, Anne added, "That is what marriage means, is it not . . . Geoffrey?"

Fitzwilliam brightened at the sound of his Christian name. Anne had not spoken it since they stood at the altar. He replied, "I would very much wish for this to be another beginning for us. We began to suit our families. Many marriages do. But, yes, after Peter was born, after the three of us had become a family of our own, my feelings for you . . . they deepened, and so very much more than I had dreamed possible."

Anne had rarely felt so warm, so fluttery, so *alive*. "I had always admired you, and I was happy to wed you. But those were childish thoughts, not truths of the heart. Those truths came after Peter, and—they *are* true, for me as much as for you, my husband."

His smile contained more joy than she had seen in him since Peter was born. This must be right and proper, for that was the measure of the joy she felt as well. How beautiful it was, after so many years of marriage, to discover love.

As he had conveniently been bidden by Lady Catherine, Jonathan set out early the next morning for the village of Faxton. Though clouds grayed the sky, he judged it unlikely to rain and so went on horseback. (Again he missed his favorite horse, Ebony, who had not come from Pemberley with them due to her dislike of pulling a carriage.) He glanced at the house as he left, half expecting—no, half wishing that he might see Miss Tilney waving farewell.

That which he had dreaded most had come to pass: he had let the curtain drop. Miss Tilney had seen that he was still as he had been when last they met: peculiar, easily overwhelmed, not like other men. Yet she had not been dismayed.

She had compassionately assisted him in his moment of greatest need, after which her behavior became precisely as it had been before. It was not that Jonathan expected less of her, for she had even seen him at his thumping back and forth and accepted this rocking behavior without a qualm. His desire to present a different face to her—one that was ordinary, one that was as others would wish him to be—had not been rooted in his fear of *her* disapproval but of his own dislike of his strange habits and ways—or, rather, the dislike others showed of them. Such pride he had taken in the curtain, and it had not even lasted two weeks at Rosings Park! Jonathan would have despaired, were it not for the warmth and acceptance of Miss Tilney . . . and the fact that her warmth was more evident now than it had been before.

Was it possible, perhaps, that Mr. Bamber's death had freed her from the hold that man had held upon her heart? This seemed wrong to Jonathan, yet he could derive no better explanation. For the time being, it was enough to know that he might yet have some chance with her. All his other attentions must be devoted to the matter of Lady Catherine's would-be killer.

The journey to Faxton should not have taken very long, but the farther he traveled, the worse the roads became. All the rainstorms that had threatened Hunsford without ever breaking had, it seemed, saved their downpours for the village of Faxton and its environs. The road became damp, then muddy, then muck that the horse could barely traverse; had Jonathan taken a carriage, he would have been obliged to turn back. As it was, he and his mount made slow but steady progress. By the time they arrived in Faxton, Jonathan was both tired and hungry, though not so much so that he would forget his purpose.

I may need more time, he thought, *and the roads will not improve much on an overcast day*. Accordingly, he took a room in Faxton's one small inn and arranged the stabling of the horse overnight. As it took a well-deserved rest, Jonathan began his explorations.

Even before he could ask for assistance, he saw an office with a painted sign in front: here Jonathan might learn much about Fitzwilliam's plans. This, however, was not the first point of his curiosity. To the innkeeper he said, "Pardon me, but I wished to ask about a person I believe may have spent some time in your fair town."

The innkeeper, an obliging fellow, smiled as he replied, "Aye, sir, and who would that be?"

"A clergyman," said Jonathan, "by the name of William Collins."

Chapter Eighteen

The weather, discourteously, does not always make itself appropriate to the occasion. Many a funeral has been held amid sunshine and birdsong; many a bride and bridegroom have been soaked with torrential rain. Yet an observer could be forgiven for believing the elements most obliging on the day Elizabeth Darcy arrived at Rosings Park, seemingly having banished the clouds from the sky. Darcy very nearly believed it so himself as he stepped outside to the gravel path to greet her even before she was announced. If asked why he did so, he might have said that he found it politic to speak with his wife regarding Lady Catherine's state of mind before bringing her into the house. This was true, but his primary motive was simply that he wished to be reunited with her as soon as possible.

"An *arrow*?" Elizabeth exclaimed as he informed her of the most recent events. "Good heavens. Whoever wishes harm to Lady Catherine is vastly determined to succeed, be the means what they may."

"So it would seem," said Darcy. "Lady Catherine bears it well, all things considered, but her temper is more excitable than is her usual wont."

Elizabeth's eyes widened, but a small smile played upon her lips, reassuring him that she would prove as adept at withstanding Lady Catherine's displeasure as she had ever been.

In the entrance hall, they almost immediately encountered Mr. Tilney. No sooner had Darcy made the introduction than

Mr. Tilney had the effrontery to say, "You have come to the lion's den, madam. May you have the good fortune of Daniel."

"Daniel was saved by the angel, was he not?" Elizabeth smiled. "That office, I think, will yet again be fulfilled by your daughter, a bright and accomplished young woman. It was my good fortune to become acquainted with her in Surrey."

Tilney said, "Given what occurred in Surrey, I find it hard to call any of it 'good fortune.'" But he spoke this in evidently pleasant humor.

In that same spirit, Elizabeth replied, "I believe that the making of friends is always good fortune."

"You have the better of me, Mrs. Darcy." Tilney seemed most engaged. The impudence he had shown to Darcy himself had melted away upon first encountering Elizabeth. Darcy had seen this phenomenon at work before. "You show great bravery in coming here, given the nature of the attacks upon Lady Catherine."

"I have been accustomed to gather my courage before entering Rosings Park," said she, "so mustering a small measure more is not too great a task. Now I must greet Lady Catherine, but I am most eager to see your daughter and, of course, my son."

Darcy, grateful for a chance to regain his wife's attention, explained, "Jonathan is gone to Faxton. He departed yesterday but is expected back today."

"May he arrive soon," said Elizabeth, with only slight dismay, as was reasonable. "But please do let Miss Tilney know how eager I am for our reunion."

"I will find her for you, madam."

Mr. Tilney went on his way, leaving them alone. Once he was out of earshot, Elizabeth murmured, "He is entirely obliging, and possessed a quickness of wit. Your portrait of him was unflattering to the reality."

"You will understand soon enough," Darcy insisted, though already he wondered whether he was the one who had lacked understanding.

Juliet had no sooner heard her father's words than she hurried downstairs, eager to see Mrs. Darcy again. This was in some ways remarkable, as at their last meeting Juliet had at times suspected Elizabeth Darcy guilty of murder. In the end, however, Elizabeth had proved herself not only innocent of any crime but also possessed of a mind that was capable of seeing beyond mere habit and convention. At times even Juliet herself felt that the pursuit of murderers was not entirely ladylike, but in Elizabeth's presence, she did not have to justify every action that differed from those of other girls her age. Elizabeth was formidable in more conventional ways as well: lovely despite her years, intelligent, witty, and mistress of no less an estate as Pemberley. This last played some role in Juliet's sense of Elizabeth Darcy as a model, though of *that* part she was not wholly aware.

Little wonder then that Juliet hastened to the sitting room, and less wonder that she stopped short in astonishment as she heard Lady Catherine's voice: "Scruple to show yourself here at last? When you would not be troubled to come before?"

"I beg your pardon, Lady Catherine," replied Elizabeth in a tone that, although civil, begged no one's pardon for any action. "During my last visit, you suggested that you would prefer to spend more time with my husband and son in my absence—'only the true family,' I believe you said. My sole intent was to comply with your wishes."

"Humph!" Lady Catherine's rejection of any opposition to

her will evidently extended even to her own previous decrees. "Well, you are here, and we are to make the best of it. That son of yours has taken long enough about his task!"

"He has given me to understand that the work can be painstaking, ma'am," said Elizabeth, "for to undertake it in haste is to invite error, and the consequences are too grave for any mistake to be allowed. You look quite well under the circumstances, Lady Catherine. In your place, I am sure I should take to my rooms."

"It is not for me to quail from such petty efforts as these," Lady Catherine said. "The miscreant possesses no great skill, as is now evident. Though it is not in my moral fiber, were I to undertake to kill someone, I should succeed at the task with the first attempt!"

Elizabeth gravely answered, "That, madam, I do not doubt."

Juliet judged it an opportunity to enter the room and was rewarded with Elizabeth's smile. "Miss Tilney! Here you are at last, and how lovely you have become."

"It is so good to see you, Mrs. Darcy, even under such circumstances as these." Juliet nodded to Lady Catherine; by this time she knew well never to suggest that anyone else held preeminence in a room.

"I very much wish to hear more about Devonshire," Mrs. Darcy said, tactfully alluding to the second murder Juliet and her son had solved together, "though I am certain the subject would not agree with Lady Catherine at this time. Your ladyship will, perhaps, allow me to walk to Hunsford Parsonage to greet my dear friend Mrs. Collins—and if Miss Tilney accompanies me, we shall have time enough on the way to speak of everything."

"Go, then, and good luck to you," said Lady Catherine with a sniff. "You will be fortunate if you find them home, for they are all running wild about the countryside these days."

Though nearly twenty-five years had passed since Elizabeth's first trip to Hunsford and Rosings, and she had crossed Lady Catherine's threshold many times in that span, she could never return without remembering that—had Mr. Collins and her own mother had their way—she would have lived out her life as his wife, in the eternal shadow of Lady Catherine de Bourgh. This arrangement would have suited none of the persons most intimately involved in it; and at times Elizabeth was amused by imagining how quickly, and disastrously, both the marriage and the patronage might have dissolved. At other times, though, the thought chilled her through. That life would not have been worth the living, and Elizabeth would have had no escape from it save death.

Charlotte had accepted that which Elizabeth refused—had in fact sought it out, as Elizabeth fully understood, but the two women had never spoken of it aloud. Their friendship had continued uninterrupted, yet transformed, and not for the better. Although Charlotte's thoughts on the nature of marriage were sensible, practical, and more in line with society's attitudes toward the institution of matrimony, they were so unlike Elizabeth's as to make both women sharply aware of how different their natures truly were. Differing natures need not be a barrier to friendship, but their discovery cannot but cause harm to a friendship nurtured upon a belief in sameness.

This history was very much with Elizabeth as she walked toward Hunsford Parsonage, but her attention was more agreeably dedicated to Miss Juliet Tilney, whose freshness of spirit had but grown stronger during the year since they had last met. "I understand it is to you my family owes thanks for our latest fascination, Miss Tilney."

Juliet seemed much surprised. "What fascination might that be, Mrs. Darcy?"

"Why, the novels of Sir Walter Scott, of course! Though of course he does not fully admit the books are his—this, I suppose, must only be because poetry is respectable, while novels are still belittled by those who should know better." Elizabeth sighed at such folly. "Were I responsible for such a tale as *Ivanhoe*, I should sing the feat far and wide. My friends and relations would be quite tired of hearing it, but would that stop me? Never."

Juliet laughed. "I am entirely of your way of thinking! Though—as you know, my mother writes, and she is still expected to keep her authorship a secret. That, however, is because she is a lady. Sir Walter Scott has not that excuse."

"No, unless he is soon to astonish us all with an unexpected revelation," Elizabeth said. "Ah, here is the path. Hunsford Parsonage could scarcely be closer to Rosings Park were it built upon the grounds."

"Were that true, I believe Mr. Collins would be delighted."

By this comment, Juliet intended to elicit from Elizabeth some information that would hint at the terrible resentment, even loathing, that Mr. Collins felt toward his patroness and could only hide through groveling humility. Elizabeth did not guess this purpose, however, for she had seen Mr. Collins's singular dedication to Lady Catherine for so long that she took it as quite a part of the scenery of Hunsford and Rosings, as much as the topiaries in the garden. Thus she only replied, "I do not doubt it, Miss Tilney! I am somewhat surprised he has not asked to be installed there," and wondered that Juliet did not laugh.

When they reached Hunsford Parsonage, they came upon Charlotte in her garden, harvesting reddish-orange fuchsia blooms. Elizabeth's earlier musings about the differences between them faded instantly when she saw her old friend once more. "Charlotte! What joy to see you, grave though the circumstances are."

Charlotte never revealed such ebullience—her nature was more taciturn—but that gave her welcoming smile even more meaning. "Elizabeth. It is so good of you to come to Lady Catherine's aid during this time, despite her insistence that she needs none."

"None from me, of course! But I am with my husband again, and soon my son as well, and I have been able to renew my acquaintance with Miss Tilney. Now I am reunited with you, too. So my journey has not been in vain."

"You two will wish to talk between yourselves," Miss Tilney said, courteously excusing herself. "I shall go to Katy and Deb, if they are about."

"Yes, you will find them inside." With that, Charlotte turned back to her old friend, and they clasped hands.

"Now," Elizabeth said, "I wish to hear how you are. Tell me everything."

Charlotte kept smiling, though she thought less of that which she would reveal, more upon what she must conceal.

Hunsford Parsonage truly was a fine home, as Juliet reflected upon being shown into the house. Lady Catherine was a generous patroness indeed—this living had to be one of the most lucrative in the land—far more so than the living her own grandfather had given to her father. Juliet had only ever minded this when it came to her dowry; her stays at Northanger Abbey had taught her at an early age that grandeur could not bring happiness. But it was difficult not to feel a bit hard done by when surrounded by such extravagance.

As Juliet was shown into the morning room and announced by the housekeeper, she found Katy standing in the middle of the room, hands clasped, evidently much afraid. Deb sat in front of her staring into space—at nothing, or at everything, was impossible to say. Juliet could not have said precisely why she knew his stare unsettled her; she only knew that it did.

"Miss Tilney," Katy began. She looked from Juliet to her brother and back again, over and over. "How good to— Will you not take a turn with— If you would meet me in the garden shortly, I could—"

Deb slumped to one side and would have fallen but for his sister catching him. Juliet rushed to their side as Katy lowered him to the floor. "Deb! Oh, what is happening?"

"There can be no concealment now." Katy seemed despairing as she took her brother's hand.

As Juliet watched in astonishment, Deb began to move strangely—his limbs and neck jerking, his head turning to one side. He made strange sounds: at first odd grunts, then a shout very like the one she had heard at Hunsford Parsonage before and had, at the time, ascribed to potential harm. As he jerked and shuddered, his free hand and one of his feet thumped loudly upon the floor.

"He is ill," Juliet said. "We must fetch a physician!"

"We have spoken to so many, have tried what little remedy they have to offer, and there is nothing they can do for my brother," Katy replied. "We can but wait and hold his hand."

Deb's face had gone very red, and Juliet realized he was not breathing. This complete lack of bodily control—it was different in appearance, but similar in its extremity, to the final throes of the late Mrs. Willoughby's suffering as she died from poison. That memory and its attendant horror returned to Juliet so vividly that for a moment she could hardly have said whether she were in that house or this one.

Yet Deb's suffering demanded her presence, and Juliet did her best to think of something, anything, that might help. "Can I fetch water? A glass of wine?" Deb was young for it, but this was of course medicinal.

"No need," Katy replied. "You see? The attack is subsiding."

Indeed, Deb had resumed breathing, and his face was no longer as flushed. His jerky movements continued, but less violently and at a slower rate. Though he as yet showed no sign of knowing where he was, of Juliet's presence, or anything else; the same blank stare remained.

Katy turned her attention back to her guest, and her countenance was so stricken that Juliet could but feel for her. "Miss Tilney, you will not tell, will you? It is so very important that you do not tell!"

"I cannot swear this, for I do not know what I have seen," Juliet replied. She wished to comfort Katy and would keep any secret that did not pertain to the attacks on Lady Catherine, but she knew she must comprehend. "What has happened to Deb?"

"Nothing that does not happen often," Katy said, lowering her gaze. "You see—he has the falling sickness."

Juliet had, of course, heard of the falling sickness. It caused people to convulse repeatedly, sometimes violently, and rendered them incapable of speech or comprehension for a time. Though sometimes it killed, she had been given to understand that many persons suffered from it throughout their lives without any other effect. "This is your secret? What you have all been hiding about Deb?"

"You realized we were hiding something, then." Katy sat down upon the floor like a child, her grip on her brother's hand easing as he seemed to slip into a more peaceful sort of incomprehension. "Our parents wish for no one to know, most particularly Lady Catherine. There is no shame in having the falling sickness, or there should not be, but, to so many, it is still thought a sign of criminality and unholiness. Some even consider it the work of demons. Sometimes I think Mama and Papa are more worried about the opinions of others than they are about my brother." This last was spoken with no small amount of bitterness.

"I am sure they love Deb very much," Juliet said honestly, "and I would wager a great sum that the principal person from whom they wish this hidden is Lady Catherine—and *there* I can understand their fear of prejudice and judgment."

"Indeed, Lady Catherine would like as not have the bishop cast us all out, lest the parsonage be stained by Deb's presence." Katy's anger appeared to ebb somewhat as she looked up at Juliet. "You asked before about the day the shot was fired at Lady Catherine, why we were in the servants' part of the house, in the hallway near the gun room. What I could not tell you then was that one of Deb's attacks was coming upon him, and we had not time to return home before it struck. So I took him to a place I thought we would not be observed. That day's attack was not a terribly bad one, but had Lady Catherine witnessed it, she would have known something was very wrong."

"That is entirely understandable," said Juliet. "Did you see anyone else moving about near the gun room?"

Katy shook her head. "Though I was so worried for Deb, an entire battalion of soldiers could have marched by, and I doubt I should have noticed a thing."

Juliet wondered briefly whether Katy had seized this opportunity to use her brother's very real ailment in fashioning a story that would conceal their true purposes on the day of the shooting. Yet she could not countenance this idea for very long. Katy was too stricken, too dismayed, to be capable of any such scheming in this moment. That part, at least, was true; Deb had fallen ill at Rosings on the day of the shooting.

Though of course there was no saying whether Deb had been seized by his attack while the Collins children were on a more lethal errand . . .

Was she betraying her thoughts by pausing? Juliet quickly asked, "How often do such fits come upon him?"

"It varies. Sometimes he will go for weeks without one, maybe even months, but then at some other time he will suffer an attack every two or three days." Katy pushed back the ringlets of hair that framed her face, and Juliet glimpsed the deep weariness that both the Collins children kept hidden. This subterfuge weighed upon sister and brother both—though, of course, the greater burden was Deb's to carry. "He has been suffering very frequent fits during the past few months. Although there is no saying what will bring on an attack, I do think that he becomes more susceptible when there is much worry and discord around us. Whoever it is who has been striking at Lady Catherine has been harming my brother, too, if he but knew it."

Would either of the Collins parents persist in murderous efforts if those efforts caused harm to their child? *Perhaps,* Juliet thought, *if by removing Lady Catherine they might provide greater peace for Deb going forward. After all, their longstanding relationship with Anne Fitzwilliam suggests that they would keep the Hunsford living, does it not?* She said to Katy only, "I am so very sorry that you are caught up in this."

Katy pleaded, "Promise me you will tell no one, please. Otherwise I will be in such trouble, and word of Deb's sickness will spread."

"If you will—allow me to tell the younger Mr. Darcy. He had already noticed many signs of Deb's distress in the past, so I do not think he will be unduly shocked by the revelation. You must know how trustworthy a man he is. Most important, we are charged with finding Lady Catherine's attacker, and Mr. Darcy should know the truth of that day, near the gun room."

After a pause, Katy nodded and took Juliet's hand in true friendship. "Let it be so, then. But as regards everyone else, may all else remain concealed!"

Jonathan returned to Hunsford that afternoon. As the roads had grown muddier on the way to Faxton, on his way back they became drier and the going became easier. He had much to consider on his journey, so much so that he would have had difficulty saying whether he passed a coach on the road (which he did not) or if he had ridden within view of a local farmer's desperate chase of an escaped pig (which he did). His questions demanded answers that rational conjecture alone would not supply. Someday, perhaps, he must put those same questions to Mr. Collins, but he first wished to discuss all with Miss Tilney.

In truth, he also greatly desired the chance to present her with an important new fact in their investigations. Jonathan did not believe that Miss Tilney liked him only as a partner in sleuthing, but he nonetheless could not help wishing to impress her in this area. Besides, he found conjecturing with Miss Tilney to be most enjoyable. So it was in excellent spirits that he first spied Rosings Park upon the hill.

His mood improved yet more when, at the very moment he rode by, two figures appeared from the small copse of trees between Rosings and Hunsford Parsonage—and these two proved to be Miss Tilney and his own mother, who cried out, "Jonathan! You are returned, just in time to make me welcome."

"Of course, Mother." Jonathan hopped down from his horse to kiss her on her cheek. "Hello, Miss Tilney."

"Hello, Mr. Darcy." Was it his imagination, or was Miss Tilney near sparkling with delight to see him again? But Jonathan was not so vain as to hold to that assumption when another explanation came to him: that she, too, had made a discovery that would prove important to the investigation.

Mother glanced from Jonathan to Miss Tilney and back again, her smile playful as she said, "Dear Charlotte was harvesting flowers, and I should follow her example. Why do the two of you not walk back to Rosings? I will be but paces behind you, plucking wildflowers as I go."

Jonathan would not have thought his mother likely to be more interested in wildflowers than in conversing with him, but he took no offense—though he did wonder why Miss Tilney blushed. Regardless, he accepted the suggestion, as this gave him a chance to speak more privately to Miss Tilney.

As soon as his mother was out of earshot, Miss Tilney said, "Mr. Darcy, you can little imagine what I have learned."

"Nor you what I discovered in Faxton. Which of us shall tell first?"

"You, please," she answered, "for I believe we shall have too much to discuss after my revelation."

Jonathan grew more curious, but he replied, "We shall have much to question after I tell you that the rector of the village of Faxton has been obliged to leave town for many months. The congregation is not inconvenienced, however, as before he left, this rector hired a man as vicar, intended to serve the population morning, noon, and night."

"That is well and good," said Juliet, clearly confused. "What has it to do with our case?"

"It relates to our case because that vicar is Mr. Collins."

Chapter Nineteen

Jonathan had previously noted the manner in which a new perspective could change one's view entirely, in both the physical and metaphorical senses. Rarely, however, had the effect been as marked as it was that day, when Miss Tilney informed him of the truth of De Bourgh Collins's illness.

"The falling sickness," he repeated as the two of them walked back toward Rosings Park. He held his horse's reins in one hand, leading it forward, but in truth he hardly remembered the beast was present. Too many memories were coming back to him, newly comprehensible. "That is his secret. I cannot see why one should be ashamed of an illness, but I cannot deny that many persons think poorly of those with the falling sickness. My grandmother Bennet believes it a sign that a family is marked by bad blood." She had cited this as the reason why she purchased from one butcher in Meryton and not the other.

"It does seem unfair," Miss Tilney agreed. "It is a superstition, as I believe more people have begun to realize—but they are not yet the majority, by any means. Although I do not know if I would walk the same path as the Collins family has chosen, hiding a child's illness regardless of what dishonesty is required, I also cannot wonder at their choice."

"The items he accidentally knocks over," Jonathan said, considering. "The strange groans and shouts. The way various members of the Collins family move him into unseen locations at odd moments—all now is rational, entirely explicable."

"Even two nights ago, at dinner, do you not recall how Deb spoke of our all having eaten partridges at Lady Catherine's table together before, when we had never done so? Katy says that this is a sign that one of his attacks may be coming—this sense of 'remembering' something that has not actually occurred previously. How strange it all is! How distressing it must be for Deb, and for all the Collins family."

Jonathan could well imagine, but already he was considering another aspect of the matter entirely. "Can we say that this fact renders Deb no longer a suspect?"

"I have wondered that myself, Mr. Darcy," said Miss Tilney. "In and of itself—I think we cannot afford to accept this as a full explanation of all inconsistencies from the Collins family. Combine that with what you learned of Mr. Collins's other work in Faxton, though, and who is to say but that these two things explain all? When we return to Rosings, let us get a pen and ink and go through our suspects once more."

"An excellent notion," said Jonathan. How differently his childhood memories now appeared! "I feel keenly for Deb. He has no doubt been trained to guard his secret closely, and yet now it has been revealed. It is very distressing to be exposed as . . . as different, when the curtain falls."

Miss Tilney was too astute a listener not to interpret Jonathan's words more fully than he had intended. "Forgive my impertinence, but—I believe you speak of your own small peculiarities of temperament?"

Why had he spoken of the curtain aloud? Jonathan could not take the word back, however, so he knew he had no better choice than honesty. He nodded.

To his relief, Juliet showed no sign of astonishment or dismay as she continued, "These seem to me so very different, yet I would not presume to correct you, for you must see the matter more clearly than I do."

"I am fortunate," said Jonathan. "My family understands my habits and needs, and they have always sought to help me rather than hide me away. Still, as you know, I have not always found acceptance."

"Your wretched schoolfellows." Miss Tilney spoke with real anger, which startled Jonathan, not least because one of those same schoolfellows had been Ralph Bamber. Her tone did not hint at a broken heart, not in the slightest. She continued, "But what do you mean by 'the curtain'?"

"That is what I call it in my head—the facade of more correct behavior that I am sometimes obliged to show the world."

"I hope you will see no further need to show this to *me*," she said. "Your behavior is not so much incorrect as—as what is correct for you may not be precisely what is correct for others. Oh, dear, I am making a mess of this, am I not? I mean only to say that you have seen truer through your eyes than most do with theirs, and this is what truly matters."

With benefit of hindsight, Jonathan could see that he had always known Deb was afflicted somehow . . . but he had distrusted this knowledge, assumed that his own differences of perception were leading him astray. He was so accustomed to considering himself abnormal, less than others, that he had failed to understand that he was not the only person who deviated from the ordinary. It was new to Jonathan, this idea that his unique point of view was not invariably a difficulty— that in some circumstances, it might even be considered a strength.

Encouraged by this, by Miss Tilney's understanding words and her lack of sentimentality regarding Bamber, Jonathan dared to add, "I must confess, I have worked very hard on my curtain this past year. I had hoped that, if we were ever reunited, I might be able to show you a face more like those of other men."

Miss Tilney looked at him in open dismay. "I hope that you will not feel the need for any such 'curtain' around me. I—I like you for yourself, Mr. Darcy, precisely as you are."

Lady Catherine remained in danger, Deb was terribly ill—but the reader will perhaps forgive Jonathan for ceasing to think on such matters during this one moment of joy.

Anne had kept to her room upstairs for much of the Darcys' and Tilneys' visit; she did so on this day as well, albeit for very different reasons, and mostly far happier ones.

"I have never been to Bath," she whispered against her husband's shoulder. They sat together in her window seat again, and Fitzwilliam held her as they looked out at her garden below. "I hear it is very noisy, very busy—but very interesting as well."

"You have never been to any city at all, have you? Suffice it to say that you will find it a very great change, but perhaps a refreshing one. There are teahouses, and libraries—assemblies and concerts—and of course the waters in the baths and the Pump Room, which will do you no end of good. To me, nothing is ever so fascinating as new acquaintance, and that is difficult to come by here at Rosings. In Bath, we shall not be able to avoid it, even if we wished!"

Anne felt very shy of new people, but then, she had so little practice with them. Never had she been introduced as *herself*, rather introduced as an appendage to her mother. That, she thought, might feel very different indeed; certainly she was willing to try. "Is our new house warm?"

Fitzwilliam squeezed her in his arms and kissed her forehead. "Warm and cozy and every good thing. I chose the best we could afford on our own means, precisely so that you would be comfortable and safe. If we discover that the air of Bath does not agree with you—why, then, we will find another place. We will locate the best house for you if we must search all England to do it."

"You are being extravagant," Anne said, delighted by his open affection. "I do not think I shall need so much help as that. Today I feel as though all I should ever need to be happy and well is to have you by my side."

"Dear girl." Fitzwilliam put his fingers to her cheek, and she felt the same dizzying delight she had known at their first kiss at the altar. If only they could remain here forever, never having to leave this room! If only Mama would let them be . . .

A rap at the door startled them both; husband and wife stifled laughter at each other, behaving like a courting couple hoping not to be seen. She called out, "Who is it?"

"Mrs. Jenkinson, ma'am," came the voice from the other side of the door. "It is time for your afternoon tonic."

"Leave it outside the door, please, Jenkinson. I promise, I will take it," Anne called, adding in a whisper for her husband's benefit alone, "but not yet."

Juliet wished for one of the little slates from school that they had written on with chalk and erased in a moment. None such were to be found at Rosings Park, however, and so she and the younger Mr. Darcy were obliged to use ink and pen to write:

Opium

Elements to consider—access to the opium, a knowledge of where it was kept, some basic medicinal knowledge
Access to the upstairs that day—Mrs. Fitzwilliam, before

archery began. Colonel Fitzwilliam, perhaps after his
supposed departure from Rosings. Mrs. Collins, if she
managed to enter the house unannounced
Knowledge—All women are taught how to make basic
medicines for their families. The colonel could have learned
something of analgesics and sedatives in the army.
No access nor knowledge—Mr. Collins, Katy, Deb

Arrow

Elements to consider—access to the archery equipment, some
skill at archery, able to be on the lawn at that time
Equipment access—unknown, as the exact time the bow
and arrow were taken cannot be determined with any
certainty
Skill—Katy, Mrs. Fitzwilliam, possibly Deb
Lawn—No one can be eliminated on this basis save for the
colonel and Mrs. Collins

"Every attempt brings us more clues, and every new clue adds to the impossibility of the situation." Juliet rubbed her temple before recalling that such a gesture was hardly genteel. She and the younger Mr. Darcy sat alone in the library, the door open for propriety's sake; they could scarcely neglect that step, though for all they knew, the would-be murderer could be eavesdropping at that instant. "I am unhappier than I should be, unhappy and fretful. Mama says that is a sign that it is time for tea."

That made Mr. Darcy smile. "Were the fretful moods of the mistress used to schedule tea at Rosings, it would be available most hours of the day and night. Instead, we have another twenty-two minutes to wait."

Juliet could see that for herself on the ornate brass clock

upon the green marble mantel. How precise he was! "No amount of tea and cakes will solve this conundrum. Thus we must seek another solution."

"I, too, have considered this," Mr. Darcy said. "To me the answer seems clear."

How alike their minds were! "To me, also. It is plain that—"

They each spoke the next at the same time:

Juliet—"One of the servants is aiding the attacker."

Mr. Darcy—"Two of our suspects are working together."

They each fell silent, weighing the other's suggestion. Mr. Darcy, she could tell, had not considered the servants as likely coconspirators, but he did not reject her notion out of hand—nor she his. Both, Juliet realized, had their merits. A servant's greater access to all parts of the house, as well as the opportunity to take the back stairs unobserved by the residents and guests, would explain much. Yet if two of the suspects were cooperating, they could potentially have accomplished all. She began, "If two of our suspects are in league with each other, which two do you believe it to be?"

"I can only say who it absolutely *cannot* be," replied Mr. Darcy, "namely, Colonel Fitzwilliam and my cousin Anne. Her shock and dismay at learning of his plans to leave Rosings Park seem to me absolutely genuine, though if that is not your judgment—at times, I do not read the reactions of others so well as I should like—"

"You read these entirely as I did, Mr. Darcy. She did not know he wished to leave, a level of ignorance that seems to me wholly inconsistent with the planning of such a crime. If they had taken so vast and dangerous a step as plotting murder, they would surely be acting in greater concert. No, they are not the conspirators. But I do not know if we can excuse either one of them of potentially working with another."

Mr. Darcy must have been thinking of her own suggestion all the while, for he next said, "The servants who would seem to have the most connection with the places and persons involved in the attempts are Mrs. Jenkinson; the maid Daisy; and Daniels, who keeps the gun room."

"There are dozens more servants at Rosings," Juliet observed, somewhat daunted at the thought of investigating them all. "Should we begin with the butler?"

"McQuarrie has already made it known that he intends to retire next year, a plan that suggests he has a vision for leaving my aunt's employ that does not require her murder." Mr. Darcy then made an excellent point: "As for the others, to me it seems highly unlikely that a servant who does not regularly interact with the family would become motivated to kill, and it is the three we have named who interact with them the most. Then again, I still do not see any motive for Jenkinson, Daniels, or Daisy, either. If one is a part of this plot, then it can only be through deception—or, at least, it would have to have begun that way."

Juliet considered his words. How easy to order a servant to perform a task that might seem completely innocent, such as providing the keys to the gun room. Afterward, how frightened the servant would be! How aware of the danger! Then this hapless person would be forced to carry out future commands, lest the blame be put on them alone. "I agree, Mr. Darcy. That could have been how all began. And if indeed a servant is being coerced into assisting in these attempts, certainly the prime conspirator would choose a servant who was ever close at hand and thus would have the best opportunity. Do not you agree?"

"I do, Miss Tilney. Yes, these three servants must be considered in turn."

She dropped her voice to almost a whisper. "We shall have

to find a way to speak to them apart from anyone else in the house, so that they will feel free to be honest."

"If they do even then. But I agree—that is how we shall begin."

Elizabeth and her husband, dearly as they loved each other, had never ceased to be two very different persons. She rather thought marriage in perfect agreement would soon cease to be tranquil and begin to be dull. It would not do, of course, to err too far in the other direction, toward constant conflict; she had been raised with such an example of matrimony and knew too well how little of happiness it afforded either party. To Elizabeth's mind, she and Darcy had achieved the ideal balance of harmony and independence.

Darcy had shared with her, more than once, his deep sympathy for his cousin Anne and the irrational yet inescapable guilt he felt for not marrying her. "Consider the girl's position," he had said once, shortly after Elizabeth had become Mrs. Darcy, usurping what the family had thought might be Anne's place. "Frail, kept apart from almost all society, unable to do more than follow in Lady Catherine's wake. The De Bourgh family is long-lived; by the time Anne inherits Rosings Park, her youth will have fled, all opportunities for happiness will be lost." At the time, Elizabeth had not been as sympathetic as her new husband might have imagined. Some of this she attributed, in retrospect, to the callowness of youth; however, her severe opinion of Anne de Bourgh had been chiefly the result of that first visit to Rosings, when Elizabeth had found Anne prideful, cross, and utterly uninteresting.

As the years had progressed, however, Elizabeth's view had

tempered. Anne's behavior could be proud, but she had been taught that behavior by her mother and was never allowed to deviate from it without reprimand. She spoke little, but this was largely because Lady Catherine interrupted every attempt. The expectation of marriage with Darcy may have been no more than a foolish fancy, but it was not Anne who had conceived of it, nor she who had so insisted upon it. And who would not be cross in such circumstances?

Yet this greater generosity of spirit on Elizabeth's part did not lead to greater intimacy between herself and Anne. Although Lady Catherine had over time gained some small measure of respect for Elizabeth's formidable will, she never scrupled to praise Anne to Elizabeth, nor to denigrate Elizabeth to Anne—often, when all three were in company together. This is not conducive to mutual goodwill, no matter how unjust either praise or denigration may prove. Anne did often have the grace to seem embarrassed by her mother's impolitic comments, but any hope of truce had progressed no further.

So, as Elizabeth descended before dinner and came upon Anne at the bottom of the stairs, she anticipated no more than distant courtesy. Instead, Anne looked up at Elizabeth with a smile, one so joyful that it illuminated her plainness into something very like beauty. "Good evening, cousin," Anne said. "How happy the Darcy men must be that you are come to stay."

Even Elizabeth's quick wit required a moment to adjust to such an unexpected welcome. "Happy I hope them to be, but in truth, I believe I came first to see Miss Tilney. She is a fine young lady I should like to know more of, and *her*, I cannot be sure of seeing again very soon."

Anne laughed, deepening Elizabeth's astonishment at her relation's sudden acquisition of a sense of humor. "Yes, of course! I shall see that the two of you are not seated far apart at dinner, so that you may speak more easily. Mama will not object." Although Anne's smile faded somewhat at the mention of her mother, she still appeared to be in a state of bliss as she walked away, leaving Elizabeth in some condition of surprise.

To herself, Elizabeth murmured, "Whatever is at work here?"

The gathering for dinner that night had taken on a greater cheer than any other during Jonathan's most recent stay at Rosings, save for one person present—the hostess herself.

Jonathan noted with pleasure the happiness with which his mother and Miss Tilney were reunited, and how cordially Mother and Mr. Tilney were able to speak. His father did not join in likewise, but Jonathan hoped his mother would work the same magic upon Father she so often did, moderating his severer opinions and bolstering his kinder judgment.

However, Jonathan did not neglect his first priorities in favor of his personal happiness. Both Colonel Fitzwilliam and Anne were in excellent spirits—so much so that he might have taken them for a couple newly affianced rather than one long married. The revelation of Colonel Fitzwilliam's plans, which might have been expected to destroy whatever marital harmony existed between himself and Anne, had evidently brought them closer together instead. If one of them had had wicked plans upon Lady Catherine's life, should those plans now be considered abandoned? On the other hand, might the would-be killer have become determined afresh to conduct marital life beyond her ladyship's purview?

Lady Catherine herself stood in contrast to the overall geniality of the gathering. Uncharacteristically, she said little, and her sharp eyes seemed to study each person in turn. Her watchfulness and severity were appropriate for one whose life was imperiled, where her confidence had been so inappropriate before. At last, Jonathan thought, his aunt comprehended the true danger, and this understanding had already begun to take its toll. Moved by compassion, he went to her side and said, "Are you unwell, Lady Catherine? Would you feel better taking your meal in your room, perhaps?" He wondered whether he or his father would be expected to stand a sort of guard even in her chambers; as much as he hoped not, he would do his duty.

"Unwell? I am very well, thank you, however much *some* would wish it otherwise." Her ladyship narrowed her eyes as she studied the entire company, apparently distrustful of all present. Yet, as it happened, her suspicions had taken on a new target, one not at Rosings Park that evening. "I have been particularly considering the many comings and goings of Mr. Collins. Always, before, his attendance upon me has been all that is correct, and more besides. In the past I have been used to consider him as my most humble and devoted servant. If his current behavior is a truer reflection of his sentiments—if all before was falseness and placation—then what else may be false? What other lies has he told?"

Jonathan glanced toward Miss Tilney, hoping she would observe and hear what transpired next. Before, he had been resolved not to tell Lady Catherine that which she did not require for her own safety and peace of mind; for instance, never would she hear from his lips the malady suffered by Deb Collins. Yet where ignorance tormented her, Jonathan could not in good conscience remain silent. "I have very recently learned the true reason for Mr. Collins's many absences of late . . ."

Chapter Twenty

"Is there any sweeter promise of the goodness of our Lord than the faith we have in forgiveness for all sins?"

So spake Mr. Collins from the pulpit the next morning. Sunday had come again, as had the worshippers of Hunsford. Lady Catherine and all her party were among them. Word had traveled, via servant, from Rosings to the parsonage of the discovery of Mr. Collins's other flock in Faxton. Had there been any doubt of her ladyship's fury, this would have been dispelled by the sight of her glowering face.

On most Sundays, Mr. Collins simply revised sermons from a book, deviating from the printed text principally by adding such allusions to Lady Catherine as would prove instructive to all, and flattering to her. Today, however, aware of the trouble in which he found himself, he had chosen to put together thoughts of his own regarding the forgiveness of sins. Yet quote Ephesians and Colossians though he might, her ladyship's heated glare never once cooled.

Most passionately did Mr. Collins wish to hurry to Lady Catherine, to attempt to explain: for surely her wisdom, the greatness of her comprehension, would lead her to the truth that he had done all of this for her! But in this aim he was to be delayed—for, immediately upon finishing services in Hunsford, he was obliged to leave at once that he might do the same in Faxton! Before expiating his sin, he was called upon to compound it. Indeed, he was unable to return to Rosings Park until that night, when he came calling with his entire family, in the hopes that their presence might soften Lady Catherine's words.

In this hope he was to be disappointed. Many times had almost all present at Rosings that evening heard the full vent of Lady Catherine's ire; most had, at some point or another, been the subject of that displeasure and endured its considerable force. Yet none of them had, at any time, heard anything approaching the wrath directed that night toward Mr. Collins.

"It is not enough that I have given you one living? One fine house? Enough tithes for any person to live upon? No! Your greed, your naked avarice, has led you into duplicity and falsehood!" Lady Catherine thumped her stick upon the floor with such force that the ornaments on their shelves trembled and a small framed silhouette on the wall tilted to one side.

Mr. Collins stood in her drawing room—he had been summoned thence with no thought of dinner for anyone in either household—unable to speak a word amid her tirade. All others stood in mute testimony to the scene, both those from Rosings and from the parsonage, in equal shades of horror at being forced to witness such a dressing-down as this.

"Have you no thought of how *I* am affected by your selfishness? How those in Faxton must look upon me as ungenerous, as a person likely to starve a clergyman with the scantiness of the living of Hunsford!"

The ardor of Mr. Collins's admiration for Lady Catherine appeared so strong, despite its current circumstance, that he found voice to defend her ere he could defend himself. "Indeed not, your ladyship! I have always described you, most truthfully, as the most generous of patronesses—"

"While scraping and bowing for another living elsewhere?" Lady Catherine demanded. "As though you were a mere vicar, or even a curate? No, I tell you now, they think ill of me for it, all because you could not satisfy your greed in any other way!"

Unexpectedly, Charlotte Collins stepped forward. "Forgive me, your ladyship, but if I may explain—"

Lady Catherine scoffed. "What is there of explanation to be had, beyond the bare fact of your husband's duplicity!"

"A great deal, Lady Catherine." Charlotte lifted her chin—as much defiance as she had ever shown her ladyship despite two decades' acquaintance. It seemed to astonish Lady Catherine into silence, which lasted long enough for Charlotte to continue. "We have ever striven to lead our lives according to your counsel in every aspect, including how we order our household and how we introduce our daughter into society. When you recommended that we purchase a carriage and horse, we did so. When you suggested certain furnishings for our home, be they velvet drapes or fine rugs, we purchased them. When you advised us to outfit Katy in new dresses upon her come-out, this, too, we did. Never did we spare expense, as you yourself have always advised us, saying that false economy was no economy at all. But—if you will forgive me, Lady Catherine—*your* economy is *our* extravagance. We obeyed your dictates to a point beyond prudence, all in an endeavor to please. At last the state of our accounts was such that my husband found himself obliged to take this drastic step."

Mr. Collins stared at his wife in horror, though it cannot be said whether his dismay arose more from the revelation of debt or from this confrontation—however polite—with Lady Catherine. The most observant of those present noted the tilt of Charlotte's head and the tone of her voice, from which they derived the knowledge that Charlotte had wished to say this aloud for a very long time.

Lady Catherine could be quite observant herself, when she

wished, but her temper continued to rule her that day. "It is my fault, I see. My fault, that the clergyman I have rewarded with a living should prove himself spendthrift! That his wife cannot manage her household! No, this falsehood shall not be endured."

"Aunt," said the elder Mr. Darcy, taking pity on all present, "it is improper for this conversation to continue further in company." The conversation had been improper from its beginning, but Darcy was too wise to mention this to Lady Catherine at this moment. He had judged that she would not stop until she had voiced her objections, but had resolved to put an end to them as soon as decently possible. "You are greatly agitated, and you have suffered shocks enough of late. Pause, rest, and gather your thoughts. Mr. Collins will no doubt be willing to resume the discussion at a later time."

"Of course!" Mr. Collins cried. "At her ladyship's convenience, whensoever that may be—"

"Be silent. I have heard quite enough for tonight." Lady Catherine showed no sign that the idea to pause was not her own. "*If* I request your attendance again, Mr. Collins—and to be sure there is no certainty that I shall!—if I do so, you shall present yourself immediately."

"Yes, indeed, your ladyship—at any hour—you may rely upon me . . ." Mr. Collins's words trailed off as Lady Catherine indignantly departed the sitting room, Darcy on one side and the ever-vigilant Mrs. Jenkinson on another, leaving behind several persons in a heightened state of embarrassment and no polite means of exiting each other's company.

Juliet was unsurprised when Elizabeth spoke first. "Charlotte, my dear, I would speak with you—you may have much news from Meryton, or I hope you do, as you know my mother is a most inconstant correspondent."

Alone among the company, Charlotte showed no sign of discomfiture. "Indeed, I have had a letter from Maria this very week." The two women moved away, to speak of more polite topics—though, Juliet suspected, greater candor would prevail when the two friends were alone together.

Mr. Collins sat heavily in a nearby chair. He was in a state of inelegance, quite as though he had been standing in full sun on the hottest day of the year, and mopped his brow with his handkerchief. "I only wished to follow her ladyship's advice, to the best of my ability," he said, to everyone and no one. "My intent was purely to live precisely as Lady Catherine would desire, in every detail."

This protestation was most unseemly, and most would have attempted to ignore it. To Juliet's relief, however, the younger Mr. Darcy spoke forthrightly as ever. "You may have misunderstood my aunt, Mr. Collins. She does not wish for an absence of reasons to criticize. I believe she is happiest where she can suggest amendment—and if no cause exists, she will invent one. To follow all her suggestions is only to invite further suggestions, on and on, without end."

"How dare you speak such calumnies upon your aunt's character!" Mr. Collins cried, in so doing losing his chance to profit from excellent counsel. "For shame, though I say it myself, sir. For shame!"

Jonathan Darcy appeared neither shamed nor surprised at this response, merely resigned.

Juliet took the opportunity to step away to a nearby window; twilight had all but ended, and the sky had taken on that piercing cobalt blue that lingers for but a few moments before darkness. At the window stood Colonel Fitzwilliam and Anne, arm in arm. Juliet had intended to speak some vague pleasantry to them that would allow all to pretend they had not witnessed such a scene, but this plan was forestalled by the colonel's whisper: "I had thought I would never again hear such a scolding as the one Lady Catherine gave me, but already I am supplanted. Poor Collins! I cannot imagine that she will not speak to the bishop about installing a new clergyman at Hunsford Parsonage, after this."

"Oh, no!" Juliet felt most keenly for the Collinses—in particular, for Katy and Deb. "She would not make them homeless, would not cast them out, surely. No one could be as pitiless as that."

"Mama could," said Anne, "though I suspect she will not in this case, not if events continue to progress."

"What do you mean?" Juliet asked.

Anne replied, "Only this: that Mr. Collins has always been an excellent listener—and Mama will be in need of listeners, very soon."

The look that the colonel and Anne then exchanged told all: Juliet realized that Anne Fitzwilliam intended to leave Rosings Park with her husband, soon, and forever.

She also found it quite interesting that Anne spoke as though her mother would certainly remain well, long after her own absence—could those be the words of a would-be murderer?

One person present suffered under near as much guilt as Mr. Collins did himself.

Jonathan felt as though he had erred—surely he had done—but what would have been the correct action? Miss Tilney was the first person he would wish to ask, but she was much engaged with the Fitzwilliams. Luckily, a presumably disinterested clergyman was at hand. He turned to Mr. Tilney (who stood nearby, uncharacteristically somber) and said, "Might I speak with you, sir?"

"Of course, Mr. Darcy," Tilney replied, drawing them both

to the side of the room. "Though, I confess, I cannot imagine what you would want with me at this juncture."

"I wish to know whether—whether my actions were right," Jonathan said quietly. "It is through my doing that the Collinses have been exposed, and the effect upon the family may prove grave indeed."

Mr. Tilney did not rush to reassurance. "Yes. A husband, wife, and two children may suffer a blow from which they cannot ever recover. You must have realized this would be the result of your interference. No rational man could assume otherwise."

It is not rationality that leads to such conclusions, Jonathan wished to say, *only an insight into the responses of others that sometimes eludes me.* From long experience, however, he knew this explanation was unlikely to be accepted as the truth it was. He sought another way to explain. "My duty to Lady Catherine had commanded that I investigate matters in Faxton to the fullest—but having learned of Mr. Collins's duplicity, I was uncertain what to do with that new knowledge. At first I only informed Miss Tilney—"

"My daughter knew this?" Mr. Tilney said. He seemed much surprised. Jonathan did not dare ask why.

"Of course. It affected our investigation—Mr. Collins's work in Faxton may explain some of his more suspicious absences. Only when Lady Catherine's fears began to settle on Mr. Collins did I speak. It would not have done to allow her to remain in folly, particularly when her ignorance of this fact caused her such pain."

Although this did not seem to wholly reconcile Mr. Tilney to Jonathan's actions, it must have had some good effect. "Mr. Darcy, the truth is that the fundamental cause of what has transpired here is not your revelation of Mr. Collins's actions. That cause lies in Mr. Collins's actions themselves."

"But the result of my speaking has been the humiliation and potential ruin of the entire family."

"That is hard indeed," said Mr. Tilney, "but had you said nothing, the Collinses might have found themselves in an identical position from false suspicion rather than true misconduct. I have been a clergyman many years, Mr. Darcy. My patron is my own father, which may seem as though it would be the most comfortable place, the most secure . . . to those who do not know my father. Believe me, I am well aware of what a man in my position, or Mr. Collins's, owes to his patron. The bishops are but putty in the hands of the great, and we are oft reminded of this truth. From the sound of it, Collins became so fixated on what he *wished* to do for Lady Catherine that he betrayed that which he *must* do for her. The results may be pitiable, but they are entirely what he should have anticipated before attempting such a ruse. No, do not ascribe yourself a central part of this, Mr. Darcy—it is Collins's doing, and his alone."

As little as we enjoy being embarrassed ourselves, it is at times more difficult to witness the embarrassment of others. In our own shame, we are either supported by the knowledge of our innocence or braced by the acceptance of our wrongdoing. Yet when opprobrium is directed at another, we often know neither what to think nor what to say; we are cast adrift from the calm shores of courtesy with no sure land in sight. Worst of all are the occasions when the misconduct is not our own, but the punishment may be. In this pitiable circumstance Katy and Deb Collins found themselves on that evening.

As their father paced the borders of the garden, utterly undone, his two children stood just beyond the threshold of

Rosings's door, in company with no one but each other. Even then, each found it difficult to speak. For a long while, they could but watch Mr. Daniels evidently debate with himself as to whether he should enter the garden, too; finally, the man decided not and returned to his tasks. Once brother and sister were alone, Katy finally began, "If it was only about my dresses—I did like the dresses so much, but I could have made do with less."

"Your dresses could not have cost so dearly as *that*," Deb said, drawing from his own estimation of what women's frills and lace were worth, rather than their actual price. "I would think the carriage cost much more, would not you?"

"It scarce matters. We kept the secret, too, so we are as much to blame as Papa." Many grown persons would have argued this point with Katy, but Deb merely nodded.

They were in misery. No person of any heart or feeling can watch the humiliation of a loving parent without agonies, and for Katy and Deb those agonies were compounded by the belief that they, too, were to blame. How fun it had seemed, keeping a secret from Lady Catherine! After an entire lifetime of being scolded that her ladyship's every whim was unbreakable law, how good it had felt to break that law, not once, but again and again! And how much easier it had seemed to break other rules once this one great precept was no more . . .

But they had failed, failed utterly. Lady Catherine remained the law; the law had been broken; the law would punish. Many a criminal behind gaol bars had felt less trapped than the Collins children did that day.

Deb ventured, "If we might speak to Jonathan, he might speak to his father, who alone has any chance of swaying Lady Catherine—"

"Say nothing," Katy said. "Nothing to Jonathan, at all, ever again. Miss Tilney has kept your secret for the time being, but she has most likely told Jonathan. If today is our judge, we can rely on *his* discretion no longer."

Unable to argue with such logic, Deb fell silent again, and brother and sister waited until they could provide some small measure of consolation to their parents—if that were in their power at all.

"My dear Charlotte," said Elizabeth as she ushered her friend into the Rosings library, where they might gain some measure of privacy and peace. "Is there anything I can fetch to provide you with some comfort? A glass of wine, or perhaps some tea?"

Charlotte's countenance rarely revealed much of her sentiments, but even one so well acquainted with her as Elizabeth could read no emotion upon her in that hour. "I am quite well, I assure you. Mr. Collins will require assistance soon, but I believe there is no person so appropriate to help him as myself. I trust you will be good enough to allow us privacy."

"I shall, of course." Elizabeth felt vaguely rebuked, though she could little imagine why. "It is a shame that Lady Catherine should give so much advice while being so heedless of the effects of its being followed."

"A shame, but not a novelty. Lady Catherine is not a malicious person, you see. She is far worse. She is willfully unaware of much that—if paid heed to—would require her to amend her actions. She could be a far kinder, more generous mother and patroness than she is if she would accept that doing so might call upon her to practice self-correction from time to time. But her ladyship will never choose humility over pride. My husband will never choose pride over humility. Thus we find ourselves here."

Elizabeth had not heard such complete candor from Charlotte since before her marriage. Can she be blamed for a moment's happiness in the hearing—in believing herself more fully reunited with the friend of her girlhood than she had been for more than twenty years? "I have never been in Lady Catherine's favor, as you know. Toward yourself and Mr. Collins—toward your children—I would have expected greater kindness, even partiality."

"Then you do not know her so well as you had thought," Charlotte said. "You, however, have no need to win her ladyship's favor, for Darcy's wealth and standing eclipse even her own. Not that she will ever admit as much—that would not do—but she is ever aware of it, as is he."

This seemed very strange to Elizabeth. "Darcy has always shown Lady Catherine every civility, all the respect that is due his aunt."

"That I do not doubt," said Charlotte, "but he has always insisted on the respect he is due as well. He is in a position to demand such, and he does so." At the look upon her friend's face, Charlotte could not repress a smile, and not a particularly kind one. "Do you not recall the pride with which he first came to Meryton? That very nearly divided the two of you, ere you were wed? I assure you he does, for I have seen it at work these past two weeks, as he silently attempts to divide your son from a young woman who cannot be his social equal."

There, Elizabeth was silenced, for she had detected this interference on Darcy's part, had in fact come to Rosings Park largely in the hopes of promoting the match her husband seemed so determined to discourage.

Charlotte continued, "You proclaimed astonishment upon my accepting Mr. Collins, yet when the time came for you to consider a more prosperous alliance, you, too, saw the merits of security."

"That was not the reason for my marrying Mr. Darcy," Elizabeth protested.

"As much as you once disliked him? Come, do not prevaricate. Let us have honesty between us."

This *was* honesty: Elizabeth believed she would have married Darcy had he but one hundred pounds per annum. Her first sight of Pemberley had awed her, had impressed upon her the social gulf he had proposed to bridge with their engagement, but had been insufficient for her to forget his earlier pride and disdain. Only when the housekeeper had spoken so kindly of him had Elizabeth begun to realize the greatness of character of which Mr. Darcy was capable. What praise is more meaningful than that of a servant?

But she could not say this aloud. If she did so, Charlotte would see it as a judgment upon her marriage to Mr. Collins— the living of which, in Elizabeth's opinion, had to be punishment enough. She was forced to endure this calumny in order to preserve even civility between them. Elizabeth said only, "I love my husband very dearly."

"No doubt you have come to do so," Charlotte said. "You are fortunate, Lizzy, for the man you wed had already come into his estate. Mine has waited many years, and it now appears he may wait many more."

Elizabeth was very nearly affronted, and it was with difficulty she remained silent. Yet to continue the conversation would have been far worse, for it sounded much as though Charlotte was impatient for Collins to inherit . . . even though this could not occur until the death of Elizabeth's own beloved father. Such is the effect of an entail on even the longest friendships and most sacred family bonds!

The sense and compassion of all decent persons will agree that, at such a time of turmoil, even the strictest of schedules must be put aside. The appetite, however, may dissent.

Jonathan understood very well that there would be no formal dinner served at Rosings Park that evening under the present circumstances. However, the more usual alternative—to ask for dinner to be brought up to his room on a tray—remained unavailable so long as matters remained in an uproar. The servants dashed to and fro, not knowing what would be next asked for, nor when, nor how; those who would have sat at table could not in politeness ask to do so. As a young man hardly done growing, and one who had recently ridden to and from Faxton, Jonathan was by far the hungriest of the lot. He felt sensations that suggested a most unseemly grumbling was likely to issue from his person if he were not able to eat soon.

I shall pull aside a servant very quickly, he resolved, *one who seems not in too great a rush, and ask for some simple bread and cheese to be brought to my room. That will suffice to allay my hunger, at least for the purposes of gentility.*

Thus he made his way into the central stairwell of Rosings; although only Lady Catherine's family and guests would use the stairs themselves, the hall beyond them was one of the conduits through which all passed at one time or another. It was not an especially bright area after sundown, but illumination was provided by lit candles in well-polished sconces upon the wall. The sound of footsteps upon the floor gave Jonathan hope, but this hope was dashed when Lady Catherine herself walked toward him, leaning upon her cane.

Yet Jonathan was more in Lady Catherine's good graces than he had been in some time. "You! You alone were able to provide the truth about Collins—he whom I should have been able to trust in any circumstance. I suppose you are not without perception, as I once was inclined to think."

This did not seem like a comment for which he should thank Lady Catherine. Jonathan tried to think of a response, could not meet her eyes as long as he would wish, and glanced upward—saw movement descending, and pulled Lady Catherine toward him in the instant before an enormous porcelain vase shattered upon the very place where Lady Catherine had been standing!

Her ladyship cried out. Footsteps sounded from every direction, as others hurried toward the commotion. Jonathan ran to the stairs, determined to seize the person on a higher floor . . . who could only be the person who wished Lady Catherine dead.

Chapter Twenty-One

In fashionable circles, it is sometimes pretended that no physical activity takes place beyond the most minimal and genteel. Were persons as weak as such inaction would suggest, they would be pitiful indeed, but this is little thought of; the illusion wished for is that wealth and preeminence have reduced the need for strain and effort, even for movement. Yet this illusion cannot survive the reality of even the most rarefied existence. Such diversions as riding and walking require exertion; the thrill and splendor of a ball comes paired with the need to dance for hours on end. Stairs must be climbed and descended, often many times a day in quick succession. All but the frailest and most invalid find themselves possessed of more strength than they may know until that strength has been called upon.

So it was with Jonathan Darcy that Sunday evening, as he dashed up the Rosings stairs in hopes of finding Lady Catherine's attacker.

"Halt!" Jonathan cried as he ran, taking two steps at a go. "Stop there immediately!" A sudden movement upstairs—already above the first story—suggested that the assailant had not heeded these commands. Footsteps echoed down the hallway on the second floor—a floor nearly vacant most of the time.

When Jonathan reached the second floor, no one was to be seen—either the assailant or one who might have witnessed this person's going and coming. No doubt the miscreant had run to the servants' stair and was already emerging in another part of the house altogether. Although Jonathan's frustration was very great, he simply straightened his waistcoat and descended the stairs toward the sounds of exclamation and dismay.

Indeed, nearly all those currently at Rosings proved to be crowding around the shocked Lady Catherine at the bottom of the stairs. Amid the flickering candlelight, Jonathan could see Anne taking her mother's arm—Colonel Fitzwilliam behind them both, drawing them away from the shards of porcelain upon the floor—Mr. Collins, ashen, staring down at the debris—Charlotte watching impassively from a doorway, and behind her, Mother. As Jonathan watched, Father entered from one direction, as through the front door squeezed Katy and Deb.

They could not have exited Rosings by any servant stair, then come back in via the front door, not in such a brief amount of time, Jonathan realized. *Katy and Deb are absolved!*

This realization—clarifying though it was—proved little consolation to him. He had had a chance to capture the person responsible, or one of the persons; he had failed.

"This cannot be endured!" Lady Catherine cried. "If my young nephew and Miss Tilney cannot identify the wrongdoer, then I must see to my own preservation. Jenkinson! Jenkinson, where are you? Begin packing my things. I depart for Pemberley in the morn!"

The shades of Pemberley, however, were not to be so honored on this occasion.

First, as Mrs. Jenkinson, Daisy, and much of the other staff knew, Lady Catherine traveled with much the same level of preparation, and quantity of items, as might normally be anticipated for an expedition to the Himalaya. There are those who cannot abide the thought of wishing for even one item of clothing or jewelry, when abroad, that might have been to hand at home, and Lady Catherine was among this number. Although the servants began work immediately, they knew that when their selection of dresses and jewels were shown to her ladyship, the same would be dismissed as inadequate. It was in fact entirely possible for Lady Catherine to declare herself to be "departing tomorrow" for weeks on end.

Second, Mr. Darcy, one of the few to whom Lady Catherine could ever be persuaded to listen, strove to discourage her plan. He told her that he thought the shock already a threat to her fragile state, which would be rendered but worse were she to undertake an arduous journey: "Do not, madam, achieve by undue exertion that which this villain has failed to do through malice." He did not tell her of his other concern, which was that, once installed at Pemberley, Lady Catherine might remain there for some considerable duration, which would not add to the happiness and harmony of his home. In this concern he was joined by his wife, who resolved that—should her husband fail to keep Lady Catherine from their doorstep—a visit to dear Jane and Bingley was most overdue.

The greatest persuasion, however, was applied by Juliet Tilney. This outcome might fairly have been doubted by observers of the conversation's beginning, during which Lady Catherine—despite having been seated near the fire—remained pale and snappish. "You promised to unearth this person's identity, and you have utterly failed to do so," she cried, gesturing dismissively at Miss Tilney. "You have abused my hospitality by wasting your time and mine."

"Forgive me, Lady Catherine," Juliet wisely replied, "but if the culprit were easily discerned, I have no doubt you would have determined his identity for yourself in a very short amount of time."

Lady Catherine sniffed. "Well. *That* is true, to be sure. But this has gone on far too long!"

"Take heart, ma'am. It is shocking and horrid that so many attempts should be made upon your life, but with each attempt, the fiend responsible gives us new clues to consider. Tonight's events may reveal much, if not all, once the younger Mr. Darcy and I are able to consider them in full."

"How many hours do you plan to spend in this pursuit?" Lady Catherine demanded. "Or days? Or weeks? Why should I remain here, endangered, throughout?"

Juliet did not enjoy saying the next, but it had to be faced: "Your ladyship, consider that we know the person responsible must be among the intimates of your household. Every such person is also known at Pemberley, are they not? They have visited that great house?" From the side of the room, Elizabeth nodded, allowing Juliet to continue, "Therefore, whoever it is who attempts to harm you . . . that person will know where you have gone, and may be able to resume their efforts there. You are not safe in any familiar place, not until this person has been caught. And truly, Lady Catherine, I believe we will have them ere long!"

Lady Catherine's head drooped then, as though she were very weary. No doubt she was, for who could sleep well in such circumstances? Although little of her ladyship's behavior had been likely to awaken much fondness in the hearts of those around her, Juliet could not but pity the woman at this instant. How terrible to know that one most trusted could be capable of carrying such hatred within, to realize that no place could be safe.

"Very well, Miss Tilney," Lady Catherine finally said. "I

shall remain. But I insist that you shall redouble your efforts immediately!"

"You need not insist, Lady Catherine," said Juliet. "This I promise."

In the hours that followed, a somewhat cold dinner found its way on tray to many different corners of the house. Lady Catherine and Mr. and Mrs. Darcy dined in their rooms. The Collinses all went home, where their cook had valiantly managed to keep some duck warm, albeit a bit singed around the edges. Anne asked that she and Colonel Fitzwilliam be served at table, even though they would sit there alone. Finally came Jonathan and Miss Tilney, who in the library (of all places!) ate a most unusual meal—sandwiches, albeit far larger and heartier sorts than the ones served at tea. Jonathan had discovered a liking for these some years past—at times, the hubbub of a busy dinner table disconcerted him, so he had experimented with eating in his room more than most persons did. Miss Tilney seemed uncertain how best to proceed, for eating such a large sandwich required both hands and could not be considered delicate. However, she hit upon a method within a few moments' time and succeeded in looking, if not refined, at least polite. Although Jonathan noted her struggle, his mind remained on more pressing matters.

"Katy and Deb must be entirely excluded from our consideration," he said. "They had left the house entirely. There is no means by which they could have traveled from the second floor of Rosings to the ground and then outside in such a short time."

"I do not know Rosings Park so well as you, but I am inclined to agree, Mr. Darcy. The young Collinses were never among our most persuasive suspects, and upon the revelation of Deb's illness, their odd absences and appearances are entirely explained." Miss Tilney considered for a moment. "Furthermore—given that Deb cannot know precisely when his fits are likely to strike—does that not make him even less likely? For he could not undertake any effort so dangerous and clandestine with certainty that he would be able to see the matter through."

"An excellent point," Jonathan admitted. "Regardless of whether or not he *would* try, it seems that he *did not*, nor Katy, either. Their dislike for Lady Catherine may be strong, but they never sought to end her life. As for their parents—I am not as certain."

"Was not your mother speaking with Mrs. Collins when this vase was cast down? That was my understanding."

"Certainly they were speaking very shortly beforehand; I will ask Mother when their conversation left off, if in fact it was not interrupted by the attempt itself."

Miss Tilney said, "The Fitzwilliams were together. I must say, their marital harmony has become most marked during the past few days. The revelation of the colonel's departure might have been expected to divide them from each other, but instead the effect is quite the opposite. Although I still believe it impossible that they were cooperating before, it is possible they could be in concert now."

"But that would require *three* persons to harbor murderous intent toward Lady Catherine. Three persons willing to act in such a criminal manner—willing to risk their lives."

"A fair point, Mr. Darcy. We would also have to assume that all three persons feel that the impending alteration of Lady Catherine's will is likely to harm them. That, I think, may bring us back to the question of a servant having been drawn into this matter against his will."

Jonathan wished he could eat by the library hearth every night, while having a truly stimulating conversation. He could not remember when he had last enjoyed a meal so. Of course, some of that pleasure came from his present company . . .

But he brought himself back to the matter at hand. "We must speak to the servants and attempt to reckon with which of them might have been forced to cooperate with homicidal efforts. Beyond that—it is difficult to know what else to do."

Although Miss Tilney appeared equally at a loss, she considered the matter carefully. "I suppose we may as well speak to Lady Catherine about her will again."

"But we know its provisions, which revealed nothing."

"We have examined everything, have we not, Mr. Darcy? Still we have no answer. Thus we must consider every aspect of the matter over again, in the hopes that we have missed something—that there is some clue still waiting to be found."

Servants hear a great deal from their masters. The usual requests and commands can be anticipated. More particular instructions are hardly uncommon. And, for all that everyone involved pretends that servants do not overhear the conversations of their betters, only a fool believes that the household's servants have not learned a great deal about what transpires within it.

Least mentioned of all, however, are the moments of true confidence between a master and servant. It is not nearly so unusual as propriety would have it for a mistress to unburden her heart to a trusty maid or a beloved cook, or for a master to admit doubts to his valet that he would confess in no other company on earth. At their best, these conversations may lead to greater trust between all involved and a more compassionately run household. At worst, however, the servants are merely given more burdens to carry, and are sometimes distrusted for how much they know. More than one soul in service has witnessed a moment of weakness their master could not endure to have remembered, and thus found themselves cast out, sometimes even without a reference.

Of all the servants, Juliet imagined that Mrs. Jenkinson was among the most likely to have been the recipient of such confidences. She reasoned that this greater intimacy could lead to more unusual requests, which in turn could draw such a servant into the position of an unwitting, then unwilling, accomplice. With Jenkinson, therefore, she resolved to begin her queries that next morning. (Juliet and Mr. Darcy had together decided to forgo their usual morning conference in order that they might undertake this significant next step.)

To start, Juliet ordered her breakfast brought upon a tray. This was done by a lower servant, of course, but this servant was tasked with summoning Mrs. Jenkinson to Juliet's room as soon as was practicable. Jenkinson appeared not ten minutes later, nervous as usual. "Is all well, Miss Tilney? Have you need to speak to Lady Catherine?"

"I take it her ladyship has remained abed this morning?" Juliet responded, for otherwise, Jenkinson would not expect others to be in search of her.

"Yes, miss, she is weary indeed. Weary and sick at heart. Better this business had been accomplished more quickly."

Juliet felt the rebuke, all the sharper for coming from a servant. Although she wished to protest that she and Mr. Darcy were doing their best, she resolved to attend to Lady Catherine's safety rather than her own injured pride. She replied only, "It must be very difficult to do much of the work of a housekeeper and yet fully care for both Lady Catherine and Mrs. Fitzwilliam, especially as you seem to serve as companion to each in equal measure. Their wishes must often be in conflict."

"It is to Lady Catherine that I always defer," Mrs. Jenkinson said. "Her needs are inevitably more pressing. Mrs. Fitzwilliam is more moderate in her requirements, and she is of a gentler nature."

"You have never been trapped between them? Nor between the wishes of, say, Colonel Fitzwilliam and the women of the house?"

"Colonel Fitzwilliam does not importune me, not in the slightest." Mrs. Jenkinson spoke with no discernible unease. Although the questioning had hardly been comprehensive, it seemed to Juliet that, were Jenkinson being forced to cooperate with efforts against her mistress's life, her inner strain would have been hinted at in some element of her speech or demeanor. Instead, all seemed calm. "Now how may I help you, miss? Forgive my hurrying you, but you see, tomorrow is laundry day."

"Would it not have been today?" It was a Monday, the traditional washday.

"In the normal way of things, yes," said Mrs. Jenkinson, "but the washing is done when we have food enough left over that the fireplaces are not needed to cook—"

"And we had no dinner last night, because of the attack on Lady Catherine," Juliet finished.

The washing of the laundry was, in any household, one of the more onerous and burdensome tasks to be undertaken, requiring many hours of drudgery to wash numerous pieces of clothing owned by both residents and guests, as well as the house linen. The preparation the night before would involve nearly the whole staff. Thus Juliet was obliged to ask for fresh flowers for her room—no other pretext came quickly enough to mind—and then to let Mrs. Jenkinson go on her way.

———

Meanwhile, Jonathan Darcy had begun his day by sending another servant to fetch Mr. Daniels to the gun room. There he was swiftly met, Daniels brushing soil off his hands, seemingly almost eager for a new task. "Good morning, sir. What can I do for you? Are you hoping for a spot of shooting today?"

Daniels seemed eager for a shooting party; he might have been happier in a house where he got to be a true gamekeeper rather than keeping charge of the grounds. But Jonathan could not abide the sport. "No, thank you, Daniels. What I wished to know was whether . . . whether there were any unusual requests made by either the family or guests at Rosings during the past few months. Anything at all that struck you as peculiar, even though it may seem unrelated to this present business."

"Not in particular, sir. To be sure, I would have mentioned it to you straightaway."

That question had not helped approach any nearer the real subject. Jonathan tried again: "Did you feel unduly put upon by any errands or requests? Something that might be not so much unusual as particularly burdensome?"

" 'Tis my job to bear those burdens, sir."

Why can we not ask what we mean straightforwardly? Jonathan thought. It was not the first time he had had this thought, nor had the question come to mind solely regarding his investigations. Perhaps he should assay an attempt. "Daniels, has anyone tricked you into doing something you should not have done? If so, has that person held that over you as a means of forcing you to do yet more?"

Daniels stared, evidently much taken aback. People did this when they had no idea what Jonathan spoke of; unfortunately, they also did this when they knew *precisely* what he spoke of but had no intention of admitting it. "Of course not, sir. I know my duty."

This is why we cannot ask such questions straightforwardly, then,

Jonathan reminded himself. *When people know precisely what they* should *answer, that is what they say, regardless of whether or not it is the truth.*

The third servant, Daisy, was sought by Juliet in vain, for she had been summoned to speak to the Fitzwilliams on a most particular matter.

"You cannot be unaware," Colonel Fitzwilliam said, "that I soon plan to quit Rosings and dwell in Bath."

"No, sir," replied Daisy. "I mean, yes, sir. I mean . . . I am aware, sir."

Fitzwilliam shared an affectionate glance with Anne as he continued. "You could scarce live in this house and not know as much. However, what is much less widely known is that my wife intends to accompany me. We shall be establishing a household of our own, and bringing Peter home from school to remain with us for another few years yet."

Daisy's responding smile seemed entirely genuine; Fitzwilliam was touched when she said, "Then I wish you both very happy, sir, ma'am."

"My hope is that our entire house shall share in our happiness," Anne added. "Which is why—Daisy, we wished to ask you to come with us, to take up the role of housekeeper."

This startled Daisy beyond the normal discourse between master and servant. "Me? A housekeeper? Is it a proper house?"

Fitzwilliam chuckled. "Yes, entirely proper. We shall not employ so large a staff nor have so many rooms as does Rosings Park, so you would not have too much to supervise."

"You have been a lady's maid many years," Anne continued, a tactful allusion to Daisy's age; while lady's maids could range from young to elderly, less physically demanding roles were understandably sought by those who had begun to feel the weight of time. And no doubt, after so many years of being addressed by her Christian name, she would welcome a more dignified title. "You have done far more besides, in the years since Mrs. Prowse passed away. Your acquaintance with the running of this house is now, I feel sure, adequate to instruct you in all that a housekeeper should know—and as I shall be a new mistress, it is only fitting that I should have a new housekeeper as well. We could find our way together, could we not?"

Daisy's smile warmed Fitzwilliam through. For so long, he had felt unable to please anyone, not under the rule of Lady Catherine. Now Anne glowed with delight, and even their future housekeeper could hardly contain her glee at her good fortune. Rarely had he been so aware of how much of our own happiness relies on providing happiness to others.

Yet Daisy's expression faltered. "But—what of my husband? I mean, thank you, sir, ma'am, but as you may know, my husband works here, too, and he could not—"

"Of course we will find something for him to do," Fitzwilliam promised. Lady Catherine would not care for these subtractions from the Rosings staff, but he judged that her ladyship's outrage could increase no further, and thus there was no deterrent to further action. "If you think he will want to come with us?"

"He will!" Daisy exclaimed. "I mean, I feel certain that he will. I take it you've yet to ask him. Shall I speak to him first, to be sure? We must decide it together."

"As you prefer." Anne looked up at Fitzwilliam as she said, "Indeed, we would never wish to see a husband and wife parted. Not ever."

While Juliet sought Daisy in vain, she instead found the younger Mr. Darcy. Sadly, each felt their morning's questioning to be inconclusive at best, and they could not persuade themselves that they would much further their inquiry by finding Daisy, though still they hoped to do so.

"Perhaps no servant has been forced into taking part after all," Mr. Darcy said. "We must return to the idea of two equal conspirators."

Juliet nodded. "And we must learn who they are in a great hurry, for the solicitor is due to arrive in but three more days—which means Lady Catherine's assailant is certain to strike once more, and very soon."

Chapter Twenty-Two

It behooves us at this moment to consider the state of Lady Catherine. Proud and indomitable, she had always been—and had, in fact, been willing to say to anyone who asked, and many who did not. She brooked no refusals, accepted no excuses, and gave precedence to no one. (This involved avoiding certain social occasions when her ladyship would have been obliged to consort with those of greater wealth and rank, but who would not prefer ruling in a small kingdom than curtsying in a larger one?) Her will had been contradicted so rarely that she lacked any practice in graceful acquiescence. Even the attempts on her life had at first bred only her annoyance and contempt; she had even vaguely felt that it reflected ill upon her to have attracted an assassin of such incompetence, however grateful for that lack of skill she might be.

However, even her mighty courage had begun to falter. Repeated blows are always more difficult to bear, and what her assassin lacked in proficiency was counterweighted in persistence. The heavy vase dropped from above was perhaps the least threatening of the attempts thus far—though it would surely have injured Lady Catherine had it struck her, the likelihood of death from such an impact was by no means certain. Yet its fall represented one shock too many for her to endure with anything resembling her usual pride.

"No, it shall not be borne," she muttered from her usual place in her throne-like chair. "It shall not be! If I am not to leave this house, then others must go this day—very nearly this instant!"

Her great-nephew, Jonathan Darcy, sat with her, Miss Tilney at his side. He said, "You would not command us to go, surely, and leave you alone. That, I fear, would not be safe."

"Nor is it safe to have murderers about me, either!" Lady Catherine said, with some justice. "You counsel that I change nothing, then, and allow this fiend to continue striking at me until at last I am dead?"

"Not at all, madam," Jonathan replied. "We wished to speak with you again, about your will—"

"I have already explained its contents. What else can you expect to glean from it?" Lady Catherine's eyes narrowed. "Surely *you* do not anticipate a bequest, Jonathan, for if you do, let me disabuse you of the notion this instant. You shall have Pemberley! Nothing else could you possibly require."

"Indeed not," Jonathan said, his countenance so stricken that Lady Catherine believed him. She did not approve of the young man's peculiar behaviors, but in all her reckonings of his faults, never had she felt the need to include greed among them.

Miss Tilney swiftly asked, "May we inquire—how great is the bequest you intend to make to Miss Pope?"

"Though it is no great fortune, it should keep Miss Pope in modest comfort, should she keep no horse nor carriage, not take a house too large for her station." Miss Pope was widely known to have been of great assistance and comfort to Anne, and had since served as governess for two other local families; all knew Miss Pope to be Lady Catherine's creature. It was to Lady Catherine that these families gave thanks for Miss Pope's efforts. To be seen to have abandoned Miss Pope to penury: no, it would not have done.

"So you do not think Anne nor any other likely to resent the loss of the sum given?" Jonathan asked.

Lady Catherine scoffed at the notion. "The wealth of the

De Bourghs is not so inadequate as you assume. Indeed, to Anne it will be as nothing. To Miss Pope it will be everything." She took a moment to imagine her former governess's fulsome gratitude. For Lady Catherine, the only drawback to leaving this sum in her will was that she would be unable to accept Miss Pope's thanks in person.

"And there are no other bequests whatsoever?" Miss Tilney asked. "Even something very small, something you might consider insignificant—"

"Do you think I would not have told you of it ere now? No, that is the entirety of my will as it shall be upon Mr. Guinness's arrival."

Jonathan and Miss Tilney seemed to find her will very interesting, to keep asking about it so. In truth, speaking upon the matter proved invigorating to Lady Catherine's mind as well. There was a certain conversation that should not be put off any longer . . .

Lady Catherine kept her own office in Rosings Park, although nearly every other person in the house could be forgiven for not realizing the fact, for it was only a small room on the first floor and she was to be found in it but seldom. In the years immediately following her husband's death, she had made more use of it, but what few tasks she had not long settled with standing orders had for some years been handled by Colonel Fitzwilliam. No doubt it had occurred to that formidable lady that she should resume her occupations in that room shortly, in the colonel's absence. At that time, however, it cannot be wondered at that Anne Fitzwilliam was astonished to be summoned there. Although she contemplated finding her husband and asking him to come with her,

Anne ultimately elected to go alone, to face that which must be endured.

Upon Anne's entrance, Lady Catherine looked up from her desk, which had been prepared for her with ink, pen, paper, wax, candles, and sand. "Here, Anne, I would speak with you," her ladyship began, gesturing toward the chair opposite. "Mr. Guinness will arrive very soon, and we shall require him to make amendments beyond that I had previously considered. To be clear, Colonel Fitzwilliam must not be allowed to profit in any way from his impudent, unchristian plan to abandon his household and family. I believe that most instruments should already provide some protections in this case, but we must determine what will be best for you, after I am gone."

"Mama, my husband does not intend to abandon his family."

This drew Lady Catherine's sharp gaze. "He has thought better of it, has he? And none too soon."

"That is not what I mean," Anne said, drawing upon her courage. "I mean that the colonel has asked me to come with him to Bath, and this, I intend to do. We had intended to tell you this together, but I would not dissemble with you."

Lady Catherine stared for so long that Anne first thought that the shock might have brought on some kind of stupor. Yet ire roused her before long. "What can be the meaning of this? You cannot be in earnest."

"I am, Mama." Anne decided it would be more endurable to muster a great deal of courage to say everything needful at once, altogether, than to have to continue summoning bravery required for several separate statements. "We love each other very much. We want Peter home with us for a few more years yet. And Colonel Fitzwilliam believes the waters at Bath will be good for my constitution. A handful of the servants will come with us—only a handful, mind—and it is our hope that we will not much inconvenience you, and that you might come to visit us often."

"But it cannot be so!" Lady Catherine's voice no longer betrayed outrage. The faint tremble—the look in her eyes—these were never witnessed by any other living person, only Anne alone. "You are my daughter, and it is your duty to remain with me."

"It is the duty of a wife to cleave unto her husband, is it not?" Anne sometimes wondered whether her mother remembered Sir Lewis very much, if at all.

Lady Catherine lifted her chin, pretending a haughtiness she did not feel; the pretense would have fooled any other. "You have heard me speak of your birth. Of how the doctor, the midwife, even your own father—all despaired of you. None believed you would live. It was I who stayed awake day and night with you, I who held you by the fire and rubbed your limbs, I alone who saved you—and this is my reward?"

Anne remembered when Peter had been so very small. How very acute that fear could be! It was this recollection that gentled her voice as she reached across the desk to take her mother's hand. "Mama, the only way I can repay you for my life is *to live.*"

The question of Lady Catherine's own survival—and who, precisely, might wish to put an end to it—remained foremost in the minds of Juliet and the younger Mr. Darcy. What little they had learned about her ladyship's estate had provided scant illumination in and of itself, yet it had focused their attention remarkably.

"There *must* be an element of cooperation at work," Mr. Darcy insisted as they sat together in the library, their various notes and lists from the investigation scattered about them. "If not cooperation, then coercion. But no one suspect could do all this alone."

"So all our lists proclaim," said Juliet, but she remained unsatisfied. "And yet—for two persons to join in a murderous plot—it has happened before in the world, and will again, I know, but two of *these* persons? That is what I cannot entirely believe. We are looking at it wrongly, Mr. Darcy. I do not know where the error is, but I am so certain that if we were able to correct our perspective, the answer would lie before us plain as day. What are we not glimpsing in those around us?"

Mr. Darcy paused, then said something that surprised her. "You are thinking, perhaps, of the late Mr. Bamber."

"Oh. I am not, truth be told. Perhaps I should be." How cold must she have become, to have all but lost sight of a man who had flattered and courted her, one whom she had helped bring to the gallows!

"On the contrary," Mr. Darcy said, "I believe most would praise your self-possession, which . . . which would be all the greater, given your connection with him."

Juliet felt her cheeks flush warm. "I had no particular connection with Mr. Bamber—none of that sort, I mean, I trust you understand me—and so I cannot claim any special dignity by having left him in the past."

Mr. Darcy thumped his chair once, a sign of inner agitation and greatly excited thought. Juliet took this as a good sign, both in terms of his trusting her to see beyond his curtain and perhaps for the progress of their investigation. Finally, he met her eyes—very deliberately—and her heart quickened to think of what else he might say . . .

McQuarrie, the butler, came in at that moment, bearing fresh newspapers for the library. His timing had rarely been worse, but he never knew it, perceiving only that the two young persons seated near the hearth seemed uncommonly quiet. No high spirits at all. Truly, McQuarrie thought, youth was wasted on the young.

Elizabeth, meanwhile, had set out for a walk through the beautiful grounds of Rosings Park. As she was an excellent walker, she had waited for no companion, but she was pleased to find one in Mr. Tilney. The two of them strolled together past Anne Fitzwilliam's carefully tended garden. "One can see precisely where the daughter's influence ends and the mother's begins," Elizabeth said, gesturing toward a line of shrubbery. On the side that belonged to Anne, rosebushes were surrounded by soft clouds of wildflowers, all of it a colorful, graceful profusion of nature's beauty; on the other, the rigidly straight garden paths traced an intricate pattern, braced on its borders by topiaries with the tops trimmed flat as tables. "I suppose Mrs. Fitzwilliam will not be able to keep a garden in Bath."

"Although land for gardens is not plentiful in Bath," Mr. Tilney said, "some is to be had, and barring that, there are always flowerpots. I shall recommend them to Mrs. Fitzwilliam myself."

"Your thoughtfulness does you credit, sir."

"You mean, of course, that it surprises you, for you have had your view of me from your husband." Mr. Tilney smiled as he held up a hand against her protests. "Do not prevaricate—it would demean you without deceiving me. The elder Mr. Darcy does not like me, nor does he wish to further any potential match between my daughter and your son. What he does not realize is that I join him in that wish."

Elizabeth was a woman of both sense and humor, but no mother can hear her son dismissed as a suitor without some sting of pride. "Why should you feel so?"

"Please do not believe, madam, that I cast aspersions upon your son," said Tilney. "His efforts on behalf of his aunt have been unstinting, and his behavior toward Juliet entirely respectful. We shared a conversation, he and I, about the ethical difficulties inherent in conducting this business, and this impressed upon me his depth of thought and his earnest desire to do good. Were that the whole of the matter, relations between our families might be very different."

"What, pray, weighs more in your reckoning than good manners and morals?" Elizabeth raised an eyebrow. She would not abase herself by pleading Jonathan's case—she had acquired just enough of her husband's pride to feel that the heir to Pemberley should have no need to beg. But she would not allow Henry Tilney to blithely dismiss her son without being forced to state his case in full.

Yet Tilney took this in apparent good humor. "He is young yet to marry, do not you think? And for all that he and my daughter have shared an extraordinary acquaintance so far, the gruesome events they have witnessed, the dark folly of man they have been forced to comprehend—surely we both wish that someday these events shall be no more than distant memories, that they will move on from such morbid concerns. Yet above all, it is your son who does not seem to possess the necessary feelings to foster a courtship." Mr. Tilney said all this with great assurance, blithely unaware of the blushing conversation taking place between Jonathan and Juliet that very instant within Rosings's walls. "My daughter has said to me that he has no designs upon her, that she is content to have him as her friend—and, I suppose, her partner in such investigations as they have been called upon to answer. Your husband and son seem to have had no such conversation, as the elder Mr. Darcy remains vigilant at all times. If I have needled your husband from time to time . . . and, I will confess, I have . . . it is because I cannot but bristle at the idea of my daughter as a conniver, when nothing is further from her character."

"Mr. Tilney, you need not convince me of that. My own acquaintance with Juliet has been sufficient to inform me of her upstanding character, her good humor and spirits, and all other merits one would wish in a young lady." Elizabeth sighed. She was certain that Mr. Tilney had misjudged Jonathan, that he was mistaken about a lack of interest—but she assumed he must know his own daughter best, and thus with sadness accepted that Juliet did not wish to marry her son. "What you say of my husband no doubt contains much truth. Jonathan has already attracted some connivers, and you can imagine how many my husband encountered in his day! You cannot blame him for caution, however little such caution was here required."

"You underestimate my mind's dexterity, for I find I can blame him and I do—but for your sake, I will not do so very much." The twinkle in Mr. Tilney's eyes allowed Elizabeth to take this in the spirit in which it was said. "Our children are friends, and friends they shall remain. Perhaps I have burned my bridges with the elder Mr. Darcy, but I hope you and I may find some measure of friendship all the same."

"Do you know, Mr. Tilney, I believe we already have."

Jonathan elected to call again upon the authority Lady Catherine had given them to ask questions; he and Miss Tilney sent notes to Colonel Fitzwilliam, Anne, and all of the Collinses, requesting that they come to be spoken with once more.

Anne made her appearance first, and so flushed and uncertain was she that Jonathan half thought she might be near a confession. Instead, she revealed that she had told her mother of her plan to go with Colonel Fitzwilliam to Bath. "It cannot be abandonment to live with one's husband rather than one's mother," she said, twisting her lace kerchief in her hands. "Not in such a case as this, where Mama has both friends and servants to care for her, to provide everything she needs. Mrs. Jenkinson shadows her every step, provides all that is required."

"I quite agree," said Miss Tilney. "But does Lady Catherine?"

"Our last conversation—she left without a word," Anne said. "Oh, if I only knew what was in her heart! I know she is imperious, and given to rages, but—she is my mother, and I would not hurt her for the world."

Was this genuine daughterly feeling, or merely a timely pretense of it? "Did any aspect of your plan strike her in particular?" Jonathan asked. "Any financial matter, anything that might involve the services of Mr. Guinness?"

"She wished to ensure that the colonel would not have access to my funds, but that matters not, if I am with him."

Katy and Deb came in next, together. They seemed to intuit through Jonathan and Miss Tilney's behavior that they were no longer suspects themselves, that their presence was wished only to illuminate the behavior of others. "You have to see that Papa cannot be responsible," Katy insisted. "Riding back and forth to Faxton nearly every day—you have made the ride yourself, Jonathan, you know how long it takes—when would he even find time to perpetrate such evils upon Lady Catherine? It is impossible!"

"He *could* have found time," Deb said, rather unexpectedly, "but not without neglecting something else. He would have had to vanish from Hunsford completely. Or not to have seen Mother. Instead, he has even had occasion to socialize with the two of you—if not so often as he would hope. After all, Jonathan, you are both his relation and Lady Catherine's, and thus quite his favorite person."

Katy smiled, seemingly despite herself. "Indeed, you make him as near a relative as can be accomplished!"

"What of your mother?" Miss Tilney asked, very gently. "She has had no unusual absences?"

Both Katy and Deb shook their heads no, though they exchanged a glance that might have meant much—or nothing.

Mr. Collins himself came next. By now afternoon had drawn on and the sky had begun to darken. "It is inconceivable to me, inconceivable that anyone should harbor such designs toward Lady Catherine. Her generosity and condescension—"

"You still feel this way, sir, after her words to you last night?" Miss Tilney did not appear to be persuaded by Mr. Collins's words.

Yet Collins would not be shaken. "How can I blame her for my own error, my own falsehoods? She has given me all, and thus have I repaid her. It was only that my desire to please Lady Catherine was so great that it led me astray. For indeed, I have no other object in life—all I do is for her sake alone."

Charlotte Collins, who followed her husband into the library to speak with Jonathan and Miss Tilney, did not take so expansive a view of Lady Catherine's generosity. "Lady Catherine is a most generous woman when she sees the need of it," Charlotte said, her hands folded in her lap. "She sees that need most acutely where others are likely to see it as well, and appreciate her generosity—but in that, I do not think she differs so much from other persons of wealth and estate."

Jonathan felt as though this were vaguely aimed at him, even if he could not understand why. "Is there a person whom you feel should have benefited from Lady Catherine's generosity but did not?"

"We benefited from such advice that it has near bankrupted us, and it may have cost my husband his position," Charlotte replied. "One can have too much, I think, of generosity."

Colonel Fitzwilliam sat with them last. He alone among those they questioned seemed to be in fine spirits, and he spoke easily of his plans. "You will have to visit us in Bath, Jonathan! And—perhaps we might ask your family, too, Miss Tilney, if you think they would be amenable?"

"Perhaps," said Miss Tilney with a smile. "Though I must warn you, my parents met in Bath, and I believe they have many strong opinions about every shop, house, and assembly there."

"We shall do our best to make all as it should be," said the colonel. "I mean to have everything done well. One cannot take pleasure in being home without a well-trained staff. Though, as Rosings proves, one can have a well-trained staff and little pleasure in one's home."

That was such an interesting way to put it. Fascinating, even. Jonathan said, "You have your staff already?"

"A few persons, as I fear we are absconding with a handful of the servants here at Rosings. Daisy is coming with us as our housekeeper, which means Daniels, too, of course—he cannot be made into a butler, I do not think, but we shall find some position to suit. He is an honest, good-tempered fellow with such skills as would make him a welcome addition to the staff of any house."

"Why should Daisy's employ with you require Daniels?" Jonathan asked.

"Oh, they are husband and wife. We do not call her Mrs.

Daniels, for Daisy she must be so long as she remains a lady's maid."

Miss Tilney sat up very straight. "I believe that is all, Colonel."

Fitzwilliam looked from one to the other. "You have scarcely asked me anything."

"But you have told us enough," said Jonathan. He understood now to what Miss Tilney responded.

Fitzwilliam rose and went to the desk to fetch something or other before he departed. This obliged Miss Tilney to whisper, "Daisy is married to Mr. Daniels."

"Yes, I see the importance of that," said Jonathan. It did not surprise him that he had not known of their marriage before; knowing would have required more attention than anyone paid the servants in another family's house. But how he wished he had known it, for this fact pointed the way to so much more! "And a master depends upon a servant in a way a servant does not depend upon a master."

Miss Tilney brought her hands together. "Of course. That is it, Mr. Darcy. That is it exactly!"

Had they not had these precise conversations on this very afternoon, Jonathan might not have seen it, even with the information about the marriage of Daisy and Daniels. As it was, however, every word they had heard from each among these suspects drew them toward one inevitable conclusion—

"I say," Fitzwilliam interjected, frowning as he rose to his feet. "Do not you smell smoke?"

How could one not smell smoke in a house warmed by fireplaces? This was Jonathan's perpetual question, but he had long ago learned he reacted more strongly to odors than most others did. Yet Miss Tilney sniffed the air as well, apparently as struck as Colonel Fitzwilliam was by the prevalence of the smoke.

Jonathan still might not have thought much of it, had he

not at that moment seen the first gray wisps appearing over the doorway. "Oh, no," he said, pointing it out to the others.

Miss Tilney gasped, and Colonel Fitzwilliam seized Jonathan's arm—just as the call went up from deeper within the house: "*Fire!*"

Chapter Twenty-Three

Surely few other words strike such terror into the heart as *fire*. Every household is heated by the blazes in its hearths; every meal is cooked over stoves that surround and attempt to control flames; after dark, illumination can come only from candles or oil lamps. Open flame is everywhere, and its very prevalence sometimes numbs us to the danger it presents. Many a maidservant or a mother has stepped too close to a fireplace and singed her dress as a result—and everyone has heard of the most ghastly situations, in which the burning clothing proves inescapable, with fatal results. Even more lamentable are those fires that devour an entire house and many or all of the persons inside.

But it was this fate someone had desired for Rosings Park, as became evident to all when the breadth of the blaze was seen.

To Jonathan's horror, fire had spread throughout the hallway and seemed to have penetrated into the morning room. From where he stood, just outside the library, he could see the dining room, which was not ablaze. Most fires began in kitchens. This had to have started from a hearth in one of the other rooms, but how could it have spread so fast?

"Anne!" Colonel Fitzwilliam called in dismay. He dashed toward the stairs; fire had already begun to claim the runner, but Fitzwilliam braved the flames, taking three steps at a time as he sought his wife. "Anne!"

Jonathan turned to Miss Tilney, who was in a great fright

but had not lost her head. She cried out, "We must flee—through the windows, perhaps?"

"That will work." Jonathan did not fancy shattering glass or leaping out onto the lawn, but it was a far more appealing prospect than remaining near. The smell of smoke seemed to have extinguished almost every other thought. "But I must find my parents! And Lady Catherine, too."

"You are right. She cannot save herself." Miss Tilney hoisted the hem of her dress to her knees, which in any other context would have been shocking indeed. "We can still pass. We must make haste!"

Anne Fitzwilliam had been attempting to collect herself in her room. Often had she displeased her mother, but on no other occasion could Anne recall having *hurt* Lady Catherine, certainly not as terribly at this.

I had no choice, she thought as she dabbed away tears with her kerchief. *No—that is falsehood. I could have chosen to remain here, but to do so would have turned my marriage into a mere sham. It would have laid waste to all our potential future happiness. Yet the cost is to be Mama's happiness . . .*

Anne frowned as she heard a shout from downstairs, then another. Who dared disturb the peace of Rosings Park? Then Fitzwilliam cried out from the hall, "Anne! Anne, open your door this instant!"

She ran to the door to do as he wished, then gasped in dismay as she saw the smoke beginning to curl gray in the stairwell—and, in front of her, a thin line of flame that stood between any person on this floor and the stair. On the other side of it stood Fitzwilliam, beside himself.

"You must not attempt to cross," he shouted over the

increasing sounds of dismay within the house. "I shall come over—"

"No, do not! I know what to do," said Anne as she turned back to her room. Although most of the floor was covered by a sumptuous floral rug, a long, thin runner marked the border between the rest of the bedroom and her beloved window seat. Weak as she was, she could drag the runner back to the line of flame and fling it atop the blaze; it was thick enough not to instantly burn through. Then she grabbed up her skirts and ran straight over the rug to Fitzwilliam. Instantly he hoisted her into his arms and ran downstairs with her. The smoke seemed to thicken as they went.

"But Mama!" Anne cried, coughing. "Where is Mama?"

Juliet saw Fitzwilliam carrying Anne through to safety and felt a moment's gladness—no more than that was to be found. She and the younger Mr. Darcy were hurrying through the ground floor, hoping to find Lady Catherine or any other person in need of assistance.

"Look," called Mr. Darcy, pointing from the hall to a window in the adjoining room that looked out upon the lawn. There stood Charlotte Collins, her arms around her daughter Katy; they, at least, had reached safety. This had proved a difficult thing to do, for though the fire seemed to have but started, it had spread to precisely those points that prevented easy ingress and egress.

The conclusion was inescapable: "Mr. Darcy, I believe this fire was set on purpose. This is the final attempt to kill Lady Catherine!"

"Final, yes!" Mr. Darcy coughed once. "If we save Lady Catherine once more, we save her entirely."

Lady Catherine de Bourgh, as it happened, had remained in her study for quite some time following her conversation with Anne. She was not satisfied with the outcome, yet could think of no means of altering it. So caught up was she in these thoughts that she detected neither the odor of smoke nor the shouts of servants in the distance until the study door swung open to reveal Elizabeth Darcy, breathing hard and in evident disarray.

"And what is this?" Lady Catherine demanded. "You look a wild thing, Mrs. Darcy."

"Rosings is on fire, your ladyship. We must to safety."

"Fire?" Was there no outrage she would not be suffered to endure? "What is the meaning of this?"

"I believe the meaning is that someone very much wishes you dead, ma'am," said Elizabeth with disgraceful forthrightness, "and if you do not come with me this moment, that wish may soon be granted."

The smoke had become apparent, and this more than Elizabeth's words persuaded Lady Catherine to move. She came around her desk, but she walked slowly with her stick, and this was a situation in which greater quickness would have been most desirable. Lady Catherine could not but be shaken by the glimpse of her house—her world, from her marriage to this day—beginning to give way to flame. The stairwell, in particular, had become perilous.

"Come, Lady Catherine," said Elizabeth, turning her body away and stooping down. "Upon my back."

"What is the meaning of this?"

"You must have been given a piggy-back ride once as a child! Or seen one given?" Elizabeth patted her own shoulder, urging Lady Catherine into this position of absurdity. "It is the only way I shall have the strength to carry you, Lady Catherine, as I believe I am obliged to do. We must away!"

There was nothing for it. Lady Catherine was forced to surrender all dignity, to clasp her arms around the neck of the upstart Elizabeth Darcy, and—worst of all—straddle her with both legs. Elizabeth merely took hold of Lady Catherine's knees with appalling boldness and began down the steps. Progress was jolting but swift. Lady Catherine could even feel some measure of gratitude for her safety, but above all, she hoped no one else could see this humiliating display. That would not do *at all*.

Jonathan must have breathed in too much smoke, for his mind could no longer distinguish truth from vision. How else could he explain the sudden glimpse of Lady Catherine riding upon his mother's back?

"Jonathan!" That was his father, hurrying toward him and Miss Tilney, with Mr. Tilney not far behind. "Thank goodness you are both safe. We must leave."

"It is not wholly ablaze yet," added Tilney, "but the fire will grow. The servants have begun a bucket train between here and her ladyship's pond as commanded, but it is so distant from the house—"

"We do not need the pond!" Miss Tilney exclaimed. "It is laundry day. There will be tubs and tubs of water sitting in the kitchen, and large wet sheets and clothing!"

The elder Mr. Darcy turned to Miss Tilney with—for once—the full measure of admiration she so deserved. "We must direct the servants. Away with us!"

Jonathan and his father hurried away. Miss Tilney made to follow, but Jonathan glimpsed her father holding her back and directing her toward the door. *Yes*, he thought, *better she should be safe. She has already given us her idea that may save all.*

As they ran toward the Rosings kitchen, they near collided

with Daniels, no doubt searching for his wife. A few words to him, and the servants' efforts shifted from retrieving the pond water to working with the laundry water, and the laundry itself. (They had been ordered to the pond by Fitzwilliam, who had both been in terrible haste and unaware of the change in the house's laundry day.) Jonathan took up some wet bedsheets—shockingly heavy, as they had not yet been wrung out—and hoisted them upon his shoulders. With this he dashed upstairs, then flung the sheet wide, so that the fabric spread out as much as possible. When it flopped upon the floor, it suffocated nearly all flames beneath it; the small ones that remained, Jonathan easily stomped out in seconds. He judged the sheet still damp enough to be used in this manner again—and in this way, already he had extinguished much of the flame upstairs.

"Fling the damp fabrics wide!" Jonathan shouted as he hurried back downstairs. "They suffocate all!"

But the others had not needed his instruction. With attention refocused on the laundry, pots and pans and bowls of water had been filled from the tubs and seized by everyone from his father to Mr. Collins to even the stableboys. Every wet linen or garment was seized and used—even mobcaps and nightdresses. Had they been obliged to use what water could be drawn from pond and pump, Jonathan thought, Rosings Park might well have been lost. Instead, though the damage had rendered a beautiful, orderly home ugly and unsettled, Rosings would survive.

They simply had to find the strength to keep going, to find every single small flame and extinguish it utterly. By this time, Jonathan felt he had a good sense where all such patches flames would be. Their placement had not been random; rather, it had been designed to trap persons inside. Such wickedness! Jonathan would be grateful to put a stop to it.

Juliet had wished to remain in the thick of things—had using the laundry water not been her idea?—but ultimately she had to accept her exile to the lawns with all the other women, as well as Deb Collins. This did provide her the opportunity to see Lady Catherine being carried out upon the back of the enterprising Mrs. Darcy; sight as it was to behold, though, Juliet wished herself more engaged in helping to put out the fire.

"Charlotte?" Mrs. Darcy, breathing hard, went to Mrs. Collins. "How shocking this all is. Are you well?"

"As well as I can be, under the circumstances." Charlotte very deliberately did not turn her head toward Lady Catherine. Was that to conceal her feelings? Or a sign that her loathing for Lady Catherine could no longer be concealed, now that Mr. Collins might no longer benefit from her ladyship's patronage?

More pointed, however, was the attention Katy dedicated to her brother. Juliet might have thought Deb would go to help—though young, he was of enough years that it seemed possible. Instead, he stared into the distance, not at the fire but seemingly through it. When his head tilted to one side, Katy glanced all around her in dismay, whispering, "Oh, no, not now, not now—"

Juliet hastened to the Collins children. Where Katy had her hand on one of Deb's shoulders, Juliet grasped the other and whispered, "Is he shortly to have a falling spell?"

"I think so," whispered Katy. "Some of the signs had showed themselves even before the fire. Mama said we ought not to remain here longer, but Papa insisted that if we remained and tried to help with your questions, it might make Lady Catherine look more favorably upon us—oh, Deb!"

Deb's arm twitched. His face had gone slack. He listed heavily to one side, but Juliet found she was able to brace him. Somewhat to her surprise, he did not collapse entirely. "Will he not fall?"

"Sometimes he does, but sometimes not. Sometimes it is— smaller, stranger, like this." Katy sniffled. "Witnessing this calamity, that is what has done it. Such a shock is difficult enough for anyone to weather; but for my brother, in his condition, it is far too much."

Nearby stood Anne, supported on one elbow by Mrs. Jenkinson. Their attention, luckily for Deb, was entirely upon the spectacle of the blaze. Anne said, "I do hope Colonel Fitzwilliam is safe, and my cousins."

Juliet replied, "I feel certain that they are. Were they not, they would not fight on in vain. It is a very grand house, but it is only a house." How acutely a fire made one realize the unimportance of material things!

Katy remained wholly devoted to Deb, keeping him mostly upright as he drifted through whatever seizure of thought and movement then compelled him. Her concern seemed less for the fit—a mild one, in Katy's telling—than it did for the chance that Lady Catherine would see him and note it.

"Take heart," said Juliet, "that at least Lady Catherine has other subjects to draw her attention at present! I believe Deb could tumble upon the ground many times over before her ladyship could look away from Rosings."

"Aye, true, true." Katy's mouth twisted in an unwilling smile. "For this we are forced to be grateful! Little as I care for Lady Catherine, I will not deny that this fate is a hard one indeed."

Yet Katy had smiled too soon, for Deb twitched again, then jerked so violently that he fell from his sister's arms onto the ground. Mrs. Darcy cried out in dismay; Charlotte knelt by her son's side. Lady Catherine proved to have attention enough to observe this. "Whatever has happened? Was the boy injured in the fire?"

"He will be well," Charlotte said. "No doubt he is merely overcome from the shock."

A very convenient excuse—and one, Juliet thought, that Lady Catherine did not believe for a moment.

The last glow of sunlight on the horizon had faded before Rosings Park was pronounced free of flame. Most of the rooms in the house were undamaged save for the heavy scent of smoke. But every hallway was soaked with water and singed with soot. Many of the carpets and sheets that had been used to extinguish the fire had been burned through, and nearly every garment in the house was filthy, many of them damaged and others destroyed. Pleased though the laundry maids were to still have their home and their employ, they cannot be blamed for a few groans as they picked up all that would require scrubbing and mending, beginning tomorrow.

However devoted and industrious the staff might be, only so much could be done in a night or even a day. As the men emerged from the house, sooty of face and hands, Lady Catherine straightened herself. Juliet had thought she might mean to thank them for saving Rosings. Instead, when they came within earshot, she said, "So! We will require a place to stay—for tonight, certainly, perhaps several days as well. I believe the parsonage can be made to accommodate some of us." With that she cocked her head, as though daring Mr. Collins to contradict her.

It was not a dare he would ever have taken. At the thought of again being of service to Lady Catherine, an almost beatific joy appeared on Mr. Collins's face. "Certainly, your ladyship! We would be only too delighted—too honored—"

"How many can you house?" Lady Catherine asked. "The others will have to shift for themselves at the inn in Hunsford."

"We have three bedrooms kept ever prepared for visitors— for you, Lady Catherine, and of course for the Fitzwilliams— perhaps Mr. and Mrs. Darcy—"

"I thank you for my share of your kindness," said Elizabeth, "but I insist that the final room be given to Miss Tilney. I do not disdain to stay at an inn, particularly not if I am with my husband."

"Before more plans are made," said the younger Mr. Darcy, "we must settle the question of who set this fire, for I believe it to be the same person who has made all the other attempts on the life of Lady Catherine."

Juliet went to his side. "Yes, we must. Our final questions made it all come clear at last."

Lady Catherine, who had been through a trying day, came closer to them. "Well, then, who is it?"

"We realized some days ago," the younger Mr. Darcy said, "that no one person among our suspects had the ability and opportunity to be behind all of the attempts upon Lady Catherine. We then began to suspect more than one person was involved—that either two people were cooperating with each other, or that one of the Rosings servants had been prevailed upon, under threat of death, to assist in this murderous endeavor."

"Yet then Colonel Fitzwilliam said something most striking," Juliet added. "He said that it was impossible to have a happy household without a highly skilled staff—but all too possible to have highly skilled staff but an unhappy home. That made us realize—"

She paused. She and Mr. Darcy had not had a chance to

confer about this yet. However, he nodded, and she knew that in this, they were in concord.

"Realize that, while none of our principal suspects could have struck without the help of a servant, a servant would have had no difficulty striking on her own," Juliet continued. "So long as she had access to every needful room of the house, all could be accomplished. The one hard place for her to reach was the gun room, for Daniels alone had the keys and kept them in his room."

"But his room," young Mr. Darcy said, "is also the room of his wife, Daisy. And Daisy encourages her best friend among the staff to rest in that space when it is available. Is that not so, Mrs. Jenkinson?"

Chapter Twenty-Four

Mrs. Jenkinson stood away to the side of the group, as indeed she nearly always did. Her soot-stained shawl remained wrapped around her shoulders; her mobcap was slightly askew. When all turned to stare at her—for once, the center of attention—she might have shrunk back. Instead, she gazed at Jonathan with her usual expression, which seemed to wonder whether he would like a cup of tea. She must have trained herself into this constant calm attentiveness, never allowing it to falter. Jonathan realized that this woman had a curtain of her own, but what it concealed was dark indeed.

Miss Tilney said, "Blame is often unfairly cast upon servants, and we did not originally consider them in this matter. The Rosings staff is paid well, and Lady Catherine"—her eyes darted over to her ladyship, understandably apprehensive, but for once Lady Catherine appeared shocked beyond speech—"is neither malicious nor capricious in her needs. Nor could anyone name any particular event or misdeed that might have goaded one of the servants to strike at Lady Catherine, who even intended to remember one former servant in her will. But the motive did not have to lie in something her ladyship had done; it could equally be rooted in something she had *failed* to do."

"What can you mean?" Anne Fitzwilliam looked from Miss Tilney to Jonathan and back again, expressing some of the horror Lady Catherine was too appalled to voice. "What did she fail to do?"

"To remember Mrs. Jenkinson in her will," Jonathan replied. "Mr. Daniels and his wife, Daisy—neither of them could have such expectations. Bequests to staff are reserved only for those who have served in those positions of the greatest trust and intimacy. Neither of them could claim as much. Mrs. Jenkinson, however, has been companion to both mother and daughter for longer than I have been alive. She has done most of the work of a housekeeper without an according increase in position and, I would wager, in pay. She would no doubt have hoped for some remembrance upon Lady Catherine's decease. Only when Guinness was called for did Mrs. Jenkinson learn that none would be forthcoming."

Mrs. Jenkinson blurted out, "She was to remember Miss Pope. How proud she was to tell it, so vain of her 'charity'! Miss *Pope*, who has not been governess here for more than twenty years! What is Miss Pope to her, compared to all that I have been and done? I vowed that never, never should I see Miss Pope made rich by Lady Catherine's generosity when I would have nothing."

The elder Mr. Darcy stepped forward, uncharacteristically disheveled from the fire and its aftermath. By the bright moonlight, Jonathan could see the gravity of his father's countenance. "You admit it, then? That you attempted to kill Lady Catherine?"

"Not at first," Mrs. Jenkinson answered. The flush of anger in which she had spoken seemed already to have weakened, but there was nothing for it now but to explain. "At first I meant only to . . . to scare her, to make her think more of her death, for then she might think more of what might become of the rest of us afterward. What might become of *me*. Yet she never did." How small she now appeared! How helpless! Yet the coldness in her voice became more and more evident as she continued. "Lady Catherine never once considered me in the slightest. Each failure gave her an opportunity. Each opportunity she squandered. What had begun as but a desire to make her see through fear what she had not glimpsed through feeling—by the time of your arrival, I was in earnest. But I knew not how to go about the business, nor is my time my own, as I am forever being summoned hither and yon. I had to take what chances I could, when I could."

"You thought not of your Christian duty to Lady Catherine, nay, to all within that household!" Mr. Collins, an enthusiastic disapprover, had rarely found such a deserving target. "You could have killed more persons besides, all from your outrageous ingratitude!"

"Ingratitude!" Mrs. Jenkinson cried. "All I have done for her ladyship over the years—close to her as any sister would ever have been—and it is ingratitude she showed me!"

Miss Tilney had been much in thought. "The marks on the gun room door," she said, "were left intentionally, were they not? To make it seem as though someone had been forced to break in, so that no one would consider who had access to the keys."

Mrs. Jenkinson bowed her head. "Daisy would have realized it, even if no one else did. For to be sure, she is the only person in the house who has thought of me at all. I have served in this house all these many years—neglected the little family I have, so much so that they regard me as no more than a stranger—and I have excited no more feeling than this."

None witnessing this could help but consider the plight of the servant known as a "companion." She is not so low as the rest of the staff, yet not so high as those who employ her. She must evidence all the gentility and refinement of a lady of family, as well as all the industriousness and humility that might be demanded from the scullery maid. The companion is at best a friend—at worst, one who must play the role of a friend regardless of her own inclinations, and with the knowledge that this friendship will be terminated with her employment should she ever fail to please. Meanwhile, the companion is often kept from finding other friends of her own—those of the gentry know she will never be their equal, and those lower in service are apt to think her "arrogant" or "snobbish," when they think upon the companion at all. Most women who take such employ consider themselves unmarriageable— for various reasons, which may or may not be evident to the onlooker. Regardless, whatever chance of matrimony might have existed previously is all but extinguished upon accepting the position of companion. Their time ceases to be their own, and any future interactions with gentlemen will take place only at a remove, as the companion acts as accessory to her lady. Companions sit through long social calls, taking tea in the parlor, without ever being addressed unless her lady wishes for a kerchief or her shawl.

Many companions are valued by their ladies and remembered with annuities or bequests. One will not end wealthy, but one need not fear destitution—in most cases. Perhaps this would have been true for Mrs. Jenkinson as well: Lady Catherine might well have assumed that, after her own death, Mrs. Jenkinson would continue to serve as companion to Anne for some years and would be taken care of thereby. Had Jenkinson distrusted this? Had she anticipated Colonel Fitzwilliam's eagerness to set up a separate household, one that would exclude her? Or had she simply been overcome by the sense that, for tolerating Lady Catherine's rages and whimsies for twenty-five years, she was *due more*? Greater fondness has turned into equal hatred for less cause than this.

Lady Catherine stepped forward, and all fell silent. Sooty and disheveled, standing on a gravel path in her garden, she had lost almost all her hauteur. Instead, she looked no more than any other haggard old woman, weary past endurance. Yet her voice still rang with authority. "You will no longer serve in this house. You will take your articles—whichever remain, after this blaze—and depart at first light. You will receive no written character from me nor anyone else at Rosings."

"Lady Catherine, I must protest!" Such was the depth of Mr. Collins's devotion to Lady Catherine that he could bring himself to oppose her only for her own sake. "The authorities must be informed! This woman belongs in gaol! She does not deserve your pity."

Mr. Tilney made a small sound—Jonathan suspected he had some thoughts about Christian compassion to share with his fellow clergyman—but no one had a chance to speak before her ladyship replied.

"It is not a matter of pity," she said. "It is a matter of propriety. Shall we lay our most private affairs before the world and allow Rosings Park to be coupled with scandal in the public mouth? No, Mr. Collins, it shall not be so. All in Hunsford shall hear only that there was a fire, contained before the damage was too great. All will be repaired, cleaned, and set back as it was before. It will be rather as though Mrs. Jenkinson had never been here at all. Where Mrs. Jenkinson will be—that is irrelevant. She will be gone, unseen, never spoken of again. That will do."

Mrs. Jenkinson looked as though she had a great deal more to say, but she could not be unaware that, should she outrage Lady Catherine further, propriety might be cast aside in favor of vengeance. Were Mrs. Jenkinson to face the law, she would surely hang for her crimes. Lady Catherine's contempt was also, in its way, a kind of charity—the only way to let Jenkinson leave with her life. Or was it, rather, a mark of how very little Jenkinson had ever meant to her mistress, that Lady Catherine could not regard her with any seriousness as either friend or enemy?

Regardless, Mrs. Jenkinson knew that the price of her survival was silence. She turned and trudged back toward Rosings, to retrieve what little she had before leaving, however she would.

Jonathan almost pitied the woman. No reputable house would hire a servant who bore no written character reference, not unless she was vouched for by another of their staff—and no one would be so foolhardy as to vouch for Mrs. Jenkinson after such events as these. She might have some small amount of money saved, but under the circumstances, she could not even ask for her most recent wages. A woman above sixty years of age would now set off into the world with no family, no friends, no home, and no way to obtain work of dignity. Most likely she would make her way to one of the cities to be swallowed up in the grime and clamor. Mrs. Jenkinson had forfeited any right to better by attempting murder—Jonathan understood that—but he prayed for her soul as he watched her go.

After a few moments, Lady Catherine continued quite as though they had not just identified and cast aside her own would-be murderer, as though there had been no fire, as though it were any other night. "Next we must consider the matter of your son, Mr. Collins. He was most overcome earlier this evening, in the throes of some manner of fit. What is the meaning of this?"

Mr. Collins's expression took on the uncertainty of a person who is soon to tell a lie but has not yet devised one. Mrs. Collins averted her face, perhaps so she need not witness the falsehood. Yet their daughter proved more forthright than her parents, or at least unable to deceive any longer. "Deb has the falling sickness. He has had it for years."

"The falling sickness?" Lady Catherine looked down at Deb without any of the contempt his family had so often predicted. "You have suffered this?"

Forbidding she could be, judgmental ever, but the Collinses had failed to consider another truth of her ladyship's character: she had been the mother of a sick child. The long hours by the fireside with the ailing infant Anne had left their mark on Lady Catherine's heart. On the rare occasions her sympathy was excited, she exercised that with as much vigor as her judgments, and nothing could so demand her sympathy more powerfully than a young person who was ill. And if she felt compassion most acutely only where she herself had endured pain, would she be so very different from the majority of humankind?

"Why am I only now hearing of it?" Lady Catherine demanded. "The boy must see physicians! He must receive the finest treatment! As soon as all is set right with Rosings, we shall travel to London, that he may take the best advice." All present stared in wonder, but she considered this part of the matter settled. "Now, Mr. Collins, you may conduct us to the parsonage."

"Of course, your ladyship! Your generosity demands no less in return! I should be only too happy for you to stay in our humble abode—Katy and Deb could make way, if the inn is not to Mr. Darcy's liking—"

"The inn will suffice," he said, rather quickly. Jonathan could well imagine that neither of his parents would relish the discomforts of staying in Hunsford Parsonage, in very close quarters with Lady Catherine. "We would not wish to inconvenience the children."

For their part, the Collins children betrayed more of the astonishment the others surely felt. Deb remained groggy, but Katy's eyes were wide. "Fancy Mrs. Jenkinson being behind it all," she whispered. "Never thought she had that much life in her."

"*Katy.*" Charlotte's voice was as firm as the hand she set

on her daughter's arm. "We must help Lady Catherine to the parsonage."

"I have an idea," said Katy. "Why does not Miss Tilney share with me? Then her father can stay with us, too."

"Yes, of course." Charlotte smiled at Mr. Tilney, a perfect simulation of calm contentment. "Do say you will come, Mr. Tilney."

"I am obliged to you, madam." Mr. Tilney then ducked closer to his daughter and whispered, just within Jonathan's hearing, "You have done marvelously well, child. Your mother will be most disappointed not to have witnessed this."

Miss Tilney prepared to go with the Collinses as well, but she hesitated a moment longer to say to Jonathan, "This must stand as our finest accomplishment, Mr. Darcy, for this time, no one has died."

"True—though to that, I believe we owe Lady Catherine's wisdom in summoning us."

"Sage counselor indeed!" she replied. Her smile was luminous in the bright moonlight, and he remembered the conversation they had had earlier regarding Ralph Bamber—the one that shone upon all his hopes, revealing them anew, as possibilities.

Juliet experienced similar optimism—but the world does not cease its spinning so that we may luxuriate in but one emotion at a time. No, despite all her eager thoughts regarding Jonathan Darcy, she had also to walk to Hunsford Parsonage, borrow one of Katy's nightgowns, and make herself as comfortable as possible in her new friend's bed. Juliet's usual bedmate was her younger sister, Theodosia, who kicked a great deal; soon she would discover whether Katy did the same.

Happily, she did not. However, the two young ladies lay awake some time, listening to Lady Catherine's querulous demands, and the endless thumping steps of the Collinses and their servants as they strove to satisfy her every need.

"I must be honest with you," said Katy. "I thought you and Jonathan rather foolish for considering Papa a likely suspect. Mama . . . she would never do such a thing, but she has no more fondness for Lady Catherine than I. So suspicion there, I could not wonder at. But Papa?"

"His admiration of her is so great, his praise so endless, I did not think it could be genuine."

Katy laughed. "It is, and yet, he speaks but a fraction of what he feels! Had I been granted a sister, I half think Papa would have insisted upon her being named Catherine, too, and how we should have told ourselves apart, I cannot imagine."

"Oh, he would not have repeated the name, surely!"

"We had an elder brother, De Bourgh, you know. He died still an infant, ere Deb was born—but they might have had the same name regardless."

"How very sad," said Juliet. She wondered whether this long-ago tragedy might explain some of Charlotte Collins's self-possession. "I promise that I will never again doubt the devotion of Mr. Collins to Lady Catherine."

"As long as she does not doubt it, either." Enough moonlight filtered through the windows to reveal the worry on Katy's countenance. "She was so fearful angry with him! We were surprised by her mercy toward Deb, but who knows whether that impulse will endure. We might yet lose all, if she tells the bishop to cast us out."

Juliet rolled onto her side, the better to address her friend. "Although I have not been long acquainted with Lady Catherine, there is no question in my mind but that she will forgive your father, and that all will carry on much as it has done—though I do think he will be obliged to give up Faxton."

"He has already written a letter resigning the post. But why say you that her ladyship will be so generous?"

"First, because her sympathy for Deb seemed genuine, and her opinions, once decided, do not seem ever to be shifted," said Juliet. "Second, because the Fitzwilliams are moving to Bath, to establish their own house there. Mrs. Jenkinson has departed, too, and under far darker circumstances. Thus Lady Catherine has lost all of her closest companions save for your family. She *should* forgive you because her own dictates and decrees led your father along this path—however, she *will* forgive you simply because she must. Otherwise she would be entirely alone."

Katy considered this for some moments before saying the precise words Juliet was thinking: "Poor woman."

"She is lonelier than any of us, I think. May we both be preserved from such a fate!"

Chapter Twenty-Five

Etiquette books may differ on the correct time for a guest's visit to end, but few would deny that it is prudent to leave after the house has caught fire. Thus it was that, upon the next morn, all those who intended to leave Rosings hastened to prepare for their going.

This number now included Colonel Fitzwilliam and Anne. Although they could not leave for Bath that very day, they began taking stock of what would and would not go with them on their way. Each and every article would need cleaning to be made ready, for soot saturated the very walls of Rosings Park. Anne pointed to each item offered in turn: "Yes, the carriage clock is mine—will I need all three of my cloaks?—not that bonnet, no, it has always been dreadful."

"Oh, thank goodness you said so," sighed Daisy as she tossed the feathered thing over one shoulder. "For the good lord knows, ma'am, I could never have said it to you." Anne laughed aloud at this—an exchange that could not have occurred between these two women before—and Daisy's answering smile hinted at the more congenial home they would work together to create in Bath.

Colonel Fitzwilliam shook his head at a white cravat, or rather, one that had formerly been white but now was likely to appear coal-stained in perpetuity. "Well, Daisy, you shall not lack for polishing rags. Ah, I can do little else here. Why do I not examine my study? The important papers are intact— that, I already saw to—but I wish to know whether all my writing paper and pens have survived."

"Why those things in particular?" Anne asked. "You can always purchase more."

"Yes, but I wish to write Peter's school straightaway and tell them that our boy shall come home at Christmas, to stay for several years at least. We shall be settled then, and our boy will have his new room ready to receive him."

Anne felt all the joy of it anew. "Yes. By then we shall have *our home*."

The Darcy family arrived midmorning, each member eager to see how all fared at Rosings Park—albeit for different reasons.

Mr. Darcy turned his attention to his aunt, who already had resumed her place in her accustomed chair in the sitting room (which she had strictly commanded to be cleaned first). "Surely it will be many days before all can be made pleasant and safe for you here," he said. "You must come to Pemberley. Indeed, we insist."

"Insist?" Lady Catherine's eyebrows raised nearly to the lace of her cap. "It is not for you to insist what I shall do. No, my nephew, I am quite resolved. All at Rosings Park must be made as it was, and this will be accomplished best and swiftest if I myself am here to observe. Besides, I must begin my inquiries about finding the best physician to help Master Collins."

"Is there nothing, then, that I may do in your service?"

"Send out inquiries to your friends and neighbors. Tell them that there is a place for a lady's companion at Rosings, available immediately. The candidate must be of exemplary character. We shall have no more errors of this sort!"

Darcy hastened to do this, which took him to the study where he encountered Colonel Fitzwilliam, who was writing to Guinness the solicitor, informing him of the fire and suggesting a postponement of his visit. There, the colonel finally made his cousin fully aware of the plans that would bring together all the Fitzwilliam family in Bath. This gladdened Darcy immensely, and he hastened to wish them joy.

"Joy I think we will have in abundance," said the colonel, more carefree than Darcy had seen him since they were lads together. "The great difficulty will be in reconciling Lady Catherine to the change."

"No doubt," said Darcy, "but I have every confidence that both her ladyship's love for her daughter and grandson, and her pride, which would not wish to admit of family schism, will equally bring her to Bath ere long."

Colonel Fitzwilliam, more grave now, said, "I heard you earlier, inviting Lady Catherine to Pemberley. She will not leave until Rosings is restored, but—perhaps your family might invite her there soon after, in a month or two, just after Anne and I have gone. I do not like to think of her in the house so alone, not when our absence is new to her. A visit to Pemberley will be just the thing to occupy her mind."

"It shall be done," promised Darcy. His wife would not be made merry upon this news, but after last night—when Elizabeth herself had carried Lady Catherine to safety—there seemed some chance that her ladyship's view of the former Miss Bennet would finally have improved.

Elizabeth, meanwhile, had immediately walked to Hunsford Parsonage in the hopes of seeing Charlotte. Pemberley was a far grander house than the parsonage, but thanks to Mr. Bennet's frequent unannounced visits to the home she shared with Darcy, Elizabeth knew well how fraught unexpected visitors could sometimes be—and the smaller the house, the greater the trouble. She found Mr. Tilney outside in the garden, purporting to read a small book of sermons, but actually watching the Collins children speaking merrily with Miss Tilney at the far edge of the property. Miss Tilney had the somewhat disheveled appearance of a young woman obliged to prepare for her day with scant help from an overburdened maid, and yet Elizabeth liked to see her lack of vanity, her freshness. "Good morning, Mr. Tilney," she said. "I would ask after you and your daughter, but it seems you are both quite well after last night's extraordinary events."

"We are indeed. I take it the inn at Hunsford did not prove too displeasing?"

"It is a clean, well-kept establishment, and they served us quite a good breakfast. We do not travel often, my husband and I, but I have heard such dreadful tales of inns! I begin to believe them all exaggerations. Do you and your family travel often?"

"Not to any exceptional degree, and I dare say we shall do less of it in future," said Tilney in good humor. "Juliet's journeys have been of such a dramatic pitch that I shudder at the thought of any of us leaving home again."

That, Elizabeth thought, was not fortunately phrased. She ventured, "You would not, of course, forbid your daughter's accepting other invitations to travel?"

Mr. Tilney considered for several moments, very gravely, before replying: "Given what has occurred in her past journeys—two dead, and one nearly so!—no, I believe we will endeavor to keep Juliet with us as much as possible. It cannot be for so very long."

There it was. Elizabeth could and would have battled her husband's reluctance to a match between Jonathan and Miss Tilney, but she could not stand against the Tilney family, too. Many might have responded in wonderment to a family's disinclination to see their daughter make such a brilliant match—but not Elizabeth, who had turned down her first offer to become mistress of Pemberley. Had Jonathan's more curious habits been mistaken for undue pride? Had Darcy made his own disapproval so clear that Tilney felt his daughter slighted? Regardless, she knew that Miss Tilney could not come to Pemberley soon.

So distracted was Elizabeth by her own dismay that she did not glimpse Miss Tilney's reaction in the distance. Miss Tilney, blessed with a good sense of hearing, had overheard enough of their conversation to feel that all her hopes, so freshly renewed, had already been dashed entirely.

Oblivious to this, Elizabeth said only, "I agree that she will not remain at your house long, Mr. Tilney. She is a remarkable young woman in every way. I wish her an equally remarkable match."

"In that we concur," said Tilney, with such a smile as to make it clear that whatever hard feelings he held against her family, for Elizabeth herself he felt only admiration. This did not much console her.

After this she went to Charlotte, hoping that matters between them might be smoothed before they parted. Elizabeth suspected their friendship would never be the same—that, in fact, it had not held true affinity and concord for many years—yet she wished to heal some fraction of the breach, if only for the fellowship they had shared as girls.

Charlotte proved to be in her parlor, apparently absorbed in a book. Elizabeth might have wondered at this ability to become engrossed in such enjoyments after a night of profound disturbance, had she not been avid enough reader herself to understand the escape that only a good novel could provide. "Good morning, Charlotte. How fare you?"

"Very well, as it seems you do also," said Charlotte. "Unexpected houseguests always create a bit of a stir, but I believe we have managed admirably."

"Indeed, achieving comfort for so many is a worthy accomplishment! You are right to be proud. You must be relieved, as well, that Lady Catherine seems willing to put all behind her."

"It is in the past," Charlotte said, "and need never more be spoken of."

From this Elizabeth understood that no true confidence would take place between them, either this morning or ever again. Very softly she said, "God bless you, Charlotte."

"And you, Lizzy."

Juliet, rather forlorn, walked across the lane from the parsonage to the outskirts of the Rosings Park grounds. From the outside, little of the inner damage was evident; any passerby might have guessed only that a thorough housecleaning was underway. This, Juliet suspected, was precisely as Lady Catherine wished.

At that very moment, the younger Mr. Darcy strode out upon the lawn and waved. No doubt he had seen her and come out, that they might greet each other. How happy this would have made her at any point before this morning! As it was, she went to meet him with a smiling face but a wounded heart.

"Miss Tilney—I am so glad to see you," he said with the artless enthusiasm she so liked in him. "My parents make ready to leave, and I am sure your father wants to do so as well."

"Our task is accomplished, and my room is burned," said Juliet. "I cannot imagine two stronger signs that departure is advisable."

"Then go we must," he said, "but—I wished to know—would you welcome an invitation from my parents to visit Pemberley?"

Juliet required some moments to fully comprehend what was meant. An invitation to Pemberley was . . . an invitation to courtship. Mr. Darcy *did* think of her as a potential wife. She had endeavored so steadfastly to put such hopes behind her, only to have them restored now that she knew them to be hopeless!

"I spoke with my father mere moments ago," she said. "He told me that he spoke to your mother, and—and no invitations to Pemberley will be forthcoming. Even if I were invited, Papa says I should not be allowed to go."

How crestfallen Mr. Darcy looked! Had she truly possessed so much more of his heart than she knew? "Why would they say such things? My mother thinks the world of you—"

"But your father does not," said Juliet. "And *that* is what my father thinks little of."

In matters of courtship, parental disapproval of a match is the most unsurmountable difficulty. Juliet knew their fathers meant only to protect their children, but this "protection" seemed likely to cost them their best chance at happiness. Ill fate indeed!

Yet Mr. Darcy did not appear unduly dismayed. He said only, "If this were no issue—if their objections could be overcome—would you then wish to see Pemberley?"

Juliet did not feel certain how to respond, but as she would not be dishonest and simper on in pretended ignorance, she must confess the truth. Very softly she said, "I should be very happy to see Pemberley someday."

"Someday soon, then," he replied. Mr. Darcy's smile warmed Juliet through. For a moment she thought he might take her hand—but she caught herself. They were not affianced; they were unlikely to ever become so. "We must not rely on what may never be."

"As water wears away stone, so does persistence overcome

obstacles," he said. When their eyes met this time, Juliet knew he was not performing for her sake, not drawing the curtain—that he wished for this connection, as surely and deeply as she. "We have never given up in our efforts before."

"True. So we shall not do so now." And then each was too abashed to say much more. What good fortune it is when silence falls only after words are no longer necessary!

From the house called the voice of Lady Catherine, "Jonathan? Where is my nephew? I have need of him!"

They exchanged a glance that admitted Lady Catherine's will could not be brooked. "Goodbye, Miss Tilney. Goodbye for a time."

"Farewell, Mr. Darcy." How long might it be ere they met once more?

The Darcys set out for Pemberley that day; the Tilneys took their carriage northward the day following. Both young persons greatly wished to meet again, but knew they would encounter great resistance. Neither of them could have guessed the shapes that resistance might take, nor the circumstance that would lead to their next encounter. For the time being, they could but take satisfaction in having saved the life of Lady Catherine de Bourgh.

Two weeks after the fire, Colonel Fitzwilliam and Anne set out for Bath, accompanied by Daniels and Daisy—or, as she was now called with greater dignity, Mrs. Daniels. Anne found the house everything that she would have wished and set about the joyous task of making it a true home. All was furnished and comfortable by Christmastime, complete with evergreen wreaths and sprigs of holly, when their son, Peter, came home for good. Although Peter had indeed been very glad to leave that school, he had not fared so poorly as his parents had feared, and their newfound independence from Lady Catherine strengthened him and formed the foundation of a happy childhood. Colonel Fitzwilliam proved to have some acquaintance from the army in town, and this soon provided the family with the company of friends, among whom Anne slowly overcame her shyness. Her health also improved, though whether this be the work of the waters or the salubrious effect of freedom from her mother's reign, none could say.

As had been hoped, Lady Catherine did in the fullness of time forgive her daughter. When she visited them in Bath, she critiqued only the draughtiness of the house, which from her ladyship was high praise indeed.

Sometimes, when Lady Catherine came to Bath, she brought with her young Deb Collins and one of his parents, or his sister. The waters had little to offer one suffering from the falling sickness, but she insisted that all that might be done for him, would be. At times her suggestions proved more burden than blessing, but they were offered in a truer spirit of charity than Lady Catherine had ever previously demonstrated. On the whole, Deb was grateful for this, for no longer was he obliged to lie and deceive. No more was he expected to act out of shame for a condition he could not help. His opinion of her ladyship rose, as did Katy's; even her most meddlesome efforts to help Deb were well-intentioned, and the Collins children could not but look upon her more kindly as a result. Society at large might yet harbor superstitions about Deb's condition, but that woeful thought was banished sooner in Hunsford than anywhere else in the realm, for Lady Catherine proclaimed the rational truth to all who would listen, including many who attempted not to do so. Officious and arrogant she remained, but she sincerely wished to do good for the young man—and this she accomplished, if only by accepting him as he was and banishing any need for further falsehood.

As for Mr. Collins: he, too, was forgiven, but he would never again hold the same estimation in Lady Catherine's eyes. This was a wound that could not heal, but Mr. Collins endeavored, through flattery and obedience, to repair the breach anew at their every meeting. What Mrs. Collins made of this, none could say, for her countenance continued to be serene, and her truths remained unspoken.

Acknowledgments

This series is a delight to write, partly because I have such a wonderful team helping me through every stage of the process. Above all, I owe thanks to my agent, Laura Rennert; my assistant, Sarah Simpson Weiss; and my editor, Anna Kaufman. Everyone at Vintage does their part in making these books come into being—so thank you to marketer Ellen Whitaker, publicist Julie Ertl, production editor Kayla Overbey, interior designer Steve Walker, copy editor Martha Schwartz, and proofreaders Nancy Inglis and Lyn Rosen.

As this is one of my all-time favorite covers, I want to send a huge shout-out for artist Perry De La Vega, who took my vague suggestion ("Maybe green?") and turned it into magic. Authenticity reader Kimberley VanderHorst helped make sure that Jonathan Darcy rings true. And Lara Hinchberger helms the Canadian team with enthusiasm for which I am very grateful.

My friends and family have always been a source of support and understanding, even when it seems like I've had to turn down eighteen invitations in a row with "I'm on deadline." Thanks to you all for trusting that I will someday emerge from the cave.

And, as ever, to Paul—thanks for taking me on life's greatest adventure.

ALSO BY

CLAUDIA GRAY

"Had Jane Austen sat down to write a country house murder mystery, this is exactly the book she would have written." —Alexander McCall Smith

THE MURDER OF MR. WICKHAM

The happily married Mr. Knightley and Emma are throwing a party at their country estate, bringing together distant relatives and new acquaintances—characters beloved by Jane Austen fans. Definitely not invited is Mr. Wickham, whose latest financial scheme has netted him an even broader array of enemies. As tempers flare and secrets are revealed, it's clear that everyone would be happier if Mr. Wickham got his comeuppance. Yet they're all shocked when Wickham turns up murdered—except, of course, for the killer hidden in their midst. Nearly everyone at the house party is a suspect, so it falls to the party's two youngest guests to solve the mystery: Juliet Tilney, the smart and resourceful daughter of Catherine and Henry, eager for adventure beyond Northanger Abbey; and Jonathan Darcy, the Darcys' eldest son, whose adherence to propriety makes his father seem almost relaxed. In this tantalizing fusion of Austen and Christie, the unlikely pair must put aside their own poor first impressions and uncover the guilty party—before an innocent person is sentenced to hang.

Fiction

Catherine and Henry Tilney of Northanger Abbey are not entirely pleased to be sending their eligible young daughter Juliet out into the world again. Particularly concerning is that she intends to visit her new friend Marianne Brandon, who's returned home to Devonshire shrouded in fresh scandal—made more potent by the news that her former suitor, the rakish Mr. Willoughby, intends to take up residence at his local estate with his new bride. Meanwhile, Elizabeth and Fitzwilliam Darcy of Pemberley are thrilled that their eldest son, Jonathan—who, like his father, has not always been the most socially adept—has been invited to stay with his former schoolmate, John Willoughby. Jonathan himself is decidedly less taken with the notion of having to spend extended time under the roof of his old bully, but that all changes when he finds himself reunited with his fellow amateur sleuth, the radiant Miss Tilney. Then Willoughby's new wife dies horribly at the party meant to welcome her to town. With rumors flying and Marianne under increased suspicion, Jonathan and Juliet must team up once more to uncover the murderer. But as they collect clues and close in on suspects, eerie incidents suggest that the pair are in far graver danger than they or their families could imagine.

Fiction

VINTAGE BOOKS
Available wherever books are sold.
vintagebooks.com